# The Grief

## of

# Wisdom

*Jane Thompson Hasenmueller*

**English Maniac**
*Santa Fe, NM*

Printed in the United States of America

English Maniac softcover edition: December 2020

ISBN: 978-0-9840819-5-0 (Paperback)
ISBN: 978-0-9840819-8-1 (eBook)

Library of Congress Cataloging-in-Publication data
is available for this title

English Maniac

Cover Design by JETLAUNCH
Book layout and design by JETLAUNCH

# PART ONE

*There is a sacredness in tears. They are not the mark
of weakness, but of power. They speak more eloquently
than ten thousand tongues. They are messengers
of overwhelming grief, of deep contrition, and of
unspeakable love.*

-Washington Irving

# Chapter 1

I sobel Allen stood at her living room window looking out at the snow capped Jemez mountains, the steam rising off her morning Americano as she raised her cup for a drink. Pink and purple hues colored the blue tinted sky with the promise of a warm April day. She watched the neighbor's cat creep along the adobe wall in her front yard, stalking early morning prey at the bird feeder. She tapped on the window with her knuckle, watching the birds take flight and the cat turn its head in annoyance. Isobel smiled, knowing the cat couldn't reach the birds, even if it leaped, but it never gave up trying. She carried her cup to the kitchen sink, then gathered her things and left for work. Friday was her favorite day of the week, just as it was for all of the faculty and students. As Principal of Sangre de Cristo High School, a small alternative school in Santa Fe, her job was rewarding, but often trying. She had a rough school population of kids who for many different reasons did not succeed in a regular school setting. Meeting their needs required a flexible attitude, discipline, and lots of love.

As Isobel pulled into the parking lot that morning, she looked forward to the day. She loved her job and her students. In her fifth year now, she had a cohesive staff and a strong reputation in the district. Grabbing her things off the seat next to her, she glanced at the time, 6:30. As she headed into the building she knew she had almost an hour to do paperwork before her day became the usual mix of issues needing to be addressed or solved. She dug in and didn't look up until her secretary arrived and popped her head in the door.

"Good morning, Isobel," Anna said, as she held the door open.

"Good morning, Anna. 7:45?" Isobel glanced at her watch as she laid aside her work, picked up her radio and walked towards the door where her secretary stood.

"Yes, and it's Friday. At least the savages are happiest on Friday," said Anna.

Isobel laughed, as she joined Anna at the door. "Okay, I'm going out. See you shortly." Isobel headed to the front doors, slipping on her sunglasses as she stepped outside. Greeting students as they entered the building gave her the chance to talk to any student who looked like they might be spinning out of control and hopefully gave them a sense someone cared. She expected her teachers to greet students as they walked into their classroom, and she expected nothing less of herself. When the bell rang, and the stragglers came barreling from the parking lot, she waited a few minutes and went in behind them. As she stepped into the office, she said, "Let the wild rumpus begin," making Anna laugh, then went to her office to try and finish a few more items before first period ended.

The day had flown by, but towards the end of the last period, she listened with her chin in her hand to Odette, who had been brought to the office by the assistant principal for disrupting class. She made time to talk with students, often finding herself patiently listening to a student's troubles wondering how they survived the lives thrust upon them. Isobel worried about Odette and checked on her often. Though Isobel had had her own issues as a teen, she felt her life had turned out rather ordinary and normal in the long run.

"Ms. Allen, they were doggin' me again. I'm gonna punch that whore, Audrey! She…"

"Please, watch your language, Odette," Isobel said. "Listen, I'm glad Mr. Andrews brought you in here before you got yourself in trouble again. You can't go around punching everyone who stares at you. Honestly, Odette, you are a striking young lady. People are going to stare at you, or at least take a second look, the rest of your life, so take it as a compliment instead of a threat."

"Thanks, Ms. A, but they weren't lookin' for that reason."

"Maybe not, but are those girls worth being suspended for? Hmmm?"

"Suspended? I haven't been in any fights this year."

"Um, yes, and let's keep it that way. A fight means you're out of here, and it sounds like you were close."

"Ok, ok. Can I come here if I need to talk? The counselor's a bitch and …"

"Odette…"

"I mean, I don't like talking to her. Ok?"

"You know you can stop by and if I'm available, yes, I'll talk to you. And if you find you can't control yourself, just come sit in the office and talk to Ms. Bassett until you cool off. But no ditching class. Agreed?"

"Gotcha!" Odette, flashed some kind of sign, smiled, and flipped her hair over her shoulder.

"Now, back to class before the bell rings, and have a safe weekend." Isobel came round the desk as Odette stood, giving her a quick shoulder hug and sent her on her way.

Isobel laughed to herself as she stacked up the last of the files on her desk. Isobel couldn't help but like Odette, even if always on the edge of a blowup with someone. As a junior in high school, she seemed to be at last recognizing the need to control herself to get on in life.

Isobel's assistant principal, Brian Andrews, stuck his head in her door, already wearing his orange safety vest. "Where do you want me today?"

"I'll take the road, would you cover the bus lane, please."

"Sure thing," as he gave her the thumbs up signal.

Isobel pulled her vest from her bottom drawer and headed to the main entrance to direct parents and students as they came and left the parking lot. Everything became gridlocked otherwise, the last thing she wanted on a Friday when she could actually go home early.

When Isobel reentered the building, the halls echoed with the Friday afternoon silence of students and staff having deserted as fast as possible. Isobel planned to leave soon too, but she could see Anna waving frantically at her to come into the office.

"Anna, what...?"

"Come look at this; isn't this where your son works?" Anna said as she pointed at the screen.

Isobel stared at the computer screen. A breaking story on an attack at a small television station at the university in Llano, New Mexico. She felt her knees begin to buckle and grabbed Anna's desk to keep from falling to the ground. "Oh my God."

Anna put her arm around Isobel and helped her to sit down.

"Where's your phone, Isobel?"

"On my desk."

Anna ran and got it, putting the phone in Isobel's hand. She looked at the screen a message from Alec appeared, "I love you mom, I love all of you." Stunned, Isobel looked to see what time the message had come through. 2:50, thirty-five minutes ago.

She tried to call him, but his phone rang and went to voicemail. She next tried Ian. He picked up. "Have you talked to your brother?"

"No. What's up, Mom?"

"There's been an attack on the station."

"What? Mom, where are you? What did you hear?"

"I'm still at school. Anna saw it on KOB just now."

Ian flipped on the television in his office, "Oh my God. It's on the Lubbock station too."

"I tried calling him and it went to voicemail, but I had a message from him at 2:50," she choked as she tried to tell Ian what it said…, "I love you Mom. I love you all."

"Mom, I'm going to head over there."

"Okay. I'm going to do the same."

"Mom, are you sure? Are you alright to drive?"

"Yes. I'll text you when I leave. I barely have service on that road though, so I probably can't talk to you till I get there."

"Okay. Meet me at Dad's."

"No. I'm going directly to the station," Isobel said. "Besides, your Dad will be at the station, won't he?"

"He's at a conference somewhere."

"Okay. If you hear anything, call me before I leave. Otherwise, I'll meet you in Llano at the station."

"I love you Mom. Be careful. I'm worried about you driving."

"I'll be fine. I love you too."

Anna hugged Isobel as she hung up the phone.

"Anna, would you call Martinez and tell him what's happened? I'll probably be back on Sunday. I'm sure Alec's fine. Right?" Anna nodded in agreement, "but just in case…," Isobel swallowed hard to choke back the panic she felt, "Remind Dr. Martinez, gently, that Mr. Andrews might need a bit of help if I can't get back, so we don't have a repeat of chaos like the last time I left."

"Don't worry, I'll keep an eye on him and be sure he doesn't burn down the school." She smiled and Isobel hugged her.

8

"Thank you. This school wouldn't run without you, Anna. I'll call you when I know something." Though Isobel spoke calmly, Anna could hear the panic in her voice.

"Thanks. Be careful. I'm praying for you and Alec."

Isobel grabbed her bag and laptop, then ran for the car. Fear coursed through her body as she drove to her house. She wondered if she should even go home or just drive straight to Llano, but she needed to believe they would all be together tonight and hear his story. Then she would stay the weekend and drive home Sunday evening.

When she ran into her house, she grabbed her suitcase from the hall closet on her way to the bedroom. She tossed in her jeans, boots, a few shirts, and a dress. She swept her makeup into a bag and threw it in the suitcase, then hurriedly grabbed up her toiletries, closed the case and ran for her car. Her adrenaline at full speed, she made herself take a deep breath before starting the car.

Her phone rang as she backed out of the drive.

"Isobel?" Isobel could hear the panic in Diane's voice, her best friend since she'd moved to Santa Fe ten years ago.

"I saw the news, Diane. I'm leaving the house now. Ian is on his way to Llano too. He'll get there first."

"Do you want me to go with?"

"No, wait. I'll call you as soon as I get there."

"I love you, Isobel. Be careful!"

"I will."

Isobel tried again to call Alec, but still no answer. She left her driveway and headed for Llano. She drove as fast as she could, making an almost four hour drive in three. Thankful to not be stopped by a state patrol, she headed straight for campus and the television station, but a barricade stymied her way. She pulled to the curb, jumped out, and ran past the barricade, a policewoman on her heels.

"Ma'am, ma'am. Stop."

Isobel looked over her shoulder and shouted back, "My son is in there." She could hear her phone in her pocket, messages catching up to her as she now had service. She stopped and pulled it out to see if Ian had messaged. The policewoman grabbed her arm and Isobel yanked away. "My son is in there and I'm looking to see if I have any messages from him or his brother."

"Sorry, but you can't get any closer."

Isobel kept walking and looking at her phone, the policewoman walking beside her, her hand on Isobel's arm, tugging. Isobel's eyes, full of tears she couldn't even see her phone. "I need to find my son, please," hysteria mounting in her voice. She managed to find Ian in her contacts and call. "Where are you? I'm here."

"Mom, I'm in the Liberal Arts building. They won't let us near the place and they haven't released any information. They are making us wait here."

"I'll be right there," and she shook free from the policewoman. "I'm going to wait with the others."

"I'll escort you, ma'am. I am not to let anyone in this area, and I have to be sure you leave."

Isobel turned and started running, desperate to see Ian. Isobel knew the campus and headed for the Liberal Arts building, where she spent most of her time during her undergraduate days. She needed to see Ian, to wrap her arms around her son and cling to the hope that Alec was safe. As she entered the pool of light on the front walkway, there stood Ian, who, when he spotted her, came running. "Mom, oh Mom," he nearly shouted, as he threw his arms around her and clung to her. They held on to each other, Isobel finally letting the tears come. The drive had been an exercise in mind diversion and she could now let it all out.

When they pulled apart, Isobel still held onto Ian's arm. "Where's Delia and the kids, Ian?" her voice full of concern for her daughter-in-law and grandchildren, but before he could respond, Nora, Ian's stepmom, joined them. Isobel turned and gave her a hug. "Thanks for being here, Nora."

"Of course," Nora replied as she handed Isobel some tissues. Isobel smiled at her in gratitude as she dried her eyes.

"Mom, Delia and the kids are waiting for dad's flight from Phoenix to get in, and then bringing him over. They should be here by midnight."

"Any word on Alec?"

"Nothing other than to just wait. We think the police wanted the FBI to get here before they did or said anything."

Isobel fought back the panic she felt inside of her. She closed her eyes and blinked back the tears. "He's going to be ok," she said, through shivering teeth.

"Mom, let's go inside." Ian put his arm over her shoulders and guided her into the building. "One of the officers told me they airlifted someone out right before I got here, but she didn't know who. Then an hour ago they sent someone in to say they'll let us know soon, and soon hasn't come yet. I want to punch something, I'm so frustrated."

The three of them entered the building and huddled together in the hall, avoiding the overly bright foyer and a few other parents who had been trickling in because they hadn't heard from their children.

"Mom, they said there weren't many people in the building when it happened. Dr. Garcia came through awhile ago and told me most of the staff and faculty had been at a campus wide meeting. She thinks the shooter didn't know or would have attacked the meeting instead. Alec might have been the only staff in the building, she said, and the rest would have been students."

Dr. Pilar Garcia had been Isobel's favorite teacher, though as dean, and now a vice president, she taught only one class a semester. Isobel made sure she took each of her classes. They become friends and stayed in touch over the years.

Isobel leaned against the wall, feeling she might collapse on the floor otherwise. "Are the kids okay?" she asked Ian.

"Yeah, they just know they're coming to see Granny for a few days, and Papa J and Grammy Nora, so they are over the moon excited."

Isobel smiled and leaned her head on Ian's shoulder. Nora disappeared and in a few minutes came back with coffee for the two of them. "Thank you," Isobel said, taking the cup from Nora.

They heard the door to the lobby open, and the three of them leaned around the corner to see a man in uniform holding a clipboard coming in the building. Isobel's stomach started churning as they waited for him to speak. Those who had been seated in the foyer stood up in anticipation and Isobel, Ian and Nora, crossed the floor to him as well.

"I know you are all anxious. We'd like to speak to you individually." Several other officers entered the building and flanked the first. "Is the family of Alec Davis here?"

"Oh my God, oh my God," Isobel murmured as she and Ian clung to each other. She couldn't catch her breath for a moment. "Yes," Isobel was barely able to say as they stepped forward. She felt nauseous as an officer walked over and took her elbow, leading all of them to an open classroom. The officer motioned for them to sit at a table. He sat across from them, but avoided their eyes, as he shifted uncomfortably in his chair.

"What is your relationship to Mr. Davis?" he asked.

"I'm his mother, Isobel Allen. This is his brother Ian and his stepmom, Nora." She managed to choke out.

"I regret to," he said, his voice breaking before he could continue, "I'm so sorry," he paused, "Mr. Davis is dead."

Isobel screamed, "No, no, no!" before convulsive sobs began to shake her body, and Ian howled with the pain as he wrapped his arms around his mother. Nora stood up as her tears slid down her face, and went behind them, wrapping her arms around them both. Everything had been normal just hours ago, and now their whole world had been rocked right out from under them. Normal didn't exist anymore. Isobel had held out hope till the last moment that Alec was alive. Until the words formed and were spoken by the officer she believed he had survived, and the delay in letting her know was because *HE* was hurt, and *HE* had been airlifted to Lubbock, *HE* was going to make it, her Alec.

The officer sat with them while they cried. He took a pack of tissues from his pocket and slid it across the table. In a few minutes he left and came back with bottles of water for each of them. He finally said, "The perpetrator shot Mr. Davis several times. I think you might want to know though, Mr. Davis shielded two of his students. The girl directly behind him is still alive at this moment, and has been airlifted to Lubbock." He then asked if he could do anything else, and Nora shook her head no. He then left them to their grief. Dr. Garcia came in and Isobel stood to allow Pilar to wrap her arms around her and hug. "Thank you for being here," Isobel said between quiet sobs.

"I'm so sorry, Isobel. So, so sorry."

"Thank you," Isobel whispered.

"Can I get you anything?" Pilar asked.

"No. I think I need to go. We will go..." she didn't know where, but Nora continued the sentence.

"To my house," and Isobel looked at her gratefully.

Pilar walked them out of the building. "I'll be in touch. Let me know if there is anything we can do for you."

"Thank you, Pilar."

The three of them walked into the cool evening and found their respective vehicles. This had been the longest day of Isobel's life and she expected the longest night was to follow.

# Chapter 2

Isobel and Ian sat on the couch at Nora's, talking through everything, glancing at the television as pictures of the "alleged shooters" came up. Ian turned up the sound for a moment, and then switched it off. "I can't bear to hear this right now," Ian said, and returned to sit with Isobel. Nora had disappeared to prepare bedrooms for everyone before the others arrived, and as she came back into the living room, they heard Delia's car pull into the drive.

Ian went out to help Delia bring in a sleeping Bree and Brian. They carried them in, followed by Jacob. He hugged Nora and let out a sob, his shoulders silently shaking. Then hugged Isobel as she joined them at the door. Ian and Delia put their arms around them both as they reentered the room. Isobel turned to Delia and hugged her close. She adored her daughter-in-law. "It must have been a tough drive for you."

"I'm okay. The kids were excited to pick up Papa J, but they fell asleep almost immediately, or it would have been harder than it was," Delia said. Isobel wrapped her arm around Delia's shoulder and they all retreated to the kitchen.

Nora poured everyone a whiskey, Irish for Jacob, and Scotch for everyone else. She passed them out and directed them to the table, where they sat, numb from the day's emotion, the waiting, the frustration, the tears.

"Our boy, Isobel, our boy," Jacob said with such force, Isobel jumped. "How does this happen? Damn I hate those people. They need to all go back to Syria."

Isobel looked at her hands cupping the glass. He had been listening to the early reports about the two shooters and the speculation over the attack being terrorist or not. "Jacob, we don't know anything about the shooters yet, or even where they are from. They are two people. They deserve our anger, no one else."

"This is not a time for your pious bullshit, Isobel. I'll be angry at whomever I damn well please."

"I'm just glad they're dead," Ian said quietly.

"Me too," Jacob shouted.

Isobel needed to be with her son, and his family. She would make an effort not to set Jacob off again, so thankful to Nora for asking her to stay. Isobel considered staying at Alec's place, but she didn't think she could be there amidst his belongings, his space, and not fall into a million pieces that might not ever be put together again. Life felt tenuous at this moment. She reached for Ian's hand and squeezed.

Delia soon left to check on the kids and put herself to bed. Jacob and Nora went next. Ian and Isobel poured themselves another Scotch and moved to the living room couch. "I just keep thinking how surreal this seems and that Alec is going to walk through the door any minute. Today was so normal. You know? I ran, dropped Bree at pre-school, I went to work, I called people, I had coffee, I..." Ian trailed off. "Normal."

"I know. I've had the same thought. I can't believe this has happened, that Alec is gone," Isobel said, choking up on her words.

"When I got to campus this afternoon, there were police cars everywhere. Then the FBI, or at least I think they were FBI, came screeching in a few minutes later in their black cars. There were students standing behind all the yellow tape, even though Dr. Garcia said they called for a lockdown. I was a crazy person, Mom. I just kept screaming for them to find Alec," Ian hunched over and began to sob quietly, his body convulsing so hard the couch shook. Isobel slid over and put her arms around him and cried with him. When he stopped and began to take deep breaths, Isobel sat up and rubbed Ian's back until he calmed. She pulled her sweater down over her hand and wiped her own eyes. Ian continued telling his story of what happened for him before she arrived. "Then when Nora got there, they took us to the Liberal Arts building. I couldn't just sit there. I kept going outside, looking to see anything, but someone would bring me back inside. I can't believe it took them so long to come and tell us about Alec."

"I drove so fast I thought I'd get pulled over for sure. I kept telling myself he's alive. He has to be." Isobel's voice broke and she took a deep breath before she could continue. "When I called him and got his voicemail, I told myself they were questioning him, or he was hurt and being airlifted to Lubbock. I told myself stories like that the whole way to stay sane enough to drive."

"Yeah, I did the same. And I kept thinking about crazy stuff we did when we were kids."

Jacob appeared in the hallway entrance. "Hey you two. No sleep for you either?"

"We haven't even tried," Isobel said. "Come, join us."

Jacob poured himself another whiskey and poured them each a bit more Scotch. He sat down on the other side of Ian and put his arm around his son's shoulders. Ian leaned into Jacob, all sitting in silence for awhile. Jacob stared off into space as he started talking. "This afternoon during my meeting I got a text from Betty to call her for an emergency." Betty had been Jacob's secretary since he'd opened his real estate business almost thirty years ago. "Betty never interrupts me. I thought something had happened to Nora since she was supposed to be driving back to Llano from Roswell this afternoon." He paused and took a drink of his whiskey. "I got out of there and called, and at the same time she picked up, I saw the headlines on CNN on the lobby television, and it registered and didn't all at the same time. That's my town. That's my university. That's where Alec works, and oh my God." Jacob, just as Ian and Isobel had done, needed to tell his story. He took a deep breath and continued. "My knees buckled and I realized, I'm sitting on the floor, Betty was talking and the concierge ran to ask me if I was ok. I know I talked to someone, I guess the concierge, and asked him to get me home. Someone put me in a cab to the airport and I managed to get on the plane. The rest is a blur till Delia picked me up at the curb."

The three of them sat on the couch, talking about Alec, remembering details of his life, till they all drifted off. Isobel's head leaned back against the cushions and Ian laid down in-between them both, his head on Isobel's lap, his legs curled up across Jacob.

Four-year-old Bree found them like this the next morning. She leaned down to her Daddy and put her face right up next to his, laying her hand against his cheek and patting him. He opened his eyes to find her smiling at him. "Daddy! Hello! What are you doing? Why are you asleep with Granny and Papa J?"

Ian sat up and snatched her up into his arms. "Good morning my little sunshine."

"When is Uncle Alec coming?"

The thought of telling Bree and Brian had not occurred to him yet. His eyes filled with tears, but he couldn't find any words to explain to his daughter how Uncle Alec would not be back. He couldn't comprehend the horror of her having to understand this at such a young age.

Isobel woke and heard Bree's question. "Come here, you," Isobel said.

Bree flung herself at Isobel, shouting, "Granny!" She hugged her as Isobel stood up.

"Let's go see what's for breakfast! What do you like to eat at Papa J's house?"

"Cocoa Puffs," Bree yelled, throwing her arms over her head.

"Well let's see if we can find some then." As Isobel opened cabinets looking for cereal, Bree ran for the table and pulled out a chair, clambering up to wait for her meal. For the moment, she forgot about Uncle Alec. Isobel knew Ian and Delia would have a hard time telling Bree her favorite playmate wouldn't be coming back. 'He can't be dead. He can't be dead.' Isobel's brain chanted over and over, as she peered into drawers, cabinets and the refrigerator, gathering the accoutrements for Bree's breakfast. But he was.

The press arrived outside Jacob and Nora's house that morning, hoping for an interview with one of them. People who came to see them, dodged microphones and cameras every time they entered or left the house. The FBI released Alec's body to them late in the day on Saturday, but they waited until midnight to go to the funeral home to avoid the melee. Ronald Gomez, the funeral director, whose sons had grown up with the boys and been friends basically their entire lives, met them and escorted them through the back door. Isobel and Ian stood on one side of Alec, and Nora and Jacob on the other, as they saw him for the last time. Isobel thought, as she looked at Alec, how little he looked like himself. Even in sleep Alec always seemed full of light, and now the light had disappeared and only a shell of the vibrant energy Alec had brought to the world remained.

Jacob and Nora said their goodbyes to Alec first, then the two of them stepped into the hall. Isobel leaned in and pushed Alec's hair back from his forehead and kissed him where she had every night of his life while he was at home. Even as teenagers she would make the boys report in and wake her up no matter what time they came in at night. She would lean in and hug each of them, take a deep whiff and then kiss them on the forehead. They never said anything about the big whiff, until years later telling her, "Mom, we knew what you were up to," smelling them for alcohol or pot. They would tease her about it years later, when visiting her, and they would come in late, though plenty old enough to drink, and ask her, "Did you get a good whiff?"

Isobel held onto Ian's hand as he leaned in and kissed his brother and whispered goodbye. Then he stepped away. Isobel pushed Alec's hair back from his forehead again and took his hand. She longed to pick Alec up and cradle him, to hug him one last time. Tears filled her eyes till her sight was completely blurred, and she saw tears dropping on Alec's hand. She wiped the tears from her eyes and looked at him again, before leaning in and kissing him on the forehead and on the cheek. "Alec, you were so brave, trying to protect your students. I can't believe you are gone. I miss you. I will always miss you. Goodbye, darling boy," she whispered. "I love you forever." Then she and Ian clung to each other as they cried.

Ronald escorted them all to his office where they sat around a small table to make plans for the memorial.

"Alec had mentioned he wanted to be cremated," Ian said. "I would like us to honor his wishes. We talked about it not too long ago, the amount of space and money wasted on caskets and all. Sorry Mr. Gomez, I mean no disrespect."

"None taken. I'm here to see we meet your needs. That's all. My staff and I have had such a hard time with this. We all knew Alec. I think you boys were in my driveway playing basketball half your lives."

"Yeah, and at our house the other half."

Ronald reached over and put his hand on top of Ian's folded hands on the table. He couldn't say anything for a few moments and they all waited. "We are here for you and we will do this as you request."

Jacob started, "We would like to have the service at our church, mine and Nora's, on Tuesday. We know there will be a crowd, but we think it will be large enough. We don't want people to come to the cemetery though." Ronald nodded in understanding.

Isobel said, "We thought it might be best to take the urn to the cemetery at dawn the day after the funeral or maybe the next. Alec loved a good sunrise. We would like the urn placed with his grandparents graves. You can do this, right?"

"Of course."

"Dr. Gordon, from the station, is putting together a film and picture montage for the service. He picked up photo albums yesterday. Everyone has been so kind and helpful," said Nora.

They finished up the paperwork and went back to Jacob's house to see if they could steal a few hours of sleep before morning.

# Chapter 3

I sobel felt weary. She found herself wandering the house at night, or sitting on the couch staring into space, because closing her eyes meant playing what happened to Alec, over and over in her mind. The day of the funeral came. They were to leave for the church early, hoping to avoid the media whom they felt certain would be in the parking lot hoping for sound bites. The church people had prepared a meal for the family and close friends, a tradition that helped make the day more bearable.

After the family meal, and the seating of all attending, they had been ushered into the sanctuary. The slide and video show of Alec's life had played in a loop as everyone entered the church, and continued now. The urn sat on a table surrounded by pictures of Alec and flowers. Ian had chosen songs from Alec's playlist and the church choir had come to sing "When

Peace Like a River," a song loved by their family, even after Isobel and Alec had quit attending any sort of church, they would still sing gospel songs when they found themselves in the car together, and this was their favorite. Those who spoke conveyed the true spirit of Alec. However, when the preacher from Jacob's church had prayed, he turned it into a mini sermon on the devil's presence in this world and how Alec would want them all to be good Christians, till Isobel wanted to yell "stop." He finally came to an end and said "Amen," as did the other good church going people of Llano.

Convened in the lobby, hands were shaken, hugs were accepted, and words of sorrow spoken. Isobel's friends, thankfully stayed close to her side. Her four best friends, Diane, Sam, Richard and Doug, had arrived in time for the family dinner before the service. The five of them, over the years, became a small family of sorts. Without fail, they came together every other Sunday evening, taking turns cooking, or having potluck, good wine. The conversation always flowed, discussing books, politics, religions, food, money, and whatever controversies that came to mind. If things got heated, Richard would always say "What about them Isotopes?" the Albuquerque baseball farm team, and they would all break into laughter. They came there to face this day with her, and for that she would be ever grateful.

At Jacob's house, where food had been arriving since the day after Alec's death, a spread prepared by the church ladies, sat ready and waiting on the table and counters. The endless day brought hordes of people with condolences, they ate, shook hands, and left, an endless stream. Isobel knew the beauty of small town life and a church community, but she did not miss that enough to ever desire coming back. When her friends left that afternoon for Santa Fe, she slipped away to her bedroom, closed the door, shut the shades and turned out the lights. The darkness settled around her, and for the first time in four days, she slept.

Isobel heard the murmur of voices, but kept her eyes closed as she slowly woke; she did not move, hoping that moment between sleep and wakefulness would last, but the reality of the last four days rushed back in. She sat up on the bed and felt tears sliding down her face into her motionless hands. She let them come, then slowly lifted her arm and wiped the tears away. Placing her feet on the floor, she found her shoes then stumbled to the dresser, turned on the lamp, and looked at herself in the mirror. She finger-combed her hair back into place, barely recognizing herself with lifeless puffy eyes, and pale skin. Making her way to the door, she realized the sun had set while she rested. 'How long had she been asleep?' she wondered. Sleep that eluded her for the last four nights, came when least expected.

The smell of food wafted over her as she opened the door. For the first time in days she felt a bit hungry, or maybe she still felt the nausea of days of stress? The thick carpet muffled her footsteps; no one turned towards her when she stepped into the brightly lit living room. 'What is with these overhead lights?' she thought as the harsh light overwhelmed her, 'Lamps, they need some lamps in here,' then caught herself, realizing what a weird random thought to have at this moment. She shook it off and stood there unnoticed, observing the crowd.

At fifty four, Isobel, fit and trim from hiking and cycling looked good. In her married days she had always been a bit heavy. Now she spent as much time outdoors as possible, keeping her weight where it should be. She liked how it felt to be healthy.

Jacob, encircled by a group of friends, looked up and saw her, crossed the room and put his arm across her shoulders, half hugging her to him. They seldom saw each other since their divorce ten years ago, and though the gesture was appreciated, she felt awkward as she glimpsed Nora, Jacob's wife, looking their way, but she gently smiled at Isobel and came towards them, wrapping her arm around Jacob's waist.

"Thanks you two, for making this part easier. I want to wake up from this nightmare, and see Alec over there with Ian, laughing and entertaining us all."

"Me too," Jacob and Nora said almost together.

As Jacob dropped his arm from Isobel's shoulders, he pulled Nora in close to him. They all stood looking at Ian, suit jacket and tie removed, his eyes unfocused, sitting quietly in an overstuffed arm chair, holding Bree, as two-year-old Brian, stood beside him, running his car up and down Ian's leg. Ian was a handsome young man, but his features were clouded in sadness.

The room was full of the people who had attended the funeral, quiet voices murmuring, with an occasional random laugh or loud comment breaking through the low rumble of voices. The kitchen overflowed with friends and family, helping themselves to the mountains of casseroles brought by neighbors and Jacob's church. The guests loaded up with food, then headed out onto the covered patio, or the living room, balancing plates and glasses in their hands or on their knees, once they found a seat. Isobel felt the tears welling up again as she saw the immense outpouring of love these people had for her son, for their family. Sometimes she wanted to resent them all for choosing sides when she and Jacob divorced, for telling tales, and basically shunning her, but that was long ago and her life, till this moment, had been far better than any she had ever had with Jacob. 'No, resentment only hurt her,' she thought, 'and they had, for the most part, been kind and caring to her throughout this ordeal.' She also realized, Alec's death, as well as the death of the others, had affected the entire community on a deeper level than a death under different circumstances. Alec was a young man who had been born and raised in this community, and everyone felt this affront to their lives.

She slipped away from Jacob and Nora as they stood murmuring to each other, making her way across the room to sit on the arm of Ian's chair. Isobel ran her fingers through his short brown hair, like she had when he was a child; he broke from his reverie and looked up at her.

"Oh Mom, what will I ever do without him? He has always been my best friend." His voice choked with tears as he tried to talk. "Remember when we would fight, you always told us, 'friends, girlfriends and maybe even spouses will come and go in your life, but your brother will always be here for you?' I still remember rolling my eyes every time you said that, but then, it turned out to be true. He was always here for me. Now what?"

"I don't know."

"I can't make sense of this. I am so angry and so, so…"

"Me too. There is no sense though. None."

"Yeah."

She leaned into him and hugged. He put his arms around Isobel's waist, like he had when he was a child. Bree took the moment to hop down and taunt her brother. Ian's wife Delia returned with a plate of food and tried to get the kids to eat, but they were having too much fun with their cars to notice.

"Isobel, did you get a little sleep," Delia asked?

Ian unfolded himself from his Mom and they both turned to her. She held out her plate to him, but he shook his head no.

"I think I slept. When I woke, I was in that twilight moment, I didn't know where I was or what had happened and just for a moment I thought, I thought everything was ok" she sighed, "What time is it anyway."

Delia looked at her phone. "7:00."

"Ok." She continued to run her fingers through Ian's hair, both of them staring off into space. No one spoke to them, not wanting to break their moment.

"Hey you two, people are starting to leave." Isobel looked up at Jacob. She had no idea how long she and Ian had been sitting there. Jacob stood in front of the chair and reached down to shake Ian's leg. "I thought you would want to say bye."

"Oh, yes," and Isobel stood up and headed to the front door to see if she could help anyone with a jacket or purse, to accept awkward hugs and mumbled expressions of sympathy. No one really seemed to know what to say. Children aren't supposed to die before their parents and a violent, senseless death is even worse. There are no words to console.

At 9:30, the house was finally empty of guests and quiet, except for Bree and Brian, both not wanting to go to bed, Brian howling for Isobel. She lightly tapped on the other guest room door and stepped in to see Delia trying patiently to quiet them.

"May I?" Delia nodded her head as Isobel bent over to pick up Brian, his arms outstretched to her. Delia smiled.

Isobel carried him to her room, laid him on the bed and curled up next to him. He put his hand in her hair and twisted it around and around till he fell asleep, just as Alec had as a baby. Her baby. Such a sweet spirited baby, who grew up to be a sweet and caring man.

Someone knocked, "Come in," Isobel said quietly. Nora poked her head round the door.

"Can I get you anything?" Nora whispered.

"No, I'm fine."

"Ok."

"Thank you again for letting me stay here. Being alone would have been too hard."

"Of course. Look, you're family, no matter." She smiled at Isobel and before closing the door whispered, "Goodnight then. See you in the morning."

"Good night."

After the divorce, Jacob dated several different women, one who refused to even acknowledge his sons. He had eventually met Nora and she was perfect for him. Uncomplicated and unassuming, an educator as well, with just a little edge to her. Nora suited him much better than she ever had. Ex's aren't supposed to like the new wife, but she did.

Isobel lay in the dark, eyes wide open, listening to her grandson's breathing. If she closed her eyes, she pictured over and over again, Alec being gunned down against the Green Room wall, shielding two of his student workers, his arms wrapped over them. The one pressed against the wall had lived, though seriously injured. The FBI would not let anyone talk to her at this point, but a kind nurse told Isobel the girl kept talking about Alec and how he saved her life. A small comfort, but all she wanted was to have her own child back.

Isobel woke with a start. She reached for Brian, only to find him gone. He had only recently been able to reach the doorknob, making him a regular escape artist. She could hear Bree's voice in the distance. Isobel reached for her house coat, but realized she was still wearing her clothes from the funeral, having fallen asleep at some point in the night. She walked down the hall and peeked around the corner.

"Granny, you're in your same clothes," Bree said, laughing and pointing.

"I know! What a silly Granny, huh?"

"You are a silly head and so's Brian. I made him breakfast."

"You did?"

"Sure I did. Come see." Bree took Isobel's hand and led her to the kitchen. There was Brian on a stool eating some sort of red jello dessert from the day before.

Isobel felt a laugh bubble to the surface. A good feeling for a fleeting second. "What a good big sister you are Bree." She bent down and hugged her and then stood and kissed Brian on the head. "I love my little munchkins!"

"Did you call my Daddy a munchkin when he was little?"

"I did."

Bree ran into the living room, plopping herself on the bean bag chair Nora kept for her in front of the television. "Granny," Bree almost yelled, "can I watch *My Little Pony*?"

"Ok, but promise to be really quiet. Everyone is still sleeping."

Bree shook her head yes and scooted down in her chair as Isobel found her show. Her brown curls the only thing visible as Isobel walked back into the kitchen to check on Brian. Red jello covered Brian's face and ran down the front of his pajama shirt.

"How's that breakfast?"

Brian grinned at her, his teeth were red too. She found a towel in a drawer, turned on the water and stood there waiting for it to be warm. Her mind wandered to the days when her boys were this little and how funny they were together. Ian almost always 'made' breakfast for Alec on Saturday mornings. Alec would appear in their bedroom doorway, holding a plastic bowl in his hands. She could hear Alec's voice in her head…"Mommy, fix my bekfest," but Ian would be right behind him, and he'd put his arm around Alec, "Come on Bubba, I'll fix it," and he'd walk Alec into the kitchen and fill his bowl with cereal and they'd watch cartoons, letting their parents lie in a bit longer.

"Granny, crying," Brian asked?

Isobel realized the water was warm, and smiled at Brian. "Yes, sweetie. Granny is sad." She went to him and wiped his face and hands and he reached up and patted her on the cheek. She lifted him from his stool and took him into the living room to join Bree. They cuddled on the couch, waiting for the others to wake.

# Chapter 4

Two days later, they were all up at five, preparing to be at the cemetery by six for a 6:15 sunrise. Jacob, Isobel and Ian had each been given a small box of Alec's ashes before the funeral and the rest were interred into the green steel urn which would rest next to Jacob's parents in the Llano cemetery. They piled into their cars and drove to the cemetery, two blocks away from Jacob's, driving between the marble and concrete pillars that marked the entrance, winding down the road to the back row. Alec had embraced his Scottish heritage and made it a part of his life especially after he and Isobel had trekked around Scotland shortly after his college graduation. "I want the bagpipes playing *Flowers of the Forest*, the REAL traditional bagpipe funeral song, when the world tells me goodbye," he had told Ian some time ago. Ian had laughed at him and called him a dork.

They'd had to send to Lubbock for a bagpipe player, but found someone willing to make the drive, and play the requested song.

A small marble slab had been laid next to Jacob's parent's graves. The urn was engraved with his name, Alec Finney Davis and the Scottish toast, "His equal will never be among us again," and would be attached to the slab after they left. Isobel's eyes filled with tears as they gathered round the marker. She looked at each face in the circle, this family that had morphed and changed over the years, the loss of the marriage so devastating at first, had been a pain that softened and healed in time, but this loss? How would it ever heal? A fracture so jagged and painful Isobel knew she would feel it each waking moment of her life.

Jacob had wanted to have the minister of his church present for this, but Ian and Isobel had balked at the idea. Alec was a spiritual person and believed in a higher power, but strongly maintained organized religion had done more harm to the world than good. Instead, they decided to recite the "23 Psalm" together and then Isobel would read Alec's favorite poem, "To S.R. Crocket" by Robert Louis Stevenson, after which, *Flowers of the Field* was played. As they spoke the Psalm, one even little Bree knew, the sun began to peek above the flat distant plain. Isobel then, through choked back tears, read the Stevenson poem and as soon as she finished, the piper began to play, the haunting sound of the bagpipe filling the morning quiet with the wailing tone, one that hit Isobel in the heart, the sound bringing back such poignant memories of Alec's short life and their time together.

When Alec and Isobel had trekked around Scotland that summer, while in Stromness on the Orkney Islands, one night as they wandered the village after dinner they heard the sound of bagpipes and peeked inside the building from which the sound came and when one of the players spotted them, he stopped and motioned for them to come in. When the pipers took a break they asked questions of Alec and Isobel, but their accent was so thick, Isobel had trouble understanding. Alec, though, had an ear for the brogue, answering for them both. They had their own private concert that night, one that had made a lasting impression.

The piper finished. They stood in the silence, each in their own thoughts, when Bree skipped over and put her hand in Isobel's. "Would you like to say a prayer, Bree?"

Bree's face lit up as she shook her head yes. She didn't truly understand what all this meant, but she knew all the grownups were sad.

She put her hands out, and as if patting a table in front of her, waved them up and down saying, "Shhhh, shhhh, shhhh. I'm going to pray," and with that she launched into, "God is great, God is good and we thank him for our food. God, Uncle Alec likes candy. Give him lots of candy. Aaaaaamen!" She smiled up at Isobel and took her hand again.

"Bree, that was perfect. Thank you sweet girl." Isobel kneeled down and took Bree into her arms and hugged.

"Granny, you're squeezing my guts out!"

Bree was the laughter they all needed today. And they did laugh.

They returned to Jacob's house, to a breakfast of fruit and banana bread one of the neighbors had prepared for them. No one really ate, but they sat around the table and talked about how beautiful their family service had been. Thankful to not have had the press or any other friends or neighbors there, they had been able to just be in their own thoughts of Alec.

They all holed up in Jacob and Nora's house for a few more days after after the funeral. Friends brought more food, and heated up leftovers still in the refrigerator. They would set the table and wait on them all while they tried to eat, but Isobel only poked at hers. She helped Bree and Brian, one seated on either side of her, with their plates, cutting up vegetables, helping Brian with his spoon, wiping their mouths, until they were ready to play again. She was thankful for their presence. They helped keep them all busy. The neighbors would clean up and then silently slip away.

Ian and Isobel had tried to venture into the grocery one evening, to pick up a few items, but they had gotten no further than the produce section before they had been surrounded by several people who knew them, or knew Alec, and though well intentioned and kind, their comments of sympathy and physical proximity were too painful. They abandoned their basket and headed for the car, feeling too raw for public exposure.

Isobel sat with her hands on the steering wheel for a moment staring straight ahead. "Are you okay?" she asked without looking at Ian.

"Yeah," he sniffed and wiped his eyes with the back of his hand. "I'm kind of ready to get back to Lubbock, but I feel bad about leaving Dad right now. He's got to be here every day. And he knows everyone in town practically."

"I know, sweetheart. It's going to be tough for him, and Nora too. When are you thinking of leaving?"

"I have to be back at work next week. You?"

"The district gave me two weeks, but I'm going to head back Saturday I think."

"How are we going to keep going? He's my brother. Damn it, I just want him back. I want normal."

Isobel put her hand on his arm. "I don't think we get that anymore."

Ian shook his head in agreement, then turned to stare out his window. Isobel started the car and pulled out of the space, heading for Jacob's house.

The next morning, Isobel stood on the porch of Jacob's house, the day already quite warm, as it can only be in eastern New Mexico in April. A cool breeze promised to turn into a hot dusty wind before the day was out. 'Thank God there are no television crews,' she thought. Waiting for Ian and Jacob to join her, she stepped into the yard and wandered over to look at a rose bush.

"Mom?"

"Over here. Looking at the rose bush."

Isobel smiled and clutched Ian's arm as they walked to her car. His was full of car seats and sticky sippy cups, so they opted for Isobel's instead. Jacob followed in his pickup.

"Are you ready for this, Mom?"

"I don't know. I keep thinking we'll walk in and Alec will be there."

"Yeah, this is so, so..."

"Surreal," Isobel finished for him.

"Yes."

She pulled to the curb in front of Alec's house, allowing Jacob to back into the drive. Alec's car sat parked under the carport, a small silver SUV, he had purchased, used, last year. He had bought the house when he moved back to Llano for the production management job. Only a block from the university, he walked to work most days. He had loved his home, a small house, built in the 1940's, with nice wood work and wood floors. There was even a basement, one his friends and coworkers gathered in during tornado warnings. Not many basements had been built in the hard rocky caliche of the eastern New Mexico plains, but it was often needed during the spring and summer here. The stucco was still the ugly military hospital green, a color he had planned to change, but had never gotten around to.

Isobel walked around to the carport and looked over into the yard. She loved the back porch, ground level concrete, with a metal roof that extended out, leaving room for furniture and a bar. They would sit here, have a few drinks, and talk for hours any time she came to visit. This was a happy place. Alec and Ian made her proud. Both had graduated college, found good jobs and started building lives for themselves. They were smart, funny, kind, and loving young men and she had a part in that. And so did Jacob.

Jacob came up behind her and looked around as well. "What a mess, eh? He never could keep this place cleaned up and the yard mowed." Just another way she and Jacob differed in their view of the world.

Isobel felt the criticism, as if directed towards her, as if it was yesterday she was standing in the backyard on Portales Circle, listening to him tell her she needed to clean up the yard, or the garage, or the kitchen, but rarely lifting a finger to help. She shook it off and turned to go in the house.

Ian held the door open for them and she stepped into the yellow kitchen with the black and white checkered linoleum floor. The familiar smell of old wood, baked bread, which he made almost daily, and the slight, lingering smell of Alec's cologne hit her full force. She put her hands over her face and began to sob. Her shoulders shaking, as her knees buckled and she collapsed to the floor. Ian sat down beside her and put his arm around her shoulders. The tears came in an endless torrent. And then it was over. She sat there, her head on his shoulder, then slammed her hands on the ground.

"I am so fucking angry! How does this happen? How can two people walk into a television station and start shooting? I can't wrap my head around this. I can't. I can't."

"None of us can, Isobel," Jacob said.

"I know. I want answers though. I just do," she said.

Isobel looked at Ian. Tears were forming in his eyes. "I'm sorry for the breakdown."

"It's okay, Mom. When I was running Sunday, out by Thompson's place, I stopped and started yelling at the sky. The cows all stopped eating and stared at me, till one started running away and they all joined in," he half-heartedly laughed. "I started a stampede." She smiled at him as he slowly stood up. Reaching up her hand to him, he pulled her to her feet.

Jacob put his arms around each of their shoulders and squeezed. "Maybe today's not the day to do this."

"No, I want to be here. I need to be here," said Isobel as she started for Alec's bedroom. She stood in the doorway and surveyed the room. It was so like him; a platform bed with a dark blue cover, one wall lined with bookshelves, the wall at the head of his bed he had bricked himself, and the low chest of drawers, under the bank of windows, were a dark wood to match the platform of his bed and side table. The closet door stood open, a t-shirt hung from the doorknob, probably the one he had slept in the night before...the night before everything changed.

His closet smelled like him. She buried her face in his jackets, shirts, sweaters, and wrapped her arms around them all, hugging them to her body, breathing in his scent. Then images of Alec and the creative outfits he put together as a toddler, continuing on through pre-school and beyond, ran through her head. She slipped his 'Mr. Rogers cardigan' off the hangar and put it on. Alec and Ian had loved Mr. Rogers, his calm voice mesmerized them while she made dinner. Ian had teased him about being a hipster when he bought that sweater. Alec just laughed and said, "Yeah, I am."

Turning to the room, she walked to the head of his bed, her hand trailing over the bedspread. She straightened a pillow and then picked up the books from his nightstand. A voracious reader like herself, they often discussed books they were reading. During July, Isobel's vacation from her job, the two of them would choose a book to read together and then she would come down for a few days and they would discuss it. So few people read anything these days, it was pure joy to find this connection with her son.

Isobel stepped into the living room and walked across the black and white carpet with a geodesic design which covered a large portion of the room. She laid the books on the grey leather couch and then sat in the club chair opposite, looking at the art work he'd covered the walls with, much of it bought from students or his travel. A small bar sat in the corner. She stood and went to the bar, picked up his bottle of Scotch, and took a deep breath of the rich peaty smell he loved so much, then poured herself a small bit and sipped it, waiting for that first slight burn as the golden liquid slipped down her throat.

Ian and Jacob's voices drifted up from the basement.

Jacob had grabbed an empty box and filled it with the food items, cups and electric kettle Alec kept there for tornado warnings. "I'll drop these at the shelter and take the rest of the food from the kitchen, too. Everyone good with that?"

Isobel shook her head yes.

"Sure, Dad, but I think Mom should take the bread making stuff if she wants."

"Thanks, Ian. Yes, I'd love that."

Teaching Ian and Alec to cook had been a means of hanging out with them in the kitchen, having someone to chat to as she made the nightly meal, and a subtle, though not always subtle, way of finding out what was going on in their lives. She savored those times of talking and laughing, time spent in the company of love. Though no longer religious in any sense of the word, she still often thought of the verse in the Bible which speaks of Mary storing up in her heart all she witnessed in her son's life. She would now have to rely on that store in her own heart to remember every detail of Alec's life. No new memories would be added. She now viciously guarded her heart against the terror of this past weekend, closing her eyes against the pictures on television or in the local paper, as she could not bear to have these memories obscure the good. She did not want to see the remains of his death, only the sweet picture of his life.

In the kitchen Jacob began to pile in the canned goods and anything from the refrigerator that was unspoiled. Ian found Alec's 'magic' clay loaf pan and the clay baking round, and handed them to Isobel. She had taught them both to make bread, but Alec had become an "Artisanal Bread Wizard," a name given to him by students who devoured his breads that he almost daily took to the station. "It's my way of feeding the masses, Mom, and kneading the bread, the best possible meditation practice ever." She could hear his voice in her head. His generosity was admirable. Isobel often feared the frugality of her Scottish heritage made her stingy instead of just frugal, so she was relieved the boys had always been generous of heart.

They left the kitchen, and trailed into his office, a long, fairly narrow, bookshelf, desk-lined, passage from the back porch into the house. Occupied by a washer and dryer as well, he laughingly always referred to this space as his 'office, slash, laundry room,' but had made plans to cordon off the offending appliances, or get the plumbing for them moved to the basement. Another project he had neither the time nor money to complete, but what they all knew, it didn't much matter to Alec. He took life as it came. He read *The Daily Stoic,* every day, and professed to be a stoic. He believed in living in the moment and knew that someday, if he had the money, he might take care of a project. Jacob found this most annoying about his son, and constantly encouraged him to "take initiative." His pragmatic business mind could not conceive of living in the moment.

"Alec loved this space," Isobel said to no one in particular. Her eyes scanned the shelves, touching a book here or there. He had all their discussion books on one shelf together.

"What should we do with all of this," Ian said as he made a wide sweeping gesture. "I hate that we have to be here now. I hate that we are walking through his house like this. I feel like he should be walking in the door any minute and laughing because he would be so surprised to see us."

"We don't have to do anything else right now," Jacob said as he stepped up and put his arm on Ian's shoulder. "Unless he left a will, which I seriously doubt, it will take a few months to go through probate, giving us time to decide what to do with...with his belongings. I'll come look through his papers and see if he left anything."

"Thanks, Dad. This is harder than I ever imagined."

Isobel went to the basement and found another empty box. She gathered the books she had left on the couch, along with his journal she had picked up off his desk, the loaf pan and round, and closed up the box. She kept on the sweater she had taken from his closet and stepped back into the kitchen.

"I'm going to go with dad to drop off the food. You headed back to the house?"

"Sure. I'll see you there."

"Love you, Mom."

"I love you too, Ian," she said as she let the screen door slam behind her, and headed for her car.

Looking down at the stairs, to avoid tripping, she hadn't seen they were there, the vultures and their camera crew lining the curb, standing around her car. Ian and Jacob were still in the house and hadn't seen them yet. One came rushing towards her.

"Ms. Allen, what are you feeling? What about your son's killers?"

Her hands, occupied with the box, she couldn't push the microphone away from her. "How do you think I feel? I just lost my son and for what? These people say we will rot in hell because we don't believe what they do, so they want to kill us to speed that up? Can't you just leave us alone?"

"Hey, get away from her." Jacob came running to fend off the reporter, slightly shoving him away. "Leave us to our grief." He opened her car door for her and put the box on the back seat, as the reporter backed away. Isobel pushed the door lock button and leaned her forehead onto the steering wheel. She could hear Jacob telling them off, then a tap on her window. She rolled down the window. "You ok?" Jacob reached in and patted her shoulder.

"Yeah, I'll be ok. Thanks for getting rid of them."

"Sure. I can't believe the audacity of these people. My God. It's ridiculous."

"I know."

"Ok, see you in a few," and Jacob turned back to the house

Isobel rolled up her window and pulled away from the curb. She turned the car towards the campus, her mind blank for the moment, she wanted to drive aimlessly, to be alone for a few minutes. The street in front of the station was no longer cordoned off with yellow tape, but tape still covered the front of the building. Students milled around outside, reading a sign on the front door. A security guard standing nearby watched them and sent them on their way. Classes had been canceled the day of the funeral for a vigil in honor of the dead, one in which the dozen or so Muslim students showed up to show their support and to display signs saying, "#not in my name," like the ones that had gone around Facebook after the Paris attacks. But today, campus was open and classes in full swing, though many students had opted to stay in their dorms or go home for a few days. Everyone was relieved the semester was almost over. Faculty and staff wanted to get the students through these last few weeks and send them home or off to summer jobs and internships. Grief counselors had been brought in for anyone who needed to talk. Isobel thought about how deeply everyone was hit by this attack. But more than anything, she thought about Alec and how much he loved this campus. Llano's campus, with its grass and fountains, was a bit of an oasis in the sandblasted Eastern Plains.

She headed away from campus and drove over to Portales Circle, parking in front of the boys' childhood home. She now knew what the term broken heart really meant. Great memories had been made in that house. Looking at the balcony reminded her of the videos Alec would direct for his brother and friends. He would assign the rolls and then shout "Action!" and begin filming whatever story he had devised. When the truth came out many years later about their escapades, which included jumping from the balcony so they could walk around town in the middle of the night with their friends, hiding from car lights, running down alleys and ending up on campus, she plugged her ears and said she didn't want to know. "Let me live in mother ignorance please." And they would laugh and tell her other stories and have her almost rolling on the floor with laughter. She knew how fortunate her boys were to grow up in a small town, one where there had been little crime and no need to worry about them being outside or riding their bikes all over town, and when they learned to drive, knowing there was such light traffic she felt comfortable when they went out. Though much had changed, the feel of community remained.

Yet, she had always hoped they would leave when they grew up. The town didn't hold much for young people these days and jobs were scarce. When Alec took the job on campus, she had been surprised, but he told her it would not be forever. He knew there was more out there for him, but he had settled in and been comfortable, loving the students and his co-workers.

Her phone buzzed, startling her back into now. A text from Ian. 'Where are you?'

She texted back, 'Drove around a bit. Parked in front of Portales Circle house. Be there shortly.'

Isobel started the car and drove to Jacob's house. The same two journalists were milling about in the yard. She pulled into the drive and ran for the front door, slamming it behind her. That night, when Bree and Brian were safely ensconced in the bathtub, Jacob turned to the news channel and there was Isobel. They had filmed her when she had come out of Alec's house. They all gasped when Isobel said, "These people will rot in hell" and the camera then came back to the reporter.

"That's not what I said. My God, they clipped that. I said, 'these people say WE WILL rot in hell. I didn't say that. Damn it. That makes me sound like a hate-filled bigot."

"Isobel, no one's going to blame you for feeling a little hatred right now. I do hate those bastards who did this to Alec and I do hope they rot in hell," Jacob said as he quickly clicked the television off. "I'm so glad the police killed them. If I had to see them, I would do it myself. I think we need to kick all Muslims out of our country. We aren't safe."

"I am angry, but hating them, or all Muslims for that matter, is not going to do anyone ANY good," Isobel shot back.

"They are ruining our country," Jacob all but yelled.

"Jacob, what's ruining our country is corporate greed and poverty, not Muslims."

"Mom, Dad, um, let's stop now. Ok?"

Jacob continued, "Isobel, you liberals just don't get it…"

"Dad," Ian said forcefully. "Stop."

"I think I'll go to bed now." Isobel stood and paused for a moment, "Good night," nodding her head towards Jacob and Nora and then turned to Ian, "Love you, sweetheart."

He jumped up and gave her a hug. "Night, Mom."

# Chapter 5

When Saturday morning arrived, Isobel, was packed and had her car loaded before anyone was up. Ian and Delia were leaving later that morning as well. They had all shored each other up throughout the week. Isobel had watched *My Little Pony* at least a dozen times and read out loud the length of a novel in children's books, been climbed on and kicked and jostled in her bed enough to keep her mind from wandering too far into a black hole. "I will miss my two distractions when I get home," she said to Ian that morning. "I'm a little anxious about being home, but I'm ready for my familiar," she paused, "and my bed," she laughed to break up the seriousness. "I'm so glad the kids were here. Now life has to go on, whatever that means."

Isobel was relieved the television crews had left them alone that day. They all gathered in the kitchen before daylight as Nora made sandwiches and cut cakes and gathered cookies for the travelers. Nora tried to press more food on Isobel to sustain her through the coming week, but she declined. She still didn't feel much like eating and knew it would just go to waste. "Take whatever's left to the teacher's lounge. You know they'll devour anything you bring," Isobel said. "Teacher's lounges are notorious food black holes." Delia and Nora laughed, knowing it was true.

"Thank you again, Nora. I know it can't be easy having the ex around."

Nora's eyes softened. "Isobel, I know I'm not Alec's mother and can't fully grasp how you feel, but if I lost one of my girls," she choked back tears, "I don't know what I would do. I love your boys like my own kids. You needed to be with family."

They hugged and then hugs all around. Bree and Brian could hardly be bothered though, they were ready to be in the car so they could watch a movie on the ride home. Isobel disliked all this over-the-top technology. But what did that matter? Everything seemed inane now.

Isobel wrapped her arms around Ian and held him as tight as she could. Then she stood back from him, her hands holding tight on his arms, "I always felt like if I taught you boys how to take care of yourselves, how to prepare for anything, to stay healthy and to be kind and thoughtful, what could go wrong? You would live these huge lives and be strong and healthy and…" she trailed off for a moment, "but I can't control anything. I feel like, like I've lost control and everything is for naught."

"Mom…"

"I know, I know," laughing and blinking back tears, "control probably sounds crazy, but the world made sense and now, it will never make sense again."

Ian hugged her. "I love you, Mom."

Isobel wiped the back of her hand across her eyes as they parted and she waved a last goodbye to all as she left the house.

Isobel took the backroad out of Llano towards Bellview, skirting the Air Force base to reach the highway. She tried to keep her mind blank, but 'Alec is dead, Alec is dead, Alec is dead,' raced through her mind to the rhythm of the tires, as if a song was stuck in her head. She brought her attention back to the highway, trying to focus on her surroundings, as she drove back to Santa Fe. She had come to Eastern New Mexico when she married Jacob and planned to attend university at Llano. The plains were miserable during the spring with high winds that blew the sand from New Mexico into Texas and with a shift in wind direction, back again. Peanut farms and cotton fields had stretched across the horizon when she attended college.

She had met Jacob in high school, when his father had moved to Albuquerque for a political job. Jacob was a handsome, home grown Llano boy who wanted to live the small town life and planned to return. A couple years older than she, they married when she graduated from high school and she had settled in to Llano, hoping the landscape would grow on her. And it did. She lived for the beautiful sunsets that occurred on windy days, all that sand in the air made for spectacular color and she loved the sunrise, when she would be out riding her bike down a highway of peanut farms. But slowly the sand hills had become dotted with dairy farmers who had sold their land for a fortune in California and bought land cheap in New Mexico, allowing them to live the high life, with their big rigs and their mini mansions. Summers became a nightmare of black flies and the putrid smell of cow manure, sweet and rancid, all at the same time.

Her marriage had also been sweet and rancid, she thought. Jacob always had a sarcastic sense of humor, making her laugh about the most uproarious things, and he had been a good dad. He loved the boys, but she had always had the feeling he never really liked her. Maybe loved her in some way, but never liked her. He belittled her in front of her friends and family. He made fun of her in front of her own boys. His jealousy though, was the worst part of their marriage, finally pulling them completely apart. She wasn't sure how many times he had cheated on her, but she now understood his constant jealousy of her, the attacks on her personality, were all just projection of his own guilt.

Isobel knew she had not made her situation any better, with her low self-esteem and willingness to take his abuse. She had also made mistakes. As the years passed though, and she gained self confidence through getting her degrees in English, being hired to teach at the high school, then the district literacy director, she eventually began to stand up to Jacob. The end occurred, however, when a woman called her one day and told her she had been having an affair with Jacob for years. Every time he flew to this meeting or that meeting it was in actuality to see her. When Isobel hung up the phone, she knew she had been released from her marriage. She felt as if a fog had lifted and she could finally see clearly. Their divorce was simple and fast. The boys were in college, she knew what their assets were, they drew up a list and split everything and they were done.

Taking a job in Santa Fe two years later had been her final split with Llano. She missed her friends from the university where she had spent her last two years in a low-level administrative position, but she did not miss this little town where everyone knew everything. Dating after the divorce had been a nightmare since someone always reported it back to Jacob, or someone wouldn't date her because they "respected Jacob too much." What a relief then to be an unknown in Santa Fe, to walk into her new assistant principal job with no baggage and to live in a city she had loved since she was a girl, when her father had been stationed in Los Alamos. They would come to Santa Fe to visit the Sears store and see the festivals, and in those days it had been a small place barely spreading beyond the old downtown. She loved the little brown houses in the hills and vowed she would live in one someday, and now she did.

When Alec had taken the job at Llano, after a few years in Albuquerque at a small station there, a job he had taken on graduating from UNM, she had been perplexed. She didn't understand why he would want to go back there. He assured her it wouldn't be forever, this job was just a stepping stone to the next, but he was glad to be living closer to Ian, a ninety-minute drive, and he told her he thought he would enjoy being around his father, to enjoy an adult relationship with him for a few years.

Her mind had twisted and turned in a million directions as she drove, but now, Alec is dead, Alec is dead, Alec is dead, played in her head again and she had to pull to the side of the road as her eyes filled with tears. "Only one more hour and you'll be home Isobel. Pull yourself together. Come on," she told herself. She wiped her eyes and pulled back onto the road, concentrating on the mountains in the distance, the last vestiges of snow visible on the highest peaks, the deep blue of the morning sky, like only a northern New Mexico sky can boast. She turned on the radio, tapping the volume up as high as she could stand, in an attempt to drown out her thoughts. Then finally she was pulling into her street, a narrow lane that wound up a hill to an adobe, two bedroom casita, she had slowly restored over her first five years of living there. Home. Her little brown house in the hills.

Isobel shivered as she rolled her suitcase to her bedroom and went through the motions of unpacking. She had been here just over a week ago throwing things in her suitcase. How strange it felt to now be unpacking as if her world hadn't completely changed. She walked through the house, built a fire in the living room, and lay down on the couch where she could look out the window. The city spread before her in the harsh light of midday, the Jemez mountains visible in the distance.

Again she started replaying the last week in her head. The news last Friday, the drive to Llano, the officer who had told her Alec was dead, and that first night. How surreal that night seemed now. When the next morning an FBI agent had shown up at Jacob's door, he'd shoved his way past the journalists waiting outside the door. He'd come to talk to the family about procedure in a case like this. "You mean a terrorist attack?" Jacob had thrown at him and the agent had replied, "Incident. This has not been termed a terrorist attack."

Nora asked, "Would you like to have a seat?" and led the agent into the living room.

"Mr. Davis, until all the facts are in, we will not refer to this as a terrorist attack and I will strongly suggest neither you, nor anyone in this family, refer to this as terrorism. We need to find all the facts before we make this assertion," the FBI agent looked sternly at each of them.

Isobel sighed and shook her head in resignation. "What about Alec? When will we be able to see him?"

"My colleagues are finishing up their investigation and looking at the coroner's report. They will decide if we need an autopsy. There appears to have only been guns used in the attack, and if that turns out to be the case, then we will release him to you soon. I would hope within the next 24 hours." He spoke in a staccato voice, harsh and defined. "We ask you stay close by for any questions we might have for you."

Jacob slammed his hand on the table next to him and asked him, "Where the hell do you think we're going to go?"

"Sir, I'm just doing my job."

"Well, you tell your people to get the job done and give us our son."

"Do you have any further questions for me?" the agent turned his head from person to person.

"Will you be able to tell us about his attackers? We've seen their pictures and heard their names, but... why? Are we allowed to know before this becomes more of a media circus than it already is?" Isobel drew a breath and went on, "I would prefer to not be blindsided by that info, but know in advance all the questions you must know we are going to have to deal with daily."

"Mrs. Davis,"

"Ms. Allen, please," Isobel interrupted.

"Sorry, Ms. Allen, I will release information to you as soon as I am allowed. Here's my card. Feel free to call me at any time." He leaned to her and gave Isobel his card, then stood and passed them to Jacob and Ian. "Thank you for your time."

"Thank you, agent..." Isobel looked at his card, "agent Dobbs," as she took his outstretched hand.

Agent Dobbs had never contacted them again. They learned the incident had been deemed a terrorist attack when the day before the funeral Jacob had decided to turn on the television to Fox News, a move causing Isobel to roll her eyes in disdain. She knew they would be playing the attack over and over, with talking heads discussing what happened to their son and four students, making conjectures that may or may not be correct, but that was Fox. Within a few minutes, there it was, a woman, her botoxed, wrinkle-free, makeup-thick face filling the screen as she declared the attack at Llano was a terrorist attack, carried out by an American nineteen-year-old freshman student, and his Pakistani father.

"Damn it! What happened to that heads-up we were supposed to get? Nora, where's my phone?"

Nora immediately stood up and went in search of Jacob's phone. Isobel went into the bedroom and found hers and the card Dobbs had given her. She called him.

"Agent Dobbs? This is Isobel Allen. We just heard on Fox news the attack was terrorist. What happened to calling us?"

Dobbs cleared his throat. "Well, Fox News did not have authority to do that."

"Is it true?"

"Yes, but that doesn't mean they should be broadcasting that already."

"You told us you would call us."

"Um, yes, but I've been inundated with calls myself."

"So are you going to give us any specifics?"

"We are searching the computer and phones of both the father and son."

"And his mother? We saw her mentioned as well."

"She is in the Air Force, stationed at Bellview."

"Was she in on it too?"

"As of right now, we do not have information that indicates she knew about the attack until it occurred, but we are searching every device she uses. She has been put on leave from her duties until she is cleared."

Isobel walked back into the living room while still on the phone. She pointed to it and mouthed, "Dobbs" to the others.

"I will call you with any news that comes my way."

"I hope you do next time," Isobel replied as Jacob held out his hand towards Isobel to take the phone and talk, but before she could hand him the phone, Dobbs abruptly said, "Goodbye, Ms. Allen," and hung up.

"He hung up."

"That bastard," said Jacob. "What did he tell you?"

Isobel related all she had learned over the sound of the blaring news. Then she excused herself and went to lie down.

# Chapter 6

The ringing of her phone woke Isobel. "Hello."
She shook her head, still groggy, and realized her
friend Diane was speaking to her.

"Hi. Just calling to check on you and be sure you
made it home ok."

"Yeah, I got home a few hours ago and I guess I
fell asleep."

"Oh, I'm sorry I woke you."

"No, it's ok. I needed to wake up. I want to take a
walk. Maybe hike the circle. I've not had any activity
this last week and I'm stiff."

"Want me to come?"

"No, no. I'm good."

"Listen, we would like to bring dinner to your
place Sunday. That way you don't have to go out and
can I take you to dinner tonight?"

"Thanks, but I think tonight I'm going to just stay in. Maybe I'll try and watch a movie. Sunday night will be great though. Thank you. And I can't tell you how much it meant to me that you were all there Tuesday. I couldn't have gotten through it without you."

"Of course. We couldn't not be there for you. We're family. Yes?"

"Yes."

"Ok, go walk. I'm calling later. One more time. K?

"You don't have to do that Diane."

"Yes I do."

"Love you."

"Love you too," and Diane hung up.

Isobel put on her hiking boots and checked her phone for the temperature. This time of day in April it could go either way. Lightweight jacket and water bottle in her day pack, she headed up the road to the path that took her to the Dorothy Stewart trail. A short two mile circle, this was her go-to daily trail. When she came to the rock bench on the back side of the circle, she sat down and sighed. She found solace here on tough days, where she could see Picacho Peak, as well as the ski mountain, but the emptiness she felt now was creeping through her like an impenetrable darkness. Tears streamed down her face as she stared at the peak until she could see nothing through the blurriness before her.

"Are you ok?"

Startled, Isobel blinked the tears away and looked over at the young woman on the trail. She wiped her face, and was about to speak, but the deluge of tears came without warning and she found herself sobbing.

The woman sat down beside her and rubbed her back. She finally gained control of herself and looked at this person, so kind to stop and see about a crazy crying lady. "Thank you," Isobel choked out. "My son died last week and… I thought a hike would help, but…"

"It's ok. I just wanted to be sure you were alright."

"Thank you."

"Oh, I recognize you from the paper. I'm so sorry about your son. I can't imagine…"

"I can't either."

They stood up and Isobel pulled out her jacket, the long shadows of afternoon beginning to put a chill in the air.

"I'll walk with you," the young woman told her and without another word, they headed down the trail, Isobel leading. When they came to Isobel's path back down to her house, Isobel turned to the young woman, "Thank you. You were so kind to check on me. And walk with me." Isobel reached out and put her hand on the woman's arm. Then the woman leaned in and hugged Isobel. "I'm so sorry you lost your son," she said. Then she waved and left Isobel standing there looking out at the city.

When Diane called that night Isobel told her what happened. "I just started sobbing and the poor thing didn't know what to do, but she was so sweet and sat there and rubbed my back till I quit crying. The grief, Diane, I can't explain how I feel. When mom died, it was a relief to see her out of her misery, and when dad went so fast, I was glad he didn't have to suffer, but this, this is indescribable."

"I can't even imagine. You're going to get through this though."

"Thanks. I'll see you tomorrow night then."

"Sleep well. Love you."

Isobel tossed and turned in bed most nights. She wandered her house. One night, she got out of bed and went in search of the box of pictures she had saved over the years. 'Thank God for real pictures,' she thought. After numerous computer glitches, and changes of phones, she had lost many of her digital pictures from recent years and had not bothered to retrieve them, not realizing how much she would regret this. Luckily, on her trip to Scotland with Alec, she had taken her digital camera instead of relying on her phone, and had the pictures printed out when she returned. The album she made was priceless to her now.

Thumbing through the pages, she ran her fingers across a picture of him sitting across from her at dinner at an Indian restaurant, the national cuisine of England and Scotland apparently, as there was at least one in every town, no matter the size, and there were hundreds in the cities. They had laughed about how ubiquitous they were, but "Thank God for Indian food," Alec had declared one night when their only other choice was fish and chips or fish and chips or fish and chips. She smiled to herself and paged on, his face smiling out at her from the top of Ben Nevis, and on the train to Thorso, where they took a ferry across the North Sea to the Orkney Islands. He had snatched her camera and taken a picture of her on that boat, her face almost green with seasickness, as he caught her leaned over the rail, her face turned towards him in surprise. The trip had been glorious, something he had always wanted to do. Ian, on the other hand, was a golfer and had chosen to go to "the homeland," for a golfing excursion, playing at St. Andrews and hitting up a few other courses. Though Jacob was not much for international travel, he had been coerced with the call of the golf club and taken the trip with Ian.

Jacob had been especially hard on Alec as he grew up. Isobel felt that Alec's enthusiasm, and his happy-go-lucky nature, had been too much like Isobel for Jacob's liking and he tried to squash it in him as he did in her. However, Alec just let it roll off his back. Jacob and Ian, on the other hand were both pragmatic, loved golf, and had business minds. Their relationship had been much easier. She had often marveled at the uniqueness of her boys. Somehow when a second child comes along the expectation is they will be alike, but then the realization dawns, they do everything differently. One slept through the night right away, the other never slept. One is covered with food from head to toe when he eats, the other has not a speck of food on him, it somehow all went in his mouth.

Isobel and Jacob's relationship had been tenuous from the first. Had she not grown up in a fundamentalist religion, one that condemned you to hell for divorce, she might have left him early-on, but it had taken fighting her way through college, raising the boys, and learning that she had strengths she never knew, before she could leave. It had also meant ditching a restrictive religion, one that sat in judgement of everyone who didn't believe as they did.

Isobel understood her strengths, knew that she was a woman worthy of love and hoped to find love again someday. She had spent the last twelve years realizing her own life. Meeting people, advancing in her work and making headway in a tough school which had never had a female assistant principal, let alone, a female principal, the position she held now.

Isobel's life was rich with friends and family. Her friends had shown up as promised that first Sunday home from Llano, for their bi-weekly dinner. They had brought an entire spread and had held her, cried with her, and fed her. She would be forever grateful to them, but now she had to go back to work, as much for her own sanity, as for finishing out the year. Dr. Martinez, the superintendent of schools, had been by to see her and talked at length to her about her needs. He had suggested taking a leave of absence for the rest of the year, but she had insisted on finishing the last four weeks with her students and staff. If she stayed home, she was afraid she would find herself in an inescapable vortex of grief. She felt she had to return to keep from drowning.

# Chapter 7

Isobel arrived shortly after her custodial staff her first morning back. She rifled through the stacks of mail and messages Anna, her secretary, had piled on her desk, sorting out what needed immediate attention from what could wait. Everything seemed inane and she fought the urge to pitch it all in the trashcan. As staff arrived, many came by the office and said hello or gave her a quick hug, but then Mrs. Griffin stepped in her office and said, "I'm so sorry, Isobel. At least he didn't suffer." Isobel felt she had been kicked in the gut. At least? At least? She fought the urge to scream and just stared at her, until Mrs. Griffin realized Isobel was not going to say anything, and she turned and left. Isobel had not given much thought to what she could say to people who made thoughtless remarks. The day of the funeral several people had told her, "God has a plan, just have faith" until she finally said to one lady, "What kind of God 'plans' to kill an amazing man like my son? Tell me? What God does this?" and the woman had backed away into the crowd. She knew most people meant well, but there are things you just don't say to someone whose child has died or been killed.

Isobel had always greeted students each day as they came into the building. She grabbed her sunglasses and left her office for the usual spot out front.

"Isobel, are you sure you want to be out there today?" Anna asked her as she walked towards the doors.

"Yes. I do. The kids need to know I'm ok."

"Are you?"

"No. But I'm trying."

"If you need back up, call me," as Anna picked up the school two way radio and waved it in the air. "I'll send Mr. Andrews your way," and they both laughed. Brian Andrews was a bit hopeless as an assistant principal, and probably had been as a teacher too.

The students were great. Many hugged her on their way in the building, and she didn't have to suffer awkward, hurtful comments; the kids were simply themselves. Lots of "love you, Ms. A!" and "hang in there" got her through the thirty minutes she stood outside greeting them, but she could feel herself trembling on the inside, a weird sensation she felt frequently now, as if the world was trembling beneath her feet, like the mild earthquake she had felt in Socorro one summer while walking the golf course at the Sun Country Junior golf tournament Ian qualified for each year. But she thought, 'Isn't that what this is? an earthquake that has cracked open the largest crevice imaginable, one she could fall into and never climb out of?'

She returned to her office and quietly closed the door. Anna would be the best interference she could hope for as she felt her way through the next four weeks. Isobel admitted to herself she had been afraid to take the leave of absence because Brian might actually destroy much of what she had worked to build over the last ten years. "Yes, I have control issues, Diane, but going back will help me keep my sanity. I can't just sit at home," she explained to her friend that first dinner they had together. They all laughed, but Diane assured her she would call her at work, "Every day, girlfriend, every day," and she did. "Just checking on you. Big hug!"

"Thanks, Diane. I'm making it." Or, "I'm struggling today." Whatever the day held, she knew she could count on Diane to give her that call.

Her first week back, a student had set off a firecracker in the hall. Isobel had heard the bang as she walked back to her office after lunch duty. The sound had caused such a feeling of terror she had cried out in complete fear, flinging her arm to her chest, and leaning the other against the wall to keep from falling. The teacher closest to the sound, Mr. Brown, had opened his classroom door and checked the hall, but no one else seemed to have heard it, or had passed it off as nothing. When he saw her, he poked his head back in the classroom, then closed the door quietly and came down the hall to her. "Are you ok?" he asked as he put his hand on her shoulder. Her back was to him and she had not heard him approach.

When his hand touched her shoulder, she gasped and turned to face him.

"Mr. Brown, you startled me." She attempted to smile at him, but the look of panic on her face must have been evident.

"I saw you standing here," he paused for a minute and looked at her closely. "I'd like to find the little prick who set that off and shake him till his teeth rattle."

Isobel half smiled at him. "Well..."

"I don't mean literally, of course. The little shit."

Isobel laughed. "Of course. Thanks for checking on me. I'm ok now."

"Ok, back to the trenches," and he went back to his classroom and she went in search of the culprit, knowing she wouldn't find the student, but felt she had to make an attempt.

As the days passed, some better than others, she found she had a constant sense of hyper-vigilance in watching over her students. Loud noises sent her heart into a palpitating panic and she jumped any time someone yelled, which in any group of teens could happen with regularity. This was new for her. Martinez frequently came by the school and would hunt her down wherever she was to check in with her. She appreciated his dedication, but somedays wished she did not have to see him, did not need to be checked on by anyone. She just wanted normal again.

Odette appeared in Isobel's office one afternoon. "Ms. A., I know I'm supposed to be in class, no ditching, but seriously, Miss Gorman is fuckin' nuts. Oops, sorry."

Isobel halfheartedly smiled at her, "Nuts? What way?"

"She shows us how to do a problem then erases it and says, 'No, wait, it's like this,'" she perfectly imitates the voice, "and she does that a few times, then we're all like, how do we do this?"

"I'm sure that's confusing," Isobel said.

"Confusing? It's, it's...confounding!"

Isobel found herself constantly amazed at this street-smart girl, who pretends she knows nothing, but is quite brilliant actually. Her grades were decent without her really trying, but she had spent so much of her time in high school in conflict with everyone around her, that Isobel feared her life would be one constant battle and she would miss her potential. Though she tried hard not to have favorites, Odette had become a student she found herself drawn to out of necessity at first, breaking up fights, suspending her, fending off her mother's wild yelling fits in the office, but then evolving into a relationship of encouragement and counseling. As Odette had matured, she controlled her temper better and began, in her own way, to blossom as a student.

Isobel sighed. "Odette, you know I can't say anything about Ms. Gorman to you. So what are you going to do to make it better? The year's almost over. Can you get through these last few weeks?"

Odette threw her hands into the air, "Whatever. Ok."

"Listen, let's look into you taking a class at the community college this summer and finishing up your math that way."

"I have to work, Ms. Allen. My mom would kill me if I took a class."

"Maybe we can frame it in a way that will make it ok."

"I can't afford it."

"Trust me, we'll work on figuring it all out. It's worth a try?"

Odette shrugged her shoulders then looked down at her hands in her lap. "Ms. A? Are you ok?"

Isobel felt tears begin to well up. She willed them not to spill over, and quickly grabbed a tissue to dab at them before they could. "No. I'm not. Not really."

"My baby brother died when I was twelve. He was four. My mom's boyfriend punched him in the head. None of us were home. I still miss him." She had said each sentence quickly and flatly, as if forcing herself to spit out the words.

"Oh my God, Odette. I had no idea." Isobel did, however, know at that moment, Ms. Gorman had not been the reason for coming to the office, but Odette's way of checking on her. Sharing her story with Isobel had taken great courage. "I know you must miss him terribly. I will miss Alec till the day I die," and then the tears did spill over and she had to grab another tissue and blow her nose.

"I know," Odette said.

Odette picked up the backpack she had slung against the wall when she walked in, and left Isobel to her tears. Odette silently shut Isobel's office door and then Isobel sunk down on her couch. The bell would ring shortly and another day would have been completed, or at least the school day. She would shuffle papers till five then head home where she would drink a glass of wine, possibly eat something then pretend to watch a movie or read a book, and then find herself roaming her house when she couldn't sleep. The routine was predictable now. Each day ticked off in the same way, till the final day of the semester arrived.

Odette had actually hugged Isobel on her way out that last day. "See ya next year, Ms. A. You better be here for my finale!"

"Of course I will," but Isobel was having doubts about returning and wondered if she could make one more year happen. "Don't forget to let me know how the calculus class goes for you."

"Oh, I won't." Odette turned and headed for the parking lot, but then turned around and pointed at Isobel, "Get some sleep, Ms. A. You look like shit!" She laughed as she ran towards her mother's car and turned and waved. Isobel returned the wave. Students continued to flood out of the building around her, some hugged her, others waved, but most were oblivious to her, or any of the staff, as they headed off to their various summers.

Ian and Isobel had talked everyday since she had left Llano after the funeral. She was looking forward to seeing him, Delia and the kids. She found some nights she would drift off to sleep then wake in a panic that something had happened to Ian or his family. She would reach for her cell phone that wasn't there, then realize a panic attack had awoken her again.

Occasionally, Isobel read Alec's last text to her. She thumbed through texts and pictures, and looked at his Facebook, as if by doing so she had proof he had existed. He had been her son. He had loved her and their family. He still existed.

72

# Chapter 8

Isobel, Sam, Diane, Richard and Doug sat around Isobel's dining room table. Isobel had offered her house for this week's dinner; she knew cooking for everyone would be a good diversion from her thoughts and a way to celebrate the end of school before she went back to Llano. Since they had kindly brought her dinner that first weekend after Alec's death, they had done nothing more than a cursory get together at Sam's a couple of weeks later and no one had lingered. Isobel had not felt up to their former discussions those last two gatherings, especially since their topic before Alec's death had often meandered into ISIS, but tonight, she felt like she needed to talk, wanted to talk, about anything at all, to not have to think, just talk.

"The problem with fundamentalism is you become attached to your beliefs, beliefs that are unchangeable and literal, so, uhm," Sam waved his hands in the air trying to come up with a word, "so rigid."

Isobel knew all about fundamentalism. 'Rigid' was a good word to describe what she observed and what she herself believed in for many years. No instrumental music, no dancing, two songs before communion and one after, services Sunday morning and Sunday night, Bible classes on Wednesday nights and if you broke from the pattern, the world was sure to fall apart, and for a girl like her, who questioned everything, her childhood and young adulthood had been very painful. "You're either in, or you're out, and it's important to maintain the distinction between who's going to heaven, and who's going to hell. That's what my childhood was all about and what my life has become about now," Isobel said.

"Isobel, I am sorry. I wasn't thinking. Let me shut up now."

"You shut up, Sam? Are you kidding me?" Isobel smiled at Sam and they all laughed, but she became serious, "Believe me, I have been thinking about this and going over and over in my head, why? Why must religion fuck up so many people? It messed with my mind for years. And please excuse the 'fuck,' I've found myself saying that word lately; not in my usual vocabulary for sure."

"You're forgiven," Diane said and reached over to pat Isobel's hand, but Isobel withdrew her hand from the table before Diane could touch her. Isobel had recently found herself bristling at the slightest touch from others. What had been so welcome in the first weeks, had become to feel contrived and pitiful now.

She felt as if there was an anger bubbling beneath her surface, ready to explode any moment, a feeling which scared her. Isobel turned towards Diane and smiled to try and smooth over the hurt she could see in Diane's eyes.

"Well let's talk food." Sam said. "This Beef Bourguignon is amazing. Why have you never made this for us before?"

"I don't know," Isobel laughed, "but today, I wanted something complicated and involved and so, voila! " She spread her arms open towards the French casserole dominating the center of the table. "Though it's really not that complicated, but wait till you see dessert."

"Bring it on, Iso!"

Isobel looked around the table at her friends. She had met them over the years and gathered them together for their similarities, and their differences. The five of them had become close and made it through each other's relationships, illnesses, tough times and good times. They had become family to each other. Isobel loved to cook and on occasion made the entire meal, as tonight, but usually they all brought potluck. She felt immense love for them at this moment for being there for her during the blackest time of her life. She stood to gather plates and Doug joined her. As they cleared the table she listened to Sam expound on the craziness in the world, something she thought about a lot these days.

Doug stood at the sink and began to rinse the plates, loading them into the dishwasher for her. "Thanks, Doug."

"Of course, my dear. But I do expect an extra big helping of dessert for my efforts here. It's not like I'm doing this for nothing."

Isobel laughed as she stepped behind him and wrapped her arms around him and hugged. "Thanks, friend."

"Good to hear you laughing a little tonight. I can't imagine what you're going through."

"It feels good to laugh. Everything seems so inane though."

"Yeah, I bet it does."

"I feel myself bristling with people sometimes. I just want to cocoon and be alone, but I know that's not what's best for me. Tonight feels really good."

"You know you can't hide from this group."

"Yeah. I do."

"Ok then, bring on that dessert gorgeous. I'm ready for my reward." He wiped his hands on a kitchen towel and then swatted her on the behind with it. She laughed as she pulled the dessert from the refrigerator.

The chocolate fondant was beautiful. A favorite of Isobel's, she had learned to make a traditional version when she lived in France for a month the summer after her divorce had been final. Escaping there for a respite from nosy people had been a revitalizing time for her. She took a cooking class and a pastry class. Both recipes this night had been from her time there. Preparing this feast for her friends had given her a sense of herself again. Just a glimpse of what life had been like before.

"You, my dear, are an amazing chef. Maybe you should cook for us full time when you retire," Richard said.

"Yeah, our own private restaurant, chef Isobel presiding," Doug said as he took his second helping of fondant.

"Maybe I will retire this year," Isobel murmured.

Diane turned to her, "Are you really considering it?"

"I don't know. I truly don't know if I can go back next year." She sighed, "I love the kids, but I am tired."

"Don't decide now. Give yourself a few weeks. See how you feel," Doug countered.

"Yeah. I will."

"When do you leave for Llano?" Sam asked.

"Tomorrow morning. I'm dreading it, but looking forward to Ian. I can't stop worrying something is going to happen to him or one of the kids or Delia. My brain does all kinds of crazy making these days." She rolled her eyes. "And what's really weird, I have this extreme fear of dying myself, and I've never been like that before."

"Maybe that's normal under the circumstances," Richard said.

"I guess." She took the last bite of her dessert and looked at her plate. "Well, you guys are good for me. I actually ate tonight."

"I'm glad we're good for something," Sam said and they all laughed. "Pour this lady another glass of wine."

"Ok, yes. Wine is good," and she held up her glass to Sam.

"Move to the fireplace?" Isobel said, pointing across the room with her glass.

They all settled in on the couch and chairs as Isobel lit a fire. She loved the Santa Fe evenings, where even in late spring one could have a small fire. She sunk into her leather club chair and took a sip of wine. "Thank you for this evening. I needed this before I go back to Llano." She raised her glass in a cheer, "Here's to the best friends one could ever have," and the others stood up and leaned into clink her glass. "Lovely."

"Did the FBI ever get back to you about the mother of the guy?" asked Sam.

"No. He has been less than stellar on follow through. I can only imagine what she has been going through, if it's true she had no idea."

"How could she not? Seriously, Isobel, it's weird you can have feelings for this woman," Diane said.

Isobel ignored Diane and took a sip of wine. "I just don't understand how something like this can happen."

"Not sure one can ever understand how," said Doug.

"I know," Isobel said.

They all started talking at once, but Isobel broke into the din, "It's the radicalization I don't understand. How did this guy, in Bellview, New Mexico come to this? How? Damn it."

"That has got to be maddening I'm sure," Richard said.

"Hey, let's change the subject," Sam said.

"Yeah, how 'bout them Isotopes?" Doug said.

Isobel started to smile and threw a pillow from her chair at Doug.

"Nightcap anyone? Whiskey? Scotch?" and Isobel went to the bar to pour everyone a final drink.

Conversation turned to what each had planned for the summer, and then they all took their turn and left.

Isobel closed the door and poured herself another bit of whiskey. She sat in her chair and stared out at the lights of the city. She had become afraid of sleep and most nights, prolonged going to bed. When she did go to sleep, nightmares terrified her. She was chased by men with guns and she held Alec by the hand, tugging him along behind her. Sometimes he was a toddler in her dreams, other times a grown man, but no matter his age, no matter how hard she pulled him along, the men chasing would shoot him and he would disappear. Isobel would wake, her heart pounding as if her chest would burst open. She finished her drink and took her glass to the kitchen.

# Chapter 9

Isobel looked at the clock. 4:00 a.m. She had tossed and turned all night. "Might as well get up," she said out loud to no one. No sooner had she put her feet in house shoes and pulled on her sweater than a panic attack hit her. Isobel grabbed at her chest and sat back down. 'Why this morning,' she thought. These attacks had been coming with more regularity in the last few days. Was it going back to Llano today? Clearing out Alec's things? Or just the terror she felt every time she thought of what had happened to Alec? Dobbs had sent her an FBI publication on surviving terror which explained that panic attacks were normal, but she was surprised, nonetheless, every time one hit her. "Breathe. Breathe." Her heart began to calm and she finally felt she could stand. She did a few sun salutations to calm herself further and then went downstairs to make a pot of espresso.

Now that school was out, there was no need to rush. In the past, she'd felt the luxury in this moment of bliss when time was hers again and only hers. She felt fortunate that Dr. Martinez had allowed her to forego the end of school paperwork and assigned much of it to Mr. Andrews. "Good practice for Brian, Isobel. I'll walk him through it." She knew he was speeding up his training since he probably doubted she would return next year.

Isobel had completed twenty five years, so she really could retire, but was she ready? What she wondered about more than anything though was, would she have to quit? The panic attacks, the anger, the sadness seemed too much sometimes. She often felt she had no control over her emotions, her thoughts, her feelings. They were an ocean of wave after wave trying to overwhelm her. How would she manage to be an effective principal another year, she wondered?

Isobel poured her espresso, then went to her chair to watch the day begin. Her journal had become her saving grace after her divorce, and even more so now, allowing her to yell on paper, something she found difficult to do out loud. Her reading choices were on surviving grief, but she avoided the ones a few people had sent to her that centered on a God who would allow this as part of his plan. She had never believed that God "planned" terrible things to happen to people, even when she had fully believed in God. Now she wavered in a half world of feeling there was something bigger than us all and believing everything was random. She couldn't really believe this world existed all on its own, with all the incredible beauty and miraculous happenings, but at the same time, didn't believe there was this guy in the sky directing everything, and she sure didn't believe in hell, though it was tempting now as she condemned in her mind her son's murderers to an eternity of torture and destruction.

She thought about the call she had finally received from Dobbs not long after she had returned to Santa Fe. "Ms. Allen?"

"Isobel, please."

"Ok, we finally have the story pieced together, though I'm sure you've heard much of this on television."

"I've tried to not watch anything. I can't stand reliving this nightmare day after day."

"That's smart, Isobel, most people aren't that wise. You knew the killers were a father and son, Zauqi Muhammad Fatah and Raheem Zaqui Fatah. There will be more investigation, but right now it appears the father radicalized his son over the last couple of years."

"His own son? Oh my God. And the mother? Where was she in all this?"

"The father deserted them when Raheem was five. He moved back to Pakistan, where he was from. We believe he may have been part of a small cell of the Taliban who has in recent years aligned themselves with ISIS. They encourage random attacks on infidels. Zauqi returned to the USA, to DC, a couple of years ago and made contact with his son. His mother, Marah Dalal, allowed him to go see his father in DC two summers ago, before his senior year in high school, and then he went again this past summer. They apparently came up with a plan while together. Zauqi bought guns over a four state area and assembled a few bombs, which luckily did not detonate. Then he drove out to New Mexico to put their plan in action."

"There were bombs? I never heard about that."

"Yes, they apparently carried them into the building, intending to detonate them at some point, but they didn't go off. We believe they were to explode after they had shot everyone, but when they didn't go off, Zauqi apparently shot Raheem then came out shooting at the police and they gunned him down."

"Shot his son? What?"

"Yes, it appears he killed his son before he walked out of the building."

"But I don't understand. Why? And why here? A small station in a small town?"

"Raheem was a very unhappy young man. His mother is an American citizen, born and raised in Philly, and Zauqi, her husband, came to the USA when he was eighteen, on a work visa. He obtained a green card and then became a naturalized citizen after their marriage. He grew up in Pakistan. Ms. Dalal met him in DC when she was in her twenties. She had joined the US Air Force when she graduated college and met him while stationed in DC."

"She's military? Stationed at Bellview?"

"Yes. But she is on leave now. She has been placed on a watch list and will remain there until every electronic device she has touched has been searched and all her contacts interviewed. She will lose her security clearance."

"Is she implicated?"

"Not yet, but…"

"But she will be? Is that what you are saying?"

"To be honest, it is hard to believe a mother doesn't know what her son is doing."

"Was he living at home?"

"No. He moved out at the end of his senior year and went to live with his dad, but came back in the fall to attend Llano. He was a member of the Muslim student association, a small group on campus, but so far, no one else seems to be connected to this. We will keep looking."

"The mom, what is her name again?"

"Marah Jabrayah Dalal."

"I want to talk to her."

"No."

"Why not?"

"Ms. Allen, it's not a good idea. What can you gain from that?"

"I don't know…"

"Listen, that's pretty much what we know for now. I'll keep you updated."

"Yeah, ok. Please do."


But now Isobel did know why she wanted to talk to Marah. She too had lost a son. Though neither the FBI nor the Air Force had found anything against her, she was still on leave. Isobel felt she needed to talk to her. What had she known about Raheem? What was he like? How did this happen? She felt she could find some peace by talking to this woman. She had obtained an address for her. She lived in Bellview and

Isobel planned to find her and talk to her while she was in Llano this week. As she finished her coffee and slipped her books and journal into her backpack, she wondered about Marah. A part of Isobel was furious at this woman. A part of her had sympathy for her. Isobel was in such close contact with her sons, she couldn't imagine how a mother could not know her son's deepest thoughts, but she knew culture might play a role in this. The researcher in her continued to hunt for information that would allow her to make sense of this murder. Talking to Marah was one way she hoped to find another piece of the puzzle, to somehow make sense of senselessness.

Isobel packed a bag and gathered her things. As she loaded the car, the sun was just beginning to shine on the Jemez mountains in the distance, and as she hit I-25, the sun rose above the Sangre de Cristo mountains. She always missed her mountains when she was gone. Her heart was there on the many trails that took her to the different peaks, with their endless vistas, grassy meadows, lakes, birds and Ponderosa pines. This was her *home* and had been even before she actually lived here. The road to Llano took her out of the mountains and into the high plains. She knew this road by heart and found herself far away in her head as she drove once again, back to the place her heart had been broken a second time but in a way she never could have imagined possible.

# PART TWO

*Grief can be the garden of compassion. If you keep your heart open through everything, your pain can become your greatest ally in your life's search for love and wisdom.*

-Rumi

# Chapter 1

Marah pulled the car into her driveway and parked. She grabbed her purse along with the groceries she had picked up at the commissary, and trudged into the house. The week had felt long and exhausting, but the weekend lay ahead and she smiled at the thought. Her small three bedroom stucco and brick house, one car garage, like all the others on the street, had been home for the last four years. She balanced the groceries on her knee as she turned the key in the lock. Dropping her purse on the entryway table, she took the groceries into the kitchen and flipped on her radio to hear NPR as she unloaded the food. The air space was dead. She pushed the tuner to see if it would come in, but nothing. Marah turned to the small flat screen television and turned on the local news, which in Bellview, meant Lubbock, Texas, two hours east.

"And we are still monitoring the shooting today at the PBS station located on Llano University campus in Llano, New Mexico. Police are not providing information yet as to the shooters or the victims. Stay with us, we'll be back with more soon."

Marah had turned swiftly around when she heard Llano, the refrigerator door hitting her in the back. She closed the door and moved to the television, looking at the last scene, an overhead shot from a helicopter, of police cars, and emergency vehicles jamming the streets of the university's main street. Grabbing her phone, she found Raheem's name and dialed. His phone rang, but went to voicemail.

"Raheem, it's Ma. I just saw what's happening on campus. Are you ok? Call me." She knew he had no classes in the TV station, but she wanted to know he was okay.

"It's after three. He should be out of class by now," she said to herself. Since Raheem had moved out last summer to attend university in Llano, she found she frequently talked to herself and to the dog, a black lab she had adopted several years ago to keep her company. Raheem had chastised her for taking in a dog.

"Ma, they're impure. Don't get a dog."

"Hadith is not the Qur'an, Raheem. The hadith is not rules, they help us think about the Qur'an and the Prophet, peace be upon him. Besides, Papa let me have a dog when I was a girl."

"Papa is not a good Muslim, Ma."

"Do not disrespect your grandfather. Now you are not being a good Muslim."

Raheem glared at his mother and left the room. His bedroom door soon slammed and she knew he had thrown himself on the bed and picked up the control to his game, shutting her out again.

Their exchanges had been like this for some time. Marah had been happy to see him embrace Islam in a more devout way two years ago, but over the last year and a half, he had become annoying with his platitudes and quotations and preaching to her.

"Ma, put on a hijab... Ma, you shouldn't drink wine... Ma, Mohammad said this, or Mohammad said that, Ma, Ma, Ma...."

She had grown up in a relaxed family, and though she followed Islam, she was private about her religion and did not make a show of it outside their home. Her father had taught her that freedom of religion in the USA gave them the right to practice their beliefs, but they did not have to parade them before others. They were good Muslims and attended to their prayers and to their reading of the Qur'an. She hated to admit it, but she had been relieved when Raheem started college and decided to live in Llano and not commute from Bellview. With him at a distance, she felt their relationship had grown stronger again. They talked on the phone frequently, and he usually came to see her every other week or so, and she would occasionally drive down and make him dinner at his place.

Marah let Bella in the house and thought about pouring a glass of wine, but glanced at the clock and realized it was barely four. She had left work early, when her patient load had been reduced that afternoon due to several cancelations. She did enjoy a glass of wine now and then, though she was careful not to have more than one, and rarely drank when she was out. She turned on the television in the living room and a commercial blared its message, giving her time to change out of her uniform and into jeans and a mid-thigh tunic. She unwound her hair from the bun she wore at work. Her thick black hair hung midway down her back and she quickly gathered it into a ponytail as she walked back to the living room. She and Bella curled up on the couch together, their usual afternoon ritual, though generally she listened to music instead of watching television.

"We are watching this scene unfold on the Llano University campus, police aren't saying yet, nor are the FBI, but an unnamed source says this is a terrorist attack. Two armed men entered the station sometime after 2:30 p.m. and began shooting. A student managed to run out a back door and notify police."

The screen changed to a young man telling a reporter, "Yeah, I heard what sounded like a really loud pop, then screaming and I just bolted. I was standing by the back exit. I know Mr. Davis was in there and a few students getting ready for the afternoon news show," he choked up and turned away. The screen returned to the newsroom where the newscaster said, "We are joining Harold Drake now, he is speaking to Dr. Pilar Garcia, Vice President of Student Affairs at the university."

"The campus is on lockdown. We have a system that alerts all cell phones. Students and instructors are required to remain in classrooms with doors locked. We are in process of emptying the non-affected buildings now. The majority of faculty and staff were in a meeting in the Campus Union Building when this started and few classes were in session. We think there is a minimal number in the station at this time."

"Hey girl, why isn't our boy calling? Hmmm?" Marah patted Bella's head and scratched between her ears. "He's probably with his friends. Right?"

She sat dazed in front of the set. Not hearing from Raheem was gnawing at her. She thumbed through her contact list on her phone and found the number for Raheem's friend, Janine, and hit the dial button, "Hey it's Janine, leave me the word and I'll get back to ya, Ciao!"

"Janine, it's Marah, have you talked to Raheem? I'm worried about him. I hope you're ok. Call me." She hung up and watched and waited for Raheem's friend to call.

The phone startled Marah when it rang a few minutes later. "Hello?"

"Marah, it's Janine," her voice sounded breathless. "We are all freakin' here. This is crazy. A bunch of us are at Dillon's house, but no one has seen Raheem since his dad got here a few days ago."

"What did you say?"

"We haven't seen him."

"His dad?"

"Yeah, his dad drove in from DC. You didn't know?"

"No, Raheem didn't mention it," Marah could feel her stomach churning.

"Yeah, we all met him a couple of nights ago."

"Ok, thanks Janine. Tell him to call me if you see him, ok?"

"Sure thing."

"You all stay safe. Be sure everyone calls home. Would you?"

"I think we all have, but I'll double check."

"Thanks for calling me back."

"No problem, Ciao!"

"Bye," and they both hung up.

Marah felt a panic she hadn't experienced since he had abandoned them almost fifteen years ago. 'What was Zaqui doing here?' she thought. She had heard from him about three years ago when he returned to the states from Pakistan, but he had not come to see her then. He had started calling Raheem though and talking to him weekly.

Marah tried calling Raheem again. No answer, just his message again. "Name, number, I'll call you."

"Raheem, call me," her voice pleaded.

Having his dad back in his life had been both good and bad. Raheem had been overjoyed when he first called, but then went through some anger, which he had taken out on Marah, blaming her for his father's disappearance in the first place. She didn't want to tell him she figured out a longtime ago, she had been a vehicle for Zaqui's citizenship and that was all. As Raheem and Zaqui built their relationship, she became less important to her son. Admittedly, it made her a bit jealous. However, being a single mom, truly raising him alone, had been tough, and so she mostly felt relieved, for herself and happy for Raheem.

Marah watched the news, both local and national, while she kept glancing at her phone hoping Raheem would contact her soon. She eventually returned to the kitchen to feed Bella and herself. She chopped vegetables and made a lentil soup. Pouring a glass of wine, she sat down at the table and opened the book she had been reading and sank into her nightly ritual of dinner, read, walk the dog and go to bed. Her uneasiness though, made it difficult for her to concentrate. 'Why doesn't he call?' she thought.

The pounding at the door woke Marah. Startled she sat up and realized she had fallen asleep on the couch. Bella began a low steady bark, one of the aspects Marah loved about having a dog. She peeked through the peephole and saw two policemen and a man in a suit. "Oh no," and her stomach began to twist into a knot and her heart to pound as she opened the door. "What's happened? Is it Raheem?"

"Marah Dalal?"

"Yes! Why are you here?" the panic in her voice had Bella barking and growling.

"Can you put your dog out?" the man in the suit said.

"What? Oh yes, but…"

"Ma'am please put the dog out."

She grabbed Bella's collar, "hush, shh, shh," as she dragged her to the garage door. "Go girl. I'm ok," and she guided Bella through the door and shut it behind her.

The men had walked into her living room, startling her as she turned back around.

"Ms. Dalal, please have a seat. I'm Agent Waters and this is Officer Miller and Officer Brown," and he pointed at the two men as she came back into the room. The two officers stood observing, but she could see they were looking around the room. Sparsely furnished, there was not much to see. No pictures, no knickknacks, just a comfortable couch, two chairs with a large square coffee table centered in the middle and bright colored curtains made with fabric her mother had brought back from Bangladesh on her parent's last visit home. "We are here about your son. We have some questions to ask you."

"Ok." She sat down in the small chair at the end of the couch, wrapping her arms around herself. Agent Waters sat down on the end of the couch closest to her.

"Do you know where your son is?"

"No. I've been worried all night. He's a student at Llano and I saw the news and I haven't been able to get in touch with him." Tears were forming in her eyes as she looked at the man in the suit, the one asking the questions. "Was he there? What's happened to him?" Panic was taking hold of her and she thought she might scream if they didn't give her any information.

"When was the last time you talked to your son?" he continued.

"This morning. He called me this morning." Tears were now streaming down her face.

"And what did you talk about?"

"Why won't you tell me what's happened?" she yelled.

"Ms. Dalal, calm down. Just answer my questions."

She took a deep breath and steadied her breathing. Gulping back fear, "He called me and told me good morning, and asked how I was, and…" she shook her head, trying to think clearly, "and he said I was a good Ma, and he loved me," she barely whispered. Crushing her brain, tightening her heart, thoughts started racing through her mind of Raheem and Zaqui, Raheem and Zaqui.

"Is your husband Zaqui Mohammad Fatah?"

"My ex-husband, well not legally, but he deserted us when Raheem was five."

"Do you know where he is?"

"He's in Llano. One of Raheem's friend's told me earlier when I called looking for Raheem."

"You didn't know?"

"No. I was surprised to hear it."

One of the officers snickered and stared at her. She glanced at him and returned her attention to Agent Waters.

"What do you know about Zaqui?"

"I know he has another wife in Pakistan, and several children," she answered angrily.

"And?"

"He came back to the states, to DC, almost three years ago. Raheem went to see him there the past two summers."

"Are you aware of Mr. Fatah's activities?"

"What do you mean?" her nerves were shot now, her patience with this questioning ended.

"What he's been doing in DC?"

"Technology director for some legal firm. I don't know more than that. Nothing."

Marah's phone started buzzing with messages. She had left it sitting on the end of the couch when she had been woken by the pounding on her door. Starting up from her chair, intending to look at her phone, Agent Waters motioned for her to sit down. "My phone. I want to see if it's Raheem."

"It's not."

She sank back into her seat and buried her head in her hands.

"Ms. Dalal."

She couldn't breathe.

"Ms. Dalal," agent Waters said louder.

Marah sat up and looked at him.

"Your son and his father were the attackers at the station today. They are both dead."

"No. You're wrong. Not Raheem. No, no, no," Marah shook her head furiously.

"We are here with a search warrant for your home and we will take all your devices, phone, computer, all." He handed her the warrant and motioned his head at the two officers. One snatched up her phone and placed it in a plastic bag.

Marah couldn't move. She stared at him.

"What?"

"For now, you are implicated through your connection to these two men."

"But...what are you telling me?" Her brain tried to make sense of what was happening. The officers had already spread out, looking in drawers and closets. She could hear one in the kitchen where her computer sat on the cabinet top, Bella faithfully barking outside the garage door.

Agent Waters started talking to her again, "You are suspended from work. Do not leave the county. We will be in touch."

"Call off your dog, lady," Officer Miller yelled from the garage. Marah went to the garage door and grabbed Bella's collar.

"Come girl." She stood in the kitchen till the officer was finished in the garage. He came into her kitchen and slammed the door shut. She immediately reopened the door and shoved Bella through and returned to the living room. Agent Waters now stood in the middle of the room, texting someone on his phone. She again sat in the chair where he had questioned her.

The officers reappeared, one held her laptop under his arm and her phone was in an evidence bag hanging from his hand. The other had her tablet in an evidence bag. Agent Waters looked up from his phone. "Finished?"

"Yeah, this is it." The officer turned and smirked at Marah.

"Miller. Enough," Waters said sharply. "Good night, Ms. Dalal."

They left. She remained crumpled in her chair as she surveyed the room where they had strewn magazines and upturned cushions. Stunned, she folded her hands in her lap, then felt herself begin to shake and soon found herself sobbing uncontrollably. She could hear Bella barking in the distance and eventually let the dog into the house. Bella nuzzled against Marah as she returned to the couch and lay on the sofa crying. She couldn't think. She didn't know what to do. Where to go. Paralyzed with fear and sorrow she clung to Bella and cried till she was spent. She had no phone or computer, no means of contacting her parents or even a friend. She turned the television on and there, a picture of Raheem and one of Zaqui were displayed side by side.

"Zaqui Mohammod Fatah and his son Raheem Zaqui Fatah allegedly stormed the public television station at Llano University this afternoon at approximately 2:45. We don't have all the details yet, but we know one student escaped out a rarely used back exit and one student was airlifted to Lubbock's University Medical Center where she remains in critical condition. Station production manager Alec Davis was killed in the attacks as well as four students, whose identities have not been revealed yet." The screen showed the station surrounded by police and emergency vehicles. This had happened hours ago. Her worst fear, as she had worried about Raheem these hours, was realized.

Marah stared at the television screen. 'This can't be real. Raheem would never do anything like this. I can't believe this.' She shook her head, trying to clear the scene from her mind. The tears welled up in her eyes, as she looked around her living room, finding her purse where she had dropped it earlier. She called Bella, snapped on her leash and opened the front door. A bright light shone in her face, confusing her, as Bella started barking and growling. Marah threw her arm up to block the light from her face and saw a microphone waving in her direction, a reporter talking to her, but she couldn't comprehend what they were saying.

"Get out of my way," but the microphone didn't move. She began to hear the questions pummeling her ears and Bella's sharp relentless bark.

"Did you know what your son was planning? What about your husband?"

"Please, leave me alone." She backed up, and turning around, put the key in the lock and re-entered her home. "Bella, come." Marah grabbed her collar and pulled her back into the house. She slammed the door and leaned against it, her hand clutching her shirt, her bag dropped to the floor. "What are we going to do?" With no way to call anyone, desperation and panic filled her with fear. Marah slid slowly down the door. Bella nuzzled up to Marah, licking her face, then sharply barking at the door. "Thanks, girl," she said through her tears. "We're ok," but she knew she was far from okay.

Marah walked through her house, closing all the shades and curtains, being sure no one could see in. At the front bedroom window, she could see someone standing in the bushes, trying to peer in, but the room was dark, and she quickly pulled the curtains closed. She pulled a quilt from the basket at the foot of her bed and dragged it to the living room, Bella padding along behind her. The two of them curled up on the couch. Marah wondered about her Pa and Mum. 'They must be sick with worry I haven't called.' She went back and forth from the couch to pacing the room, Bella following her every move, panting. "You know something's not right, huh, girl?" Marah scratched her between the ears, patted her head. "What would I do without you?" Marah was in shock. Every time she closed her eyes and felt sleep coming, her head would jerk back up. The television blared reports of what had happened today, naming Raheem and Zaqui, and occasionally mentioning her name.

Marah woke and for a moment she had no idea where she was, but soon enough the events of last night filled her brain and she caught her breath. Her stomach wrenched again with pain. Grabbing a tissue she blew her nose. The alarm in her bedroom was going off, five a.m. Time for prayer. She got up, her entire body ached as she trailed down the hall and turned off the clock at her bedside. She didn't go to her prayer mat, but instead went to the front window and peeked out. The news truck was still parked in her drive. Marah went to the bedroom again, changed into loose running pants, and put on an old t-shirt and jacket. She again walked past the spare room where her prayer mat lay and went to the garage and grabbed Bella's leash. She found her running shoes and laced them up. She went to the sliding door that led into the backyard, a slight hint of light was visible in the eastern sky. Carefully lifting the latch on the back fence, she pulled her hood down over her eyes as far as possible then she and Bella stepped into the alley and headed away from her house as fast as she could run.

The cool morning air cleared her head. 'Why had no one, not one single friend, come to her last night?' She had left with no thought about where she should go. She needed to call her parents. Who lived closest? Janet? At the corner, she turned in that direction, running down the quiet streets, knowing Janet would be awake this early even though it was Saturday. She always complained about not being able to sleep in on the weekends. They had a seven a.m. to four p.m. hour shift during the week. Janet was the pediatric physician assistant and Marah was the gynecological nurse practitioner. There was a general practice physician, Joe, and several nurses. They made a good team and had become friends over the years.

Marah tapped on the door, hoping not to wake Janet's three kids, and waited. Within a few seconds, the foyer light came on, then the porch light, and someone looked through the peephole, but the door did not open. She tapped again and stood on her tiptoes, thinking maybe Janet didn't see her, but the porch light turned off, followed by the foyer light.

"Ya allah, allah," Marah gasped as she leaned her hand against the door and bent over, again sobbing. She pounded on the door, but this time, no light came on. Turning back to the street, tears clouding her sight, she found her way to her alley. Bella led the way back to her gate and they slipped through, the sun beginning to show above the distant horizon. Marah left Bella in the backyard and entered the dark empty house. She went to her bed, dropping her jacket before she got between the sheets and pulled the covers over her aching head.

# Chapter 2

Marah met Zaqui in Washington D.C. when she was twenty four years old, soon after she had earned her nurse practitioner's license. She had joined the United States Air Force after graduating university with a Bachelor's in Nursing, and then the Air Force had paid for her further training. She was sent to the Pentagon in Washington D.C. for her first assignment. She loved the city and this placed her close to her parents in Pennsylvania. Zaqui had finished his Masters and was looking to find a Muslim wife. They met at the Convention of Islamic Society, when they each attended the Matrimonial Banquet, Marah with her father, Zaqui by himself. While waiting in the lobby to enter the event, she kept her head a bit lowered, but stole glances around the room. She spied Zaqui and thought him handsome. He was somewhat tall with dark features and beautiful dark brown eyes.

The banquet was a speed dating event, but in the Muslim community, parents often trailed along behind their sons or daughters and also asked questions. Pa didn't like that Zaqui was alone, but once they started talking, he was impressed with Zaqui's determination in coming to the USA, finishing university and searching for a Muslim wife. During the socializing which followed, Zaqui remained with Marah and Pa, entertaining them with stories of Pakistan and his time in university. He asked Marah questions about why she joined the Air Force and what her plans were for her future. She liked this, as many Muslim men she had met only asked if she would be a traditional Muslim wife, wrapping herself up and staying home. She did not picture this for herself at all.

After the event, Zaqui had single-mindedly pursued her. He was far more traditional than she, but she was attractive and intelligent. He soon had asked her to marry him. The wedding and reception were arranged by Marah's parents where they lived in Philadelphia. The ceremony was Muslim with a mix of Pakistan and US traditions. His mahr, a marriage gift, to her was a set of gold bracelets his mother had passed on to him for this purpose, and a bolt of the most beautiful blue silk Marah had ever seen. He also promised ten thousand dollars should he ever divorce her. Together they decided she would remain in the Air Force and he would follow her on assignment, easily finding work in the technology field wherever she was stationed.

Zaqui and Marah found a small apartment in Alexandria, VA. Marah commuted to the pentagon each day where she was a triage nurse in the clinic there. Though she and Zaqui had known each other only a short time, they got along well. He found a job with a start-up computer technology company in Alexandria. When she realized she was pregnant three months after they married, Zaqui was excited. Marah had found a female Muslim doctor, and the two of them had convinced Zaqui being in attendance at the birth would be fine. As soon as Raheem was born, the doctor handed Zaqui his son and he whispered in his right ear the adhan, "There is no deity but God, and Muhammad is the messenger of God," then handed him to Marah.

"Look at my two precious ones," Zaqui said to her as she made her first attempt to breastfeed Raheem.

"Isn't he beautiful?" Marah exclaimed.

"He is, and so are you my love."

Once Marah and the baby were cleaned up and settled in, Zaqui returned to the room. "I called Pa and your Mum. They will be on their way soon."

"And the Aqiqah?"

"A week from today. Pa said he would cook for our party and I set up the donation. It is difficult for me to be away from my country for this time in our life. We should be in Pakistan. Then I could do the sacrifice meat myself. I do not like to call someone up to donate meat."

"Zaqui, it's ok. We live here." She felt frustrated when he brought up Pakistani rituals. She had been born in the United States and Pa had learned to adapt, why couldn't Zaqui? "The nurse is insisting I tell her a name for the baby."

"No!" Zaqui's face became angry, as it often did when he felt someone challenged his beliefs. "One week, not a day before, insha'allah. They will have to wait."

Marah knew not to argue with him. "I will let her know." They had already decided on Raheem, which meant servant of the merciful. Marah liked the name and had wanted to pick a middle name too, but Zaqui insisted it was wajib, an obligation, to give the baby his own name and his grandfather's name. He would be named Raheem Zaqui Muhammod Fatah. And his name would not be said out loud until announced at the Aqiqah, the ceremony of sacrificing an animal on the occasion of a birth, and the meat being donated, according to his Pakistani tradition.

Marah woke with the ringing of the doorbell. Again she felt startled back into reality. The bedside clock said it was noon already. She tiptoed to the front door and looked through the peep hole. Colonel Joe Horowitz stood on the porch, the camera crew focused on him, microphones stretched out to him. "What part did Ms. Dalal play in this attack? Is she being discharged from the military? What are your thoughts Captain?"

"That's Colonel, now get out of my face."

Marah opened the door, standing behind it so she could not be seen by the cameras. "Come in, Joe."

Joe Horowitz was the presiding doctor in their division. He and Marah had become friends over the years, as had the whole department. She was relieved to see him.

He squeezed through the opening and slammed the door.

"I …" and the tears choked her words, as she bent over crying. Joe grabbed her shoulders and pulled her up into a hug and held her against his chest while she cried and tried to gather herself. He then led her into the living room, one arm around her shoulder and motioned for her to sit on the couch.

"Have you eaten anything?"

She shook her head no, "I can't."

"Tea then?"

"Yes please. That would be nice."

Joe left her there and went to the kitchen. Her dinner from the night before still sat half eaten on the table. He cleared the dishes and looked around for tea and started the kettle boiling. Bella was barking now, knowing someone was in the house with her mistress. Joe went to the sliding glass door and let her in. "Hi Bella, how's my favorite girl?" as he scratched her between the ears and rubbed her back. Bella came with Marah to the office picnics they held frequently during the summer. "How ya doing pup?" Marah came to join them and then both stood there petting the dog until Joe heard the kettle click off. "Go sit down, I'll bring our tea."

Joe sat in the side chair and handed Marah her tea. "Thanks, Joe."

"No problem. I make a pretty damn good pot of tea after my years in England."

"Not just the tea. For coming."

He reached in the bag he had brought in with him and handed her a disposable phone. "Our unit was called to come in for a debriefing this morning, by Colonel Rankin. When I heard those bastards had come over here last night and taken everything, I thought you might need this."

"Thank you, thank you, Ya Allah, I need to call my parents. They must be worried sick."

"Of course. We have been instructed to not have contact with you until they clear you, but Rankin gave me permission to come give you the news. Go call them. I'll be here."

Marah took the phone and retreated to her bedroom. She started to dial, "I can't remember the number," she mumbled to herself and started frantically searching in her bedside table for her address book. Tears began to blur her eyes. It wasn't there. Blindly she ran to her office in the spare bedroom and sat at her desk, wiping her eyes with the sleeve of her shirt, she saw the book tucked into the center drawer. Finding the number, she dialed, but she only got Pa's message. She then tried her Mum, but the same. She left a quick message on each and gave them the number listed on the box of the phone.

Joe had moved into the kitchen and was doing her dishes from the night before. He had opened the refrigerator and stuck his head in, when she came to find him. "Hey, checking to see what you need."

"My parents didn't answer."

"Think they are headed out here?"

"I hope so, but I'm hoping they flew. My father doesn't see so well at night anymore. It would be like him to try and drive. I left them a message."

"Feel like talking?"

She shrugged her shoulders.

"I'm staying with you till you hear from your parents, ok?"

"Are you sure?"

"Of course. Do you want to tell me what happened last night?"

They went back to the living room and sat down. Her tea had gotten cold. Joe took her cup and emptied it and refilled it from the pot he had carefully wrapped in a towel to keep warm.

Marah lifted the warm cup and felt the steam on her face. She closed her eyes and saw Raheem there smiling at her. She opened her eyes and looked at Joe. "I don't know what time they came. They just barged in when I went to put Bella in the garage. But I knew something had happened. I thought," she hesitated, "I thought Raheem must have been in the television station for some reason and been hurt." Her shoulders began to shake with held back tears. "I had tried calling him, but got his message and then I talked to his friend, Janine." Marah choked and couldn't go on for a few minutes.

Joe went to the kitchen and found a box of tissues. He held one out to her and he watched her as she blew her nose, her long dark hair with its few silver strands, falling around her shoulders. He had only seen her hair loose one other time, and she had quickly pulled it up in a bun at the back of her head. "Such a beautiful woman," he thought to himself, then quickly chastised himself for thinking about her beauty at a time like this, instead of her grief.

"Janine told me Zaqui was in Llano with Raheem. I had no idea. No idea. How could he do this?" Again she had to stop speaking. "When she told me Zaqui was there, I had this terrible feeling in my gut, but I couldn't believe it. Why? Why would he come out here?"

"I had no idea Raheem was involved with his father like this. I always knew Zaqui was a strict Muslim. Much more than I, but that doesn't mean you become a killer! And Raheem. He never really read his Qu'ran. I would chide him about it, but he would make fun of me and go back to whatever game he was playing," her voice grew louder and the anger she felt made it tremble. "I don't understand."

"Marah, no one does right now."

"No, but they think I do. They think I'm part of it. Janet wouldn't even open her door to me."

"What? When did you see Janet?"

"When I couldn't get out of my own house, I finally thought of her and she lives close, so Bella and I snuck out through the alley before sunrise and went there. I thought she would let me use her phone. She turned on the porch light, she looked through the peephole, I saw it darken, then she turned off the porch light and didn't open."

"My God." Joe was genuinely horrified for her. Anyone who knew Marah would have to know she had no hand in this. There was not a kinder, more gentle person than Marah. "I'm sorry. She didn't even mention it when we all went in this morning."

"And you're not even supposed to be here, right? Because they want to be sure I'm not in on this." The tears came in a flood again. Joe moved to the couch and put his arm around her shoulders.

"I'm here, Marah. And I'm staying. Damn them."

Marah lay on the couch with Bella, she could hear Joe opening and closing cabinets, clanking dishes, rummaging in the fridge.

"Are you ready to eat something? You have to eat something. Keep your strength up." He poked his head around the corner and smiled at her.

"I'll try." She wiggled free of Bella and stood up. Her head began to spin and her eyesight went dark for a moment. "Whoa" she exclaimed as she quickly sat down, landing on Bella who whined and pulled free.

"Hey, you ok?" He was across the room and sitting beside her in three steps.

"Yeah, just a little low blood sugar. Hits me now and then if I stand up too fast."

"And haven't eaten."

"Yes, and that. It passes quickly. No worries."

"Ok, but you are definitely eating some of my soup."

As they stood up, her new phone rang. She snatched it up, "Hello?"

"Marah, it's Pa."

"Pa…" she couldn't force any other words to come, she cried as she listened to him.

"Marah, Mum and I are in Dallas. We will be in Lubbock by 4:00 and to you by 6:00. Ok?" He could hear her crying.

She shook her head yes, still unable to say anything.

"Is anyone there with you? Marah?"

"Yes. My friend."

"Let me speak with her."

Marah handed the phone to Joe. "Hello?"

"Who is this?" Joe could hear the question her father's voice conveyed at hearing a man's voice.

"Colonel Joe Horowitz. I work with Marah."

"This is her father, I know Marah must be in shock. I'm glad you are there." His voice was clipped with a strong Indian accent. "We are in Dallas. We should be in Lubbock by 4 and to Bellview by 6:00. Can you stay with her until we arrive?"

"Yes, Mr. Dalal. I will be here. Do not worry."

"Thank you. We will see you then."

"Sir, I think you should know, the press is camped out in front of her house. It would be best if you come down the alley. Call and I will meet you there."

"Thank you. Yes. This has been a shock to us both. My wife is having a very difficult time. That might be too much for her, walking through that."

"Yes, sir. I will take care of it."

He hung up the phone and handed it to Marah. She slumped against him, relieved to know they were on their way and someone was helping her through this ordeal. He put his hand on the back of her head until she pulled away.

"Come on, let's try and eat a little."

Marah sat at the kitchen table, an old barn door wood table she had picked up at a garage sale when she and Raheem first moved to Bellview. "Ma, seriously, this old piece of junk? This is what you want?" But he had dutifully helped her carry it from the truck she had borrowed, into the house. She had found mismatched chairs, all old, worn wood, and added cushions to each one, her favorite being one she had made from the blue silk she had received in marriage. A large rug from India which she had inherited from her grandmother covered the floor on which it sat. The table felt cozy and comfortable. There were always fresh flowers in the center and a table for herbs and other plants sat in the corner windows which looked into the backyard.

Joe ladled up the soup and placed the bowls in front of them. He found some stale crackers in the pantry and laid them out as well.

Marah took up her spoon and half heartedly took a few spoonfuls of soup. "It's good, Joe. I didn't know you could cook."

"It's amazing what you can learn to do when push comes to shove."

"What do you mean?"

"When my ex-wife left me with two girls to raise, I had to figure out pretty quickly how to feed them. My mom came and lived with us for about a month and taught me some basics. Said she regretted not having taught me to cook as a boy, but in those days, moms didn't teach their sons to cook."

"I didn't know your wife left you. I thought she had died."

"Well she did in a metaphorical way I guess." He could joke about her now. "She hated the military life and when I came home and said we were moving again, she left. We didn't hear from her for years then out of the blue she showed up one day. The girls were in their teens by then, Jill a senior and Kris a sophomore.

Neither wanted anything to do with her, but I think Jill sees her mother periodically now that she has a child of her own."

"You're a grandpa. That must be nice."

"Yes, it is." They sat in silence and ate their soup. Marah finally broke the silence, "Zaqui left me when Raheem was five. He went back to Pakistan. It took me a while to figure it out, but I'm certain he married me to get his US citizenship, though I was never sure why he went back to Pakistan afterward. I guess he wanted to be able to travel back and forth easily between the two countries."

"When Colonel Rankin met with us today, he said you were married to the man who had done the killing, but I didn't know you were married still."

"Yes, we were still technically married. When I signed our marriage contract, I agreed if we had children, and for some reason we divorced, when my son was seven or eight, his father could take him. That is the fundamentalist Islamic rule. For a girl, a mother can keep her until she is nine, sometimes, ten, but fathers always get the children. So I never took any action. I was afraid if I did he would come for Raheem."

"He could just take him from you?"

"Yes." Marah leaned forward, her face in her hands, shaking her head back and forth. "And now, in the end, he got him anyway." The tears began again. Joe reached over and put his hand on her shoulder till she was able to stop crying.

"I told your father I would stay with you until they arrived, but don't feel obligated to talk. I'm sorry I brought up your relationship with Zaqui."

"Joe, it's ok. Until he showed back up in Raheem's life, I hadn't thought much about him, and always felt guilty for the relief I felt when he left us."

"Relief?"

"Yeah, he had seemed so nice, so supportive of my career and independence, but after we married and Raheem was born, that all went away. He became a tyrant. Constantly berating me for something. Telling me I was not a good Muslim wife." Marah sighed and looked away from Joe. "American Muslim women lead such different lives. Why our parents want us to marry men from India or the middle east is beyond me. We always disappoint those men." She turned her attention back to him and half smiled. "And I'm not the first one who married a man who solely wanted citizenship, that's for sure."

"I had a friend that married a Slovakian woman and as soon as she got her citizenship, she was gone. I felt bad for him, but behind his back everyone used to say, 'What did that drop dead gorgeous woman see in a schmuck like him?' so no one was surprised when she left, except him, poor schmuck."

Marah half-heartedly laughed. "Poor guy. Poor me."

She ate a little more of her soup, though it had grown cold and then they cleared the table.

"Go lie down if you'd like. Take a nap."

"Not sure I can."

"Try?"

"Okay, I will."

He watched her as she left the kitchen and heard Bella get up and follow her down the hall. Her bedroom door clicked closed and Joe began cleaning up the dishes.

Joe heard her door open a couple of hours later. Bella appeared first and went straight for the door. Joe let her out and Marah stepped into the living room. Her hair was pulled back neatly in a bun, and she had changed out of her running clothes into loose pants and a long shirt that flowed around her as she walked. Even though her eyes were puffy and red, she was still beautiful.

"Did you nap?"

"I think I did for a short time. Yes."

"Your parents should be here soon."

"Joe, thanks again for being here. Did you tell anyone from the base you were here?"

"No, but unfortunately the press may have done it for me. Not sure if I made the news this afternoon or not, but seems like they are always looking for any little tidbit to spice up a story. Creating controversy from nothing."

"I don't want you to be in trouble on my account."

"Marah, it doesn't matter. You have done nothing wrong. The only people in the wrong here are those who think you are somehow involved."

"And Raheem and Zaqui," she barely whispered as she leaned her head back onto the chair and sighed.

Joe recognized that shock was setting in. He went to the kitchen and brought her back a large glass of water. She shook her head when he held it out to her.

"You need to drink some water, Marah. Becoming dehydrated will only add to your lightheadedness and the shock, which I think you are experiencing. Come on, Doctor's orders."

She took the glass and drank half. "Ok?"

"Ok and the rest, sooner than later."

"Yes, Doctor."

They sat quietly in the living room. Joe glanced at his phone, looking for messages. He had received a barrage earlier from several members of his and Marah's coworkers, asking what was happening and did he think Marah was in on it. He couldn't believe their ignorance and judgement, as he defended her in each reply.

Marah sat looking off into space, her phone clasped in her hand, waiting for her parents' call. She felt no desire to reach out to any friends for fear they would all respond as Janet had so callously done and she did not think she could bear the pain.

Again, they sat in silence, waiting.

When the phone finally rang, Marah nearly jumped up and ran to the back door as she answered the phone. "Pa? Ok. Yes. Ok." She hung up and turned to find Joe standing behind her.

"They are almost here. Main street. Should be less than five minutes." She spun back around and began to open the sliding glass door. Joe put his hand on hers and stopped her.

"Marah, I don't want you to go out there. We don't know if there might be some journalist lurking around. Let me go wait at the gate and you stay."

She hesitated for a moment. "Yes. Ok. You're right."

He left her standing there as he went to open the back gate and step out as soon as her parents appeared in the alley. Their rental car turned into the narrow lane and he slipped out to greet them. He motioned for them to be silent as he went to the trunk of the car and waited for Mr. Dalal to pop the switch. They disappeared into the backyard and he gathered their things and put them inside the gate. Then he jumped in the car and drove it around to the next block and parked. Walking back down the alley, he saw someone turning into the other end and ran to Marah's gate, slamming and latching it behind him. Hopefully, no one saw him park the car and her parents could be here without the press's knowledge.

Marah felt the unbearable emotions hit her in a wave as soon as she saw Pa step through the gate. He held Mum's hand, but as soon as she saw Marah, she ran to the door and threw herself at her daughter, clinging to her. Her father wrapped his arms around them both and moved them away from the door, trying to shield them from any possible prying eyes. Joe found them like this as he stepped inside with their luggage and slid the door shut behind him.

"Marah, Marah, how did this happen?" Her mother had Marah's face between her hands, looking into her eyes. "Why oh why? Our sweet Raheem."

Pa took his wife and daughter by the hand and led them to the couch in the living room where they all sat down. Joe took their luggage down the hall. When he came through the living room again, Pa motioned for him to sit down.

"I knew you should never have let him see Zaqui. That devil."

"Dara, that's enough."

"No, it's true, Pa. I should have said no."

"Marah, if you had kept them apart, Raheem would have defied you. You cannot blame yourself."

"But I do."

Shariq adored his two children, but Marah had a special place in his heart. As the oldest, she had followed him around from the time she could walk. Her curiosity led to long discussions with him as she grew up. She would often come to his building during his office hours at the university. He was a much admired mathematician, and Marah would sit and listen to his conversations with students and colleagues. His heart ached for her now, for all of them, at the loss of Raheem and the devastation his acts created.

Marah leaned her head on Pa's shoulder, sighed and closed her eyes. Mum held tightly to Marah's hand. Joe felt awkward, as if a spy to their grief. Marah sat up and looked at Joe, as if she had read his mind. "Oh my, I didn't introduce you all. Joe, I'm sorry. This is my Pa and Mum. Shariq Dalal and Dara Patil. Mum, Pa, this is Dr. Joe Horowitz. He is my colleague at work, and my friend."

Shariq and Joe both stood and shook hands. "I'm sorry for your loss, Mr. Dalal, Mrs. Patil."

"Thank you. And thank you for staying with Marah till we arrived. We are indebted to you, Dr. Horowitz."

"No. I am happy to be of service. This is such a bad situation with the press and government. I am afraid none of you will be able to leave here for at least this week. It's a zoo out front."

"Yes, we saw pictures on the news at DFW."

"Sit down, please," and Pa motioned with his hand to the seat.

"Marah, has anyone told you where they took Raheem?" Pa asked.

"No, Pa. They came last night, took my phone, my computer, my tablet and left."

"Did they leave a card?"

"I don't remember."

"It's in the kitchen," Joe said. "I saw it earlier." Marah half-heartedly smiled at Joe. "Would you like me to call and see what I can find out?"

"Yes. Please."

While Joe went to call Agent Waters, Marah struggled to explain everything to Pa and Mum, but finally finished. Mum shook with silent tears throughout Marah's recounting. Raheem had been special to her, he was the only grandchild living in the US. Marah's sister had left the country after graduating college for a job in London, where she met and married her husband, and now lived with their three children. Mum saw them only once a year, when she and Shariq returned to Bangladesh, what had been East Pakistan when they had left so many years ago, and Marah's sister would meet them there. She hugged Marah to her now and softly stroked her bowed head.

All eyes turned to Joe as he rejoined them. "Agent Waters did not want to speak to me. I finally convinced him I was calling for you, Marah, when I described his not so kind invasion of your home last night. He said Raheem's body is still at the hospital in the morgue. They've tried to suppress that information from the press so there is not an attack on the hospital. They would like to remove him to the funeral home in Llano. Waters suggested cremation so his body would not have to…"

"No! That is haram," Shariq slammed his fist on the couch arm as he spoke.

"Marah, you must not allow them to do this," her mother whispered.

Joe just looked from one to the other. He had no idea why what he said had caused such a reaction. "I'm sorry. I told Waters I would speak to you about your wishes and call him back."

"No, Joe, you're fine. In Islam, it is forbidden to cremate. Allah does not allow the destruction of the body. I will call him back."

"I will be glad to if you'd like."

"Thank you, but I should."

"I left his card on the kitchen cabinet. I can help with the arrangements, whatever you like."

"Joe, you are so kind. There is so much…" she couldn't finish the sentence. "Thank you."

Joe left after making them dinner. Then Marah got her parents settled in Raheem's room. She eventually collapsed in her own bed. The house was quiet, but she could vaguely hear murmuring voices. Maybe she was imagining them. The crowd of journalists waited like vultures on the front lawn to pounce on anyone coming or going from her house. She felt her heart pounding in her chest and tried deep breathing to calm herself.

Marah stared at the ceiling. She remembered the day Raheem was born, holding his perfect tiny body in her arms. Smelling his skin, counting his fingers and toes, looking into his eyes and watching him latch onto her breast the first time. She remembered the sound of his voice as he said his first words and how it changed to a deep resonant sound as he grew into a man. She sometimes felt so inadequate as a single mom raising a boy, but she had found support for him at the various mosques they had attended over the years. However, skipping around from base to base, having to restart their lives over every time had probably not helped him gain the foundation he needed to be the man she had envisioned. And Bellview had been the hardest. There were few Muslim's on the Eastern Plains and only a small mosque. School had been difficult for him here. Her heart pounded with grief and guilt. Then she thought of Zaqui and how he had stolen her son from her in the end.

# Chapter 3

M arah found Pa in the kitchen when she woke the next morning. He had completed his prayers with Mum, who then went back to bed. Marah had slept right through her prayer alarm. She had no desire to pray. "Pa, did you sleep?"

"Ah, Marah. Yes. Some. It was easier last night since I knew you were in the next room."

"Good." She poured a cup of tea and sat down beside her father. "I never knew I could hurt this bad. The pain is...I don't know how to describe it."

He took her hand in his.

"I wonder…" tears choked her words, "where will Raheem be in the afterlife? What will Allah do with him?" She turned to Pa, looking for an answer.

"We must be strong. We do not know what Zaqui did to influence him. We must pray Allah will forgive Raheem, that he will pass over Siraat to paradise."

"I cannot pray. My mind is blank. I keep asking how can Allah let this happen?"

"Marah, you must not think this. We must subject ourselves to Allah's will. Pray and the words will come again."

"No, Pa. I'm afraid."

"You are in grave pain right now. It will come. Inshallah."

They sat in silence. Flashes of Raheem played through Marah's head. The little boy running through the house with a light saber. The boy jumping off of anything he could climb. Her little boy. Her little boy who had grown up to be a murderer. How could she not have seen it?

Both Marah and Shariq jumped when Dara walked up behind them, placing a hand on each of their shoulders. Bella padded in behind her and went straight to the back door. Marah jumped up and hugged Mum, then opened the door to let Bella out. "Tea?"

"Yes. Thank you."

She made another pot of tea and set it on the table.

"You slept, Marah?"

"Not really. I can't stop thinking how I missed the changes? Why couldn't I see them, Mum? Why?" She breathlessly went on pacing back and forth, "When he started being secretive about his father? When he started berating me? Why didn't I question him? Why couldn't I have stopped this? What if there hadn't been a staff meeting, and all those people had been at the station? How many more would they have killed?" She stopped when the tears began to flow.

Dara stood and wrapped her arms around her daughter. "Marah, mothers see their children with eyes of love. You mustn't blame yourself."

"But I should never have let him see Zaqui. I let him spend the summer with him. And it was my own selfishness; I wanted a break. Mum, it was so hard sometimes."

"There now." Dara stroked Marah's back and made almost a cooing sound in sorrow for her daughter. For all of them. She struggled to fight back her own tears. The loss of her grandson, was so overwhelming, so raw, she felt she could hardly breathe. She steered Marah to the table again and they all sat down.

Shariq poured Marah and Dara tea and sat waiting for them to settle down. He was a practical man and knew they must make decisions regarding Raheem today.

"Marah, I will call Agent Waters and let him know that Raheem must not be cremated. We need to find a resting place for his body. One where no one will defile his grave," Pa said.

"What? Defile his grave?" Marah was horrified at the thought.

"Yes. I think there is a possibility. We must try and make all arrangements today. It has been too long already."

Marah sighed and looked into her tea cup. "Please call him and tell him no cremation."

"Yes, I will and let him know the body must not be embalmed. They will want to do that I'm sure."

Marah knew that Pa was right. Burying him here in Bellview would open the door for his grave to be defiled, and what if someone went so far as to dig him up. She waited for Pa to get off the phone and find out when she could see Raheem.

"The hospital morgue is expecting us at ten this morning. Mr. Waters said he will be sure the press is not hanging around the hospital, but says he can't do anything about the ones camped out here."

"I feel like we're in prison," Marah said.

"Agent Waters also suggested I talk to the funeral home director in Llano. He may know where to bury Raheem safely."

"Is Joe coming back today?" Mum asked.

"I think so. Maybe soon."

"Why don't you call him. See if he'll drive up to the back gate and take us," Pa asked.

"Pa, I hate to burden him with more."

"Marah," Mum interrupted them, "He is more than willing to help you. That was evident yesterday. Call him. It is best."

"Ok."

Joe arrived in the alley at 9:30. Marah, Pa and Mum, slipped out the back gate, Marah patting Bella on the head and telling her to stay. They all got in and he slowly crept down the alley, trying to keep the sound of the truck from alerting the press camped out front. They had attacked him last night when he had left Marah's for home. He knew they would be looking for him to come back this morning.

They were all lost in their own thoughts, and no one spoke as Joe drove them out of town. He had chosen the back road, a small two lane road that connected the air base with Llano. Marah gazed out the side window, watching the tumbleweed-covered sand hills and scattered farm houses go by. Marah always took this road when she went to see Raheem. High Desert Sands state park was off this road and Marah and Raheem had occasionally camped there on weekends as an easy get away from town. After Raheem moved to Llano last summer, she sometimes took the side road to the park and walked around the pond there before going home. She loved the wide open plains and their endless vistas. The tears began to fill her eyes again, blurring her view into a haze of muddled colors.

When they arrived at the hospital, Joe drove around back as Waters had suggested. They piled out and quickly crossed to the back loading dock, following the ramp up to the double doors. An orderly met them and escorted them to the morgue where they were greeted by Agent Waters and the doctor on call. Ronald Gomez from the funeral home, arrived just after them, coming up the rear. Marah was in a daze as introductions were made all around, then the doctor escorted them into the small morgue, where there were two drawers, one she knew held her Raheem and the other Zaqui. The room was ice cold; she shivered from head to toe and couldn't stop shaking. Joe led her forward and they stood on one side and her Pa and Mum on the other as the doctor pulled the drawer out for them. Mum shrieked and began to sob and the others stared horrified at Raheem's body, his face covered with a large pork chop and bacon stuffed into his mouth.

"My God," the doctor exclaimed and yanked the pork chop and bacon off of Raheem's face. He turned and opened the other drawer and found the same applied to the face of Zaqui. The orderly found a waste basket and held it up for the doctor.

"What is this?" Shariq almost roared. "Who has done this?"

"Mr. Dalal, I do not know. This is inexcusable. When I find who is responsible, I will not rest till he is fired. My God! I am so sorry. Please, step outside for a moment. Let me clean their faces. I...," and he trailed off, unable to say anything else.

Joe held the door as they left. They huddled in the hall, Mum was crying uncontrollably and Pa was trying to soothe her. Marah was in shock and stood there with tears pouring down her face.

"How could someone do this? I do not understand how the hospital could let this happen," Shariq said.

Joe's anger was palpable. Tears had filled his eyes too, that someone could be so hateful that they defiled his friend's child so completely.

When the doctor had finished with Raheem and Zaqui, he called them back into the room. He opened the drawer again and allowed them to gather.

Marah stood over Raheem weeping. She touched his beautiful thick black hair and ran her hand down the side of his face. "Why Raheem? Why? How could you do this?" Then she stepped back and turned away. Joe escorted Marah and her mother from the room. The doctor asked if Shariq would identify Zaqui and opened the other drawer upon his nod.

Pa stood staring at Zaqui. Anger was all he could feel as he looked at his former son-in-law. Bitter vile anger filled him and without a second thought, he spat in Zaqui's face. "You monster."

They were next escorted to a small conference room to make plans with Mr. Gomez. "Ms. Dalal, I am sorry for your loss. This is very difficult for you, no doubt, but I must tell you, I have been threatened with violence if I have anything to do with you and your son or husband, so I must ask you not to speak about the arrangements with anyone."

Mr. Gomez realized fatigue and shock had set in for all of them, including himself. He turned to Marah again, "I can't help thinking what it must be like for you, all the unanswered questions. I'm sorry you had to see your son violated like that, here in the hospital. This is a small town and ignorant people can be very cruel." Mr. Gomez paused and looked down at his hands. "My own anger at this situation has made my choice to help you difficult. Alec Davis grew up with my sons."

Marah turned away from him for a moment. When she looked at him again, her eyes were filled with tears. "I am so sorry. I realize this is a loss for you too. Thank you for your kindness, Mr. Gomez. I'm...we're grateful for your help." She looked to Pa for his input, but he was still seething from seeing his grandson defiled, feeling the defiling of Raheem's body as an insult to them all. Shariq collected himself and turned to Mr. Gomez, "I don't know if you know much about Islam?"

130

"I have assisted with other Muslim funerals. I know embalming cannot be carried out. Is that right?"

"Yes. No embalming."

"He needs to be buried soon then."

"Today," Shariq snapped.

"Yes. Under the circumstances…"

"Under the circumstances of having a hospital staff who defiles bodies, we must get him out of here today. I am prepared to do the Ghusl and Kafan, are you familiar?"

"Yes. I think I can arrange for the hospital to let us do that here. With no embalming, he must stay cold."

"Where do we bury him? I'm afraid of what will happen if he is buried in Bellview," said Marah.

"Well, I had a call this morning from a friend who lives on a ranch about thirty miles south of Llano. She said, um, well…she is appalled at what your son and husband have done, but she feels people are not going to treat you right, Ms. Dalal, and would like to help. She would like to offer you a burial spot for Raheem. Only Raheem."

"Oh. But why? Why would she do this? I mean offer a place for Raheem?"

"Because, Ms. Dalal, she is one of the kindest people you would ever hope to know."

Pa stopped pacing and put his hand on Marah's shoulder. Mum clung to her hand.

"Do you think we can do this today?"

"Today will work. She said give her the word and she'll have the place prepared."

Marah choked back tears, "Can we keep this secret? The staff?"

"We can if Dr. Baxter will keep everyone away from the morgue, but then there is the question of taking his body out." Gomez took out his phone and called Marah's benefactor. He stepped out of the room, leaving them to their thoughts. Mum and Marah sat in the chairs at the desk while Pa paced and Joe leaned against the wall. Once the door shut behind Mr. Gomez, Joe walked to Marah and bent down beside her. "I will be glad to help with all of this. If we need to use my truck to take him to the ranch, I will be glad to do so."

"Thank you. You are a good friend to me."

When Mr. Gomez returned, Joe stepped back to his place at the wall.

"Kate is digging the spot. It will be at the end of an abandoned road, a place that should discourage anyone, even if it is ever discovered. We will go as soon as your father has finished with the body."

"Thank you."

"The body must face northeast. Can you let her know," Pa interjected.

"Yes, I will call her back. Now what about your husband?"

"Zaqui was not my husband. He left me fifteen years ago."

"I understand, but you were still married and that means you have to decide what will be done with his body."

"Do what is easiest for you. I don't care. He stole my son from me and killed him. Cremate him."

"Marah," Pa spoke sharply. "You cannot do that."

"Yes. I can."

"Marah! I will not let you do this. I am angry too, but we cannot do something forbidden for our own satisfaction." He turned to Mr. Gomez, "The Imam from Bellview can help you. I will get you the information."

"Ms. Dalal, I can only do as your father wishes if you give me permission."

"Yes, do that. I don't care."

"Ok. Let me call Kate again and give her the direction for the grave."

"Yes, thank you."

Mr. Gomez stuck his head in the door and let them know he had talked to Kate about the grave, then he gently closed the door and went to speak to Dr. Baxter and gather what Shariq would need for the preparation of his grandson's body. With the air base close by, Gomez had helped with several Muslim funerals and knew the body must be washed by a relative, not embalmed, and must be wrapped in a certain manner. He seethed inside at the senselessness of Alec's death and found this situation difficult. However, after talking to Marah and her parents, he felt certain they had no idea Raheem was being radicalized. Marah looked confused in fear and uncertainty. She did not consider her son a martyr. Her anger at Zaqui was palpable.

The four of them remained in the conference room until Gomez came for Shariq. He escorted him to the morgue and rolled a gurney to the drawer side of Raheem. The two of them lifted his body onto the table and moved him to the middle of the room where Shariq was able to wash the body. He covered his grandson with a towel from the middle of his waist down between his legs, the Auwra, and then he washed Raheem's face and beard. Gomez knew this was to rid Raheem's face from any remaining touch of pork. Shariq then started on the upper right side of his body, gently washing the arm, hand, underarm and torso, carefully avoiding the area where bullets had entered his body; he then moved to the upper left side, then the lower right side, finishing with the lower left side of his body. This ritual was required to be completed a minimum of three times. Gomez had found a rosemary bush outside the hospital and cut numerous branches for Shariq to use as a perfume for the body. Camphor was generally used, but Gomez could find none available in the hospital. He had prepared a basin for the last wash with small branches of the rosemary for the perfume wash. He then sat in wonder, watching Shariq's loving care to his grandson knowing how difficult this must be for him.

Once he had finished the Ghusl, Gomez helped Shariq move Raheem to the second gurney, prepared with three white sheets Gomez had talked the hospital laundry into giving him. Shariq removed the towel covering Raheem's Auwra and placed a clean towel in its place. Then Shariq laid Raheem's left hand on his chest, then his right hand on the left, as if Raheem was in prayer. He placed pieces of the rosemary on Raheem's forehead, nose, between his hands, on his knees and feet. Then he folded the right side of the first sheet up, then the left, until each layer was securely wrapped around Raheem. Gomez then handed him strips of torn sheet to use as rope and Shariq tied the sheets together above Raheem's head, then wrapped and tied two around the body and lastly one below Raheems feet. He then stood back and closed his eyes, silently weeping. Gomez left him to his tears and went to notify the others that Shariq had finished.

Ronald Gomez worried about how they would remove Raheem's body from the building unnoticed. He knew his small hometown was notorious for gossip and the last thing they needed was someone following them to Kate's ranch. Her kindness was well known in Llano, but this was going above and beyond in his mind. Having reporters inundate her would be cruel payback for her thoughtfulness to a stranger. He finally came up with an idea he hoped would work and went to speak to the family.

Joe gave his keys for the truck to Shariq. Marah put on a doctor's lab coat and let her hair down from a tight bun, into a ponytail hanging down her back. She then put on her father's reading glasses. Hopefully, if anyone from the media was outside, they would not recognize her, as she never wore her hair down and didn't wear glasses. Her father went to Joe's truck and drove it up to the ramp beside the loading dock. Marah wheeled her mother out to the truck in a wheelchair and helped her into the front seat of the truck, standing there as if talking to her. At the same time, Gomez had backed his transport van up to the loading dock and Dr. Baxter wheeled Raheem's body, zipped up into a body bag, into the back of the van. Joe walked alongside the body, his head covered with a baseball cap pulled down over his eyes, and he bent over as if in tears, as he walked to the passenger door of the van and slipped inside. When Marah's mother saw Raheem being loaded, and no one seemed to be paying any of them any attention, she motioned to Marah, and Marah slipped in the backdoor of the truck and closed the door, sliding to the middle of the seat to be sure she could not be seen through the dark windows. Dr. Baxter slammed his hand against the door of the funeral home van as he closed it, and Gomez put the van into gear and drove away, followed closely by Shariq, driving Joe's truck. Marah looked over her shoulder and saw no one following them. She breathed a sigh of relief as she slipped out of the borrowed lab coat and handed her father's glasses back to him.

Marah's phone began ringing as soon as they were clear of the hospital parking lot. "Hello?"

Joe's voice broke her nervous reverie, "Anyone following us?"

"Not that we can see."

"What a relief. I was afraid someone would catch on to us with all the activity, but maybe that's what kept them from noticing."

"Yes. Hopefully."

"Is your dad okay driving? We can stop and I'll come back there." He could hear her cover the phone with her hand, as she asked her father whether he was ok driving.

She came back on the line, "He says he's fine." Her father followed the funeral home van as Gomez made his way along the edge of town, passing by the university, heading for the highway to the south. Marah had never been to this side of town and never seen this part of the university. She had always driven straight to Raheem's little house when she came to town and had never really explored the area. They passed a half empty strip-mall and grocery store, both rather faded looking and sad. The highway south passed tumbleweed-covered fences and rolling sand hills. Farm houses here and there were set back from the highway, most surrounded by a few trees, that may have at one time been more profuse, offering a wind block from the eastern New Mexico winds. The blazing sun made everything look washed out, as if it all was one bland color.

Her parents murmured to each other. She didn't pay much attention to their conversation. Looking out the window, she watched the blurring scenery as they picked up speed. Her thoughts raced from anger to sadness to disbelief. She wanted to scream with frustration and fall to the floor in uncontrollable sobs. Images of Raheem as her sweet little boy, so full of joy and happiness, were obliterated by the pictures of him on the surveillance cameras she had seen on TV, his shaggy beard he'd started growing, not quite filled in, holding a gun, a large gun. Then following his father down a hall. She did not know that person. She was not burying that person. The camera also showed Zaqui shooting Raheem as the police finally stormed the doors. That image would never leave her.

As they approached the ranch, her father slowed behind the funeral home van, and slowly made the turn onto the dirt road. A farm house could be seen down the road, surrounded by trees. Off in the distance from the house, a ramshackle building sat as if leaning into the wind. A dog ran out to meet them as their vehicles turned into the yard. Mr. Gomez had asked them to remain in their car until they arrived at the burial site. He hurried from the van and greeted a woman as she came from the house. She pointed down the road and off to the south. They stood talking for a moment. Marah was transfixed on this woman who would be so kind as to think of her.

Kate wore faded blue jeans and a short sleeve button up white shirt. Her grey speckled hair was cropped short and lay in tight layers against her head. She smiled easily, as she and Mr. Gomez talked. The two of them got into the van and Pa followed them down the dirt road. It eventually faded into more of a dirt track, but they continued on. Marah could see a tractor just ahead, its shovel poised in mid-air. Her heart lurched at the sight.

Pa stopped behind the van, after allowing Mr. Gomez to turn around and back up close to the hole. Once they were situated, Mr. Gomez came to the window of Joe's truck and Pa rolled down the window to talk to him. "What would you like us to do? We will help in whatever way you would like."

"Thank you. Would the three of you mind sitting in the truck here while we recite the Salat al-Janasah? Then I will ask Joe to help me lower him into the grave. We will need some rocks to prop Raheem on his side. The body is not laid flat. And we must find something to lay on top of him before he is covered." Pa sighed as he looked around at the barren landscape. "I think we can use those dried plants against the fence there."

"Tumbleweeds, Pa."

"Yes, they will have to do."

The three of them, Pa, Mum, and Marah stepped out of the truck and walked around to the grave. Kate, Gomez and Joe went to the truck and got in, softly closing the door behind them. Pa helped Mum over the ruts in the road and Marah followed behind them. They went to the grave and looked into what seemed a huge deep pit. Pa led them to face the northeast. Women did not usually attend funerals, and the Salat al-Jarazah, a prayer required in Islamic tradition that seeks pardon for the deceased and all dead Muslims, was not usually said at the grave, but in a side room of a mosque, but they must do what they must. Pa stood at the front facing northeast, Qiblah, then Marah stood behind him and Mum behind Marah, forming the required three rows as they could. "Allahu Akbar," Pa started and they each joined in as they repeated four times, then Pa began the ritual, reciting and raising his hand. Marah and Mum stood behind him as he went on. When he had finished, Pa went to the truck and asked Joe, Kate and Mr. Gomez to join them.

"His body must be propped on the side so Raheem faces Qiblah. Would you all mind helping us find some large rocks if possible?"

"I'm sure I dug up quite a few, let's look in the pile."

They gathered enough rocks to hold Raheem's body in place.

"Joe, will you help me move Raheem's body into the grave?"

"Of course."

Mr. Gomez opened the back of the van and slid the body board forward, then unzipped the body bag.

"We must enter where his feet will be placed."

"Hold on, I've brought a ladder out on the tractor." Kate went to the machine and untied the ladder from the side. She placed it in the grave. "What if you move him to the side of the grave and then once you are in, Ronnie and I will slide him to you. Will that work?"

"Yes, thank you."

Shariq slowly climbed down the ladder. Then Joe followed. Once they were in the grave, they reached up to receive Raheem from Kate and Gomez. They gently laid him on his side facing Qiblah with his back against the wall of the grave. Shariq recited, "In the name of Allah and in the faith of the messenger of Allah," as they laid him down. The rocks were then piled in front of him, keeping the body from rolling forward. They then removed the ties from above his head and from below his feet. "Are there any more rocks? We need just a few more to cover him. Marah came to life and went searching for more. She carried a few large ones to the grave side and Joe took them, handing them to Shariq who carefully laid them on his grandson. They then climbed out of the grave. Shariq went to the fence and pulled tumbleweeds away, laying them on top of Raheem below. Then he took a handful of dirt and dropped it on top of Raheem, and did this three times. Then Marah followed suit, as well as Mum. When they were finished, Mr. Gomez directed them back to the truck and Kate went to the tractor and began to carefully push the dirt back into the grave. The three of them watched in silence.

When Kate had finished, Shariq went in search of a rock to place at the head of Raheem's grave. Kate started to back the tractor away, but Shariq waved her down and asked her to make the grave convex as required by the Prophet. She backed up and put the front loader on the hard dirt and moved enough to make a small pile over the grave, while he continued to hunt for a large rock. Finding a large flat one, Joe, who had been following him, picked up and carried it to the head of the grave. He stood the stone up as best he could and stepped back to allow Shariq to stand there. He waved Marah and Dara over to him and put his arms around their shoulders. "Oh Allah, forgive him; Oh Allah strengthen him."

Kate had parked the tractor and joined Gomez and Joe. The three of them stood quietly nearby as Sahriq, Marah and Dara huddled together in their pain. When they left the grave, they held hands, carefully picking their way around the ruts and weeds, making their way to the others. Gomez approached them and went to Marah.

"Ms. Dalal, I am sorry for your loss. None of us can imagine what you are going through, but I will say, the media has been very unfair to you. Please let me know if there is anything else you need."

"Thank you, Mr. Gomez. I don't know what we would have done without you, and without Mrs. Wilson."

Kate Wilson stepped over to Marah and held out her hand. "Marah, I am sorry for your loss."

"Mrs. Wilson," Marah began, but she choked on tears and could not speak.

"I am Shariq Dalal. Your kindness to complete strangers is hard for me to understand."

"Mr. Dalal…"

"Shariq, please."

"Shariq, I was horrified at the way the media was treating your daughter. I know the local family whose son was killed, and love that family, but I think we have to look after the living, and frankly I have no doubt Marah's life is going to be hell for awhile. I thought I might be able to help in some way and this is what I came up with."

"Thank you." Marah had collected herself and was able to respond. "You are so kind."

"No, just doing what I think is right."

"Do you live out here by yourself," Marah asked?

"No, my husband is away on business, and my daughter is at college. She is due home in a couple of weeks."

"Oh." Marah looked away across the empty plains, thoughts of Zaqui shooting people filled her head. How could her sweet son turn to this?

Kate cleared her throat, "I didn't mean to upset you."

"I know, I just thought of the students who won't be going home from Llano."

"Is it ok if I ask you about your son?"

Pa and Marah exchanged looks, he nodded his head at her, as if encouraging her to talk.

"I just…I don't know what to say. He was such a kind hearted young man. Always considerate of me, of others. I don't know the man who went with his father to kill. I don't." She shook her head and looked into Kate's eyes. "That was not my son."

"Marah, we must remember him as we knew him, not the man his father made of him," Pa said.

"Yes," Marah nodded her head as she spoke. "Yes, because no one else will."

The weight of the last two days weighed her down, she felt so tired, drained of all feeling and emotion. She looked at her parents and knew they felt the same. Joe somehow kept them all going, but she just wanted to be home in her bed.

"Thank you again, Kate. I'm overwhelmed with your kindness." She put her hand out to Kate, but Kate took her in her arms and hugged her.

"I'm sorry for your loss," Kate said before releasing her. "I know you have a tough road ahead."

They said goodbye and returned to Joe's truck. Pa and Mum sat in the back seat, her head leaned on his shoulder. Marah looked at them and sighed. She felt they had aged ten years since she last saw them only a few months ago. The stress of their trip and burying their grandson was too great for them. And she felt the guilt of all that had happened gripping her heart in a steel vise. How would they ever recover from this?

# Chapter 4

M arah slept for the first time since her world had imploded. Exhaustion had finally caught up to her. Bella slept on the floor next to her bed, Marah's hand had stroked Bella's head until she drifted off. She was surprised she had slept when her alarm awoke her for prayers. She slipped out of bed, and found Pa in the hall, silently closing the bedroom door where he and Mum slept. The sound of Mum snoring made them smile at each other. "Shhh, she needs to sleep," Pa whispered as they entered Marah's office. Marah covered her head with her scarf as they knelt to pray, he on his mat in front of her, both of them facing towards qibla, Bella in the hall, her head laying on her crossed paws, watching them both. She knew she was not allowed in. When finished, they retreated to the kitchen. Marah let Bella out to the backyard and then made tea. They sat together, quiet in their own thoughts while the sky began to lighten with the early dawn.

"I have not been praying, Pa. I can't. This morning I had to try, but I felt nothing."

"Marah, Allah is there to help you through this. You must rely on Allah."

"I know. Thanks for being here Pa. I couldn't have gotten through yesterday without you and Mum."

"Of course we are here." He reached for her hand and held it for a moment.

"Pa, I'm scared. I will have to go back to work and I am worried about what will happen there."

"Marah, life is going to be hard for a long time. None of us who knew Raheem can understand his motive, how he got pulled into this, we can only put our trust in Allah and keep living our lives."

"But Pa, I do know. Zaqui did this."

"Yes, however, Raheem wasn't forced. The videos make that clear. He joined his dad willingly."

"Why? I just want to know why? I thought he was doing well. He had friends at university, he liked his professors, his studies, he seemed like he was finally having a good time after his high school experience."

"What do you mean?"

"He never really had friends at the high school. His teachers thought he was 'surly and uncooperative.' And he got harassed a lot."

"You never told us this."

"I didn't want you and Mum to worry. I thought he would get through it and be okay. And he was till Zaqui came back into his life." She shook her head and looked into her cup. "I knew he harbored a lot

145

of anger toward his dad before Zaqui showed up, but then he appeared and Raheem went running to him, so hungry for the man who deserted us."

"Oh daughter, I wish you had told me. Maybe I could have helped."

"But that's not all. I could have paid closer attention. I was selfishly so relieved when he left for school. He had been unhappy and berating me all the time." Her throat started to constrict and she could feel the tears building as she choked out, "I was glad he was gone." She pulled a tissue from the box near her chair and blew her nose. "It's my fault. This is all my fault. I should have seen the signs."

"Marah, Marah," Pa said and reached out his arms to her. "You mustn't say that. You are not responsible for his actions."

She pulled away from him and looked up with tear-filled eyes, "Am I not? 'Oh believer's save yourselves and your offspring from the fire whose fuel is humans and stones.' I have not saved him from that fire."

"But you are not the reason he chose the fire Marah. And we do not know what was in his heart."

"Thank you, Pa." She hugged him quickly, and got up to refill their tea cups as Mum walked into the kitchen.

"As-salamu alaykum," she said to both of them as she walked to Marah and hugged her. "How are you this morning, dear?"

"Mummy, I'm so tired. So so tired, but what about you?"

"I'm afraid I didn't sleep much." She looked at her husband, "Thank you for leaving me to sleep this morning. I was awake till almost 4:00."

"Certainly," Shariq replied.

Dara took her cup of tea and joined Marah and Shariq at the table. "Has anyone looked outside this morning? Are they still out there?"

"I don't know. I feel like a prisoner in my own home."

"Well, I'm glad Joe brought you that phone," Dara said.

"Yes, me too. I was so relieved when you called me."

They fell silent. Marah finally set down her cup and sighed. She went to the cabinet and found oatmeal to make for their breakfast. Another day to stumble through. She wasn't even sure what day it was and took a quick glance at the calendar. Monday. 'Today is Monday,' she thought. And she measured out the water and put it on the stove to boil.

"Why don't you come home with us for awhile?" Dara asked.

Marah turned to look at her mother, "I don't know. I feel I need to go back to work."

"When are you going back?" Pa asked.

"I think in two weeks. I'm not sure. To be honest, I don't know." She paused and took a deep breath as she stirred the oatmeal. "I don't even know if I can leave the city. I don't remember what the FBI agent said to me. They just stormed in here and took my things. It was awful."

"I think we need to enlist Joe's help and see what we can find out. You cannot leave this house and I think it best if no one knows we are here." Pa tapped the table with his finger tips and continued, "I will talk to him about going to see the agent and getting your computer returned and your phone. They can't charge you with anything, so they need to clear you and let you get your life back in order."

"Pa, I think my life is going to be out of order for a long time." She scooped the oatmeal into bowls and took them to the table. "If I can, I will go home with you. I can't stay here and be a prisoner in my house forever. I'll call Joe and see what he can find out for us." No one spoke while they ate their breakfast, each in their own thoughts. As Marah stood to gather their bowls, she said, "I got such mixed messages from Raheem this past year and we didn't talk to each other like we had before..." she trailed off as she turned towards the sink.

Pa nodded his head then said, "Remember, I tried talking to Raheem about being more devout a couple of years ago and he said, 'I am good with Allah, Pa. No worries.' Then he went back to the game he was playing."

Marah came back to the table and joined her parents. "You know, when I think back on this past year, I thought he was getting more serious about Islam, but maybe he wasn't really. He rarely came up to go to mosque."

"I think we might drive ourselves crazy trying to figure this out, darling," Mum said. "Let's try to think about something else for awhile." Mum took Marah's hand and held it between her own, "I know this is going to be terribly hard, but we must not dwell on what we do not understand."

Marah nodded her head yes and leaned over to hug her. Then she gathered the teacups as Pa and Mum left the kitchen and went to dress for the day. Marah stood at the sink rinsing the dishes, going over in her head the accusations the media were purporting. The word 'alleged' made her crazy every time they said it. 'Alleged murderer, alleged terrorist,' were they afraid to just name Zaqui and Raheem for what they were? Murderers? 'My God, Raheem is a murderer.' The thought made her sick to her stomach and she left the half washed dishes and ran for her bathroom.

Joe arrived several hours later to find Marah asleep and her parents talking on the couch. Marah had given him a key to let himself in so that the press would not catch a glimpse of any of them when answering the door. He brought in two bags of groceries, carried them to the kitchen and started putting things away. Shariq followed him and began helping.

"Did you sleep last night?"

"Maybe a little," Shariq said. "What is happening out there? Any chance they might be going away?" indicating with his head the media outside.

"Not yet, I'm afraid. They're like wolves waiting for prey every time I walk through them. They want a statement from Marah."

"No, no, no." Shariq shook his head. "They want to attack her, is what they want."

"I know it would not be easy. I've wondered if she should get a lawyer."

"What? She has done nothing wrong."

"True, but a lawyer could help get her phone and computer back, and see that she is exonerated in this.

A lawyer might also be able to make a statement that will get the media off her back."

"I think we should contemplate this for awhile. Maybe when Marah awakens I will bring it up with her."

"Okay. Good."

"She's napping?"

"Yes, since breakfast. We thought it best to just let her be."

"How about I make you all some lunch?"

"Thank you. I think that will help."

Joe and Shariq talked as he put together a meager meal for them all. "Where did you grow up, sir?"

"East Pakistan. My family lived in a small village for many years. When I went away to university in England, I thought I would go back to my village, find a wife, and settle for the rest of my life."

"What happened?"

"When I returned in '65, there was so much unrest. East Pakistan, which you probably know is now Bangladesh, wanted independence from West Pakistan. I felt my opportunities were going to be very limited and I did not want to bring up a family in this uncertainty. I married Dara in '66 and after Marah was born in '69, I moved us to Philadelphia. I was a math professor at Penn."

"That's great."

"It has been a good life. Till now. We will get through this though. We will. Inshallah."

"Yes."

They fell silent as Joe cut the vegetables for a salad. He soon had bowls laid out and silverware set on the table. "Ok, I think we have lunch."

Dara had just walked into the kitchen as he finished his preparations. She turned around and went to wake Marah.

They appeared in the kitchen together, Marah's hair had quickly been pulled into an uncombed ponytail, and her tunic was wrinkled from having been slept in. "Hi Joe. Thank you for cooking again."

"No problem. I'm here to help."

"I don't want you to help yourself out of a job."

"Hey, my worry, not yours."

"Where's Bella? Is she still outside?"

"I'll get her," Pa offered. He went to the sliding glass door and opened it slowly, expecting Bella to come running, but she was nowhere to be seen. He stepped outside and called her name. Nothing. No sign of her. Marah appeared in the door behind him.

"Bella," she called, but she still did not appear. Marah went to the dog house and peered inside. No Bella. She checked the gate. It was latched. "She's never gotten out of the yard. I don't understand."

Joe and Mum had now both come outside and the four of them stood there, frozen not knowing what to do next.

Marah started for the gate, but Joe stopped her. "Let me go."

"But I have to find her…"

"I will find her. I don't want the media crowd to pounce on you."

"Oh." She could say nothing else. Her mind was in a panic at the thought of Bella being gone. "Okay."

"Marah, let's try and eat. Yes?" Mum had come up and put her arm around her daughter's shoulder, hugging her close and guiding her back into the house.

"I'm not sure I can."

"Let's try."

Marah had not eaten anything when Joe reappeared an hour later. She jumped up from the table and ran to meet him in the backyard. "No Bella. What has happened?"

"I've looked everywhere. I've been up and down every street. No sign of her. I even went around front and asked the circus out there if they'd seen her. No one had."

"This can't be. She has never gotten out of the yard. And I can see no place where she could. I'm scared, Joe. Something has happened to her."

Joe reached out and took her hand. "I'll put up signs, I'll keep searching. We will find her. Ok?"

"Ok." She stood there, comforted by the feeling of his warm hand.

Shariq stood at the window watching his daughter. He opened the back door, "Marah," he said sharply, and she pulled her hand away from Joe, lowered her head and walked into the house.

The printer was spitting out LOST DOG signs, when Joe came back from a second search. He picked them up off the printer, took a roll of tape and headed back out to plaster them around the neighborhood. He had told Marah to put his phone number and name as the owner so no one would make the connection to her. When he had finished, he came back and they all waited. He made dinner. They halfheartedly talked about inanities and Marah stared off into space frequently. When the phone had not rung with information and ten o'clock approached, Joe said his goodbyes and left for the evening. "I'll be back tomorrow. Call me if you need me to pick up anything. I think I brought enough groceries for a couple of days, but if there's anything you need…"

"Thank you, Joe."

"She'll show up tomorrow. I know it," Joe said.

"Yes. I'm sure," Marah sighed.

"Ok, get some sleep."

"I'll try."

After tossing and turning all night, Marah drug herself out of bed for early morning prayers. She again met her father in the hall and the two of them entered the office. When they were finished, Marah headed straight for the back door. The yard was still dark as she silently slid the door open and stuck her head out. "Bella," she called. Then as she was about to shut the door, she noticed something hanging off the back fence. She turned on the porch light, flooding the yard with its brightness, making clear what was hanging from the fence. She began to scream, a gut wrenching scream which brought the last of the hangers-on from the front yard to peer over the side gate, to see Bella, cut open from her throat through her stomach, hanging by a rope over the fence. A head scarf was draped around Bella's head to resemble a hijab.

Pa stepped outside and the sight made him physically ill. Mum came running and as soon as she saw Bella, she ran to Marah, who had sunk to the pavement and was crying hysterically, put her arm around her, lifting her up and propelling her into the house. The camera's were flashing, although someone else could be heard throwing up and someone said, "What the fuck?" Pa wiped his mouth and went back into the house, turned off the light and slammed the door shut. "Allah! Is there no decency in this world?"

Mum had Marah, sitting on the couch. She rocked back and forth as her entire body shook with hysterical cries. "Allah! Allah!" Losing her son and now this, how would she cope? Mum kept rubbing her back, shushing her like a crying baby. "Come, darling. Let's go lay down. Come, take Mummy's hand." Marah reached out and took her hand. They walked to Marah's bedroom. Mum helped her to the bed, helped her lay down, then crawled in beside her and took her in her arms. She held her until Marah stopped crying. Held her until she stopped shaking. Held her until she fell into a fitful sleep.

# Chapter 5

"Marah, you have to eat something." Mum was at her bedside again, urging her to eat, but she could not force herself to even sit up, let alone swallow food.

"I'm so tired, Mum. Just let me sleep." She rolled over, her back facing her mother, and pulled the pillow over her head. Her mother tiptoed from the room, tray in hand.

"She won't eat a thing," Dara said to Shariq and Joe. The two men were sitting on the couch talking about everything that had occurred over the last few days. Shariq had called Joe after discovering Bella and asked him to come as soon as possible to assist him in pulling Bella from the fence. Together they had lifted her down, Shariq averting his eyes and allowing Joe to lead him. Then Joe dug a grave in the back corner of the yard and placed Bella gently down. He found her favorite toy and placed it beside her before covering her with dirt. Marah had been unresponsive to any questions they asked. They proceeded without her. Bella tipped Marah's emotions over the edge, something she had been fighting since the night she found out about Raheem. But seeing her dog split open like that, understanding the hate that could cause someone to commit such a vile act, knowing that her own son had also acted out of hate, was more than she could bear.

Dara carried the tray to the kitchen and then joined Shariq and Joe in the living room. "When I arrived this evening, one of the guys out there told me they were all shaken by what happened to Bella. He thinks they will all be getting out of here sometime today. He gave me his card and told me that if Marah would like to make a statement, to call him. He seemed like a decent guy."

"Decent? Hanging out in front of the house? Keeping us prisoner? I don't call that decent," Shariq said.

"No, but I would recommend calling this one if the time comes. He was not aggressive and seemed very sorry Marah has had to go through this ordeal."

"He is part of the ordeal."

They sat silent for awhile until Shariq crossed the room and turned on the television. The constant coverage had dissipated somewhat, but Bella's murder had brought new activity and commentary was non-stop on social media. 'Marah deserved it for raising a monster;' 'Why does she have a dog? Muslim's can't have pets;' 'Her son was evil, she got what was coming;' but then there were those who were simply outraged at the murder of the dog, 'the only one to feel sorry for is the dog;' and the occasional sympathy for Marah, 'no one deserves to have their dog murdered.' The stream was endless.

When the reporters had looked over the fence the day of Bella's murder, they had seen Shariq and Dara. This brought a barrage of reports with their pictures and information about where they lived. Afterward, they had heard from the Imam at the mosque they attended telling them people were being very supportive. "They know you and your family, Shariq. I am reminding people here that Allah does not approve of this kind of Jihad. "

"Thank you. We hope to bring Marah home with us for a few weeks. As soon as the FBI releases her, we will come. Inshallah."

"Inshallah."


Dara stood in front of Shariq, Marah's food tray in hand. "Shariq, you must go to Marah and tell her to eat. She must get out of bed now. It has been five days since Bella. She must stop now."

"I will try."

"I tell you, she will listen to you. I have become a clanging gong to her and she doesn't hear a word I say." Dara held out the tray to Shariq.

"Okay. I will try."

He tapped on the door at the end of the hall, "Marah? May I come in." There was no answer. He tapped again a bit louder and longer. "Marah? Are you there? It's Pa. I'm coming in."

The curtains were drawn, leaving the room dark and dreary. He could make out her form on the bed. He went to the side of the bed and set down the tray, then reached over and tapped her on the shoulder. "Marah. Marah," he said gently.

"Wha...?" She sounded drugged as she struggled to say something to him. "I can't..."

"Daughter, you must get up today. You can not go on this way. You must accept Allah's will now." He sat down on the side of the bed and lifted her up. She slumped against his shoulder and began to cry. He patted her back as he had when she was a child. "There, there." He rocked her for a few minutes. "Marah, you must eat something. Then Mum is going to come help you shower and get dressed. Okay?"

"Okay."

"Yes? Good. Mum is very worried about you. We all are."

Marah shook her head in agreement. She knew she had to get out of this bed and she felt hungry. "I feel hungry today, Pa."

"That's good," he said.

"Would you have Mum come in?"

"Of course." He hugged her and kissed her forehead. "How about if I help you get your feet on the floor. No laying back down."

"I can do it." She slid to the edge of the bed, as he stood up, and she sat there with her feet on the floor. Her head felt dizzy and her body weak. "Thanks, Pa."

Marah stood naked in front of the bathroom mirror waiting for the water in the shower to heat. Her uncombed hair was matted and dirty. She looked thin and gaunt. But most striking was her face. She hardly recognized her gaunt pale face. She stood staring at herself, a woman who looked ten years older than a week ago, shattered like a glass. Turning away from her reflection she stepped into the shower and let the hot water flow through her hair, over her face and down her aching body. She recalled voices coming and going, rising and falling, over the last five days, yet could remember nothing said, just Mum stroking her head, whispering in her ear to wake up, to eat, to get out of bed, but Marah had been unable to respond, body frozen in a state of suspension, her mind shutting out Raheem and Bella, Zaqui and his evil. She wanted to scream and shout in pain, to beat the walls with her fists, to punch someone or something till her pain went away, but instead she leaned her head on the shower wall and closed her eyes.

"Marah, are you okay?" She heard her mother through the bathroom door.

"Yes, Mum. I'm washing my hair. I'll be out soon." Marah reached for the shampoo and soaped her hair then watched the soap suds wash over her body, wishing her life would wash away as well. She shook her head as the thought of death encompassed her. "No." The thought of Mum and Pa going through this shook her back into reality. 'They have lost a grandson, they can't lose me too.'

Mum was waiting for her when she came out of the bathroom. Marah's body and hair were both wrapped in towels. Mum motioned for her to sit on the edge of the bed and then she towel dried Marah's hair and combed it out, twisting it into a bun at the nape of her neck. Marah dressed and joined her parents in the living room. Pa came to her as she entered the room and hugged her to him. "Ah, Marah."

They filled her in on the happenings of the week. Joe had called the FBI to give the agent Marah's new phone number. The agent called this morning and said she was cleared and they would return her devices. The media had left her front yard. Now they needed to make plans for the three of them to travel to Philadelphia. "But I haven't talked to Colonel Rankin yet. I'm not sure I can leave," she said to that bit of info.

"Joe talked to him. The Colonel would like to meet with you as soon as you feel able. He said he would come here to see you. He doesn't want you to have to go there."

"He doesn't want me to, more likely."

"Well, either way, I told him you would contact him as soon as you could."

"Thank you. Pa, I think I will email him and I should check to see what has come in. May I use your computer? I don't want to wait until my computer comes back."

"Of course."

Marah sat at the kitchen table and signed into her email. She scrolled down the list, deleting the news and sales emails. The majority were the usual mail she got everyday, but there were a few from people she knew, including one from another Muslim woman she knew from the mosque. She was cordial with this woman, but not friends so she was surprised to see the email and wondered how she got her address. Marah clicked on it.

*Salaam!*

*Do not dwell on the death of your son, Marah. Put it behind you and praise Allah.*

*He is a martyr. He is united with Allah.*

She sucked in her breath and breathed out. She closed the computer and laid her hands on top. Frozen there, contemplating the message, fighting hard to not hate this woman, she pictured her and wondered how many others felt the same? If the FBI read that, did they question this woman? Would they follow up?

Marah didn't want to find herself curled up in a ball in her bed again, so she reopened the computer and deleted that email. She then composed a note to the Colonel, telling him she could meet with him at any time, or he could just email her and let her know her status. She then emailed Joe to let him know she was out of bed and on her feet again. That being done, signing out of her account and closing the computer, she had no idea what to do with herself. Time had come almost to a standstill, yet it seemed a month ago that her world had fallen apart, but in actuality, it was a little over a week.

Sunday evening Joe came to check in with them and make dinner. He brought more groceries and news from the base.

"Marah, I think the Colonel is going to put you on leave for a month, at least that's what I'm hearing. Friday, Lois told me when people call in for appointments, they request to not be placed with you." He watched her face and saw her eyes brimming with tears. "I'm sorry. I hate telling you this. I know it hurts you." She could only shake her head in agreement.

She wiped her eyes with the back of her hand. "What can I do to help you with dinner?"

"Marah, do you want to talk about it?" Joe asked.

"No. I do not."

"Ok. But when you do, I'm here."

"I know. I've spent a week in bed. I'm not going back there. I have to do something besides think about this. Ok?"

"Ok." He looked at her face. She was resolved for the moment. "Then find me some oregano, would you?" She half-way smiled at him and then began to search her spices.

# Chapter 6

The FBI cleared Marah, but the press chose not to pick up the story. "They destroy me and then refuse to clear me. I get it, Raheem is my son and so I am the reason he did this. Do you think people will eventually forget about me and let me live my life?" she asked her father.

"Marah, I do not have an answer. I wish I did." The three of them sat in the Lubbock airport, waiting for their flight to Dallas. They would arrive in Philadelphia that evening. Marah had on her sunglasses, hoping to avoid being recognized. It had been two and a half weeks, but she was nervous about being out in public. "The American public is fickle. They have already moved on to something else."

Their flights went smoothly, landing in Philadelphia on time. When Marah and her parents entered the baggage claim area, her sister was there waiting, a surprise for them all. Marah ran to her and they fell into each others arms, both crying, both exclaiming how wonderful it was to see each other. Marah's parents wrapped their arms around them both, laughing and crying with their girls. "Why didn't you tell us you were coming?" Marah asked.

"I wasn't sure till the last minute, so I wanted to surprise you. I had to make arrangements for the kids because Amal has no time right now for the day to day stuff, but he sent me with his blessings. I needed to see you."

"And I you. Thank you my sweet sister. I love you! Thank you for being here."

They held hands as they went to the baggage carousel. Mum and Pa trailed behind them. Marah leaned her head on Suraiya's shoulder while they waited for their bags. "I can't imagine what you have been through. I hated not being able to come to you right away and then not being able to contact you on the phone was excruciating. You poor darling."

"You sound so British!" Marah half-heartedly smiled at her sister.

"How are you holding up?"

"Better now. After…." she choked for a moment, "Bella, I collapsed. Mum probably told you."

"What? No, she didn't tell me anything. Not really. Just kept assuring me you all were fine and it would just take time."

"Oh. Well, now is not the time. Later. I can't talk about it now."

"Okay."

"Tell me about the kids. About Amal. Fill me in on London."

Marah and Suraiya slept in the same bed that night. When Mum poked her head in the door the next morning, they were curled up around each other, just as they had been when they were little girls, sound asleep. She sighed with a mixture of pleasure and sadness. How sweet to have them home together, but her heart was breaking for the pain they were all going through, but especially Marah.

Suraiya stayed two weeks. They played games, went for drives, shopped, but most of all talked.

"Marah, come stay in London for awhile. Play with the boys; they haven't seen their Auntie in a long time."

"I would love that, but I have to get back to my life. Or find out what my life will be now. I think I have to get out of Bellview though. I hope the Air Force will allow me a transfer, especially since no one wants to be my patient any longer."

"What?"

"Yeah, Joe tells me when people call for appointments they tell the secretary they don't want me."

"Oh no."

"I'm struggling with not being angry. Like really struggling. How could Raheem do this to me? To himself? I just want to scream at him. It's maddening to have loved this person that it turns out I didn't even know. How does this happen? How?"

Suraiya had no comfort for her. What was there to say?

"Think about coming to see us. Okay?"

"Okay, I will. Maybe in the fall. It might be nice to get lost in the streets of London. Yes?"

"Yes." They hugged and made plans to Skype when Suraiya arrived home. "There's my ride. I love you."

"I love you too! Mum! Pa! Her ride is here."

They appeared in the foyer and hugged Suraiya one last time. The three of them stood there together, waving as the car pulled away from the curb. The two weeks had flown by and now the house was quiet again. Mum, Pa and Marah all sought solace in their own ways. Marah walked quietly down the hall and shut herself in her old room, drew the curtains and went to bed, though only mid-afternoon. She was soon asleep, the only place where she could escape what had happened, at least when the nightmares didn't steal her peace.

The nightmares started soon after she spent the six days in bed. For those six days it had been as if she didn't exist. She would surface for awhile and then sink back into a black dreamless sleep. She felt cocooned in the darkness and wanted to just stay there, her mind a total blank. After she came out of that sleep, and back into the world, a week later the nightmares started. She would find herself standing in front of Zaqui and Raheem, their guns pointed at her and she would start to scream at them, but they would start shooting at her and she couldn't move as she stood there screaming, 'Stop! Stop! Why are you doing this?' but neither answered her. They just kept shooting and before she would hit the ground dead, she would wake herself screaming. The last two weeks had been such a nice reprieve. With Suraiya sleeping beside her, the nightmare didn't come, though she still started awake from dreams, at least she hadn't had THAT dream or awakened herself screaming.

Marah could feel someone watching her. She opened her eyes and saw Mum sitting beside the bed. "What are you doing, Mum?"

"It's 7:00 o'clock. I am worried about you."

"I was tired. I had to lay down. I didn't mean to sleep through dinner."

"Come eat something."

"Ok." She smoothed her hair and pulled her tunic down over her jeans as she stood up. "I'm as okay as I can be right now. Don't worry. I won't spend another week in bed. I promise." She helped her mother out of the chair and they went to the table together. Mum sat and watched her eat. Refilling her glass, asking if she wanted more of this or that. The television was blaring in the office where Pa sat watching one of the news stations. She knew another two weeks lay ahead of her here, a surety she could rely on, when the future seemed all but sure.

Almost four weeks with her parents had shored Marah up with their affection and love, something she had experienced so little of over the last decade or more of her life. Any time she visited them, she always went home energized and happy; however, she now simply felt calm, a calm she needed to face work and neighbors and people in this town. This was not going to be easy.

During the flight home, Joe left her a message to call him when she arrived home. They had spoken a few times in the month she had been away, but mostly relied on email. He was a good friend to her, but he was not Muslim and this presented a problem; she could feel his attraction to her growing every day. It would be so easy to love him. So easy, she thought, but she could not let her loss of Raheem, the loss of her life as she knew it, to throw her into the arms of a man who was not of her beliefs. Marah knew, she must somehow break away from him, and likewise this town. There was nothing for her here now. Joe was the only one who had believed in her and stayed by her side throughout this ordeal, but she worried he wanted more from her than she could give.

Marah pulled her car into the garage and waited for the automatic door to close before she got out. She grabbed her suitcase and backpack off the backseat and carried them into the house. The silence was enormous. She felt like Bella would come running around the corner to greet her at any moment, her head nuzzled up against Marah's leg until she scratched her ears and went to the door to be let out. But there was no Bella. And there would never be another. She struggled to not feel as if losing Bella was her punishment for having a pet in the first place, when they were considered unclean. Worse yet, she was a bad mother and losing her son meant she had to lose Bella too. "Don't go there, Marah." Her voice echoed in the kitchen. She shook the thoughts out of her head and went to her room, unpacked and fell onto the bed.

The phone rang and she dug in her purse to find it. Joe. She set the phone down and let it ring. Then she listened to his message. "I left some soup and salad in the fridge for you. I thought you might like to stay in and not have to go to the store. I'll call tomorrow. Maybe we can get together? See ya." Hurting him was something she wanted to avoid, but she felt breaking away from him was her only choice and she knew it was going to be painful for both of them.

When she checked her emails, there was one from Colonel Rankin asking her to not report to her office, but to come to see him at 0800 hours Monday morning. She hit reply and said she would be there. It was Friday evening which meant she had all weekend to think about her plans, plans she had been formulating in the back of her head for the last several days. Planning how to get out of Bellview might be just what she needed to keep moving forward.

Marah avoided Joe over the weekend. She went to the grocery store, her hair pulled up on top of her head and wearing the clear glasses she had bought in a small shop in Philly to give herself a different look whenever she left the house. So far, no one had recognized her, but here in Bellview, that might be different. When she backed out of her drive, her neighbor was in his front yard. She waved and he turned the other way, then walked into his house. She sighed and headed to the store.

No one recognized her. She let out a huge sigh of relief when she had returned to her car. She felt as if she had not been breathing the entire time she was in the store. The rest of the weekend she did chores that were long past overdue and prayed five times a day. 'If I can get in a ritual of prayer, maybe my thoughts can turn back to Allah.' She had felt so abandoned, so bereft of faith, since she'd lost Raheem. 'Why?' she asked herself over and over. But no answer came. She wanted desperately to feel Allah's presence, but it eluded her. 'Keep praying, Marah. Pray. You will see. Allah is with you,' Pa had told her many times over the last four weeks.

The weekend passed and her meeting with the Colonel arrived. She waited in his outer office, his secretary taking peeks at her from around his computer screen. He obviously knew who she was. Ten minutes later the Colonel appeared at his door and invited her in.

"Good morning, sir." Marah entered her mentor's office and waited for him to take a seat before she sat down.

"Marah, we both know why you are here. We have a situation we need to figure out. I am told your patients are refusing to see you. Of course one or two have requested you, but the majority have requested someone else. This obviously is clogging up the schedule with overbooked staff."

"Yes, sir."

"I am sorry about your loss. I know you have been completely cleared, but that doesn't seem to make a difference to those who need our services."

Marah fought back the tears. She had vowed she would not cry, but she could feel the tears tipping over the rims and running down her face. The colonel stood, came around his desk and handed her a box of tissues. He sat on the edge of his desk, his arms crossed, waiting for her to wipe her eyes.

"I'm sorry, sir."

"No need to be sorry. I cannot imagine what you are going through. However, I don't think it will get any easier for you if you stay here. Have you thought about this?"

"Yes, sir. I know I will have to leave. In July of next year I will be eligible for twenty year retirement. I've been considering...."

The colonel cut her off, "Yes, retirement is what I was thinking too. I might be able to find you a desk job."

"But... Sir, are you saying I won't be able to practice medicine my remaining time?"

"Marah, I'm recommending a permanent change of station and a new beginning, and I may be able to get you transferred to another base in the meantime, which might mean you could still practice medicine until retirement."

"Yes, sir." Marah fought back tears.

"I'll get the paperwork in motion then." He stood up and Marah did as well.

"Thank you, sir." She turned to leave.

"Marah."

She turned back to face him. "Go ahead and go home today. I'll start looking for someplace for you to work here until your retirement is settled."

The knot in her throat grew. She nodded her head, and choked out, "Yes, sir." He nodded at her as she turned and left his office. She didn't even see or hear the secretary as he stood and told her goodbye, she only wanted out of that office. Her feet carried her down the hall and out into the morning sunshine. Everything in her line of sight was a blur, but she made it to her car, slammed the door and the tears exploded. When she finally collected herself, the parking lot around her was full. She put her car in gear and headed home.

# PART THREE

*Grief is in two parts. The first is loss.*
*The second is the remaking of life.*
-Anne Roiphe

# *Chapter 1*

Marah found herself isolated in a cubicle at the back of the clinic where she had worked since she arrived at Bellview. She entered through a seldom used exit in the far recesses of the building and went out the same way, rarely seeing anyone. Assigned digital paper work, she sorted through the nurse's and doctor's notes looking for errors, worked on files the Colonel sent her, and surfed the net. The tedium made her want to scream. She missed her patients, the constant interaction with others, the satisfaction at the end of the day. She missed her life. "Raheem, how could you do this?" She rested her head in her hands and sighed.

Seven weeks had passed. Every day Marah struggled to get out of bed and report to her job. She had been avoided by colleagues, yet pursued by journalists and a few Muslims who told her Raheem was a hero. A martyr. She despised both with a passion. And she felt hatred for Zaqui.

Zaqui's wife had contacted her last week, sending an email with pictures of her three sons and herself. Her name was Bahja; she and Zaqui had been married nine years ago in Pakistan. 'I had no idea he had a wife in America until an American showed up at my door to tell me Zaqui and his son were dead. I thought they meant one of my sons. I kept asking them, what were they talking about, my sons were here, Zaqui in the US. Then they told me about you. I am still angry he did not tell me. I did not know, Marah. I did not know. I would not have married him. I found your email in a file hidden at the back of the desk. I also found a life insurance policy. You are named in it.' Bahja had attached a scanned picture of the policy. 'I and my sons have been living with Zaqui's family while he has been away. We only saw him twice a year, but he sent me money. His mother says we must leave. They believe Zaqui a martyr and I do not. I will return to my parents and find a job. I ask you, please to send me some money so I can return to my home. I will never ask anything of you again. I know this must seem terrible. I have no one to ask here.'

Marah had read the email and opened the document. She was stunned to find Zaqui had continued to pay this policy all these years. They had both taken out policies when they married, but she had long ago switched her beneficiary to Raheem. Marah had not answered Bahja. What could she say to this woman? Marah had heard from Zaqui's cousin, that Zaqui had married a woman in Pakistan, but

Marah had never contacted him, her fear of losing Raheem was too strong. She had not even asked him about her when he came back to the states for a job and requested to see Raheem. 'What if I hadn't let him see his father?' She had thought a million what-ifs since Raheem's death.

Four o'clock was quickly approaching. Marah gathered her things and started closing down her computer. She had spent most the day looking at websites about why people become terrorists, asking herself how she contributed to Raheem's decision to do this with Zaqui, but she could come to no conclusions. She knew she had often been absent from his life, letting him drift into constant video games, and had told him to get along with people when he faced discrimination or harassment at school. Trying to downplay his feelings and concerns had been her approach and she regretted this now. This seemed to be the most likely reason he latched onto his father. Marah shook her head to banish the downward spiral of thought and turned to the door, ready to leave. There was a soft knock, and she knew it was Joe checking up on her before she headed home.

"Hello there," he said as she opened the door.

"Hi Joe."

"How about we grab some dinner? My treat."

"Thanks, Joe, but not tonight. I've kind of had a rough day and I just want to go home."

He looked like a hurt puppy every time she told him no, but she was resolved to avoid a relationship with him.

"Ok. But soon. Alright?"

"Yeah, ok."

He gently squeezed her arm and headed back up the long dark hall, back to civilization, as she turned the other way and headed out of the building.

Marah could see the 'For Sale' sign in her front yard as she turned the corner for home. The sight always made her sad, but she could not stay in Bellview. There was a car parked in front of the neighbor's house. Though the media had eased off, she was still on guard against their intrusive manner, and was wary of any unknown vehicles or unusual activity near her house.

She pulled into her drive and opened the garage door, quickly pulling the car into the bay. Her hand reached up to the remote to close the door, and as she did, she saw the car that had been on the street slowly pull away, the driver looking Marah's way. She waited for the door to close then went inside.

# Chapter 2

Isobel pulled into the drive-thru of the Taco Spot in Llano and ordered a veggie burrito and a taco. As she sat at the window waiting, she thought of all the times their family had come here before or after whatever sporting event was on the agenda that weekend. They had some great times as a family. She could acknowledge that easily, but her relationship with Jacob had always been so hard, her stomach always in knots, due to his jealousy and his need to control her. His inability to take responsibility for his own actions had always left her feeling like a crazy person. When they finally divorced, he told her it was her fault he cheated on her. That really was the final straw. It had taken her a year or more to stop getting panicked about how long she stayed at the grocery store, or worrying if a man looked at her too closely, or any number of other things that would set Jacob off and end up with her head in a spin wondering what she had done. She knew she had contributed to their divorce in her own ways and had her own regrets, but she loved her independence and the ease of her life now. Life had been good. Until this.

"Ma'am, your food…"

Isobel had been staring at the last of the sunset, lost in thought, and had not heard the window open. Startled, she turned toward the teen thrusting the food bag at her. "Oh, sorry. Thanks." She took the bag and left, driving the two blocks to Alec's house. Pulling into the drive she noticed the glow of the back porch lights, lighting up the yard. She wasn't expecting Ian till the morning and she knew she had not left the lights on. Isobel grabbed her purse and her dinner and headed for the gate. She peered over and saw Jacob sitting on the couch, staring off into the yard. "Hey, you. What's up?"

Jacob looked at her and smiled. "Hi. I didn't realize you were here. I thought you were coming tomorrow."

"I came down this morning, but I've been out for awhile." She came through the gate and sat in one of the side chairs. "Want a taco?"

"No, but I'll take some Mexican Fries." He grinned at her.

"I didn't get any."

"What?"

"Those were yours and the boys favorite, but come on, tater tots called Mexican Fries? Not so much for me. I only ate them because you guys ordered them." She smiled at Jacob and took a bite of her burrito.

"Can I get you something to drink?" He shook his highball at her.

"Sure, just some water for now, though. I'll have some Scotch when I'm done here."

"I don't know what you and the boys see in the stuff. I hate that peaty taste." She nodded at him, her mouth full. Jacob left her to eat and went into the house. He came back with large ice waters for them both.

"What are you doing here, anyway?"

"Sometimes I just have to get out of the house. I walk over here and just sit and have a drink. Makes me feel close to him I guess." His voice cracked. "I was always so hard on him."

"Yes, you were."

Jacob looked at her and grimaced, "You'll never give me a break, will you?"

"Nope. Not anymore." She smiled at him.

"I loved him, though. You know that."

"Of course I do."

He bowed his head and began to cry. "I can't believe…, I can't believe he's gone. Our boy." He sat there for a moment, then looked up, staring out into the yard. The twinkle lights gave the dark back yard a warm glow. "He loved it back here. That's why I sit here when I come." Jacob turned to look at Isobel. He leaned over and took her hand and pressed it between both of his. "He was an amazing man. We did that."

"He was, wasn't he?" She could feel the tears welling just waiting to fall.

"You know I loved you, don't you?"

"Yes, but what…?"

"Losing Alec has made me realize…made me feel so bad, my relationship with him, with you, it's just all…I mean we never know what can happen."

"Yeah, I know what you mean." She leaned over and kissed him on the cheek, and pulled her hand slowly from his. "It's ok, Jacob. We all have to forgive ourselves and live the best we can right now. Right?"

He looked down at his empty hands and shook his head, as if to clear his thoughts. "Yes, yes, I guess." They sat silently now, both looking at a cat that had jumped into the yard and appeared to be stalking something in the grass. "How about that Scotch now?"

"That sounds good. Shall I?"

"No, I'll get it. Neat?"

"Yes, please."

Jacob went into the house, letting the screen door slam behind him. Isobel saw the bathroom light come on as she stood up to throw her cold food away and move back to the chair she had occupied. Jacob returned with their drinks, holding hers out to her, then clinking his against hers. "Cheers," and he returned to the couch.

"How's the real estate business?"

"Finally better. I really thought we might go under after 2008, but we pulled through. Looking good now. The base in Bellview adding personnel last year really helped."

"That's good."

"So where were you this afternoon? I didn't even realize you'd come to town."

"I went up to Bellview. I wanted to see where his mother lived. I sat in my car just looking at her house. I saw her pull into her drive. I don't know what I expected."

"That's kind of weird, Isobel."

"Yeah, I know." She could see that Jacob wanted to say something, but he refrained. They finished their drinks and Jacob headed home.

Isobel sat there for a long time. She went inside for a blanket, then turned off the lights and the porch light, before coming back outside. She curled up on the couch and stared into the dark, thinking about how strange the day had been. Thinking about seeing the mother of her son's murderer and then finding Jacob here when she returned. She sat there until she fell asleep. When the cat they had seen earlier jumped up beside her, its tail hitting her in the face, she woke with a start, not knowing where she was for a moment. Pushing the cat off the couch, Isobel gathered her blanket around her, picked up her glass and moved inside to pour herself another drink, hoping the Scotch would allow her to drift into sleep again.

"Mom," Isobel felt a hand on her arm and slowly opened her eyes, "Mom, what are you doing on the couch?"

"Hi, honey." Isobel sat up and pushed the hair out of her eyes. "I guess I fell asleep. Did you just get here?"

"Yeah. I knocked, but you didn't come to the door..." He leaned over and gave her a hug.

"Oh, sorry."

Ian picked up her highball glass and carried it to the kitchen sink. Isobel followed him, the blanket wrapped around her shoulders. "How about some coffee?" she asked.

"I'll make it."

"Thanks. It's in that jar in my grocery bag there. I'm going to go wash my face and change clothes."

"Yeah, ok." Ian busied himself with the coffee.

Isobel looked at herself in the bathroom mirror. Dark circles ringed her eyes. She sighed as she bent to splash her face with cool water. The soft grey hand towel still hung next to the sink where Alec had placed it. His shaving items sat on the shelf. Dirty clothes lay where they'd been thrown into the basket hamper. There were even a few stray hair stubbles from his last shave in the sink. His presence still so strong, yet he was gone. Isobel dried her face and went to change clothes.

A few minutes later, Isobel heard Ian yell to her in the bedroom, "Hey Mom! I'm taking our coffees outside." She shook her head, Ian's voice so much like Alec's, that for a moment she thought it was him calling her.

"Ok, be right there." She zipped her jeans and ran her hands through her hair, and started for the door, her eye glanced at her makeup bag on the dresser. She stopped and applied some lipstick. 'Maybe that will make me look alive,' she thought.

They sat on the couch together sipping their coffees. Ian had found a box of shortbread cookies in the cabinet and they each took one.

"So, when did you arrive yesterday?"

"I was here by noon. I hung around here for awhile, but then I drove up to Bellview. I went to the mom's house. I parked and waited for her to get home."

"Seriously, Mom? Why?"

"I don't really know, other than I wanted to see her and it turns out she looks just like the picture we saw on the news."

Ian looked at her and smiled. "What did you expect?"

"A Muslim woman in an abaya?" she said and shook her head. "I know, cliché, but damn those media images get in your head and I, I don't know, but she just looked ordinary and sad from what I could see through the window."

"It's hard to believe she knew nothing, but what do we know?"

"Yeah, what do we know?" Isobel said.

They sat for a moment in silence, then Isobel reached over and hugged him, tousling his hair like she did when he was little.

"Mom, don't mess with the hair," and they broke into laughter remembering Ian's middle school years when his hair was gelled so stiff if she even came near it he would shriek, 'Like a girl,' Alec always said.

"Ok, ok!" They finished their coffee, talking about his family, how he was managing and how hard he felt the loss every day.

"I think about him constantly. I feel so detached from my life, like I'm watching a movie and this can't possibly be real."

"Me too. And the anger...."

"Yeah. I have to remind myself the kids don't understand. I mean I started yelling the other day when Bree knocked over her glass at the table. The look on her face, Mom. I don't want them to have lasting scars from this because I turn into a crazy person."

"You're human, Ian. Apologize and she'll remember that, not that you yelled."

"Delia said the same thing."

"Is she doing ok?"

"She's my rock, Mom." He choked up, tears welled in his eyes as he looked at Isobel, "She's amazing. I couldn't get through this...."

"I know. I'm glad you've got each other."

They sat quietly, listening to the birds, Isobel with her arm on Ian's shoulders. He leaned his head onto hers. Then the cat from the night before showed up, meowing at their feet.

"This cat was here last night too. Is it Alec's?"

"He probably fed it Mom, even if it wasn't his. You know how he is...was."

"Ok, let's get going. Maybe we'll find some cat food lying around in there."

They gathered the boxes they had brought and began going through Alec's belongings. Jacob had already gone through his paperwork, so Isobel shuffled through the books on his shelves, taking those she had never read and boxing the others into the giveaway pile. Ian started in the living room, asking Isobel what she wanted from the bar and putting the rest in a pile to take home or to Jacob. They worked their way through the rooms, calling out to each other, "Come see this," or fighting back tears over something special they ran across.

When Isobel started clearing out Alec's closet, tucked on the shelf at the back, she found his 'blankie' that had never been toted around in his hand like other kids carried theirs, but always worn as a cape, no matter where they were going. He was Superman and even had refused on many occasion to remove his Superman pajamas that he wore nightly. A flood of memories brought her to her knees, the blanket clutched to her chest. She pictured his little cherubic face asking her questions, patting her cheek, studying a bug, running in circles around the yard, listening to his prayers, his laughter. She saw him running down the basketball court, the soccer field, his first date and his last prom night. Graduation from high school, college and his master's degree. Posing for a picture in front of this house, so proud. And his sorrow at losing the woman he thought he would marry to another guy. She pictured his face, heard his voice, felt his love, his pain and began to cry.

Ian found her on the floor, tears rolling down her cheeks. "I'm so sorry. I lost it when I found this." She held out the blanket, to show Ian, a pale green thermal, its satin borders worn to holes in many places. "His Superman cape."

"No need to be sorry. I've almost lost it a few times myself. I found a box of Star Wars men in the basement. We spent hours with them. I didn't even know he still had them."

They leaned against the closet door, talking about Alec.

"Hey, anyone here?" Jacob called out from the kitchen.

"We're back here, Dad."

Jacob popped his head around the corner of the doorway. "What are you two doing down there?"

"Just talking. We had one of those moments, you know I'm sure," Isobel explained.

"Well, come on. I came to take you two to lunch. Nora has made a feast." He walked over and put his hand out to Isobel. She took it, and he pulled her to her feet. Ian stood and hugged his dad.

"Sounds great, Dad."

"Yes, thanks."

Isobel, still clutching Alec's blanket, carried it to her box, folded it neatly, and laid it on top of the other items. She ran her fingers over the frayed edges for just a moment, and closed her eyes, seeing him as her little boy again. With a deep sigh, she picked up her purse, locked and closed the door, and followed Jacob and Ian to the car.

# Chapter 3

Marah woke sometime after midnight. Hunger pulled her to the kitchen. Rummaging around in her cabinets, she realized she hadn't been to the grocery store in a long time. She pulled out crackers and peanut butter, and stood over the sink eating. Nights were the hardest. Sleep often eluded her and she would wander the house or turn on the television. Having never been much for watching in the past, Marah now found it distracted her and gave her relief from the emptiness and loneliness that were her constant companions. She mindlessly brushed the crumbs from the crackers into the drain and put things back in the cabinet.

Curling up on the couch with a blanket, Marah thought about all those who'd loved the people who died and felt the stabbing pain of what Raheem and Zaqui had done. 'Two people had so profoundly changed the lives of how many?' she thought. Like a tidal wave generated from its epicenter, the damage they had caused was immeasurable. And she alone was left to deal with the aftermath of their evil. She struggled every day to keep despair from drowning her. Mum called her daily to be sure she had not taken to her bed again. Anytime she felt as though she couldn't get up, she thought of Mum and those calls. 'I have to get up. I have to keep getting up everyday.'

The light of day was beginning to show when she fell asleep on the couch. Her dreams were so vivid of Raheem as a baby, his sweet face, those eyes so dark, like pools of chocolate, looked into hers and she could see him change into a man before her, the image of him morphing into Zaqui and then Zaqui pulled a gun out from under his thawb, pointing it at her face, his mouth twisting into a hard grimace that began shouting at her the rules of Islam. She tried to run, but couldn't pull herself from his grip. His yelling turned to a prayer, his eyes drilled into hers.

Marah wrestled with the blanket she was wrapped in, she felt herself in that state between sleep and awake, where she desperately wanted to wake up, but her dream held her in a vise grip. She felt Zaqui's presence in the room with her and had to break free so she could run from him before he attacked her in her own house. The prayer was endless. His angry voice, droning on, and as he came to the end, she could see him pulling the trigger, his eyes still locked onto hers, locked in his grip, and as he yelled Allah Akbar, the gun exploded with her scream that finally pulled her from the dream. Her heart pounding, her breath a labored pant, she found herself sweating, tangled in the blanket on her couch. "Oh, Allah, Allah, Allah, please help me." She threw the blanket from her body and rose from the couch.

"I have to get out of here today," she said out loud. Marah decided she would pack a picnic and drive somewhere, anywhere, to get out of Bellview for the day. If she went to the grocery store at opening, she was unlikely to run into anyone she might know. She kept her incognito glasses by the door for the occasions when she had to go into public, always fearful someone would recognize her or she would run into someone she knew. She tried to blend in with those around her.

As Marah walked down the hall to her bedroom, she glanced into Raheem's room and saw the boxes of his belongings she had piled up on the bed. When the FBI had given her clearance to clean out his house, she had just thrown everything in haphazardly, trying to get out of there as quickly as possible. She left many things behind, taking only his most personal items. The landlord had harassed her for the last month's rent, money she really couldn't spend, but when Zaqui's 'wife' contacted her about the life insurance, she went ahead and paid so she could be left alone. The life insurance money would still be another month before coming, but they assured her she would get the settlement. She found it ironic, she would have received 10,000 had she and Zaqui ever divorced, but now she would receive $250,000. Blood money, but money she needed to put this behind her and start a new life when she could walk away from the Air Force. 'Just one more year,' she thought. She also had decided to send Zaqui's wife money, so she could start a new life too. Marah sighed and leaned her forehead against the door frame. She would tackle Raheem's room tomorrow.

Marah wandered through the harsh lit aisles of the grocery store, ticking off items on a vague list in her mind. A summer Saturday morning, people sleeping in, no one in a hurry to be doing chores, left her with empty aisles and no unwanted looks. She took a deep breath, realizing she had been holding it since she stepped out of her car in the parking lot. Marah picked the last of her items and headed to the front of the store, choosing the self-checkout line. She hurried through the process, but when it held her up on an item, an agitated clerk came her way. Marah ducked her head and avoided eye contact with the cashier and thankfully the distracted woman cleared Marah's screen and allowed her to finish. She finished bagging her items and headed to the car.

Safely inside, the car already warm with the promise of a hot summer day, she wondered if she would ever be able to look anyone in the eye again. Would she constantly have the fear of recognition, the fear someone would call her out for raising a son who so callously killed others, a husband who was a terrorist? She had always been friendly, open to others, smiling easily, but the ease in which she had negotiated her life was gone. There was nothing but fear and shame left in her now.

After packing a picnic lunch, Marah backed out of her drive and turned into the street. She didn't even bother waving at her neighbor, edging his lawn, his face turned towards her, quickly turned away. He had turned his back on her since 'that' day and she saw no reason to keep trying. The clock on the dashboard read 11:00 and the hot air had heated the car while she had made her lunch. She turned on the air conditioning, turned up the music and headed to the highway. She had no idea where she was going, she just wanted to get out of Bellview for awhile. At the crossroads that cut the town into quarters, she headed south towards Llano. She passed several dairies, the cheese plant in the distance, and soon she was on the outskirts of Llano. The sun created heat waves on the pavement in front of her, mesmerizing her, keeping her car headed in their direction, skirting the city, heading out of town towards Kate's. Though she hadn't intended to visit Raheem's grave, yet as if the car had a mind of its own, she found herself driving that direction.

She spotted Kate's road and pulled off the highway onto the dirt and gravel caliche that led past the house. There was no pickup in the drive, no sign of life, except for the black and white dog that came barreling after her car for a short run. She continued down the road till it turned into the narrow overgrown ruts they had traversed two months ago. She saw the gravesite in front of her and stopped the car. Her heart raced, a cold sweat breaking on her forehead. When she opened the door, the hot air hit her in the face. Swinging her feet out of the car, she sat there for a few moments, taking in the land around her. Tumbleweeds piled against the fence beyond Raheem's grave. The scruffy landscape spread out in all directions, a tree here or there stood strong against the harsh elements, a diminished sand hill covered in scrub, and in the distance, that old shack that seemed to lean into the wind.

Marah suddenly felt terribly weary, wondering what had made her drive here today. She took another survey of her surroundings and could see thunderclouds on the horizon. A late afternoon shower might be in store, but for now the heat hammered down on her head and she wished she had brought a hat. Searching the back of her car she found a towel and draped it over her head, covering her exposed neck from the sun. Marah stepped carefully through the clumps of prairie grass and made her way to Raheem's grave. The stone still stood, but the mound of dirt seemed to have sunk a little. She waited for the tears to come, but they did not. She stood dry eyed staring at the stone. She had learned at a young age she was not to cry and carry on at a grave. She was there to remember her dead son and to say a du'aa for him, a prayer of forgiveness, to think of him in this still place and hope that he would find paradise and not hell, but she found it impossible to not think of hell. She walked past the grave, removed the towel and placed it on the ground in front of her, then slipped out of her shoes to stand on the towel bare foot. She raised her hands:

*Peace and blessings be upon you Raheem. In sha Allah I will join you, I ask Allah to keep me and you safe and sound. Peace be upon you and the mercy of Allah. Amen.*

Marah slid her feet back into her shoes, picked up the towel and shook off the debris that clung to it. Returning to the car, she took her lunch from the cooler and placed the towel over her head again. She walked towards the shack, picking through the rough terrain, keeping an eye out for rattlesnakes. As she walked, the tears began to flow down her cheeks. The hot breeze drying her tears almost as quickly as they fell. She stopped and looked up at the sky, "Why?" she whispered. "Have mercy, insha Allah." She stood stock still, looking at the clouds, white puffs drifting across the plains. Clutching her bag to her chest, she started moving towards the shack again.

When Marah came close, she could see it had not been for storage, as she had assumed, but someone had possibly lived there, the small space just big enough for one. The dirt floor was hard and clear of debris. Entering through the narrow doorway she thought the shack had visitors frequently, why else would the floor be clean? She removed the towel from her head and spread it on the ground in front of her. Facing the large window missing its glass, she sat to eat her lunch. She pulled the hummus and vegetable sandwich from her bag, and stared off into the plains. They seemed endless before her. She longed to set off and see how far she could go before running into anyone or any town. She could lose herself here and no one would come looking for her. Kate might notice her car eventually, but it was far enough from the house and obviously on an unused section of her land, it might be weeks before it was noticed. Joe. Joe would be the one who noticed. He would go in search of her.

Marah finished her lunch and laid the bag aside. The towel stretched out behind her, she laid back and stared at the ceiling, or what was left of it. The roof was missing at least every other shingle, making a patchwork quilt of sunshine on the floor. She closed her eyes and moved her head where the sun shone directly on her face. Her mind emptied for a moment, just a moment, and she felt a peace come over her, relaxing her body, her eyes, her jaw, and she breathed in deeply, but Raheem's face drifted through her mind and she quickly opened her eyes, only to squeeze them shut again from the glare of the sun.

The chill in the air woke her, the sun no longer warm against her skin. She could see the sky above had turned dark and the clouds threatened to break open at any moment. Hail. She knew the change in temperature signaled the plains' worst enemy, and before she could gather her things, a bright flash of lightning lit up the sky around her and the clap of thunder seemed to have been right over her head. She ran for the car and could feel the large drops of rain and hail slapping against her bare arms. As she yanked open the car door the clouds broke apart and the hail beat the roof of her car. Then a torrent of rain came in a deluge around her. She had quickly jumped in and pulled the door shut just in time. Marah knew the road would become impassable if she didn't leave right away. Hard dirt roads turned quickly into rivers in the dry southwest.

Her eye caught the stone on Raheem's grave as she put the car in reverse and did a quick turn. How could he have done this? Would that thought ever leave her head?

The rain pounded the windshield and roof of the car, the vibration hard enough she could feel it shake her body. The road filled with water, gushing down the crevices dug deep into the hard dirt. She could see the highway in the distance and the lights of Kate's home and her truck in the drive now, as Marah's car bumped along through rocks and holes. When Marah reached the road she pulled the car onto the asphalt turnout and parked. The rain came in sheets now and she could barely see a few feet in front of her. Rain pounded the roof, and she had to cover her ears with her hands to stand the noise. There was no way she could drive in this. She would have to wait out the storm, knowing a storm like this quickly petered out and turned into a hard rain and then nothing but sunshine and maybe a rainbow.

# Chapter 4

Lunch with Nora and Jacob had turned into a yelling match, or at least Jacob was yelling. What he hadn't said the night before came spilling out. "You think she looked ordinary and sad?" he shouted at her. "She's Muslim, damn it. Don't you get it Isobel, they are all in this. All of them. They need to all go home."

"Jacob, this IS her home. The news said she was raised in Philadelphia for God's sake. She's in the Air Force. How much more American does she need to be?"

"I don't fucking care. She is as guilty as that son of hers and husband."

"Jacob, please, honey, stop yelling. Sit down." Nora tugged on Jacob's arm. He took a breath and looked down at her. "Please?"

Jacob sat down hard. He glared at Isobel as he ate the last of his brisket. Isobel quietly finished eating, then Ian leaned over to her, "Mom, you ready to go back?"

"Sure. I think I'll walk though. Is that alright?"

"Yeah, I'll meet you over there in awhile. I'm going to help dad with a few things first."

"Nora, Jacob, thanks so much for lunch. I know we don't see eye to eye on this Jacob, but I hope you can calm down enough to realize she is probably not our enemy. She must be hurting too."

"Our son is dead, Isobel. I will not forgive her or anyone of her like. Do you hear me?"

Isobel turned from the table, picked up her purse and went to the front door. Nora tagged along behind her, opening the door for her. "He'll calm down, Isobel."

"Maybe. Are you doing okay?"

"Yes. Being off for the summer has been a relief. It's been hard having to answer everyone's questions, especially since I rarely have an answer for them."

"I sometimes forget what it's like to live in a small town where everyone knows your business." Isobel leaned in and hugged Nora. "Keep in touch and thanks again," Isobel said as she opened the door and left.

Isobel noticed the blackening sky and picked up her pace. She hadn't realized how ominous it looked when she stepped out of the house. A flash of lightnings startled her and a clap of thunder made her jump. She started to jog, her purse slapping against her thigh as she ran. She didn't want to get caught out in a hail storm, and the sudden drop in temperature made her sure that's what was about to occur. No sooner had she turned onto Alec's street, when a few drops splashed her nose. She ran a little faster, but before she could reach Alec's house, the hail began and the rain poured. Isobel was soaked to the skin before she ran under the carport. She searched for her keys in her wet bag, digging them out from the bottom and finally opening the door. A hot bath was calling her name. And though it was only two in the afternoon, she stopped and opened a bottle of wine, poured herself a glass and went to seek solace in a hot soak.

"Mom? Where are you?" Isobel had drifted off in the tub, her head against the tile wall. She started awake when she heard Ian call out to her.

"I'm in the bath; I'll be out in a minute," she yelled out.

"No hurry, Mom. I'm going to the basement."

"Great." She stepped out of the tub and dried herself, noticing how thin she had become in the last two months. She found she often forgot to eat these days, and it was starting to show on her frame and in her face. Losing a child affected every single thing in life. Everything. "I can't think straight anymore," she muttered to herself.

Ian and Isobel continued packing up Alec's things, then boxing up the different piles for their final destinations. Next week, there would be an auction of his furniture and other items, then the new owners would take possession a few weeks later. They had a hard time coming to the decision to sell, but Jacob felt to leave the house empty would possibly make it vulnerable to vandals and none of them could stand the thought of renting it out since their obvious renter would be college students and might not keep Alec's home the pristine show place it had been.

Jacob listed the house and within a month, they had a buyer, a young couple expecting a baby. They all agreed this would be perfect, but as Isobel lay on the couch that evening, looking around the stark living room, now devoid of Alec, art taken from the walls, the bookshelves empty, glasses and bottles from the bar boxed and sent home with Ian and Jacob, she worried they had acted in haste. The last bit of Alec would be gone now. She sighed and pulled the blanket around her shoulders, took a sip of her whiskey and settled in to a book she had pulled out of the stacks.

Early the next morning, Isobel finished mopping the kitchen floor, rinsed the mop, dumped the bucket and in her bare feet traversed the house to be sure she had left nothing behind. She had loaded up her suitcase that morning into her car and then started cleaning, but there wasn't really much that had to be done. Alec kept things spotless. She just wanted the ritual of the moment. When she had walked back through, there was only the furniture, and the auctioneer, Delia's father, would be picking it up this week. After spending the week in Lubbock with Ian and Delia, she would come back Saturday morning to be at the auction barn, then drive back to Santa Fe.

She stood in the center of the kitchen. "This is so fucking unfair," she said outloud. Alec gone, just like that, in the blink of an eye. She twirled around and looked into the dining room, remembered their shared dinners, his friends, Ian and his family, Jacob and Nora, she had sat at the table with all of them at one time or another, all fed by Alec and all adored by him and they all adored him right back. How could one imagine a life without their child? How could this even happen? She pulled out a chair and sat down for a moment. The house so perfectly quiet, she felt his spirit here with her. She closed her eyes and wrapped her arms around herself, as if hugging Alec one last time. With a sigh, she opened her eyes, stood and pushed in the chair, took her bag from the counter and stepped out of the kitchen, into her shoes, pulling the locked door behind her.

"Ian, Delia, my little munchkins," Isobel exclaimed as she opened the car door and they came spilling out of the house, Bree and Brian running towards her and throwing themselves into her open arms. "I'm so happy to see you." Bree wrapped her arms around Isobel's neck and hung on as she tried to stand up and Brian wrapped his arms around her leg.

"Granny, Granny, Granny. Will you sleep in my bed tonight? Please?" Bree begged.

"Yes, yes, yes, my little warrior princess. I will sleep with you." She nuzzled her nose up to Bree's and then they kissed. Isobel knew they would start out the night together and then Bree would find her way into her parents room to snuggle up with them. Brian would stay the whole night with Granny though, cozied up next to her, his heavy breathing a comfort to Isobel. He really did remind her of Alec. She knew Ian felt the same.

"Hey, Mom. I'm glad you're here," he said as he hugged her, then reached for her bag.

"Hi Isobel," Delia said as she wrapped Isobel in a tight hug. "I'm so happy to see you. I was worried about you this weekend trying to get the house closed up, but Ian said everything went well?"

"It was hard, but I'm ok. We had some great times in Alec's house, but it's just a house. Our memories will have to hold us."

"Right."

"And we have to just keep making new memories together." They smiled at each other.

She and Delia walked into the house together, arms wrapped around each other's waist, Bree and Brian led the way, running and laughing, as Ian grabbed Isobel's suitcase from the car and followed them all in.

Isobel settled into the guest room. Bree and Brian sat on the bed watching her unpack. Bree, always full of questions, asked about her clothes, her shoes, her makeup, as she removed items from her suitcase. "Granny, when will Uncle Alec come back? Did you see him in Llano? Is he with Grandpa Jacob? Daddy says he can't come back."

"Bree, my sweetie," Isobel sat down beside her and pulled her close, "Your Daddy is right. Uncle Alec can't come back anymore, not as he was. His heart is with us though, in our hearts." Isobel patted her heart and then touched her hand to Bree's. "We get to remember all the fun times we had with him and that makes our heart feel happy."

"My heart feels sad though."

"Mine too right now, but we can still feel the happy when we think about his laugh, or when he twirled you around, or played Barbies with you, or held you until you fell asleep."

"I don't remember that, Granny."

"Well, he did. You were crying and crying and he picked you up and rocked you in his arms and kept rocking you until you fell asleep. Then he put you in your bed and covered up your head."

Bree burst out laughing. "I couldn't breathe if he covered my head, Granny."

"You're right." Isobel smiled at Bree. "Maybe he didn't cover your head, but I'm going to..." and she picked up Bree and ran with her to her bedroom, laid her on the bed and pulled the covers over her head. Bree was laughing hysterically and Brian followed them, "Me, Granny, me now." And she ran to pick up Brian and laid him on his bed and covered him up as well, until Bree sat up, her hair a mess, laughing in that high pitched sound that only little girls have. Brian did the same, then they threw themselves back down so she could cover them up again. They played this game and when they grew tired of that, Isobel found a stack of books and they curled up next to her as she read them story after story. When Brian had fallen asleep, Bree and Isobel tiptoed out of the room and quietly closed the door behind them. Isobel had not felt this relaxed and happy since Alec had died. She picked up Bree and hugged her close, knowing this would be a good week.

"What can I do to help?" Isobel said, as Ian poured her a glass of wine.

"We've got it, Mom. Just sit."

Isobel sipped her Saint-Veran and watched Delia and Ian make a salad for the evening meal. They each chopped different vegetables, throwing them in the large bowl as they finished. She envied them, just a little, their ease with each other, their shared passion for cooking, and their close friendship.

"Are you sure you want to go back for the auction next Saturday?" Ian asked.

"I think so. I know it will be hard, but I feel like..I feel it's the right thing. It's just his furniture, but he picked everything with such care. Do I sound crazy?"

"No, Isobel," Delia said. "Not at all. You have to do what feels right for you, like thinking about meeting that mother. I admire you for trying to find your own peace. Oh, and by the way, Dad said he would have the coffee waiting for you when you get to the auction barn Saturday. And knowing him, he'll have a few breakfast burritos for you too." Her father owned the auction barn outside of Llano, and had volunteered his services.

"Dinner is ready." Isobel started to stand up, "No, stay there. I'll get the kids." Ian wiped his hands on a towel and crossed the living room to find Bree and Brian. Delia picked up the salad bowl and brought it to the table. She had set the table with her Santa Fe pottery and woven place mats. Next, she pulled a loaf of bread from the oven and set it next to the salad.

"Beautiful, Delia, and the bread, oh it smells so good. Tell those kids to hurry up, I want to butter while it's hot."

Delia laughed as Bree and Brian ran in and climbed into their respective seats. "Hurry, Granny wants her bread."

"Me too," Brian said, and reached out for the hot loaf.

"Hold on there, Bucko, let me slice it up."

Ian sliced the bread and Delia served the salad. Isobel coveted the moment, promising herself to remember these moments always.

Delia, an elementary school teacher, was off for the summer, and she and Isobel spent the week by the pool, swimming and playing with the kids, reading, talking, laughing, crying, and making margaritas of all kinds. Ian joined them after work each evening, grilling up something for dinner each night, and after the kids were asleep, the three of them would find themselves sitting under the stars, reminiscing about Alec.

"Mom, remember the reading hour?" He turned to Delia, "In the summertime, after lunch, she would make us both pick a stack of books, then we would all three lay around on pillows and blankets we spread on the living room floor and we would read for an hour. When we were little, we would fall asleep, but as we got older, and protested the reading hour, inevitably we would both get caught up in our books and read for longer than an hour. I was never as good of a reader as Alec though. He really loved to read."

"He did," Isobel agreed.

"And then there was boot camp."

"Boot camp?" Delia asked.

"Yeah, the week before we had to go back to school in the fall, Mom would start making us get up at school time so we would be back in the swing of early hours on the first day. She would already be back at work, so she would call us several times and make sure we were up and moving. She ran a tight ship."

Delia giggled, then started laughing, and hiccuping till they all were laughing loud. Bree opened the back door and stuck her head out, "What's so funny, Mommy?" Then they all laughed even louder, as Bree walked over to Delia and climbed into her lap.

Then Isobel felt the tears in the corners of her eyes, happy and sad at the same time.

"You okay, Mom?"

"Yes. I'm good. This has been a great week. I think when the emotion starts coming out, I sometimes can't make it stop, but I'm good," she said as she wiped her tears with the back of her hand.

Ian stood up and came to hug her. "Time, Mom. I know this will never go away for us, but time will help."

She shook her head yes and hugged him to her. "Thanks. Thank you both. I will miss you."

"You can come back anytime. We loved having you here," Delia said.

"Yay, Granny. Stay. Stay. Stay," Bree chanted over and over, raising her fist in the air with each 'stay.'

"I'll come back soon, sweetie. I've got some things I need to take care of at home."

"Promise?"

"I promise!"

"Okay then," and as she slid off of Delia's lap, she came over and took Isobel's hand and led her to the door. "It's time for bed, Granny. Let's go." And off they went, Bree pulling Isobel along behind her.

# Chapter 5

Isobel pulled into her drive that evening, glad to be home, but dreading the quiet that would greet her behind her front door. Delia's father had been more than kind to her this morning, offering her coffee, and the burrito Delia had predicted. He had sat up a cozy chair for her where she could see the proceedings, but not have to be in the crowd. She felt relieved all had gone as planned, the money ready to be deposited into an account for Bree and Brian's college, as Alec had requested in the will Jacob hadn't thought existed. She pulled her suitcase and backpack from the car, but left her items from Alec's house for tomorrow.

The refrigerator was empty, the cabinets bereft of food, but she found a frozen veggie pizza in the freezer. She stood there holding it in her hand, then put it back in the freezer. El Sitio. 'A drink, rellenos, that will help me sleep.' She went upstairs, reapplied makeup, changed into a summer dress and boots. Grabbing her bag by the front door, she did one last check in the mirror and headed for the bar, a mile walk from her house.

Santa Fe was known for the intense light and had attracted artists for decades. She had been attracted even as a child to the beauty here, the blue skies, the mountains, and the eclectic buildings. The little sleepy town she remembered as a child, had grown into a busy city, or at least when the tourists were in town, which seemed to be longer and longer every year. 'Couldn't they buy their hat and boots and get out of town?' Isobel laughed out-loud at the thought she and her friends often said when they had to fight the traffic, or got stopped behind a gawking tourist when all they wanted to do was get home. Just as the thought passed, a car ambling up her narrow road, nearly hit her, as the driver was busy looking around instead of paying attention. She smacked the hood of his car and startled him. "Sorry," he yelled as he went past her.

Isobel said hello to the hostess, the ever changing pretty young girl at any restaurant, and headed for the sunken bar. Cindy waved at her as she sat down, then came down to talk to her and take her order.

"How ya doing, Isobel?" Cindy leaned across the bar and took Isobel's hand in hers. "I'm so, so sorry about your loss. I have been thinking about you and hoping I'd see you now that summer is here."

"Thanks, Cindy. I'm doing ok," she swallowed hard, willing the knot in her throat to go away.

"Thanks. I just got back from...from a trip, and I needed to get out of the house."

"Well, good for you. What can I get you? Margarita? Wine? First drink is on me, my dear," she said.

"Instead, how about one of your famous Bloody Mary's?"

"You got it." Cindy winked at her, squeezed her hand again, and turned to take more orders and make drinks. The bar was starting to get busy and Isobel felt relieved. She didn't really want to chat, even though she appreciated Cindy's concern. Isobel had met Cindy the first night she moved into her house up the hill. She had wandered down to have a drink and find some food after a day of unpacking. They had hit it off right away. Cindy was down to earth and loved people. The bar had been fairly empty that night and they had chatted easily. Cindy was a mainstay at El Sitio, a rarity in a city that was a revolving door of restaurant people.

"Here you go. Do you want food?"

"Sure, a relleno plate, but don't put in the order just yet, please."

"Gotcha." And Cindy left her to her drink.

Isobel surveyed the bar, she had an eye for tourists, and saw that most were the summer tourist crowd, here for some weekend fiesta or to enjoy the cooler air. Carefree and relaxed, she remembered what that felt like and hoped she would some day feel that way again.

The Bloody Mary went down easy and Cindy brought her a glass of her favorite white. She read the news on her phone app, anything to keep her mind occupied.

"What's going on in the world?" The man sitting next to her had turned to her, his question startling her out of her reverie. "Sorry, I couldn't help noticing you were looking at the news."

"Oh," she said, and quickly tapped the screen off. "Nothing really. Politics as usual." She turned back to her drink and her phone, hoping he would leave her alone.

"No police shootings? Terrorist attacks today?" He smiled at her, waiting for a response.

Stunned, she turned her face towards him, "What? Why would you ask that?"

"Just trying to make conversation."

"Well, don't."

"Sorry. No reason to be a bitch about it."

Isobel took a deep breath. She could feel the tears, feel the anger, and didn't want to make a scene. She took a drink of her wine and motioned to Cindy, "I'm moving…" she mouthed and pointed her finger to the end of the bar, picked up her glass and started to stand up.

The man grabbed her elbow, "Let me buy you a drink and make it up to you."

"No, thanks."

"What a bitch."

"Look, asshole. I came here to have a drink and eat dinner. I came by myself to be by myself, not to be picked up by some guy in a bar. I don't want to talk to you, especially about terrorists. My son was killed by a terrorist two months ago. I don't want you to buy me a drink, because I don't know you. I just want to be left alone. Got it?" Her voice had raised at least an octave. Everyone was staring at her. "Now if you don't mind…" She stood up and moved to the end of the bar, as a table of women in the corner of the room, clapped for her and raised their glasses to her in cheers.

"I'm sorry, I mean, I…" He looked around the room and realized all eyes were on him, snatching his wallet from his pocket, he threw a twenty on the bar and left.

"You okay?" Cindy brought Isobel her food and offered another glass of wine, but Isobel shook her head no.

"Yeah, I'm sorry about that. I didn't mean to get so loud."

"Hey, he was a jerk. Got what he deserved."

"Would you put this in a box for me? I think I'm going to head home."

"Sure thing. Be right back."

Cindy boxed her food and brought her the tab. Isobel paid, and then walked home in the golden light of approaching sunset.

Isobel put her dinner in the refrigerator, then took her whiskey bottle, a glass, and a light blanket up to the deck. A deep orange layer of light lay across the Jemez and faded into pink, then purple, and the dark blue of approaching night. She poured herself a drink, watching the light fade from the sky. Once the sun set she wrapped the blanket around her shoulders and settled in to watch the stars appear. Slowly at first, but as the night sky darkened, it came alive with the starlight. She looked for the big dipper, then poured herself another drink. She imagined Alec amongst the stars and picked out a star for him.

Isobel's glass hitting the deck startled her awake. She felt chilled and realized she had drifted off. Picking up her glass and bottle, wrapping her blanket tight around her, she went back into the house and saw it was after midnight. 'I can't believe I was out there so long.' She felt hungry and headed to the kitchen where she slid her meal from El Sitio onto a plate and put it in the oven to heat up. While she waited for her food, she wandered from room to room, checking that doors were locked and windows closed, then settled at the dining room table and scanned the mail that had stacked up over the last week. On top was a note from Diane, 'Give me a call when you get home. Let's go to dinner.' Isobel set it aside intending to call her tomorrow.

The smell of green chile brought her back to the moment. She pulled the plate from the oven and took it back to the dining room to eat. This was her favorite comfort food, green chile stuffed with cheese and green chile sauce on top with a side of beans. In her mind, there was no better dish. She ate a few bites, but a feeling of despair washed over her. She tried to eat a bit more, but the food stuck in the back of her throat. Picking up the plate, she carried it to the kitchen and went to bed.

"What the fuck is that pounding?" Isobel glanced at the clock. 9:00 a.m. Diane. Isobel crawled out of bed and headed for the door. As she entered the living room the door opened and Diane stepped in. "Hey you! Sorry to barge in but when you didn't come to the door I was worried. You okay?"

"Yeah, I was up late last night…"

"Did I wake you?"

"That's okay. I needed to get up anyway."

"I'm sorry."

"No, really, it's ok."

Diane came across the room and hugged Isobel to her. "Let's go get coffee before I open the shop. Yes?"

"Sure. Let me wash my face and change clothes. I'll be right back."

Isobel shuffled back to her room and pulled up the bed clothes. She stripped to her bra and panties and found her yoga pants and a tunic to slip into. She combed her hair and put on lipstick. When she walked back to the front of the house, Diane had dumped the rest of her dinner from the night before into the sink and placed the dishes in the dishwasher.

"Hey, thanks. I tried to eat…."

"El Sitio? Why didn't you call me?"

"I didn't see your note till I sat down to eat last night."

"Oh. I thought you would call when you got back to town." Diane looked hurt, but Isobel ignored her. She really didn't care.

"Well, let's go so you're not late."

The Coffee House was close to El Sitio, allowing them to leave Diane's car and walk. The cool morning air was refreshing and helped Isobel shake off the hangover. They found a table in the back corner of the outdoor seating, and sat down.

"I ordered all the fall sweaters yesterday. I have one in mind for you when they arrive. It's soft blue and will look great with your hair and eyes. All organic cotton."

Isobel just nodded her head and distractedly looked around the courtyard.

"I talked to the guys and they want to get together this Sunday. Are you up for it?"

"Sure."

The server took their order and Diane went on. "I thought we could all do summer salads and white wines. Does that sound good?"

"Yeah, that will be fine."

They grew silent. Diane shifted in her chair, looking uneasy. She stared at Isobel, then looked away. "Are you still intending on meeting that woman?"

"You mean his mother? Yes. I think so."

"I still can't believe you want to? I mean…."

Isobel took a deep breath and looked at her friend. "I need answers." She sighed, "And I get it, there are no answers, but I still need them, and I think talking to her would help. I shouldn't have to explain myself to you of all people."

"She raised him. She should accept some blame for what happened to Alec."

Isobel shook her head. "I want to meet her because I have felt hatred for her and her son and I don't hate people. I think meeting her will help me find some peace."

"Whatever."

"I don't want to talk about this right now. Ok?"

"Ok, but…"

"You don't have to understand, Diane. Just let it be."

They finished their coffee with small talk, then walked back to Isobel's house. Diane gave her a quick hug. "I'll let you know where and what time." She turned to get in the car, "See you Sunday."

"Yeah, see you then." Isobel managed a smile, then waved as Diane backed out of the drive. Why was she the one having to step around people's feelings? Resentment lingered in her as she went into the house and crawled back into bed.

# Chapter 6

Isobel knocked on Sam's door, her famous Mango Tango salad in hand, as she walked in. "Hey, everyone!"

Sam's head appeared around the corner of the kitchen as she walked across the room, shouting back, "Hey, you," and his head disappeared. She came around the corner in time to see him pop the cork on a bottle of Prosecco. He leaned over and kissed her cheek as she set her salad on the counter. Once he set the bottle down he opened his arms and squeezed Isobel in a bear hug. She hugged him back and they separated laughing.

"I haven't seen you since…"

"Dinner at my house?"

"Yes. Way too long."

Isobel smiled. "Yes, too long. Maybe we can get back to a regular schedule now."

"I hope so."

"Where is everyone?"

"Running late I guess. You're the first here."

"Really? I thought I was late."

"Nope." He picked up a champagne flute and poured her a Prosecco. "Just what the doctor ordered," as he held out the glass to her.

"Ha! You love saying that."

"Well, I am a 'doctor' you know."

"Yeah of Social Sciences."

"That's why I ordered up Prosecco, darling. It's the perfect social drink."

Isobel started laughing, and then they heard the front door open and Diane, Richard and Doug all came in together talking.

"We're here!"

"It's about time," Sam called out as he walked into the living room to give each one a hug. Isobel watched, her back leaned up against the wide adobe doorway, smiling at her friends as they each came towards her, salad in hand.

"What's this, already drinking without us?" Doug said as he air kissed Isobel on his way into the kitchen.

"That's right my friend, you're late to the party."

Doug sat down his salad and poured the three remaining glasses, handing them out as they each came into the kitchen, their voices all talking over each other, till Sam held his glass in the air for a toast, "To the best group of friends, and to our darling Isobel, I am so happy we are all together again. Salut!" They all held up their glasses, clinking with each, "Salut!"

"Thanks, Sam. I'm really glad to see you guys!"

"Well come on. Let's go sit out back and enjoy the first round."

Sam had set a beautiful table with his French dishes and Provencal table cloth; candles stood at the ready as soon as the sun set and he had lightweight blankets on the back of each chair, much like a proper café would have in France. French music played on the outside speakers, setting the mood. "This is lovely, Sam," Isobel exclaimed. "I love a French café!"

"Just for you, my friend." He pointed them to seats around the fire pit. Each place had a four-piece escargot plate on a stand, set over a small candle to keep them warm. The butter still sizzled as they sat. He also had his signature 'faux gras,' a mushroom mixture so delicious a person would swear it was the real thing. Each person had a small crock accompanied with tiny toasts. "Sit, sit," he motioned them, as he pulled a chilled white wine from the bucket by his chair. He circled them, filling the wine glass at each place. "I loved Diane's idea for a summer salad night, but I thought we should start off with something, well, more substantial."

"Show-off," Diane shot at him.

"Yup. That I am."

Isobel looked at her friends and felt such relief that for a moment, she thought her life was back to normal. Those little moments, like waking in the morning and thinking for just a second all is well with the world, gave her momentary joy, and though reality always intervened, for now, this was enough, to sit amongst friends and be transported out of her grief. She would take that.

Doug leaned over to Isobel as the others chatted, "Truly great to see you my friend."

"Thanks. I'm glad to be here. You guys are the best reprieve in the world."

"Is it the charming repartee or my good looks?"

"Both," Isobel laughed.

"Eat, people. The escargot cannot go to waste."

"These are incredible, Sam," Richard said as he popped one in his mouth and then picked up a piece of bread and sopped up the butter left in the cup. "Superb!"

"As always," Diane agreed.

The idle chatter continued as they ate their appetizers, and Sam did not let a glass go dry. As the sun started setting, Sam lit the candles and brought out all the salads. They joined him at the table. The salads passed, plates filled, Richard turned to Isobel, "Ok, tell us about seeing the mother. Is it okay for me to ask?"

Isobel had just filled her mouth. She held up her hand, and nodded yes. Washing down the bite with wine, she began, "Yes, it's fine. I couldn't go in."

"I think you were pretty damn brave to give it a go, personally," Sam said.

"Thanks, Sam, but I don't think I'm brave." She swallowed hard, focusing on the candlelight for a moment, "I'm sorry I keep saying this, but I want to know why. And the damn thing is, there is no why."

"I can't believe you would ever want to meet her," Diane said.

Isobel's face froze as she turned to look at her. "You have got to quit judging me, Diane. You have no idea what it is to lose a child and what it takes to get through this." Isobel's voice grew louder. "You have none. And your fucking dog doesn't count." She threw down her napkin and left the table. Diane's mouth stood open as she watched Isobel's disappearing back.

An uncomfortable silence ensued for a moment, "Why is she so mad at me? I don't get it."

"Diane," Doug reached over and patted her shoulder, "she has to figure this out for herself. None of us can understand what she is going through."

"I get that, but she just snaps at me...."

Richard left the table and went in search of Isobel. "Hey, sorry I started that." He came up behind her standing in the dark living room looking out at the lights of the city.

Isobel started when she heard his voice, then she turned, "It's ok, Richard. Diane wants me to be the same ole Isobel and I never will be again."

Richard hugged her. "Yeah, I get that. I can't imagine losing one of my kids. I guess no one can."

"Until you do."

He took her hand and led her back to the table. "Sorry, everyone, Diane," Isobel said, returning to her seat.

"Sorry, Isobel," Diane mumbled and took up her fork.

"Ok, ok, eat, drink." Sam made the rounds with the wine bottle. "How about them...."

"Isotopes," they all yelled together. They continued to eat, everyone in their own thoughts for a moment.

"Iso, what are you going to do this summer?" Sam asked.

"Yikes, I'm afraid to tell you after my little outburst."

The others all looked around at each other, waiting. "I started reading the Qur'an."

"Wow, now that should be interesting," Richard commented.

"Obama keeps saying how it's a book of peace, but I'm finding it not very peaceful in places."

"I've never read it," Richard said and the others said likewise.

"Mohammad tells the people to cut off the hands of thieves. Brutal."

"Is that metaphorical?" Diane asks.

"No. This is a very literal read."

"Well, the Bible is so metaphorical, I thought maybe..." Diane continued, but Isobel cut her off.

"I'm sorry, but the Bible is not metaphorical if you're a fundamentalist; it's as literal as the interpreter decides. I grew up in a pretty fundamentalist religion. I know how literal people can take religious instruction. I think Mohammad just wanted to get people in line and do what he said and if you believe you are a prophet of God, then hey, you can say whatever the hell you want. Right? At least the Bible is a bunch of different writers. The Qur'an is just one man's attempt to control the world around him. Not unlike the formation of the Catholic church."

"So, some light summer reading," Doug said.

"Yeah, something like that," Isobel smiled, glancing at Diane, "I just want to know why some people say Islam is a religion of peace, when all we see in the world is violence. I have no peace now," she could feel the raw emotion just below the surface. "Maybe I never will again, but understanding might help."

"Let us know what you find out," Sam said and winked at her.

"Of course. Obviously, you can't shut me up when I get on a roll."

Richard reached over and squeezed her hand, but Diane said nothing. She sat silent, staring off across the yard.

"Dessert," Sam said, and jumped up to stop the awkward silence that had ensued. "Give me those plates..." and he stacked them up and went off to the kitchen.

The evening ended with a Herisson, a small individual tart Sam had modeled after a tart he once ate in Lyon, France. They all exclaimed as their "hedgehog" was placed in front of them a shortbread crust, filled with almond paste, covered in a meringue and then topped with ganache pulled up into spikes to resemble its namesake. He served the espressos next and they finished up the evening with a tawny Port. The conversation remained light for the rest of the night. Deciding on their next meeting, they said their goodbyes and Diane, Doug and Richard headed home in the taxi Sam had called for them. Isobel had a short walk back up the hill to her place.

"Thanks, Sam. And thanks for just being here for me. That's really all I need right now."

"I know, sweetheart. I'm here. Come down anytime."

She leaned in and kissed him on the cheek as she stepped out into the cool summer evening. This was what she loved about New Mexico in the mountains. The days could be hot, but the nights always cooled

off. She pulled her wrap around her shoulders. The moon was so bright, it lit her path back up Canyon road. She turned down the alleyway that led to her house, a long rambling little drive lined by other casitas. Hers was the last at the end of the alleyway. Sitting on a bit of a hill, hers was isolated from the others, giving her total privacy except on the front porch. She often sat there in the early evenings, later moving up to her bedroom deck once the glaring sun had sunk low enough. She found the key and let herself in. The quiet felt oppressive after an evening of talking with her friends. She had always loved the quiet, but now, all she felt was suffocated. She grabbed a glass and Alec's bottle of Scotch, then headed for the deck. Once again, she fell asleep in her chair, and only woke when her glass rolled out of her hand, thumping on the wooden deck when it landed. She gathered up her blanket, curled up on the bed, and drifted back to sleep.

Two hours later, Isobel was wide awake. She wandered down to the living room and stood at the front window looking out over the city. The lights twinkled, a soft orange glow hung above the downtown area. Isobel pulled on the sweater she left draped on the back of the couch and sat down on the window seat. She pulled her knees up under her chin and wrapped her arms around her legs, emitting a long sigh. 'When will I ever sleep all night again?' Her thoughts wandered to Raheem's mother. 'Is she sleeping? Is this the plight of mothers losing children?' And she knew the answer was yes. The nights were the worst. Interminable. Thoughts running rampant. Out of control. She hated being out of control.

Isobel switched on a light and went to the kitchen to make a cup of tea. The bird clock chirped 3:00 am at her as she flipped the switch on the kettle. She pulled out her proper British tea pot, the one she had bought at a charity shop when she and Alec took their trip to Scotland. It brought to mind his smiling face, his insistence she could find the very same pot in the states, chiding her for buying something she would have to lug around with them. She didn't mind though. She placed it, wrapped in bubble wrap the shop keeper scrounged up for her, in the middle of her pack, and hoped she could keep from breaking her prize. When they ran across a tea shop, she popped in for a good strong loose leaf tea and made Alec carry all two ounces in his pack. She had laughed when he fell to his knees after she slipped the package under the top flap. Putting out her hand, she yanked him to his feet again. She pictured the scene as if it was yesterday, standing with sweater pulled tight around herself, a faint smile on her lips, looking off into space, until the sound of boiling water brought her back. She poured water over her tea bag, placed the pot and her cup on a tray, and headed to her office.

Isobel turned on the lights and set her tray on the footstool by her sofa. She picked up the pictures she had left in a pile there and started flipping through them. Then the thought occurred to her that if her house caught fire, she would lose the pictures she had found of Alec. She would lose all her pictures. A desperate feeling set her in frenzied motion, dragging a box from the closet that contained all the pictures she had of her family from over the years. She had sorted them into envelopes after her divorce eleven years ago, but had never bothered to put them in albums. Now she yanked pictures from their envelopes and started scanning them. One after the other. The boys when they were young, family pictures, camping, hiking, road trips, school pictures, she thumbed through each stack as she placed picture after picture into the scanner. Her tea grew cold, forgotten, as she stood next to her computer and the printer, scanning pictures.

Hours later, Isobel realized the sun had come up. She glanced at her tea pot and cup. What time was it? "Shit. Almost nine." Diane would be here any minute, but too late, she heard Diane knocking on the door. She went to let her in, still in her clothes from the night before.

"Hey! Long time.... Didn't you sleep?"

"What? Oh," Isobel looked down at her clothes. "I slept for a few hours."

"In your clothes?"

"Well, I fell asleep on the deck and then crawled into bed late."

"Oh."

"Anyway, I can't go this morning. I should have called you."

"Come on, just change, let's go."

"No. I'm not finished yet. I'm...working on something.... I have to stay here and finish."

"What is it? Can I help?"

"I've got to finish scanning all the pictures. Then I'm putting them all on a flash drive so I can carry one in my purse and have one at home."

"Isobel, you don't have to finish right now. When did you start?"

"It must have been around 3:00 or 3:30. I had a panic attack when I stepped in my office. What if I lose the pictures? They are all I have left of Alec.... and, and what if something happened to Ian? I have to get these done. I have to."

"I'm worried about you."

"I don't need you to worry about me," Isobel snapped at her. "Just let me be. Please."

"Yeah. Ok." Diane turned around and put her hand on the door, then turned back to Isobel. "Scanning pictures won't bring him back, Iso."

"For God's sake, Diane, just fucking leave me alone if you can't support me. I don't need this from you." Isobel turned and went back to her office, leaving Diane to let herself out.

Isobel picked up another packet of pictures and started scanning again.

Sam knocked on the door mid-afternoon. Diane had called him that morning to let him know about Isobel. "I don't think she's sleeping at all. Can you stop in and check on her? I'm tired of her snapping at me."

"Sure, no problem."

Isobel came to the door after he knocked a second time. She still wore her clothes from last night.

"Hi Sam. Diane sent you, didn't she?" Isobel opened the door wide and motioned Sam in. He gave her quick hug and stepped into the living room.

"Yeah. She's worried about you. What's up?"

"She got mad because I was scanning pictures and wouldn't go to coffee with her this morning. Want something to drink? I was about to make tea."

"Sure. Why don't you let me, though. Sit down. You look really tired, my friend."

"I am."

"Okay, I'm making the tea. Why don't you go out front and I'll be there shortly."

"Yeah, I'll do that." She was definitely not herself, Sam could see this. She seemed distracted and he could smell whiskey on her breath when they hugged. He put fresh water in the kettle and found all the accoutrements for tea. Ten minutes later he carried the tray to the front porch, but found Isobel asleep on the lounge chair, her head leaned over on her shoulder, one arm had dropped off the side of the chair. Though a warm day, he found a lightweight throw in the living room and draped it over her to keep her from waking up chilled. He poured himself a tea and sat back in his chair, watching a neighbor's dog pacing back and forth in its yard. The mail truck came down the alley, stopping at each mailbox. When he finished his tea, he went inside and put things away. He then cleaned her kitchen and did the dishes. She had obviously been stacking things since she returned from Llano last week.

Sam walked down the hall and glanced in her office. He literally gasped at the mess that greeted him. Pictures were scattered everywhere. He was afraid to pick them up, even though there seemed to be no rhyme or reason to how they were laid out. He thought the scene looked as if she had just thrown them over her shoulder after she scanned each one. There were still piles on her desk. He knew the long tedious process of scanning on a home computer. "Geesh." He picked up all the pictures on the floor and tried to organize them by son. There were some great shots of Alec and Ian when they were little. Sam had gotten to know the boys over the years, seeing them when they came to visit Isobel. He enjoyed them greatly. He thought of Isobel's kids as his surrogates, since his own had been turned against him by his ex-wife. Isobel and Jacob had done a great job raising their boys. After picking up pictures from the floor, he went back to the front porch to check on Isobel. A little drool sliding down the side of her jaw, made him smile. That would be one to give her a hard time about next time they were all together.

Not wanting to leave her out on the porch by herself, he went inside to look for a book or magazine to occupy him while she slept. The Qur'an she had ordered, lay open on the dining room table. He read the opening page, but couldn't make himself keep reading. He found *Blood and Thunder,* a book about Kit Carson and the southwest, on the bottom shelf of the bookcase. Isobel's eclectic taste in books always allowed him to find something to read on her shelves. This looked interesting.

Sam had been reading for an hour when Isobel finally woke up. She sat up groggy and confused. Then she saw Sam and smiled, remembering that Sam went to make them tea. "Hey, where's my tea?" She looked around the porch, but saw no cups or pot.

"Well, sleeping beauty, you've been asleep for an hour and a half. I have had tea, cleaned the kitchen, picked up a few pictures, and now..."

"Picked up pictures? Shit!" Isobel jumped up and ran inside. Sam followed.

She walked into her office and breathed a sigh of relief. Sam only picked up the pictures she had dropped on the floor. "Is everything all right?" he asked looking over her shoulder.

"Yeah. Sorry. I've been working on this since three this morning."

"Three? Really? Isobel, you've got to get some sleep."

"I just did." She smiled at him.

"You know what I mean."

"Yes. I do need to sleep. Thanks for letting me get a nap. I feel better."

Sam put his arms around her and drew her to him. She laid her head on his shoulder. Without warning, she began to cry. He held her till she finished. "I just want to preserve what I have," she choked out. "These pictures are all that's left of him. I can't let something happen to them. Do you understand, Sam?" She pulled away and looked at his face.

"Yes. Of course I do. My kids are frozen in time for me and pictures are all I have, so I do understand. I do."

Isobel found a tissue and blew her nose. "Thank you, Sam."

"Why don't we find a scanning service? I'll help you, if you'd like."

"I don't want to send them away though."

"Ok. Well, how about instead of going crazy scanning in the middle of the night," he paused and smiled at her, "Why don't we set up a table in here and sort through them and then you scan a few piles everyday until you finish?"

"I got in a panic last night. What if there was a fire. That's what kept going through my head. I couldn't stop thinking about something happening. I know I was in crazy mode. That seems to be happening to me a lot."

"Time, Isobel. Time will pass and though the pain will never go away, the pain will soften and the panic will go away."

"Yeah, I guess."

They stood there a minute looking at the mess. Sam glanced at his watch, "It's almost six. Go shower and for God's sake, change your clothes. I'm taking you to dinner."

"Oh, no. I can't."

"Yes. I won't take no for an answer. Then I'm bringing you back and staying with you until you fall asleep. No bottle is putting you to sleep tonight. Got that?"

"What?"

"It doesn't take a genius to figure out you're drinking yourself to sleep every night. I've been there. Done that. Now get going. You know how I am when I get hangry!"

They laughed and she hugged him as they parted in the hall. She went upstairs to clean up, and he went back to the porch to read while he waited for her.

# Chapter 7

Two weeks passed, and Marah had continued every
night to walk down the hall, pause at Raheem's
door, and look at the boxes piled on his bed. Each
time she kept going, afraid of what she might find.
Tonight, however, she stepped in and opened the box
where she had placed the plastic bag with the items
returned to her from the FBI. She sat it aside and
started removing the other items. Piling his clothes
up in neat folded stacks, she picked up a sweater and
buried her face in it, catching a whiff of his cologne.
Tears formed in her eyes as she refolded the sweater
and placed it on top of the pile. She broke down the
box and laid it by the door.

The next box was full of his books. She sat down
on the edge of the bed and picked up the stack.
History, English, Math, Communications and a
religious studies textbook were all massive books she

had found in the pile. Then she saw, *Our Master Muhammad,* at the bottom of the box. There were two volumes. As she thumbed through the pages she noted Raheem had written notes throughout in the margins, underlining passages and putting stars beside others. She had thrown them into the cartons when she'd gone to pick up his belongings, but now she wondered how the FBI had missed them. Wouldn't they have taken these too? She remembered finding his books in a pile on the floor, as if they'd been picked up and thrown there or rifled through. With all the notes, she puzzled over why they had not taken these. They had also left his Qu'ran behind. However, she noted at the time, it had been picked up and examined, then thrown in the pile, on top of the other books. She placed the books on his desk, broke down the box and placed it with the other.

Marah picked up the plastic bag and dumped it on the bed. Raheem's laptop slid out with a thump, then a pile of papers, a journal and another book, one she had never seen before, a commentary on Tawhid. She thumbed through the pages and saw Raheem had notes in the margins and on the numerous blank pages throughout. She took the stack to her bedroom and laid them on the nightstand. While she readied herself for bed, she went over when she started seeing changes in Raheem. After visiting his father for the first time he had become more serious about Islam, praying five times a day and going to mosque regularly. He shortened his pants and donned a tunic, but this was not unusual for a man who has become devout. His senior year in high school he had withdrawn from his few friends and taken up with another Muslim boy, the only other Muslim student at Bellview High School. The two had been inseparable, playing video games together and going to mosque, though he had stopped after he left for university. But then, after the mid-year break, when he had returned from his father, he had started being harsh with her. That's when he started complaining that she didn't cover her hair, except during prayer, that she had a dog, and that she occasionally drank a glass of wine. "Ma, you are not a true Muslim. I don't want you to go to hell." She could still hear his voice in her head.

Marah sat on the edge of her bed and looked at the pile. She pushed the covers back, propped up her pillows, and pulled the stack onto her lap. The papers were random notes about the Qur'an and about his studies at the mosque. They looked much like what she had written when she was in high school attending classes at the mosque after public school each day. Then she opened the commentary. Tawhid meant the indivisible oneness of God, the concept of monotheism, but she had never seen this book. Each chapter dealt with different verses of the Qur'an, then the corresponding hadiths, which were explained by the author. She thumbed through the first chapter and read Raheem's comments to the side, his thoughts on the importance of monotheism. However, as she looked further, there was another handwriting at what appeared to be key points in each chapter; Zaqui's. He must have given Raheem the book.

Marah closed her eyes and vividly remembered Zaqui's hand slapping her face in the first year of their marriage. She disagreed with him about money he spent on a computer, money they didn't have, and he slapped her. Astonished, more than hurt, random slaps came more and more often, and punches any time she disagreed with him. His literalist beliefs were kept hidden until after they married. She had not been raised in that way. Though her parents were from Eastern Pakistan, they had quickly adopted an American way of life and brought their children up in such a way as to understand Islam as more egalitarian. The women in her family knew their place, but Pa had never hit her or her sister, and he never hit Mum.

She turned her attention back to the commentary and continued reading the notes. When she landed on a chapter about judgement, Raheem wrote in the margin, "Jews are all liars, including Professor Goldberg" and he had underlined "hypocrites are worse than the Jews; accepting bribes is prohibited and that is one of the bad manners of the Jew" in the text. Her eye then fell on several passages heavily underlined, "Applying any law other than that divinely revealed to the Messenger is an act entailing apostasy; killing is the penalty of apostasy; referring matters of dispute to any law other than that of Allah entails violating one's belief in Allah and in his book," and next to these underlined passages Zaqui had written, "Understand, Raheem, this is why only Allah's judgment matters. Do not trust the infidels of this country. Their laws cannot be applied. Only Allah's. Only Sharia. This is why it is our duty to kill infidels. Reformers of sharia are polytheists and apostates, my son, they too must die."

Marah, her eyes filling with tears, laid her hand on her chest and closed her eyes. 'How could Raheem be pulled into this? How? How?' She turned back to the text and saw, "Good intention does not justify acting in violation of the Sharia." Boldly underlined, Raheem had written, "We will not stop fighting till this country accepts Sharia and all infidels are dead." Tears rolled down her face, her eyes blurred till she had to lay the stack down and find a tissue. She wiped her eyes and continued looking for Raheem's notes. In the last chapter she found another underlined passage, "Muslims are obliged to fulfill their pledges and oaths. Muslims are prohibited from breaking their oaths and pledges. The verse attests to Allah's Omniscience and to the verity that nothing is hidden from Him, Exalted be He. There is a threat to whoever breaks his pledges or covenants." Then Raheem had recopied the verse from the Qur'an, "And fulfill the covenant of Allah when you have taken it, [O believers], and do not break oaths after their confirmation while you have made Allah, over you, a security. Indeed, Allah knows what you do." (Qur'an: An-Nahl: 91) Under this he had written the date, April 15. Marah gasped. "My God!" She threw the book across the room; it slammed into the bedroom door jamb, before falling on the floor. She closed her eyes and wept.

Marah called Agent Waters the next day hoping for some answers. 'Why?' She thought, 'Why did they do it?' Did the FBI know more than what had been reported in the news? Waters did not answer. That evening, she called her father to talk to him about this commentary.

"Pa, I need to talk to you about this book the FBI found in Raheem's belongings."

"What is it, Marah?"

"It's a commentary on Tawhid, and Raheem and Zaqui have written notes in the margins. He underlined parts on Jewish people and listed a professor's name. I have tried to talk to Agent Waters, but he has not returned my call yet. And the thing is, that professor is Jewish. But Pa, the worst is in the last chapter, the commentary talks about taking an oath, how we do not go back on our oaths, and then gives the Qur'anic verses. Then Raheem wrote at the bottom of the page the date of the murders." By now Marah was crying. Her words caught in her throat and she could barely say anything.

"Marah?" He could hear her crying, "Marah, are you listening?"

"Yes, Pa."

"Zaqui was an angry man. Yes?"

"Yes."

"He was a Salafist and unfortunately, many believe in violence against anyone who believes differently. We both know he dealt in violence with you."

"Yes, but his own son?"

"Marah, yes. Yes, his own son. He believed he was taking his son to paradise. He distorted and misquoted verses and texts and took them out of context to further his own extremist ideas. Pakistan, unfortunately is rampant with extremist ideology."

She sucked in her breath and stifled a scream, feeling as if her head would explode.

"Marmar," he used her childhood nickname, "I know it's hard to understand. We have to trust in Allah."

"Do you think Allah approves of this? Do you?" She sensed a hesitation in his answer, a hesitation she did not want to acknowledge.

"Allah has decreed everything that will happen, Marah. 'Ask not questions about things which if made plain to you, may cause you trouble.' You remember this passage in Surah 5? This is what you have to remember now."

"I'm not sure...."

"Mum wants to talk to you, I'm giving her the phone."

"Hello, Marah?"

"Hi Mum, I'm here. Are you well?"

"Oh yes, of course. When will you come again? Soon?"

"I will try, Mum. I don't even know if I have any time-off left. The Colonel is looking for a transfer spot for me. He said he would check the bases close to you, but it's not looking good. I may end up in Albuquerque, at Kirtland."

"I will hope you come near us then, inshallah."

"I love you, Mum." Marah could feel tears welling up and wanted to get off the phone, as to not upset her mother.

"Peace to you, daughter."

Marah heard the phone click and Mum was gone.

She hoped Agent Waters would call her back Monday. If not, she would call him. Until then she had another lonely weekend to fill. Her gaze wandered to Raheem's journal on the bedside table. She ran her hand across the cover, a simple notebook she had bought him at the beginning of the school year. Fear of what she might read made her heart race, her throat constrict. Marah picked up the journal, but couldn't open the cover. Her eyes blurred with tears, as she threw the journal on top of the bed and left the room.

Mid-morning, Monday, sitting in her closet of an office, her cell phone rang. She snatched it up and answered without looking to see the caller i.d. on the screen.

"Hello."

"Waters here."

"Agent Waters. Thank you for returning my call."

"What can I do for you?"

"I looked through Raheem's items you returned last week. One was a book I'd never seen before, a commentary on Tawhid. Do you know which one I'm talking about?"

"Yes."

"I just wondered...I mean...is there a reason not mentioned on television about why Zaqui and Raheem, why they killed...murdered those people?" Marah could feel emotion building in her voice. She stared at a vase on her desk and repeated over and over in her head, 'blue vase, blue vase' a technique someone had taught her years ago to keep from crying, and waited for his answer.

"You will have to be more specific."

"I saw Raheem had listed a Professor Goldberg in the notes he took in the margin, on the passage about Jews. Did he target this man?"

240

"Yes. I believe he did, but Raheem didn't realize there was a school-wide faculty meeting, and Professor Goldberg had left the station to attend the event."

"Why didn't the media carry the story?"

"We didn't release that information. We felt someone else might target the professor."

"Who is he? I mean why him?"

"Ms. Dalal, I think you know."

"Because he was Jewish?"

"Well?"

"Agent Waters, I didn't bring up my son to hate Jews. They are the people of the book, and, and…"

"His father did though. And Professor Goldberg was Raheem's communications professor. Have you read Raheem's journal?"

"No. I haven't been able to make myself yet."

"I think you will find answers there."

"Oh." Marah didn't know what else to say. "Ok."

"If you need to call again, that will be fine, but keep in mind, we have kept Professor Goldberg's name out of the media for a reason."

"Yes, of course."

"Ok, then?"

"Yes. Thank you. Goodbye." She hung up her phone and sat staring at the bookshelf in front of her. Folding her arms in front of her on the desk, she laid her head down. She knew she had to read his journal.

# Chapter 8

Home from work at 4:30, Marah changed into her running clothes. She glanced at Raheem's journal, still lying on her bedside table. 'Later,' she thought. In the kitchen, she decided on a vegetable curry, a comfort food from her childhood, but she made a quick, modern version, much less intensive than Mum's. She heated up leftover rice and smothered it with her curry. Life had become one chore after another with no joy. She took her food to the table and opened the book she'd left there, reading mindlessly while she ate. When she found herself just staring at a page, she closed the book and carried her half eaten meal to the sink, dumping it down the disposal. Marah then took her time wiping down the cabinets, loading the dishwasher, and throwing out the trash.

Marah spent the early evening watching television, and avoiding her bedroom. As soon as the sun set, she put on her running shoes, pulled her cap down low and headed out for a run. She thought about her faith as she made the first turn on her route, wondering how God could let this happen? 'This was predetermined? How could this be Raheem's destiny?' Then her mind wandered to her failings, having a dog, drinking wine, having Joe for a friend, and worst of all, questioning God. Any of these, or all might take her to hell.

She thought about Raheem, his messy hair, his wonderful smile and his hugs. She reached up and touched the heart around her neck, the present he had given her last time he saw her. She knew now, he meant this as his goodbye to her. The note he enclosed said, *You are always at the center of my heart, Ma. I love you. Raheem.* She kept the note in the drawer by her bed, looking at his words each night before she turned off the light.

When Marah made the last turn towards home, she ran as fast as she could, wanting to wear herself out. When she reached her drive and pressed the code to open the garage door, her heart was pounding so hard, she could feel her head throbbing with each beat. She slipped into the garage and hit the close switch, waiting for the door to come fully to the ground. Fear a journalist would jump out of the bushes and run in, or worse, someone set on hurting or killing her, kept her standing there until the door completely closed, always aware of her vulnerability.

Stopping in the kitchen to fill up her water bottle, she noticed the motion light in the back yard was on. She went to the window and looked out, but saw nothing. Then she realized the back gate was open. Marah pulled her phone from her pocket and dialed.

"Joe?"

"Hi Marah."

"I went for a run and when I got back the motion light in the backyard was on and the gate is open. I hate to ask you, but…"

He interrupted her, "I'm on my way."

"Ok. Thanks."

"Stay on the phone with me. Are you in the house?"

"Yeah, the kitchen." She could hear the engine of his car start.

"Do you hear anything in the house?"

She paused, listening to the tomb like silence that surrounded her. "No."

"Good, but stay right by the door to the garage. Did you see anyone when you were out?"

"No. I waited for dark so no one would notice me, and I didn't see anyone."

"That's good."

"This is weird. I've got to get out of Bellview, and soon."

"I'm glad you're still here."

Marah sighed with the hopelessness of their situation. He kept her on the line, telling her each turn he made, the cross streets, the landmarks he passed. Then, she heard a car in the drive.

"Is that you in the drive?" she said before he could tell her he had turned in.

"Yes. Just pulled in."

She opened the door to the garage and hit the switch. Joe bent down and came under the garage door and Marah immediately reversed the door down.

"Thanks for coming!"

"No problem. Stay here. I'm going to walk through the house first." He pulled his handgun out of a shoulder holster and started through the house, flipping on the lights as he went, opening closets and looking behind the shower curtains. "Marah," he called her name, and she followed the sound of his voice to her bedroom. "Did you leave this window open?" He pointed to the window beside her bed, open an inch or two.

"No. I don't think so. But…"

"The screen is missing."

"I sometimes open the window a crack at night to make the air circulate back here, and might have last night, but I know a screen was on the window." She began to shake and had to sit on the edge of the bed. Joe came and sat down beside her, putting his arm around her shoulders.

"You okay?"

Marah shook her head yes, trying to keep the fear from overwhelming her.

"I'm going to go look out back."

"Yeah, ok." He left her there and headed for the sliding door in the kitchen. She saw the lights come on and flood the backyard. She went to the window and saw Joe walking the perimeter of the fence, his phone flashlight on, lighting every corner. No one was there. He stepped through the gate and looked both ways in the alley, but saw no one. He then came to the bedroom window.

"I didn't see anything in the alley." She nodded her head as he worked the screen back into place. "Okay, shut the window and bolt it. I'm coming around." She did as he instructed, then he was there beside her, checking the other window, making sure the bolt was in place. They walked through the house, checking each window. Joe checked the front yard and made sure that all the screens were in place and hadn't been touched. When he finished, he joined her in the living room.

Tears pooled in her eyes. Now even her own home wasn't safe. Joe sat in the chair beside her and waited for her to regain her composure. She wiped her eyes with the back of her hand and took the running cap off her head.

"I can't thank you enough," she said.

"Marah, it's ok. You don't have to keep thanking me."

"It's just I haven't been very nice to you lately, and then I called you, but I knew," she took a deep breath, "I knew if I called the police I might get one of those guys who came here the night…you know, and they were hateful. I didn't know who else to call. Actually, I have no one else to call."

"Anytime. You know that."

"Thank you."

"Ok then, go pack a bag. You can't stay here tonight. You're coming to my place."

"Joe, really, I can't."

"Yes you can. No one would want you to stay here. I will lock my bedroom door so I'm safe from you and…"

She looked up and saw the laughter in his eyes and she smiled.

"Marah, I don't want to make light of your beliefs. I get it. You are a single woman. You are not supposed to be alone with a man, especially one who is not a family member. Is that haram or halal? But you cannot stay here tonight. I'm not sure you can stay here any more at all."

"Haram. It's haram. Forbidden."

"Ok. So go pack and let's go. I'll follow you. You can park in the garage so no one sees your car. Does that help?"

"Yes. But please do not tell anyone."

"Of course."

Marah went down the hall to her bedroom, packed a few days worth of clothes, and before she zipped the bag shut, she laid Raheem's journal on top of her clothes.

"Okay. I'm ready."

"Let's go."

They walked to the garage, Joe loaded her bag in the backseat of her car and then waited for her to open the garage door. He climbed into his pickup and backed out of the drive, waiting for her to do the same and the door to close. He followed her to his house and as she pulled into his drive, the garage door opened in front of her. She drove into the bay, turned off the car, and waited for the door to close behind her. She laid her head on the steering wheel and sighed. She jumped when her door opened. She slid out of the car, and Joe grabbed her bag and they went into his house.

# Chapter 9

J oe settled Marah in the guest room. He laid towels
out in the bathroom for her, brought her a bottle
of water, and said goodnight. She watched him walk
to his room, a few feet away, and he turned back to
her, "I'm locking myself in now. No sneaking in,
little lady." He winked at her and closed the door
behind him.

As she unpacked, she heard Joe's television,
muffled through the wall. She felt safe for the first
time in a long time, and realized how stressful every
night had been for her since Raheem. She gathered
her nightclothes and crossed the hall to the bathroom.
After a quick shower and brushing her teeth, she came
back to her room, to Raheem's journal she had laid
on the bed.

Marah opened the cover and thumbed through
the pages, Raheem's small neat print covered most

the pages. He never learned cursive well and always defaulted to printing. She paused on a page or two that had passages written in, Urdu? Panjabi? Arabic? She was unsure, but since Zaqui had known all three languages, any of them could be possible. Returning to the first page she began to read:

*Sept. 1*
*Praise be to Allah. I am happy to be away from home. I love Ma, but she's not a good Muslim. I beg her, I tell her she is bad, but she doesn't listen. 'The righteous are not in any way held accountable for the wrongdoers; their only duty is to remind them so that they may be mindful of God.' (Surah 6:69) I'm really glad Papas was able to swing a place for me. I can study without all the noise, like at Jeff's place. And I can make plans. No sharing rooms with an infidel. That would be the worst. Inshallah.*

*September 7*
*Praise be to Allah. Summer with Papas was good. He's teaching me to be a good Muslim. He gets it... what I am facing here. He gave me a book to help me understand Tawhid. Allah is one. These other religions think their Jesus is God too, but he's not. 'how could He have children when he has no spouse, when He created all things, and has full knowledge of all things.' (Surah 6:101) The people of the book, they are stupid. they will live in painful torment in hell. There is only one God. Allah. The most gracious. The most merciful. Muhammad, peace of*

*Allah be upon him, brought us the message. I am
understanding so much more. Inshallah.*

Marah read many entries where he repeated these
same ideas over and over. He also quoted passages
from the Qur'an and from the commentary, but his
Qur'an verses were often out of context. His writings
were tinged with his building fundamentalism. She felt
distanced from him reading his growing distaste and his
continuous judgements for those around him. This was
not the son she knew, nor raised. When she reached the
second half of his journal, dated soon after his return
from D.C. to see Zaqui over the Christmas break, his
words stabbed her like a knife through her heart.

*January 23*
*Praise be to Allah. I have communications with
Goldberg. I can't believe I have to sit and listen to
this jew. He is already talking about Israel and the
semester just started. Fuck this. What a hypocrite.
They kill our brothers. They steal our land. I am
disgusted by this man. He is an ape. He is cursed.*

*January 25*
*Figures Goldberg works at the television station.
jews run the media. they control the infidels. Papas
and I have taken an oath. We will be blessed. I
will some day see paradise. Inshallah*

*February 26*
*I hate Goldberg. And all he stands for. This class
sucks.*

*March 15*
*Classes are useless now. I have to keep going though.*
*Papas says no matter what, go to class. Whatever.*
*I got a new game this week. The guys came over*
*and we played all night.*
*Really cool.*

*March 30*
*Praise be to Allah. Paradise is promised. Cowards*
*will have to face the wrath of Allah, praise to him.*
*God needs soldiers who will take out the infidels*
*wherever they are. I will be the example. I'm not*
*afraid. I will have peace and tranquility from*
*Allah. This liberal decadence must end. People will*
*know me. They will speak of me. And my brothers*
*will praise me. Inshallah*

*April 1*
*Praise be to Allah. The day will come when Sharia*
*is the law of the land. It is God's law. The only law.*
*All law comes from God. Inshallah*

*April 5*
*Praise be to Allah. I am a soldier. 'God is your*
*protector--an excellent protecter and an excellent*
*helper.' (Sura 22:78) Inshallah*

*April 15*
*Praise be to Allah. I am a witness to the truth!*
*Paradise will be mine. Inshallah*

Marah lay the journal down on her bed, rolled over and buried her face in the pillow, allowing herself to cry. When she could control the tears, she turned over and stared at the ceiling, the tears rolling into her ears, soaking the pillow. She reached over and turned off the light. Eventually she drifted into sleep.

The next morning, she ate the oatmeal Joe made for them both, and drank down the green smoothie he insisted would pump her up for the day. She gathered her things and then Joe handed her the garage door opener. "You'll need this." She took it from him and headed for her car. "I'll see you later," Joe said as she went through the garage door, pulling it closed behind her. She slipped behind the wheel of her car and headed to work.

Marah did not go to her little closet at the clinic. Instead she drove to Colonel Rankin's office several streets over and took a chance she might be able to speak to him. "Is the Colonel in this morning?"

His secretary hesitated for a moment, not sure he should bother the colonel for her. "Well, I need to check his calendar. Give me a minute." Then he took his notebook and went into the Colonel's office, quickly closing the door behind him.

Marah looked around the office. She fussed with her uniform, glancing down to be sure everything was in place.

He reappeared and without looking at her said, "You can go in."

"Thanks." She entered the Colonel's office and found him standing behind his desk. "Good morning,

Sir. I'm sorry to come without an appointment, but...," she trailed off and he motioned her to sit.

"Marah, how can I help you this morning?"

"Sir, I have to get out of here. Have you found a place for me yet?"

"Looks like Albuquerque is our best bet. They have a nurse practitioner retiring at the end of the month and the base commander has agreed to take you. He is keeping your circumstances hush, hush. We want you to finish out your duty without being harassed or otherwise encumbered. I'm sorry I couldn't find a position closer to your family."

"Thank you, Sir. I will manage. I just need to leave Bellview. I had an attempted break-in at my house last night. People here know who I am and won't leave me alone."

"I understand, Marah. I sincerely do. Give me a couple more days and I think I'll have your transfer completed."

"Thank you."

"Sure. I will send notice when I get the paperwork."

"Ok."

"How's your office working out over there?"

"Well, since no one ever sees me, it works just fine. I come and go through the back door."

"I know you must be ready to get back to what you do best."

"Yes, sir."

"Alright, I'll let you know."

She knew this was her dismissal; she picked up her hat and left. Back in the outer office, the Colonel's assistant ignored her, his eyes directed at the computer on his desk. She stopped and stared at him for a moment, but he would not acknowledge her. He should have, by all rights, stood as she passed by his desk, but she didn't care. She just hoped she could keep her connection to Raheem a secret when she got to Albuquerque.

Friday her transfer came. She sent Joe a quick email to let him know his guest room would be free soon. Ten minutes later there was a knock on her office door.

"Come in, Joe," Marah called out, knowing he would be coming to talk about her news.

"How'd you know it was me?"

"Umm, because I just emailed you I'm leaving... and no one else ever comes to my door. Take your pick."

"Well, I'm happy for you. I know it's what you wanted. Let's celebrate tonight. I'll make you something special."

"You don't have to, Joe, but..." she hesitated, "I'm really, really glad you will do that for me."

"That's what friends do, Marah."

"Yeah, well you're my only one left, so thanks."

"Okay then, a night of steak, salad, and my dark chocolate, cherry crisp."

"You had me at chocolate."

"What? Not steak?"

"Hardly."

"Ok, ok, ok. I'm going back to work for a few then headed to the grocery. Anything else we need?"

"No. Thanks, though. I'll see you in a bit then."

# Chapter 10

J oe had the grill heated, the salad made and the crisp
ready for the oven when she walked in. She had
stopped at her house for a few more things, pulling the
suitcase she had filled behind her. When he saw the
bag, he frowned, "Why didn't you let me go with you?"

"You have done too much as it is Joe. I was fine.
All is good there. No signs of any more breaking in.
Maybe it had nothing to do with me."

"Maybe..., but please let me go with you if you
need anything else."

"Ok." She saluted him and headed to her room.

"You better salute me," he called after her.

When they finished their meal, Marah and Joe
settled into chairs on the deck outside. She drank
another small glass of the Brut Joe bought for her
celebration and he poured himself a beer. Tall trees,
a tinkling fountain, trumpet vines, and a garden of

vegetables and flowers made Joe's backyard a sanctuary. She felt relaxed and peaceful, wondering if this might be what it feels like to be a long married couple, at ease with each other, enjoying the end of another day. She closed her eyes and breathed in the subtle scents of the evening air.

"Marah," Joe spoke her name softly, "are you alright?"

She opened her eyes and looked at him, "Yes, I'm the alrightest I've been in a longtime. Thank you for letting me, I mean, making me stay."

"Still uncomfortable about staying?"

"Yeah. I am. But staying at the Sands Motel seemed worse." They both laughed.

"Any bites on your house?"

"No. Who wants to live in the home of a terrorist? I'm hoping I can rent it though. I don't care as long as I can get out of here."

They were quiet for awhile, listening to the birds, watching the light fade.

"I finally read Raheem's journal." Marah's gaze focused on the garden. Joe waited for her to go on. "I am heartbroken. I don't understand how he turned into a person that hated Je..." She realized what she was about to say and stopped. "I mean this wasn't the boy I raised."

"Jews? Is that what you were about to say?" Joe said this without anger or malice.

"I'm sorry Joe."

"There is no reason for you to be sorry. I know you. I always thought Raheem was a great kid. But

I didn't see him as much this last year, so I didn't see the changes you've mentioned."

"His Dad gave him this, this commentary on the Tawhid, that can be misconstrued in every direction. The notes both he and his dad wrote in the margins made me sick to my stomach." Marah couldn't look at Joe. She kept her gaze focused into the yard. She felt relieved Joe did not get up to turn on a light, even after the sun had completely set. He lit the candle in the middle of the table and leaned back in his chair.

"What is the Tawhid?"

"The belief there is only God. No other. So Christians believe Jesus, peace be upon him, is the son of God, but we believe he was a prophet of God; the whole trinity thing is strange. God is God. Praise be to God, 'He is God the One, God the eternal. He begot no one nor was he begotten. No one is comparable to him.' That is why."

"From the Qur'an?"

"Yes. 112: 1-4. I was a good Muslim daughter. I memorized the Qur'an." She smiled.

"I'm impressed. I know little about my Jewish faith. I did not grow up in what one might call a practicing home. We celebrated Christmas right along with Hanukkah."

"Well, we are a very Americanized version of Islam, I'm pretty sure, though Pa is not so much. My parents grew up in Eastern Pakistan, that's the part that is Bangladesh now, but left in 1969 and came to the US. He always taught us that the Qur'an is the word. He has always been against the faith people put in the hadiths."

"Excuse my ignorance again, what are the hadiths?"

"They are the sayings and actions of Muhammad, peace be upon him, but they were written centuries later, much like the New Testament in the Christian bible was written long after the prophet died. There are four major books of hadith in the Shia tradition, but many many more in the Sunni tradition, which is my parents. They are Sunni. Most of Bangladesh is."

"Ah, thanks for the lesson."

"Thanks for asking."

"His journal? Is it that bad?"

"Yeah. I don't even know the person, who wrote that," she paused and looked up at the sky. "What was strange though, was the kid in him was still there too. One day he wrote about getting a new game for his PS4 and then the next about hating his Jewish professor."

"Does this professor have something to do with what Raheem and his dad did?"

"Yes. Zaqui hated Jews because India and Israel are aligned. We argued about this a few times, but..." Her eyes filled with tears and she felt her throat closing up. "But then he started hitting me when I argued with him, so I quit."

Joe sucked in his breath. "He hit you?"

"Yes. Not regularly, but if I disagreed or argued, then he would. I tried to be a good wife, but our cultural differences were just too much."

"No one deserves to be hit, Marah. You know that, right?"

"Yeah, but I didn't then. I was relieved when he left and felt so guilty for feeling relieved."

258

Marah could see Joe shaking his head.

"I didn't divorce him because I was afraid he would take Raheem. Didn't matter though, did it?"

"I'm sorry you have had to go through this, Marah." He paused, and then quietly said, "I wish our cultural divide didn't exist."

"Joe, you have been such a good friend to me. You helped me so much through that first part, but then I knew you wanted more. Sitting out here like this, spending this week with you, has made me wish we didn't have that difference too, but we do."

"Couldn't we work around the Muslim Jewish thing?" He said it laughingly, but she knew he was serious.

"I have broken so many rules. I also was not a good example to Raheem. I plan to spend the rest of my life making up for that by being a good Muslim woman."

"Marah, you are a good person. You are. These rules limit you."

"No, Joe, they make me who I am."

# Chapter 11

Marah spent the next few weeks gathering the personal items she wanted to pack herself and driving back and forth to Albuquerque to look for an apartment or house she could rent. She and Joe did not talk any more about the conversation that night. She came to his house after work each night, always nervous someone would notice, but no one had said anything. She would pull into the garage and quickly close the door. Sometimes she made dinner, sometimes he did, they would small talk then each go to their rooms. She could always hear the news on his television, then nothing, as she lay there as always, awake, staring at the ceiling. Relief from thinking came only when she fell asleep.

She finally found a small house in the university area and made arrangements with the moving company the Air Force provided. They arrived early on a morning in July to pack up her house. A truck would come the next to day to load and move. She planned to leave as soon as they closed the door on the last of her items and arrive in Albuquerque shortly before the truck's arrival. Two bedrooms, a living room with a kiva fireplace, and a kitchen area with a small dining area separating the two made up her new home. Two big shade trees made the back yard inviting. She felt safe. The neighbors on both sides came to meet her the weekend she came to clean before her move in and they seemed nice; a military couple, and the other a single woman, a nurse at one of the hospital day surgery wards.

When the truck arrived, Marah directed as they unloaded. She didn't own much, so the whole process did not take long. Once they left, she collapsed on the couch with relief. 'No more Bellview. No more stares.' She hoped she could live anonymously here. A weight lifted from her shoulders as she looked around her new home. She hoped to feel the same when she reported for work on Monday.

A clerk handed Marah the customary list of places to check in and people to see before she started work. She made her way around the base, finding the post office, the commissary, payroll, and what seemed like dozens of other offices where she met the required people, ending up at the end of the day next to the hospital, in the women's clinic where she would be working. Colonel Ramona Jarrell directed the clinic, however, Marah arrived after the Colonel left for the day. A lieutenant showed her around and escorted her to the office assigned to her. "Sorry you missed Colonel Jarrell. She had several meetings to attend, then she has rounds at the hospital."

"I had so many places to sign-in before I could come here, the time totally got away from me."

"No problem. Colonel Jarrell said she didn't expect to see you until tomorrow."

"Great. Thanks for showing me around, Lieutenant. I appreciate your time."

"Nice to meet you, Colonel Dalal. I'm looking forward to working with you." The Lieutenant returned to her desk, leaving Marah standing in the doorway of her new office. 'Much better than my closet, that's for sure,' she thought. She sunk into the desk chair and let out a sigh of relief. "So far, so good," she said, and turned to face the window. She gazed out and saw a few trees, and a yucca plant semi-blocking the parking lot from view. "Much better than my closet, much better."

# Chapter 12

Isobel received a call from Jorge Martinez's secretary, asking her to come by the next morning. She meant to check in with him when she came back from Llano, but she seemed to have trouble sticking to any plans, or even remembering what she should be doing. Isobel set her alarm for 6:30 to give herself plenty of time to work-out, have coffee, get dressed and actually put on a little make-up. When she arrived, she was shown straight into his office.

"Isobel. I'm so glad to see you," Martinez exclaimed as he came around his desk and hugged her.

"Thanks, Jorge. I'm glad to see you too. Makes me feel kind of normal coming here today." She managed a smile.

"I guess it's been pretty rough," he said.

"Yeah. But I've got some good friends and of course, Ian and his family. We hold each other up."

"Good. I'm glad to hear it. I think I have a plan you might like."

They sat down at the small table by the window in his office. A pot of coffee in a thermos sat on the table and he poured her some as she pulled up her chair, a ritual they often shared when sitting down to discuss her school or district happenings. Their friendship had developed over the years and he often relied on her for her insight, giving him a different perspective than long time employees of the school district might.

"Ok, Jorge. What is it? Are you ready for me to tender my resignation?"

"No, Isobel. I really don't want to lose you from the district, but I know you may not be ready to come back in August. I'd really like to see you take my place in three years when I retire."

"I've often thought about that, but now...," she trailed off.

"Yes. But right now that might not seem doable. So, this is what I'd like to offer. Don't retire. This next year, be a literacy/writing consultant for us. Work with teachers on their curriculum, give them help on best practices in teaching writing, and run a few workshops. I know that's your expertise. Then next year, I think there will be an assistant superintendent job available. A win win for all of us."

Isobel felt overwhelmed with the offer. "I don't know what to say. That's so generous."

"Isobel, you're good. We need leaders like you in this district. You don't have to give me an answer today. Take a couple of weeks. I leave on the 3rd of July for vacation. Can you give me a call before then?"

"I can do that. I just need to sort it all out in my head."

"Ok. Take your time."

As they finished their coffee, she asked about his wife and family, and asked to see the latest pictures of his grandchildren. He scanned through his phone and found the latest. "We're lucky to have grands, aren't we?" She said.

"Yes. We are." Martinez was a good boss and in many ways a good friend. "There are not many people I can bore with my pictures, you know." They both laughed.

Then she pulled out her phone and showed him pictures from her recent trip to Lubbock. "It goes both ways, my friend." He took her phone and looked through, then handed it back. She took the phone and stood. "I better let you get back to work."

"Thank you for coming in Isobel. I haven't wanted to intrude on your grief, but my door is always open if you need to talk."

"Thanks, Jorge." They stood and he gave her a quick hug. "I'll be in touch before you leave."

"Great." He walked her to the door and saw her out.

Isobel drove through the city, dodging tourists, not only in cars, but as pedestrians oblivious to crosswalks and sidewalks. She worked hard these days at remaining patient. She often felt frustrated at the least little thing that went wrong. At home, Isobel called Ian to tell him what Martinez had offered.

"What do you want to do, Mom? I can't imagine you're ready to retire yet."

"No, I can't either. I mean, not really. I've always loved to write and have been thinking lately what that would be like, to write full-time, but I'm not sure. Taking his offer would probably be the best thing. I would still have some options. I forgot to ask him what my pay would be. I'm guessing less than I make now."

"Can you make that work?"

"I have savings."

"Good. You've got time to decide, right?"

"Almost two weeks, although I think I'm going to take the offer."

"Sounds good." Ian said. "How are you holding up?"

"Ok. I've had a few moments of what seems like insanity, but ok. My friends are checking in on me. However, it's been kind of weird with Diane."

"In what way?"

"It's like she wants me to just get over Alec and move on. I've lost my patience with her a couple of times."

"Yeah, I think no one knows what this feels like unless they've been through the same thing."

"She never had kids, so I think that makes this even harder for her to understand."

"Probably so."

"How are you holding up?"

"Good, I guess. The kids keep us busy, and we spend evenings in the pool so we're all exhausted at bedtime, which is good. I'm sleeping better. What about you?"

"Ok." She didn't tell him about how often she drank herself to sleep.

"I miss you, Mom."

"I miss you, too. I'll come down around the 1st. Does that work?"

"Sure. We're throwing the annual pool party for the 4th. You in?"

"Of course."

"I thought about canceling this year, but Delia said no. We have to try to get some normality back in our lives, and we haven't been seeing our friends much, so..."

"She's right. Definite wisdom for all of us in that."

"Yeah, I'll have to agree."

"I'll let you get back to work, just wanted to check-in."

"Thanks, Mom. And I do think taking the job is a good idea."

"Thanks, Ian. Love you."

"Love you too, Mom."

# Chapter 13

Isobel spent the next couple of weeks scanning pictures during the day, cleaning out closets, throwing things away, and trying not to drink. Hiking got her out of the house and she would wander the Dale Ball trails, mindlessly trekking in circles at times. She didn't trust herself yet to take any of the high mountain trails, fearing her mindlessness would get her lost, something impossible to do on the Dale Balls. She also contacted Martinez and told him she would accept the position. Though not a drastic cut in pay, the trade off gave her a flexible schedule, one she set herself. The rest of the summer gave her time to make plans for workshops, to set up appointments with each school principal, and to put together a list of teachers who needed assistance.

After Isobel cleaned out every closet, cabinet and drawer in her house, she decided to tackle her office before her secretary and her vice principal left for the summer. When she entered the building, Anna saw Isobel and went to meet her at the front door, giving her a big hug. Anna mothered Isobel, as she did everyone, making Isobel feel cared for, even though she was Anna's boss.

"I'm so happy to see you. I've been worried I haven't heard from you."

"I'm sorry. I was away for a week or so, then I've just been taking care of things at home."

"Of course. I know it must be so difficult." Anna hugged Isobel again, and when she stepped back, Isobel could see tears in her eyes. Before Isobel could say anything, Anna rushed on, "Dr. Martinez came by, he says you're leaving us."

"Yes, he's offered me a position which will allow me to stay on. I thought I would retire, but I think I might not know what to do with myself if I did. But... um, I just couldn't imagine coming back and dealing well with everything here. The stress..."

"I understand. I think it's the smartest thing the school board has done in a long time. Good for Martinez for going to bat for the position. You'll be great."

"Thanks, Anna."

"Do you have time for coffee?"

"I came to start packing up my office, but let's have coffee first."

"Did Dr. Martinez not tell you? He sent over a couple of people and they boxed everything up and moved it to your new place at Central Office."

"Wow. No, he didn't." She felt herself relax at the thought of not having to do that right now. "That was nice of him. I'll make the pot of coffee, but they probably packed up all my cups."

"I kept one of yours out so anytime you come here, you've got a cup."

"Anna, you are a genius." Isobel smiled to herself as she made the coffee. She truly felt grateful for the kindness of her friends and colleagues.

The sun hovered below the flat horizon as Isobel loaded her suitcase in her car, and hugged Ian and Delia bye. Though the three of them struggled a bit the night of the 4th of July party, the other's happiness helped them get into the party spirit. Alec, always the life of any party, was sorely missed by everyone. Isobel lingered several more days, but now she felt the need to go home.

"Mom, thanks for coming. It was good to have you here."

"I'm glad I came."

"We'll see you in August before school starts here," Delia said and hugged her again. "We always need a little Santa Fe time."

Ian opened her car door, "Love you, Mom," and he hugged her tight, nuzzling his face into her neck for a moment, as he did when he was little. "Be safe."

"I love you, too," she choked out. "It's always hard to leave you."

"I feel the same way." They smiled at each other as she slid into the driver's seat and he shut her door.

"Ok. Here I go." She rolled down the window and waved at them as she headed down the street.

The road stretched before her, a five and a half hour drive back to Santa Fe. Lubbock grew dusty on the outskirts before it turned to farmland, cotton fields, pecan groves, and soybeans. Dairies were interspersed among the fields, sucking the Ogallala Aquiefer dry, even more so than the crops. As she entered New Mexico and drove through Bellview, she thought of Raheem's mom. Impulsively, she turned off the highway and drove to her house. A 'For Sale' sign stood in the yard. As she pulled in the drive and went to the door, she noticed there were no curtains or shades on the windows. She walked over and peered inside and saw an empty house. 'I wonder where she's gone,' she thought, returning to her car. Isobel then headed for the highway and home.

The eastern New Mexico landscape changed to scruffy grass, sand hills, and cattle scattered here and there, roaming the hard land searching for their dinner. Small farm windmills dotted the rolling landscape, capped by huge commercial windmills visible on the Caprock to the east. When she hit the interstate, the mountains appeared in the distance, urging her home. She headed north at Clines Corner and made her way past the turnoffs for movie sets, red sandstone cliffs, the road to Lamy, climbing the hill into Eldorado, and turning west for home. She pulled into her drive right before noon, glad to be there.

Isobel unpacked, but the afternoon stretched ahead of her. She took a book out to the front porch and sat in the shade. Her eyes wandered to the road, a small dirt lane really, that led down to Canyon Road. Through the leaves of the trees, she could just glimpse the apples hanging from the limbs, and the windows of the casita with the bright blue trim that sat on the far side of Canyon. The heat was heavy and not even a hint of breeze touched her skin. Her mind slipped around between memories of Alec and Ian; her own childhood; the loss of her parents; and all her achievements between the time she divorced Jacob and now. She let it all float around in her head, concentrating on nothing, yet thinking of what seemed like everything. The book lay unopened on the pillow next to her as she drifted off, her head leaned back on the wall.

"Alec?" She woke herself up as she spoke his name. Shaking her head to clear her mind, she could have sworn Alec was talking to her. Isobel realized her phone was ringing somewhere inside the house and went in to answer. She looked at the screen and saw Nora's name. "Hi, Nora."

"Hi, Isobel. Are you doing okay?"

"At the moment I am."

"Listen, I know this seems strange, and please don't tell Jacob I called you, but that boy's mother has been transferred to Albuquerque. I know you wanted to talk to her and my friend, Linda, is friends with one of her former colleagues and anyway, you know how things are here…"

"I can't believe you called. I drove by her house on my way home today and it was empty. I wondered what happened to her."

"Do you still want to talk to her?"

"I do, but how do I find her now?"

"I've got her phone number. I'll text it to you."

"Okay, this is so freaky."

"I know."

"I guess I can call her. She'll probably just hang up, but I can try."

"Just don't tell anyone I called you, okay?"

"Of course not."

"Thanks."

" Are you and Jacob doing okay?"

"For the most part. As you know, some days are better than others."

"Yeah. And others worse."

"I've got to go. I just wanted you to have the info."

"Thanks, Nora."

As soon as they hung up, a text came through with the phone number. Isobel stared at the number for a moment, then pressed it and waited for Marah to answer.

"Hello?" Marah, sitting at her desk had unthinkingly answered. She usually screened unknown numbers.

"Is this Marah Dalal?"

"Yes."

"This is Isobel Allen, Alec Campbell's mother."

Marah paused, not recognizing the name right away. "I'm sorry, I don't..."

"Your son, killed my son," she said quietly.

Isobel could hear Marah gasp.

"Why are you calling me? How did you get my number?"

"I just want to talk to you. I want to understand why. I thought...well...I thought maybe you could give me some insight."

"I don't know what I can tell you. I don't understand myself."

"Can I come see you?"

"I don't live in Bellview anymore."

"I know. You're in Albuquerque."

"What? How do you know that?" Isobel could hear the fear in her voice.

"Ms. Dalal, I promise, I don't want to hurt you. I just want to talk."

Marah didn't respond.

Isobel said, "I found your phone number, I can probably just find where you live and show up. Or we can meet somewhere and talk."

"Okay, but I think you should come to my house. Someone might recognize me if we meet somewhere."

"Saturday?"

"Sure." Marah gave Isobel her address and told her to come at 1:00.

"See you then," Isobel said and hung up. She felt her hands trembling slightly as she looked down at her silent phone. As much as she wanted to know why, at the same time, she didn't. A feeling in the pit of her stomach began to wash over her, bringing on a nausea she hadn't experienced before. Her knees buckled and she sank to the couch. Her heart pounded. Slowly, she began to take a deep breath, drawing in and breathing out till she felt her body relax and the nausea pass. That night she needed her old friend and poured herself a tall whiskey.

# Chapter 14

Isobel woke long after the sun rise. Still dressed in yesterday's clothes, she stumbled to the bathroom and began to strip them off. She kicked the denim shorts and white t-shirt towards the hamper in the corner, then stood in front of the mirror, assessing her tired, weary face. Always a hiker and healthy eater, the person standing in front of the mirror did not resemble that woman. Her eyes were bloodshot and red, her face drawn and tight, the wrinkles standing out as if she were eighty instead of 55. She stripped her panties and bra off, threw them to the pile, and stepped into the shower, letting the water run over her face, covering her entire body.

When she finished, she wrapped herself in a towel and opened the window to let in the morning breeze, but the air was hot and heavy like the day before. She dried herself and wiped off the mirror. The shower had revived the color in her face a bit, she noticed. After she dried her hair and ran the straightener over it, she looked better, and the final touch of a little make-up brought her face back to life. She dabbed on a bright lipstick and went to dress. Isobel found her jeans in a crumpled pile inside the closet, but as the room was already heating up, she thought better of them, and donned a light, body skimming t-shirt dress, with comfortable sandals. Looking at the clock, she realized she still had a couple of hours till she needed to leave.

Isobel begged off coffee with Diane again, not wanting to deal with Diane's questions any longer. She made herself a coffee and took her cup to the front porch. Her book still sat where she left it, the sweater draped over the arm of the settee. Curling up with her feet beside her, she surveyed the street and settled in. Last night bothered her. She could only keep up this drinking herself to sleep routine a little longer. Once she returned to work, dragging out of bed like today, would be too much. Now that she had finished scanning all her pictures, she needed another project, one to keep her mind busy.

The Qur'an she ordered came to mind. She laid down her cup and went to find it. Still on the dining table, she picked it up and took it back to her place on the front porch. The Oxford edition had been suggested as the best translation, and now, thumbing to the contents page, she saw an introduction she had skipped over when she started reading last month. She found the background of Muhammad and the Qur'an explained there. Finishing her first cup of coffee, she made herself another and continued to read.

Isobel recognized references to the Christian Bible. A devoted bible reader for much of her young life, when she returned to college as a grown woman, with two children, she began to understand where literature came from. She saw how it was influenced by the times in which something was written, and realized the Bible, a book rich in history and explanations of happenings people wanted to understand, became easily manipulated for the benefit of the reader. She believed in more than just this life here on earth, but did not believe in a God looking down at them, knowing every move and overseeing every person. She felt Alec's energy still present in her life, and knew he still existed in their minds and hearts. She often told people she was a spiritual agnostic, as she could think of no better way to describe her despise for organized religion, her understanding that possibly no God existed, yet maybe the possibility of something more and that connections existed in all beings.

Engrossed in the reading, she came across a passage, 'Do not contribute to your destruction with your own hands, but do good, for God loves those who do good.' "Wouldn't this mean, don't commit suicide? But also, not to kill anyone?" she said out-loud. Isobel paused in the reading, feeling her stomach growl with hunger. She gathered up her items from the porch and went to the kitchen to see if she could find anything to eat. Finding a jar of peanut butter and a box of whole wheat crackers, they would suffice till she could go out this evening. Her head ached from drinking herself to sleep the night before, and the fat and salty in the peanut butter would do her good.

Plate in hand, she settled at the dining room table to eat and continue reading. Isobel found the Qur'an read much like a set of rules to follow. Some made sense, others seemed like a means of controlling people, much like her experience with religion. As she finished her last cracker, she glanced at her watch. She needed to leave for Albuquerque to meet Marah.

# Chapter 15

Isobel pulled into Marah's drive. No one knew she was coming. Her head ached from too much whiskey the night before, but the drink allowed her to stop obsessing about this moment and get some sleep. She walked to the door and knocked.

Marah turned on the kettle when she heard Isobel at the door and went to let her in. She had laid awake all night, wondering what she could say to this woman.

They stood staring at each other for a moment, then Marah held out her hand. "I'm Marah."

Isobel took her hand. "I'm Isobel."

"Come in." She stood back and motioned Isobel in. "I've put the kettle on for tea," she said as she shut the door and then led the way into the kitchen. "Please, have a seat." She indicated a chair at the table.

Isobel sat looking around the kitchen, the kettle rattled as Marah placed tea bags in the tea pot. "Your table is lovely. Antique?"

"In a way. It's a recycled barn door I refurbished myself. Raheem hated how..." she looked away, embarrassed at bringing up her son's name.

Isobel stood up and walked to the window, gazing into the backyard, she said, "I'm sorry what they did to your dog. She didn't deserve that, nor did you." Isobel returned to the table as Marah brought the cups and pot over and set them down.

Marah could feel tears, but fought them back as she poured their tea.

"Thank you for seeing me."

"I'm not sure I can help. The man who killed your son is a stranger to me. I don't know him."

"But surely you saw something?"

"No!" Marah answered sharply. "He was in school. I rarely saw him."

A silence descended as they sipped their tea. Isobel looked at the woman in front of her, Marah's head bowed over her cup, her hair pulled into a tight bun at the back of her head, a few strands of grey evident, and thought she had made a mistake coming here. She thought she should leave, then Marah started talking, still staring into her tea cup.

"Raheem was always a quiet kid. He was only five when his dad left us. But he would clown around when it was just the two of us. I felt bad for making him move around so much. Then we landed in Bellview, I was promised an extended stay. I thought he would make friends and come out of his shell some." Marah looked up at Isobel, "But he was bullied and never quite found his place. When his dad moved back to the states a couple of years ago, he contacted us. I thought a relationship with his dad would be good for him." She looked away again for a moment. "When he took an interest in Islam, I was happy. He even made friends at college, but now I look back and I knew something was off."

"What do you mean, off?"

"He lost his tenderness with me. He actually sort of bullied me." Tears started to slip down her cheeks. "I was happy when he decided to live in Llano for school. Mom's are supposed to be sad," wailing now, "I'm sorry. I'm so sorry."

Isobel sat frozen in her chair. Tears poured down her own face. She felt angry at Marah. For mourning her own son? She wanted to scream, 'Your fucking son killed mine! Stop crying!' Her frustration bubbling up over this woman crying for her son.

"I know you must hate me," Marah said.

"I don't hate you. I can't. I'm just…." Isobel stopped. She looked outside for a moment. "I should go. I'm sorry I disturbed you." She started to stand up, hesitated, then sat back down. "I'm angry. I feel like I want to scream at people, and hit things, and throw things. I find everything inane to the point I want to tell people to fucking shut up and I don't even use that word, but now I seem to say it all the time."

Marah nodded in agreement.

Isobel continued, "In the grocery store the other day, I heard this mother being loud and mean to her toddler and I yelled at her. I said he could get sick, or get shot or die and she needed to be nice to him and love him and hug him, and I was screaming at the top of my lungs and crying, when I finally realized what I was doing because of the look of horror on her face, and then her son burst into tears. All I could do was grab my purse and leave. I went to my car and broke down." Isobel reached for a napkin and wiped her eyes. "The anger. The anger is the worst."

"I feel angry all the time too. Zaqui stole my son from me, that's the worst, but he also stole my life." Marah paused and then whispered, "I'm a pariah. In the eyes of the world, I am to blame."

"I've been blaming you. I have. And hating you a little too."

"Oh," Marah replied.

Isobel hadn't really admitted that before, but now that she did, she didn't feel better. "I think we actually are both sad and missing our sons. Nothing will ever be normal again."

"Yeah, I sometimes think, where did my normal boring life go?" She half-heartedly smiled at Isobel.

"Ian and I talk about missing normal."

"Ian is your husband?"

"No, he is my son. Alec's older brother. I'm not married."

"Another son...." Marah's voice trailed off.

"Yes. This has been hard for him. They were very close. He's married though, and has two children, Bree and Brian."

"They must be a comfort to you."

"Nothing is a comfort to me right now," Isobel said harshly.

Marah looked away. They sat in a tense silence.

"I'm sorry. I know you were just stating the obvious, I...people say ridiculous things to me and I snap. It's becoming my natural response. Do you know what I mean?"

"Not really, because no one talks to me but my one friend, Joe." Marah looked up from her cup into Isobel's eyes. "No one. I think that's why I gave in to meeting you. I didn't care if you screamed at me, punched me or even killed me, I just needed to talk to someone."

They sat at the table in silence, each in her own thoughts. Marah had no answers for Isobel. She had no answers for herself. She wanted to know how she could keep living forward.

"What was he like? Your son?" Marah said. "Is it okay if I ask?"

Isobel, startled at Marah's voice, turned back to face her. "Yeah. It's ok." She swallowed hard to choke back the emotion she felt each time she talked about Alec. "He was a good man. Everyone really loved him. He never met a stranger." She paused, then smiled, thinking of him and Ian when they were little. "Ian was a serious kid, always looking out for his baby brother. The two of them would make me laugh so hard. Ian, always Alec's straight man. They had a great time together." Isobel took a deep breath, and blinked back tears. "The boys and I loved to hike, and the two of them would go backpacking somewhere every summer."

"What was his job at the station?"

"He was the production manager. The student's loved him. His boss said he was brilliant, but then, I knew that." She smiled.

Marah smiled too.

Isobel felt the shadow that often crept in at moments like this, crushing her heart. The joy in the thoughts of Alec were always struck down at the sorrow of him being gone. She turned away.

"Isobel, can I tell you something I learned about Raheem and his father?"

"Sure," she said, turning back to Marah.

"When the FBI brought back his belongings, there was a book there I'd never seen before." Marah stood up and went to a table in the living room, bringing back the book, she thrust it at Isobel.

Isobel looked at the cover. The word Tawhid was printed there and she started to thumb through the pages as Marah spoke. "This book is about the oneness of God and comments on the Qur'an and the Hadiths." Isobel noticed the writing in the margins and paused now and then to read. When she saw what Raheem wrote about his Jewish professor, Isobel gasped.

"This is terrible." She looked up at Marah. "It's sick." She closed it and set it down, her hands pressed together between her knees, "Professor Goldberg was the target?"

"You know him?"

"Yes. Alec respected him greatly. He was a mentor to him."

"The FBI told me they didn't release the information to the press because they thought it would put the professor in danger of another attack."

"Oh my God."

Marah said nothing.

"Do you feel this way? About Jews?" Isobel asked sharply.

"No! I never taught Raheem this way. Never."

"Where does this come from?"

"Zaqui hated Israel. He was Pakistani, and he resented what they were doing to the Palestinians."

"But for God's sake, why here? Why one Jewish guy? And they didn't even get him, they killed my son instead!" Isobel's voice had risen to the point she was nearly screaming. She stood up and walked into the living room. Marah followed and stood in the doorway.

"Are you okay?"

"I can't believe this. I don't understand."

"I know. I was shocked."

"How could you let your son be this man?"

"I ask myself the same question every day. What if I'd said no to him seeing his dad? What if I'd not let him go to DC? Would he have defied me and gone anyway? Would Zaqui have come and taken him away? I thought he needed his father, you know?"

Isobel understood that, having seen way too many kids deprived of a relationship with their dads and the damage that caused. She felt deflated and sat down on the couch.

Marah sat in a chair waiting for Isobel.

"Why did you come to Albuquerque?" Isobel asked.

"I couldn't work in Bellview. None of my patients would see me any longer."

"So they transferred you?"

"Yes, at my request. The Colonel kept it quiet, so I'm hoping no one will recognize me and I had hoped no one in Bellview would know, but I guess things always leak in a small town."

Isobel slightly smiled. "Yes, I don't miss that."

"Hopefully no one will spread the word up here."

"I won't tell anyone and I'll let my friend know to keep it quiet."

"Thanks."

They again sat in silence. Isobel looked around at Marah's living room. She finally spoke again, "About that book, Marah, where did Zaqui get it from?"

"I've asked Pa," Isobel looked puzzled, "My father, he believes some schools might be using the book. That really scares me. The interpretation of the Qur'an and hadiths in this book are harsh."

"The hadiths are what Muhammad said?"

"Yes, but in our family, we were taught that the Qur'an is the only word. The hadiths are for consideration because they were recorded much later so who can say they are for sure."

"I am reading the Qur'an."

"You are?" Marah was visibly surprised.

"There is much that is like the Bible I grew up reading. Even many of the same people."

"We both believe in the Abrahamic God."

"Well, not exactly. Yours believes it's okay to kill people, mine, or the one I grew up with forbids killing." As soon as the harsh words left her mouth, she regretted them. Isobel could see she'd hurt Marah, and she hadn't meant to. "I'm sorry. There I go again letting the anger speak."

"It's okay."

"I don't feel quite the same way about God as I did in my younger years. Too many things put a bad taste in my mouth for religion."

Marah turned her gaze back to Isobel, startled out of her thoughts. "We cannot give up our teachings so easy."

"I wouldn't say it was easy for me, but I guess for a lot of Christians, yes, we can give it up easier than maybe a Muslim can. Maybe. I don't know. I have no room for the rules of religion anymore. They just seem a way of controlling people. Do you know what I mean?"

"Yes...," Marah hesitantly said, "uhm, but not really. I mean, I could never stop being a Muslim so it's difficult for me to understand how Christians can stop."

"I think all the different Christian religions teach so differently, who knows why some give it up and others cling to their beliefs."

"I don't cling, I just believe," Marah said defensively.

"I'm sorry, I didn't mean to offend."

"It's okay, really...."

"What are you going to do about the book, Marah?"

"What do you mean?"

"If some Muslim schools are using it, don't you want to warn parents?"

"I don't know."

"You don't know?" Isobel felt indignant. "Do you want others to go through what we are going through?"

"I'm not sure what I could do…"

"Contact schools? Make a public statement? Please don't sit back and do nothing, Marah."

"I don't think I can. I mean, that's not something…"

"You are the only one who can." Isobel felt her frustration rising, anger bubbling to the surface and tears welling up at the back of her eyes. She looked away for a moment and took a deep breath. "You have to do something. I could try, but who would listen to some white woman whose son was killed by a Muslim terrorist? They would consider me prejudice and racist."

Marah was chewing on her bottom lip, obviously upset.

"Marah, please think about it. You could make a difference."

"It's not just the book, Isobel. I was not paying attention. Zaqui was behind this."

"Yes, but the book influenced him. Maybe he would have self-radicalized if he'd had the book. I think you need to alert parents."

"I'll think about this and call my father."

Isobel refrained from telling her to think for herself, but thought it nonetheless.

"Okay. You'll let me know?"

"Yes."

"Thank you for thinking about it."

They sat in silence for a few minutes then Isobel glanced at her watch and stood up. "Marah, I'm going to head home. I think I've disturbed you enough for one day."

"I'm glad you came."

Isobel picked up her bag from the couch and Marah walked her to the door, stepping out on the porch with Isobel as she left.

"Thanks for the tea, Marah." Isobel started to hug Marah and stopped herself, unsure what to do, when Marah leaned in and hugged Isobel.

"Thank you for coming. I'll be in touch."

"Okay." Isobel waved as she got to her car and opened the door, started the car and headed home.

Marah thought about what Isobel had said, but what could she really do? She did not want to bring attention to herself. She hoped for anonymity at the base, and in Albuquerque. Speaking out about this book could only hurt her in the long run. She was sending Joe an email telling him about Isobel and their conversation, when her phone rang. She glanced at the screen and saw her father was calling. She answered as she hit the send button.

"Hello, Pa."

"Marah, we were calling to check on you. Are you settled in now? How is Albuquerque?

"I'm fine. Really. All settled in and I'm starting to see patients at work."

"Good, good. That makes us happy."

"Thanks, Pa." She could hear her mother in the background telling him what to ask her.

"And what else, Marmar, are you sleeping?"

"Ok. Yes. Some nights I wake up, but ok."

"That's good."

"Pa, I have something to talk to you about."

"What is it?"

"That book, the one Zaqui gave Raheem, I wonder if parents know what it is teaching their children?"

"It is not for you to concern yourself, Marah."

"I'm wondering if I should…" she trailed off.

"Should what, Marah?"

"Should warn parents about it."

"No! Only grief comes with wisdom. This is not our business, Marah."

"Maybe it is, Pa."

"You must not think of this. We must put this behind us and move on."

"Yes, I guess, but…"

"But nothing. No more talking about this. You are fine. Your job is good. You will come home soon."

"Yes, Pa. I will. I should be able to take some time soon."

"Mum wants to talk to you."

"Marah, you are well?"

"Yes, Mum. I'm good."

"Come see us soon."

"I will. Soon. I promise."

"Very good. Bye bye." And like always, Mum hung up the phone and was gone.

# PART FOUR

*Do not grieve. Anything you lose comes round
in another form.*
-Rumi

# Chapter 1

Isobel spent the last weeks of her summer, hiking, reading, cleaning, and setting up her new office. Before school officially began, she decided to host Sunday dinner at her place; she had not seen everyone since before the fourth of July, and Diane had drifted away, avoiding Isobel's constant pain. Now mid-August, Isobel felt a deep sense of loneliness and longed for their company, for a night of friends. She cleaned the house and bought a few bottles of wine; a Prosecco for aperitif and the La Cana Albarino 2013 for appetizers. Sam was bringing the reds. She had been lucky and found halloumi at the cheese shop and was making her favorite appetizers.

Sunday morning, Isobel hiked to Picacho peak from the Canyon road side. She had been making herself hike the trail every day, rising before sunrise and leaving the house as the sky began to softly lighten.

Each day she attempted to hike the trail faster than the day before to get her heart racing and to keep her from letting her thoughts wander too much. She dressed, pulled on her boots, picked up her small pack already loaded with water bottle, sunglasses, reading glasses and a journal. Outside, Isobel pulled her bike from the storage under her stairs and mounted. The cool, crisp air felt good on her face as she rode up the hill to the trailhead where she jumped off her bike and locked it to a tree at the bottom of the trail.

Isobel set off to the peak, passing the old waterworks pipe, stopping for a moment to take a few deep breaths and a few gulps of water, she walked on at a fast pace. Some days were easier than others, and today she felt lighter than she had in the last week, finding herself almost running as she headed to the peak. When she summited, the sun was just coming over the Pecos wilderness in the distance, a beautiful sight when she was able to hit it at the right moment. She stood in the light and let the rays soak into her sweating body. Even this early in the morning, she could feel the heat. The day promised to be hot, but hopefully the rains would come and cool things off before dinner.

She slipped the backpack off her shoulders and pulled her journal out before sitting down. Everyday she wrote, her feelings flowing through her pen to the page, giving her just the slightest relief from the sadness, and voice to the anger. Isobel had never been an angry person and she found this the most difficult emotion she had to abide through all of this. Today though, the anger did not come. She wrote instead about how strong she felt climbing the trail, summiting the peak as the sun came up, and the comfort of knowing her friends were coming this evening. The pain she felt, her constant companion, had quieted, even if only for a few moments. She tucked her pen into the pages and slid the journal back in her pack. As she stood to leave, she could hear voices coming up the trail. A couple came into view and greeted her.

"Good morning," Isobel said, then slipped on her sunglasses and headed down the trail. Half-way down she looked up to see Sam headed her way. "Hello, you," she said, and he looked up to see her.

"Hello, yourself. What brings you out so early?"

"This is my 'stop drinking myself to sleep every night' remedy, climb Picacho before sunrise as fast as possible. Makes it impossible if I spent the night before drinking."

Sam laughed, "Well I'm glad to hear it. I've been worried about you."

"Yeah, I think the look on your face that day you found me rather out of it hit home. I've had a few nights where I couldn't help myself, but this seems to be helping."

"Good for you. I'm looking forward to tonight."

"Me too. It will be great to have us all together."

He hugged her and they said goodbye. Isobel continued down the trail, thinking of her friends. She felt they had all pulled away in some ways, except for Sam, but at the same time, she had pulled away too. She found so much inanity in everything, she couldn't stand to hear idle conversation. She also knew, most people didn't have the guts to look death in the face and be willing to bear someone else's pain as they went through tragedy. 'Maybe no one did,' she thought. 'Maybe that's why I feel drawn to Marah. She gets this pain. She is dealing with it like me. Maybe even more. Her son intentionally put her through this.' She reached the end of the trail and shook her head as if to dispel the thoughts.

Isobel unlocked her bike and headed for home. The whole day lay before her, but with her friends coming this evening and school starting tomorrow, she had plenty of tasks to keep her busy. When she pulled into her drive, she put her bike away and as she climbed the stairs to the house, she decided to dress and walk to the coffee house, 'a great way to start my morning', she thought.

Isobel cleaned and readied everything for the evening. She worked in the yard some, cleaning out the flower beds and picking tomatoes to slice for dinner. Long past noon, hunger hit her and she made herself a salad. She put everything on a tray and carried it to the front porch where a slight breeze made the heat bearable. The clouds building up in the distance for an afternoon rain promised to dissipate the heat. By the time she finished her late lunch, the clouds moved closer and the skies turned grey. She went to clean up and as she stepped out of the shower, the rain began to pour, pounding her flat roof, drowning out all sound, even the thoughts in her head. She pulled on a robe and lay down on her bed, her face towards the door to the porch and she watched the rain, the drops bouncing off the deck as they hit, puddling in low spots, splashing the rails, rain so hard even the roof of the deck could not keep the water from hitting the furniture and door.

Mesmerized by the rain, she closed her eyes and drifted off to sleep, her dreams took her to Alec and Scotland where they got caught in the rain while out hiking one afternoon and when they arrived at a village, they took refuge in an old bar, where an elderly man, whom they could hardly understand what he was saying, told them to order a Glayva to warm their insides. Nothing ever tasted better. She woke with a start when the rain stopped, a smile on her face, that faded with the recognition of knowing she was in her bed. She sighed as she wrapped her robe tightly around her and went to her closet to dress.

# Chapter 2

"Hello in the house," Isobel heard Sam call through the screen door.

"Come in," she called back, wiping her hands on a towel as she went to the front door.

"We meet again," and Sam leaned in and kissed her on the cheek, his hands full with the casserole he carried and the bottles of wine hanging off his arm in a carrier.

"Let me take this," and she grabbed the casserole from him and led the way to the kitchen. "What's in here," she said as she lifted the lid, sniffing the wonderful aroma.

"Vegetable Au gratin."

"Smells divine!"

"Thank you very much. Only the best for you."

They laughed and she placed the dish in the warm oven.

"You're early," she said as she turned back to cutting a pear into slices.

"I am. Thought I could help. Or get a head start on drinks."

"Both then." She threw him a towel, "Would you dry the rest of the dishes there and put them away?"

"Of course."

"And pour yourself a whiskey, the soda's in the fridge."

"Even better. Can I fix something for you, my dear?"

"No, I'm good, thanks."

They chatted as they finished up their tasks. Isobel dried the chairs and table on the deck, and she and Sam set the table, the sun heating up the evening, dispelling the chill the rain had left. Perfect weather for dinner. The others arrived each bearing a dish of food. Isobel opened the Prosecco and poured everyone a glass. "Here's to us. Sante," and they clinked glasses all around. They moved to the front porch and all settled in to the settee and chairs. Isobel sat on the footstool so they made a circle of sorts. She relaxed into the moment. Happy to see her friends and for once, the angry knot in her throat and stomach seemed at ease. She sighed and let herself just be.

When they had finished their drinks, Isobel directed everyone back to the kitchen. "My friends, I have a special treat for you tonight," and she turned the flame on under her skillet, heating the haloumi, then she placed the cheese slices into the larger skillet with dates and pears and poured ouzo into the skillet. "Are you ready?"

"Wait, do we need cameras for this?" Diane asked.

"Oh, yes, my friend. I think you do."

Everyone grabbed their phones and got their cameras ready. Isobel took a torch and lit the skillet to the 'oohs' and 'ahhs' of the collective. "And voila!" she said as the last of the flames died away and she began to serve up the appetizers on plates.

Isobel was in her element when she was feeding people. "Do you like?"

"Are you crazy?" Richard said through a mouth full of date, "these are amazing!"

"Yeah, damn good, Iso" said Doug and the others concurred.

"Ah, perfect then!"

"Who needs anything else now, that was fantastic. We can all go home. Give me my dish. It's unworthy." Sam had them all laughing.

"Uh, no way. I'm hungry!" Isobel opened the oven and took out the dish Sam had brought and carried it to the table on the deck. He took the decanter of wine and bottles of water and the others brought their dishes.

"Beautiful, Isobel," Diane said as she stepped outside.

"Thanks." Diane had seemed cold towards Isobel on her arrival, so she welcomed her comment, hoping the ice was broken and they could all talk with ease. And they did, for awhile.

"Iso, have you talked to the boy's mother yet?" Doug asked.

"I saw her a few weeks ago. She's in Albuquerque now, so I asked her to let me come see her."

"Why is she in Albuquerque?" Richard asked.

"She requested a transfer. She said she was a pariah, and her patients wouldn't see her."

"What did you talk about?"

"We talked about our sons. She told me she didn't know the son who killed mine. She also told me about a book she found in her son's things. One the FBI had originally confiscated. It was really disturbing to her, and to me when I saw it." She explained to them what Marah had said and what she herself had read. "I told her she has to speak out about it, to let other parents know, but she said she would have to ask Pa. Her dad. I wanted to shake her and tell her to make her own decisions."

"Has she said anything since?"

"No. I'm sure he must have advised her against it, and I realized later it would ruin her anonymity she has right now, so...I haven't pressed her. But I am really, really frustrated. I feel angry all the time. At least until today. I've felt pretty good today. I think knowing you all were coming, made my day better. The knot eased up some."

"Let go, Isobel," Diane said. "You'll feel better every day if you just move on. I don't get it why you hold on."

Isobel sucked in her breath and looked at Diane hard. "I hold on, Diane, because Alec was my son. Because I will carry him with me everyday of my life. All I have left of him is memories and I will not let them go. And if I can keep one other parent from facing this tragedy, this gut wrenching, life ending tragedy, I will." No one knew what to say, but Sam

301

reached over and rubbed Isobel's back. Richard and Doug sat silent, until Doug said, "Diane, she has to grieve in her own way."

Diane sat frozen in her chair. "I'm just trying to help."

Isobel took a deep breath. "I'm sorry I got so angry. I'm doing the best I can."

"Iso, you don't have to apologize to us," Doug said.

Isobel knew that while time would heal the heaviest pain, her life would never be the same, and she would always, every day miss her Alec. She would find a way to make a difference for other parents one way or another.

Everyone got up from the table and cleared the dishes. They blew out the candles and retreated to the kitchen. Isobel had made a cherry pie, and while she cut the pie, and dished the ice cream, the guys loaded the dishwasher and someone made a pot of decaf. They took their dessert and finished the evening in the living room. The conversation was subdued and quiet till one by one they left, leaving Isobel to herself.

# Chapter 3

M arah dragged herself out of bed in time to pray every morning. She found solace in what she felt was her only place of refuge. Attending the mosque felt impossible, as someone might recognize her, and she didn't feel ready for that yet. She remained anonymous at work, her colleagues assuming she came from the base near Philly, an assumption she allowed the day someone asked where she was from. Philly allowed her to state a truth without stating a lie.

The dry and hot days, left her with no choice but to run early in the morning. She donned her running clothes and left her house before sunrise, the air still cool and crisp. Her route took her through the UNM campus, up and down sidewalks, quiet and free of people this early in the morning. Once home, she showered and dressed in her uniform, a tunic and pants, then tied her hair into a bun at the nape of her neck. She made herself eat breakfast because she could rarely make herself eat dinner. Her days ticked off minute by minute, seeing patients, picking at lunch, seeing patients, then coming home to her tree-lined street, taking off her uniform, putting on loose pants and tunic, to sit in her backyard, with her loss. Loss of her son. Loss of her life. Anger flowed through her like the waves of the ocean, sometimes pounding her head and other times softly slapping the shores of her heart. Some days she felt as though she didn't exist, but at least her parents and sister acknowledged her life. She found herself going through the motions of living in a semblance of who she used to be.

August slipped into September. Marah ticked off the days. One by one. When the light began to change towards the end of the month, the air to smell like fall, she called Isobel. Having not spoken since the day she told Isobel about the Tawhid, Marah hesitantly tapped Isobel's name in her contacts and pushed the call button. Unsure if Isobel would answer, Marah startled when she heard Isobel's hello.

"Isobel? It's Marah."

"Hello, Marah. How are you? Is everything okay?"

"Yes. I guess."

"Did you learn something new?"

"No, I noticed how beautiful the mountains are in the fall light."

"Yes, my favorite time of year." Isobel waited, but Marah stayed quiet, "Is that what you called about?"

"I've never been hiking," she paused, hesitating to ask anything of Isobel, "I wondered if you would take me sometime. I've always been a runner, but I never really see anything when I run."

Isobel hesitated for a moment, a million thoughts running through her head at one time, but finally, "Yeah, sure, I'll take you."

"Would Saturday be okay?"

"Yes, that will work. I take off pretty early most days, but how about you be here by 7:30? I'll make us breakfast after."

"Isobel, thank you. Yes, that will be great. I'll see you then."

Saturday morning, Marah headed to Santa Fe by 6:15. Earlier in the week she told a colleague she was going hiking for the first time. She recommended Marah go to REI, they would help her pick everything she needed. She went after work one evening and bought hiking boots and asked someone what kind of clothing she would need to hike in Santa Fe. The sales associate had been wonderful, showing her different layers, and even found a hiking skirt for her that she could wear over pants or leggings. She also bought a small day pack, water bottle and hiking poles. Now driving towards the mountains, for the first time in a long time, she felt happy. She wanted desperately to hold on to this all day.

Marah pulled into Isobel's drive shortly before 7:30. She picked up her bag and backpack and carried them in with her. She hesitantly knocked at the door, as if Isobel wouldn't be expecting her, then made herself knock harder. As she stood there waiting, she noticed the trees with green and varying shades of yellow, and some were already beginning to lose leaves. She took a deep breath and smelled the pinon smoke from an early morning fire.

The door flew open and brought Marah's attention to Isobel, standing there in her hiking clothes. "Marah! Did you knock?"

"Yes."

"I didn't hear you. I happened to look out the kitchen window and saw you standing here."

"Oh, that's ok. I've just been admiring the trees and enjoying the smells. It's beautiful up here."

"Come in," and she stood back from the door to let Marah enter. "That's a big bag you have there."

"Well, I didn't really know what I needed, but the lady at REI went over the basics with me and so…" she held the bag up and pointed at it.

Isobel laughed, "They are my favorite hang out for sure. It's like a playground for adults."

"My first time, but I can see that. Raheem and I used to camp sometimes out at High Desert Sands and I would have loved to have some of that equipment. Ours was an old tent I bought off a colleague, and sleeping bags I got at the discount store."

"Alec and I went to Scotland when he graduated college and hiked all over. We had such a great time on that trip." They looked at each other and smiled.

"Oh dear, I'm sorry Isobel. I…I shouldn't talk about Raheem." Marah looked away embarrassed. Isobel took her hand and led her to the couch.

"Here, give me your bag. Sit down." Isobel laid the bag by the door and joined Marah. She took both Marah's hands in her own and fought back tears. Marah turned to look at Isobel. "It's not easy for me,

Marah, but I'm trying to understand that your Raheem is not the Raheem that killed my son. I don't want to be angry with you. I don't want you to bottle up your grief and then have to listen to me spill mine."

Marah's eyes filled with tears as she looked down at her hands clasped in Isobel's. Isobel hesitated only for a moment, then pulled Marah to her and let her cry it out. Her own tears slid silently down her face. When she finished, Isobel grabbed a tissue for each of them.

"Here you go."

"I don't deserve your kindness Isobel."

"That's not true."

"But I, I have had no one to talk to. I can't even mention Raheem at work. I…"

"Listen, you can call me. If I can't handle it, I'll let you know, but we both lost our sons, Marah. We have that in common. And yours got caught up in something that maybe he didn't intend and mine got caught in that too."

"You are very generous. You are," Marah choked out.

"Thanks, but I'm as desperate as you are to talk to someone who understands."

"Yes. Desperate."

They sat there for a few moments, each leaned back into the couch and looked out the window at the mountains in the distance. Marah reached for Isobel's hand and squeezed it. Isobel put her hand on top of Marah's. They sat in silence until Marah released Isobel's hand.

"Hey, we've got a mountain to climb," Isobel said. "Let me see what's in that bag and we'll get you set up."

They went through all the items Marah had bought, and Isobel assessed her clothing. The air had turned chillier this week and she wanted to be sure Marah was warm enough and she wanted to be sure she knew what to pack, even if for a short hike. Isobel showed Marah the whistle on the backpack strap and then packed her up with a full water bottle, the lightweight emergency blanket, matches in a plastic tube, and a bandana. "This is fine for our short hike, but I'll make a true hiker out of you yet." Isobel grabbed her own pack and they were on their way. They drove to the trailhead in Marah's car, Isobel pointing the way.

Once they hit the trail, Isobel took her time, waiting for Marah to catch her breath now and again. "I'm a runner so I thought this would be easy," she laughed.

"It will be. Your first time is the hardest even though you're in shape. Your muscles are having to work differently. You'll be fine."

And she was. They spent the hike quietly ensconced in their own thoughts, only occasionally talking. Isobel showed Marah how to properly use her hiking poles and she soon looked like a pro. When they got to the top of Picacho, Isobel took Marah to her favorite perch and they sat together looking out at the Pecos Wilderness. Isobel gave Marah a homemade power bar and they sat in silence for a moment. The air was cold this morning, even though the sun was shining.

"Isobel, this is amazing. I can't thank you enough for bringing me."

"No problem."

"I wasn't sure I should even ask you, but I was too scared to go on my own. I love running, but I mostly see the sidewalk and when I come home from work every day looking at the Sandias, I thought how nice it would be to hike."

"Yeah, I've always loved hiking. I think from my Girl Scout days."

"We never got to do anything like that, my sister and I. After school we went to Islamic studies, so there was no time."

"Is it just you and your sister?"

"Yes."

"Are you close?"

"We are, but she lives in London with her family." Marah took another bite of her power bar, "this is really good, by the way," she said with her mouth full and they both laughed.

"We better head back. I'm feeling the chill now."

"Me too."

They picked up their packs and headed towards the trail. Isobel felt a comfort she hadn't in a long time. No one can feel your pain, except someone who has experienced the same. At work she felt smothered by pity, and uncomfortable with how people tiptoed around her. Marah knew the pain of loss, and this soothed Isobel for the moment.

As they made their way back down the hillside, Isobel explained the importance of staying on the trail and how even the most experienced hiker can get turned around even when just a few yards off the trail. Though this set of trails would be easy to find the way out, once a hiker entered the mountain trails, getting lost became easy if you didn't know what you were doing, and didn't have a compass. "I'm sorry for the hiking lecture. I want you to be safe though if you go up to the Sandia's on your own."

Marah laughed, "Thanks, really I appreciate it."

Isobel pointed out the old water pipes and the nature conservancy that was once the reservoir for the city. When they reached the bottom, they returned to Marah's car and then to Isobel's house.

Isobel had made red chile sauce after work the day before, and for their breakfast she threw together Huevos Rancheros with beans on the side. "A breakfast well earned this morning," she said as she handed Marah her plate.

"I'm going to be feeling that mountain for a few days I'm afraid."

"Yes, but your runner legs will keep you from getting too sore."

"I hope you're right."

They sat side by side at the bar in the kitchen. The silences were no longer awkward and neither felt compelled to fill them.

"You are a really great cook, Isobel." Marah broke the silence as she ate her huevos.

"It's just huevos."

"I don't care. This is really good."

"Well, thanks. I've always enjoyed cooking, especially for friends and family. Not so much for myself."

They finished eating. Marah picked up both plates and took them to the sink where she rinsed them.

"Marah, I've been thinking about how hard this must be for you, not having anyone to talk to. I know you have family, but if you can't even talk to people in your community or at work, it must be very hard."

Marah still had her back to Isobel. She shook her head yes. She felt her throat constrict. She took a few deep breaths then turned to face Isobel. "When I knew Raheem was dead, that was the worst moment of my life. But when I started registering in my head what he had done, my head felt like it would explode." She took deep breath, "But I think the worst has been the isolation. Joe was the only one who spoke to me."

"A friend?"

"No. A work colleague mostly. No, I mean yes, he was my friend. He wanted more than a friendship though. I don't have male friends, but he got me through the worst. He helped when Mum and Pa came. He was wonderful."

"Sounds to me like you like this guy."

"I do. But he is Jewish. I am Muslim."

"Oh, Marah. After all we've been through? That still matters?"

Marah nodded her head yes and turned to look out the window above the sink.

"I'm sorry, Marah. I didn't mean to offend you."

"That's not it." She turned back around, "This happened to Raheem because of me. I didn't pay attention and I have not been a good Muslim woman. 'Whatever misfortune befalls you, it is because of what your own hands have done....' Raheem tried to tell me, but I didn't listen. Even being here is not good."

"Did you just quote the Qu'ran?"

311

"Yes."

"I'm not sure how you have been a bad Muslim, but I do get how these 'religious rules' get in our heads and make everything confusing. I'm way past that, Marah. I don't have a lot of tolerance for fundamentalism anymore. I grew up that way. But I'm not going to tell you what to believe, what not to believe."

"I should go."

"Are you sure?"

"Yes."

"Okay."

Isobel followed Marah to the front door where she helped her gather her hiking things and waited while she put on her shoes, then held the door open for her. A warm breeze hit them in the face as they stepped onto the front porch.

"Marah, I don't really get what happened right now, but if you want to hike again, let me know."

"Yes, of course. I will." Marah went down the stairs and tossed her items in the backseat, then as she stood at the driver's side, ready to slide into her seat, "Thank you again, Isobel. This was really nice. Thanks." And she dropped to her seat, pulled the door closed and backed out of the drive as quickly as possible. Isobel watched until she took a right on Canyon and was gone.

# Chapter 4

Marah's eyes blurred with tears as she turned up Canyon and headed towards I-40. She pulled into the church parking lot on the corner and found a tissue to wipe away the tears and blow her nose. 'Just get through this year, Marah, then you can retire and go live in Philly.' The tears continued and she felt the anger bubbling up and her tears turned to sobs. "Why, why, why, Raheem? Why?" She pounded the steering wheel as she screamed the words unaware of her surroundings and uncaring whether anyone saw her or not. When she finally calmed herself, she looked around, but saw no one there, just the sun glinting off the house across the street. She wiped her nose, took a drink of water from her bottle, and pulled back onto the road, climbing the hill to St. Johns, rounding the curve by the monastery, heading down Old Santa Fe trail towards her turnoff for the interstate.

Though the mornings were cooler now, the sun still heated the day to almost summer temperatures and turned the sky a glaring white hot. Marah berated herself in her head for her behavior towards Isobel. She traversed two worlds, her Muslim upbringing and beliefs, and the secular life she led at work. She felt frustration at the ambiguity of her life, now more than ever. Isobel's irritation with Marah hurt her and she hated that Isobel used the word fundamentalism, an extreme and unbending word. This is what becomes of someone who lives in two worlds, but after Zaqui left her and Raheem, her choices ended. She set the cruise control and concentrated on the road, blocking out the morning.

When Marah pulled into her drive, an overwhelming sense of tiredness rolled through her. She dragged herself into the house, and lay down on the sofa. The emotions, the anger, the loneliness, and sadness, these were what exhausted her. She stared at the ceiling for a long time. Tomorrow she would go to the masjid and worship. Tomorrow she would find herself again.

Isobel sat on the front porch, puzzled over Marah's actions. 'She called me and wanted to hike. What happened,' Isobel thought. Her mixed feelings for Marah added to the complexity of having a friendship with her. Yet something seemed right about it. She blamed their mutual grief on Zaqui, a man she didn't know. She could hardly even think his name, let alone say it out loud. She wondered what kind of man chose death for his son. And worse, death for hers. The anger hit her like a brick wall, causing her to emit the scream of a wild animal caught in a trap. "Damn him to hell," she screamed before she caught herself and darted into the house, letting the screen door slam behind her. She flung herself on the couch and lay there tightly clutching her hands together over her stomach, her eyes squeezed tight, until she took a deep breath. "Breathe, Iso. Just breathe." When she opened her eyes, she lay there, staring at the vigas, until she started counting them and knew she had to get up and find something to keep her busy and get through the day.

# Chapter 5

As the days of October shortened, the sun slipping behind the Jemez earlier and earlier each evening, Isobel left work as soon as possible, to hike in the last of the fading sun since she could no longer hike in the morning. She rushed into her bedroom, stripped her work clothes and pulled on hiking pants, two layers of shirts and a jacket. Sitting on the front porch bench, she quickly stuffed her feet into her hiking boots, then drove up the road to the trail head. She could make Picacho peak as the sun hovered to the south, over the Jemez, poised to set within the hour. Isobel couldn't pause longer than a moment to look across the darkening city nestled in the valley where one swath of light lit a path through its middle, the rest already in the shade of the mountains. To the south she saw the Sandias, a dark mass on the horizon. Occasionally, the ski mountain to the north, lit up in the red light that gave these mountains their name, Sangre de Cristos, made her realize she stood in that very light, just a speck on the mountain, no different than the scrubby Pinons which surrounded her. Then she would turn back down the trail, her headlamp at the ready when the light became too dim. Back in her car, the heat turned up, she headed home.

Isobel's dinners consisted of salads and soups. She ate, she cleaned up, she turned off the lights and went to her room. Once she showered and slipped into pajamas, she nestled into bed to read. She finished the Qu'ran and moved on to other books about Islam, trying to understand a religion full of hard and fast rules, growing so quickly. Is this what people want? To be told how to conduct their lives at all times? She thought about Marah and how she pulled away from friendship because Isobel was not Muslim. She found a verse in the Qu'ran which explained Marah's actions to her.

For Isobel, her childhood religion had always been about the rules, and now she saw the same thing in Islam. Around the age of twelve she started questioning her religion. She heard preachers say, "We follow the New Testament only, and the Old Testament is for reproof." Yet she heard many quote the verse from Proverbs, "Spare the rod, spoil the child," as a defense of spanking their children and this seemed such a contradiction, because in the New Testament in Ephesians, fathers were called to not provoke their children to anger, and anger was the only thing a child could feel on being spanked. She saw many contradictions. Jesus himself spoke of kindness, of treating all people fairly, of service and non-judgement. Yet, she found many religious people, strangely, to be the most judgmental. Currently reading a memoir by a female journalist who spent a year studying with a well respected Imam and teacher, she thought she might understand Islam. This woman's journey was helpful to Isobel in understanding Islam, but she still felt it to be a controlling ideology.

Marah's alarm woke her at 4:45. She gave herself plenty of time to wake-up so that she would not miss the Fajr prayer. She had been lax with her prayers over the last few years, but she now felt an urgency to pray, to feel the presence of Allah, and to know the angels of the night and the angels of the new morning were intently listening. She kicked back the covers and let the cold seep through her pajamas, she reached for the silk caftan beside her bed, and pulled it on over her pajamas, covering her from head to toe. At her mat, she waited for the call to prayer, a call that came from an app she downloaded to her phone. Once finished praying, she donned her running clothes and put on her shoes, and went for a thirty-minute run.

Colder weather set in, but she ran just the same. Then she showered and readied herself for work. She ate breakfast. She drank tea. She made herself a lunch. She gathered her things and left for work. She arrived at 6:45 and went straight to her office where she clicked on her computer and scanned the list of patients for that day. Then she pulled her lab coat on over her uniform and checked in with the clinic receptionist before seeing her first patient. As a gynecological NP, she saw only female patients. Mid-day she paused to eat her lunch at her desk, then finished seeing her remaining patients. After completing her paperwork, she packed up her things, took off her lab jacket, carefully placing it on the hanger behind her door. She shut and locked her office, walked to her car and went home.

She laid her messenger bag by the door, went to her room and changed into something comfortable, made herself some dinner, though often only cereal and milk. She might watch some television or read. Then she readied herself for bed, donned her caftan and said prayers again, after which, she collapsed into bed. Everyday the same. Marah stared at the ceiling. Only eight more months till she could retire. She scrawled the word ENDURE on a piece of paper and stuck it to her bathroom mirror. She said it out loud. "Endure, Marah." Then she turned out the light. Only eight more months.

Isobel opened the front door and set down her backpack, glad to escape the cold wind that battered her from the car to the door. In the kitchen she turned on the kettle, then changed into fleece pants and an oversized sweater. Evening hikes were over once daylight savings ended, making them slow and agonizingly long. She made a cup of tea and sat at the dining room table to look through the day's mail. Nothing but junk. She flipped on her laptop and checked her personal email, finding nothing but junk there too. *The Year of Magical Thinking* lay where she left it this morning, and she picked it up and read a few paragraphs. Richard gave it to her, a book Didion wrote following the death of her husband. Isobel found it engaging, and she understood the sentiment. She found her own magical thinking endless. She read a few pages, then warmed up some soup, taking her bowl and the last glass of the Barolo Sam had brought her this weekend, to the living room where she started a fire in the kiva fireplace, tucked into the corner of the room. She sat in her club chair watching the flames, feeding them when they began to die. She pulled her chair close, and felt the heat on her feet, propped on the adobe hearth.

Isobel's thoughts drifted to Ian and Delia. She pictured the end of their day, curled up on the couch with the kids enjoying a movie. She smiled at the image in her head. The sweetness of their marriage. Their love for their children. She'd dreamt of such happiness for her child, and she hoped they could outlast the tough years sure to arise as the kids demanded more time, their activities stretching them thin on time for each other. She and Jacob certainly had not survived those years.

Then Alec. She thought of him every day. She pictured him on the couch in her living room, his legs stretched out to the hearth, a Scotch in his hand, a book at his side, talking about work, or his students, or philosophy. Did she agree with him? What did she think about this? How would she help this student or that student? In turn, she would ask him questions, feeling she learned much from his perspective on life. They would sit up talking into the wee hours of the night, until she begged off to go to bed. He made up the couch and passed out there, tired from a long week at work, and the drive up to see her. Then they spent Saturday wandering the city, stopping in art galleries and cafes. Sometimes Sam joined them for dinner on Saturday evening, but they always ate out, giving Alec the chance for his Northern New Mexican food, so different than that available to him on the eastern side of the state. After lunch on Sunday, he headed back to Llano, where he made a loaf of bread, ready for his students on Monday. She smiled at the thought of his generosity.

Isobel sighed. She glanced at the clock. Eight. Too early to go to bed? Yes. One more hour. She picked up a stack of catalogs thrown in a stack by the door, ready for the trash. She mindlessly thumbed through them, pausing now and then at something she liked. But she didn't really need anything. She took the stack of catalogues back to their pile beside the door, and pulled a legal pad from her bag. 'I'll plan Thanksgiving,' she thought. Ian, Delia and the kids were coming as always, but she had invited Jacob and Nora as well, thinking maybe they would like to all be together this year, their first year without Alec. They said yes, as Nora's girls were planning Thanksgiving with their dad this year. Divorce. Complicated.

When Jacob and Isobel divorced, to make things easier, the boys decided on Thanksgiving with her, and Christmas with Jacob. When Jacob questioned their choice, asking if they wanted to rotate, Alec had explained, 'Umm, Dad, Mom can cook. Need I say more?' Isobel had laughed when Alec told her about it later. Thanksgiving, her favorite holiday, made having the boys with her even better.

Isobel scratched away at the pad, making lists of dishes, the usual favorites, and thinking she might try something new. She thought about who else to invite, but didn't really feel up to a full house this year. "Just us I think, but maybe Marah would like to come," she mumbled. She would have to talk to Ian about this. 'I think Ian would be fine, but maybe not so much Jacob. I don't want to make Marah uncomfortable. Damn. What am I thinking? I can't invite her. Besides, she is uncomfortable with our relationship. Okay. Going to bed now,' ending the stream of thought. Isobel laid aside the pad, stirred the flames down and went to her bedroom. But she couldn't stop thinking about Marah and how Isobel felt drawn to her.

Isobel crawled into bed and pulled the covers around her shoulders. She tried to read for awhile, but distracting thoughts kept interrupting her, and she lost track of her place in the book. She laid the book aside and turned off the light. The darkness cocooned her like a thick blanket, and as she lay there, she stared at a ceiling she could not see, took long deep breaths, then eventually slipped into sleep.

# Chapter 6

Thanksgiving holiday arrived. Ian and family pulled into her drive Wednesday afternoon. Bree came running up the stairs to Isobel as she stepped out onto the porch. "Granny," and she threw her arms around Isobel's legs, hugging her tightly. Brian followed closely behind, climbing the stairs like a ladder. He too threw his arms around her, overlapping Bree. Isobel reached down and lifted Brian into her arms.

"Hello, you two," as she ruffled Bree's hair, and opened the door for them all as Ian and Delia stepped onto the porch. Ian leaned in and hugged his mom with his free arm, Delia, hands full, air kissed her and they filed into the house. "I'm so happy to see you all!"

"Granny, where is my puzzles?"

Delia gently corrected her as she carried her bags to the table, "Where ARE my puzzles, PLEASE."

"Where are my puzzles, please?"

"In the closet sweetheart."

Bree turned to leave the room, but Delia stopped her, "What do you say?"

"Thank you, Granny," and she went running through the kitchen and down the hall to find her puzzles, her favorite thing to do at Granny's house.

"I'm trying to teach her to be polite," Delia said, "but she is always in such a hurry, she forgets."

Isobel laughed and cuddled her head against Brian. He was a hugger and still clung to her like a little monkey. "She's fine, but good for you," and she smiled warmly at Delia. Ian had taken their bags to the guest room and helped Bree bring her puzzles to the dining room table. Delia made herself comfortable on the couch, and Isobel stood at the picture window with Brian, pointing out the Jemez mountains in the distance and other sights visible from her house. He began to wiggle in her arms then he turned towards her and put his hands on each side of her face, and patted her, and then at the top of his lungs said, "Let me out of this love jail!"

Everyone started laughing, and Isobel let him slip to the floor so that he could join Bree at the table. "Oh my, I didn't know hugging could be a love jail. That boy, the things he says."

"Never a dull moment at our house, Mom," and Ian stepped up and gave her a bear hug. "Now you're in my love jail," and he lifted her off her feet for a moment. Isobel laughed as he set her back down. "Mom, you seem awfully thin," his face now serious. "Are you eating?"

"Yes. I'm fine," she assured him, "besides, it's Thanksgiving, I'll eat plenty this weekend. So tell me what's up? How are things in Lubbock?" She joined Delia on the couch and Ian sat in the Club chair.

"Um, that's called changing the subject," Delia said, and smiled at Isobel.

"Seriously, I'm fine. I've only lost a few pounds."

"Well, I'm going to make sure you do eat plenty this weekend," Ian said.

"Ok, ok," and she laughed them off, but knew she had lost too much weight. She just found eating by herself difficult these days. "When is your Dad getting to town?" she asked Ian.

"I don't think Nora was able to leave until noon. She had some sort of meeting to attend this morning."

"Where are they staying?" Isobel asked.

"Inn on the Alameda, I think. Is that right Delia?"

"Yeah, I talked to Nora last night. That's what she said."

"Well, that's good. Not too far away," Isobel replied.

"Mom, it was really nice of you to include them."

"Thanks. I thought maybe we should all be together. Ya know? It just seems right."

"Yeah, I thought so too. And it will be good for Dad. He's been really having a tough time lately."

Isobel felt the slightest bit of pain at the mention of Ian's concern for Jacob. The two of them had always been closer than she and Ian, but then Alec had been closer to her than to Jacob.

"Yes, yes, good for all of us I think." She stood up then and looked at her watch. "Who needs a snack?"

"Meeeeee!" cried Bree and then Brian followed her lead, "Me too!" Ian trailed Isobel to the kitchen and watched as she stacked cookies on a plate.

"Are those the Mombo Combo cookies?"

"Of course. I made them with you in mind."

Isobel had fashioned a chocolate chip, peanut butter, oat cookie for the boys when they were little, trying to give them something that was at least a little bit healthy, and they had become the family favorite. She had even continued to make them after the boys left home, sending them care packages when they went away to school. They had gone down in the family history as the Mombo Combo cookies. Though she rarely made them these days, she thought it was time to introduce the grandkids to their father's favorite.

"Hey, you guys don't get any of these," he yelled to the kids, "I'm eating all of them. They're my favorite."

"Daddy, you can't." Bree marched into the kitchen and stood between her father and Isobel, "I'll take that plate, Granny."

Isobel handed Bree the plate and she marched back into the dining room and put the plate between herself and Brian. "Here you go bubbah. I didn't let Daddy eat any of them." Brian grabbed a cookie from the plate and started to take a bite, but Bree stopped him by putting a hand on his arm, "What do you say, bubbah?"

"Thank you."

"Good boy."

Ian and Isobel dissolved into laughter and Isobel could only think how good it felt to laugh.

# Chapter 7

Thursday morning, Isobel woke at 5:00. She set out the homemade cinnamon rolls to rise, a family Thanksgiving tradition. Then she put together the tray of smoked salmon, cream cheese, capers, purple onions and lime slices for the bagels Jacob and Nora would bring at 9:00. Arranging the pies on the buffet she'd made earlier in the week, she thought of Alec saying, 'All nine kinds that Harold liked best,' a line from his favorite childhood book, *Harold and the Purple Crayon,* a line they shared anytime someone mentioned pie.

Next, Isobel finished two of many side dishes and made a timetable for when each dish should go in, and come out, of the oven. The roasted turkey, prepared Wednesday morning and removed from the bone, waited in the refrigerator for reheating. Lastly, she set the table for eight, then stood back to admire everything. 'Perfect,' she thought, as she started a pot of coffee before going to shower and dress.

Nora and Jacob arrived and everyone scrambled to toast bagels and pile them with cream cheese and salmon, then stood around the kitchen eating and drinking mimosas. When finished, Ian cleaned up the kitchen, and made Bloody Mary's for everyone. Afterwards, he took the kids out to the living room to watch a movie while he and his dad talked. Isobel, Nora, and Delia busied themselves with the meal, lightheartedly chatting about work and raging about the state of education.

Isobel invited Sam to join them when his brother canceled on him at the last minute due to his mother-in-law becoming ill. Sam arrived sometime after the Bloody Mary's were served and joined the milieu in the kitchen. Ian made him a drink, then Sam took over the proceedings in the kitchen, directing the show. Isobel stood back and smiled. She loved her dear friend, and though she felt bad for his brother's mother-in-law, she felt selfishly happy to have Sam here today. The chatter continued as Sam saw to the proceedings and within the hour the food lined the buffet ready to be served.

"I think everything's ready, even the bread." Isobel said.

"Mom, are you kidding? You never have the bread ready with dinner."

"Sam's a genius scheduler, what can I say?" and she shrugged her shoulders and winked at Sam.

"I say the blessing," Bree ran from the television, and stood amongst the adults, putting her hands in the air.

"Turn off the television first, please," Delia asked her. Bree ran back and pushed the off button on the remote then came to the center of the group again.

Isobel held a tray in front of her with eight shot glasses, six filled with Drambuie and two with apple juice. "Bree, let's have our toast first, okay?"

"But Alec's not here and he always says it."

"Well then, we will toast to him. How's that?"

"Okay, but Brian and me, we get juice."

"Yes. I have yours right here," and Isobel held the tray down to her so she could take a cup for herself and one for Brian. Then Isobel passed around the glasses. They started this tradition of a Scottish toast after Isobel and Jacob divorced. Alec would say a few verses of some sort then Isobel would thank everyone for coming and get teared up, then the collective "Cheers!" and after Ian said a blessing, dinner would begin. She thought about skipping it this year, but decided Alec would not want that. And so she began, "Here's to our Alec," she swallowed hard to keep her voice from breaking, "A true Scottish toast, 'his equal will never be among us again.'" She held up her glass and with tears in their eyes, everyone said, "Cheers."

Then Bree, who stood in front of Ian for the cheers, came back to the center of the circle. "Please hold hands." She looked at Delia for approval on saying please. "Bubbah, come hold my hand," and she extended her hand to her brother. He grasped hold and stood beside her in the center of the circle of adults "Bow your head," and she pushed his head forward. "Ok everyone," and she proceeded, "Dear brother God, thank you for our food. Thank you for our friends.

Thank you for taking care of Alec in heaven." There was a collective sigh from the adults as she said the words, then she hurried on, "Feed him lots of turkey. He likes it. And thank you for cookies. Amen."

Tears welled up in everyone's eyes. She looked around the circle and ran to Delia, "Did I say it wrong? Why is everyone crying?"

"No darling, you did everything just right."

Brian crawled up into his chair with the booster seat and looked at everyone expectantly.

"I think Brian is reminding us it's time to eat," Jacob said."There's enough for an army, Isobel."

"I know. I forgot to scale back, because, well, most years we almost do feed an army."

"Thanks again for having us," Nora said as she picked up her plate and waited for Jacob.

"Yes, Isobel, thank you. I'm glad to be here. Makes this easier somehow." He choked up and turned away from her. Nora patted his back and they turned to the buffet and started to fill their plates.

Isobel's eyes clouded with tears. She blinked and felt them roll down her cheeks. She reached for the tissue stuffed in her pocket for such a moment, and dabbed at her eyes. Sam put his arm around her. He leaned in and whispered, "You okay?"

Isobel turned to him and smiled, nodding her head yes. "Thanks. I am."

Sam and Isobel filled the wine glasses and water glasses. Then the room became almost quiet as everyone started to eat. Knives and forks clinked on plates. Glasses raised and lowered. Even Bree and

Brian hungrily ate their food, quiet for a moment. Isobel looked around the table and smiled, happy to be surrounded by family. Glad to have Jacob and Nora with them. Though she and Jacob saw each other once or twice a year since Bree and Brian had been born, they had not spent any real time together until Alec's death. The death of their marriage tore them apart, but the death of their son had brought them back together, for now, in a strange way.

"Isobel, everything is delicious," Nora said.

"Yes, you could always cook a great meal," Jacob said, but added, "Well, maybe not always."

Isobel laughed remembering their early years of marriage, "Yeah, but I made great chocolate chip cookies and a mean taco in those days."

"Yes you did."

"Umm, you still make a great chocolate chip cookie. Just saying," Ian added.

"And a mean taco, though I've upped my game on both," she replied.

The talk remained light hearted, but there was a pall that lingered in the air. In past years, Alec and Ian were like a comedy team, making everyone laugh, teasing Isobel, and teasing conversation from the many different people who joined them each year. Isobel always invited those who needed a family to call their own for the day because their's was too far away, or they had none. They would sit around her table and enjoy a Thanksgiving of plenty. She looked at everyone now, happy to have them all here, and tears welled up in her eyes. "Mom, remember..." Ian trailed off as he looked at her. He got up from his chair and came and hugged her close to him. "I know, I feel the same way," he said.

"Ok, I'm fine now. Really. I'm so happy we are all together, but I just started thinking, and well..." she trailed off and Ian hugged her one more time before sitting down again.

"Pie, Daddy, I want pie, pleeeaassse," Bree giggled.

"Me too," cried Brian.

"And me," chimed in Sam. They all laughed as Ian and Delia started clearing the dinner plates and Isobel cut the pies. She brought ice cream and whipped cream from the kitchen and served everyone up their choice. Before she could even sit down, Bree and Brian had finished and climbed down from the table. They ran to the living room and Bree found a puzzle for them to do together.

"Isobel, have you talked to that woman?" Jacob asked.

"Do you mean Marah?"

"Of course."

"Yes, she lives in Albuquerque now so we have seen each other."

"I still don't understand why you would talk to her. She raised that boy. And she married that man."

"Jacob, should we really talk about this now?"

"Yes. I feel you are betraying Alec by even speaking to her." He shook his fork at her and pie fell onto his plate. He stabbed at the pie and brought another bite to his mouth, this time he managed to eat it, before he said anything else.

"I actually thought about inviting her today, but she said she was going to Philadelphia to see her parents."

Jacob stared at her, "Invite her? Here?"

"The thought crossed my mind, but I didn't."

"Mom, Dad, come on. Let's not. Okay?"

"Ian's right, let's not argue, Jacob. We each have to deal with this in our own way. You have Nora. Ian has Delia. I have found that even though my friends are here for me," she looked at Sam and smiled, "no one can really understand what this feels like for a mother, except another mother who has gone through the same thing."

"My God, Isobel, join a support group," Jacob said.

"Jacob, look at us. Look at all of us. We have each other. We have the memories of our boys together, loving each other, laughing, caring for one another. We taught them well. We did that. You and me. We will always have that. Always. And we have friends and jobs where we have been able to keep on going. People feel sorry for us, even if they don't know what to say, but they don't revile us. Marah will never have any of that. She lost a son she discovered she didn't even know. She is denigrated at her work. She had to leave her job and move to a new place, and live every day in fear someone will discover who she is. I think she is being punished enough and if I can offer her the slightest comfort because I understand what she is going through over the loss of her son, then I will do that for her." Isobel threw down her napkin and took her plate to the kitchen. She stood at the sink for a moment, looking out at the mountains, and wondered where that had come from. She didn't even know she felt so strongly about Marah.

# Chapter 8

Marah left Albuquerque late afternoon, on Wednesday before Thanksgiving. She felt her spirits lift and her heart ease as the plane left the ground. She breathed deeply for the first time in months, and felt the stress release. Her father met her at the airport and took her home. When she walked into her childhood home, greeted by her mother, her arms wrapped tight around her, she burst into tears and cried on her Mum's shoulder.

"Marmar, here, here, it's ok daughter. You are home."

Her mother held her while she let out the deep sadness she daily lived with, and held her till her tears turned to sniffles.

"Mum, I'm sorry. I…"

"No, stop. You needed to cry. You are good now?"

"Yes, Mum. Yes." She glanced at her father who looked perplexed at her, unsure of how to help.

"You are okay then?" he asked.

"Yes. Thank you. I'm so happy to be home for a few days where I can just relax." She looked at her parents who were both starting to grin at her. They now stood side by side and Pa put his arm on Mum's shoulders, the two of them almost giggling. "What? What are you up to?"

"We have a surprise for you," Mum said. And as she spoke the words, her sister stepped out from the hall and ran to her. Marah burst into tears again as her sister grabbed her and rocked her back and forth.

"What are you doing here," Marah was finally able to ask.

"I needed to see you and hug you, of course. And besides, I miss Thanksgiving. I'm not letting you have all the fun by yourself this year."

"Thank you for coming. I am so happy," and she felt the tears flowing down her cheeks again.

"Then stop crying, you. Come on. Let's have tea." They wrapped their arms around each other's shoulders and went to the kitchen with Mum, while Pa took Marah's bag to her room, where he knew Marah and Suraiya would spend every night whispering till the late hours of night before sleeping through prayers and into the middle of morning.

The call to prayer woke Marah from her sleep. She meant to turn off the app, but forgot, so she got up and pulled on her caftan, joining her parents for prayer in her father's study. He looked at her puzzled as she walked in, then the three of them began prayers, her father in front of her and her mother. When they finished, her father said, "I didn't think I would see you this morning, daughter."

"I'm trying, Pa. I really am."

"Good. Allah is with you."

Marah hugged her parents and went back to bed, where she curled up around Suraiya and dozed back into sleep. They woke when the smell of Sheermal enticed them awake, their mother's tradition for any special occasion. They both pulled on leggings and tunics and held hands as they walked to the kitchen, as they had when they were little girls.

"Good morning, daughters."

"Morning, Mum," they said almost simultaneously, and they went to her and each kissed her cheeks. Marah went to the table, pulled out a chair, grabbed two of the Sheermal for herself, and took a bite. "Ahhhh, so delicious." They loved these little festive breads filled with candied fruit, and as children begged Mum to make them. But they had always been for special occasion only. "I love these. Thank you for making them."

"Certainly," Mum said.

"Me too, Mum. Yours are the best. I get them in London sometimes, but they always disappoint."

Mum placed tea on the table and she joined her girls, but kept jumping up to check on things she had in the oven or on the stovetop. "I'm so happy you are both here again, and for a happy occasion."

"We are too," Suraiya spoke for them both and smiled at Marah. "Especially since I can't get Marah to come visit me."

"Maybe this summer. My retirement papers go through in July."

"September then, after the holiday travelers are gone."

"Okay. September. I really would love to."

"Perfect. And maybe you'll decide to just stay," she winked at Marah.

"No, no. At least one of my children must be in the USA with me," Mum protested.

"Maybe I will come live with you, Mum."

"Yes, yes. You can do that. I will tell Pa."

"Mum, I'm kidding. But maybe I'll live in Philly. I miss the city."

"But maybe you will live here." Mum stood at the stove, stirring the cranberry sauce. Marah went to her and put her arms around her, kissing her on the cheek.

"Thanks, Mum. You're the best."

The three of them spent the rest of the morning preparing for their Thanksgiving meal, reminiscing about their childhood years. Pa came and went, tasting this or that. Mum sent him on his way each time, shooing him away with a towel, or handing him a little plate with a sample of something. Marah loved watching her parents together, the way they treated each other kindly, or teased each other. Pa had been a tough disciplinarian, but had always been kind to them. Tears threatened to spill over, as she watched her family now. She knew they all loved her and loved Raheem, yet they were so removed from what she was going through.

Mum made sure everything met her specifications, the table set with the best linen and china, each dish presented in a beautiful serving piece, then she sent Suraiya and Marah to dress for dinner. When their mother had come to the US as a young woman, she struggled to adapt to a new culture so different from her own. However, after she and Pa spent their first Thanksgiving with an Indian family who had lived in the US for several years, Dara couldn't wait to have her own dinner the next year. She soon came up with a mix of dishes from her adopted home, and included her own that her mother had made for special occasions. When Ramadan fell during the Thanksgiving holiday, their meal became the feast at the end of the fast that night, but in other years, they ate at 2:00. Marah had no tradition of her own because Zaqui wouldn't allow her to celebrate an infidel holiday, and after he left her, she and Raheem spent every Thanksgiving with Mum and Pa.

Marah and Suraiya dressed up, donning dresses and heels, as their mother insisted they all do every year. They both pulled their hair back in knotted buns, Marah at the nape of her neck, Suraiya in a topknot on her head. Each wore the pearl earrings and necklace Mum had given them when they turned sixteen. Mum always wore her most beautiful silk sari wrapped over a long sleeve slip and Pa wore his silk sherwani, an ankle length collarless jacket. When they came to the table, they stood behind their chairs and waited for Pa. He came to stand at the head of the table, Mum on his left, Suraiya on his right and Marah at the other end. Then he said the Du'a.

before I could get to my turnoff. If they made train travel affordable, maybe people would leave their cars at home, but the cost is ridiculous and if you don't book in advance, forget it. No one can afford those tickets, so people drive to London. That's when I want to move to the Cotswolds and live in a cottage." Suraiya, always the dramatic one, had them laughing at her waving arms and exaggerated faces.

"You in the country? Yeah, right!" Marah said laughing. She felt comfort in their stories, but ached for normalcy in her own life. Once the kitchen was spotless to Mum's specifications, Marah went and retrieved the book on Tawhid and took it to Pa in his study. She loved his room, with its book-lined shelves, big desk, little sofa and leather chairs. As a child, she often took a book off the shelf and curled up in a chair while Pa worked, grading papers or preparing lectures. She loved to be close to him. She always looked to him for guidance and he helped her tremendously after Zaqui left her, but this time she might be on her own.

"This is it," she said as she passed him the book. He took the book and opened the cover, thumbing through the pages and stopping to read comments Zaqui or Raheem made in the margins. Tears filled his eyes and his face contorted in rage.

"Zaqui has perverted our beliefs. He stole our Raheem from us. In the name of Allah, I would kill him."

"I've had those same feelings," Marah said.

"I will read this thoroughly, but I will tell you now, Marah, I don't know about speaking out on this.

I raised you to believe the Qur'an is the final word, but hadith's help us understand the prophet and give us instruction outside of the Qur'an. You would be bringing ridicule to yourself to condemn this."

"Does that really matter now? I am a pariah, Pa. I had to leave my job in Bellview and move to Albuquerque, where I have no friends and must stay away from colleagues at work for fear they will find me out. I just have to get through the rest of this year, then I could speak out about this. And this commentary can be used to radicalize young people, Pa. That's wrong."

"NO," and he emphasized his shout by banging his fist on the arm of his chair. "I'll read this. Then we will talk again," and he threw the book on his desk.

Marah was quiet. She looked at her hands in her lap. With tears in her eyes, Marah looked up at her father, "I can't let this happen to anyone else," then she stood and left the room. Marah had never defied her father. Shariq went to his desk and slumped in the chair, then picked up the book and started reading.

# Chapter 9

"Marah, come sit with me. Let's talk," Pa said, as he stepped into the kitchen, where Marah, Suraiya, and Mum sat having tea. Pa spent most of Friday going through the textbook, examining the message, and the points, Zaqui and Raheem made throughout.

"Okay, I'll be right in. Can I bring you tea?"

"Yes, that would be nice. Thank you."

Marah fixed a tray for him and gathered her courage to hear what he had to say. She sat his tray on the small table in the midst of the chairs and sofa and then sat down.

"Well, what do you think?"

"Marah, I'm glad you brought this for me to see. The hatred directed to Jews and Christians is disturbing, I agree with you on that. However, most of this book is simply teaching Tawhid. I can see though, young minds should not be reading this, especially if they have a teacher like Zaqui."

"Pa, this book is being used in Muslim schools. Right here. In the USA. The writer calls Jews apes and Christians swine, and pushes for killing these people. This text also makes women out as worthless, basically."

"Still, Marah, I don't know what you can do about this."

"Tell parents. They should know."

"I don't know how you would do this."

"Like I told you before, how much worse can my position be? All I have to do is make it to retirement, then I could send letters to schools and ask them to review this book."

"Well, daughter, I think you should wait and see. You still have time. Let's put it aside until then."

Marah sat on the sofa, head down, eyes tightly closed and pictured Raheem. He loved her. He had been a good boy. She missed him dreadfully. "I just want him back. I want him back. Here, now. I just want him back." She stood up and loudly said, "I. Want. Him. Back."

Shariq sat stone faced, staring out the window, the book grasped firmly in his hands. He dropped it on his desk, then left the room, grabbed his jacket and left the house to a snow softly falling in the late Saturday afternoon light.

Marah and Suraiya each returned home on Monday. Before she left Philly, she went to her father's study and picked up the book from his desk. It now sat ensconced on the windowsill in her spare bedroom, where she vowed it would remain until next summer. Another week passed, and she spent a weekend doing nothing. She would endure.

# Chapter 10

I sobel spent the rest of Thanksgiving day keeping the conversation neutral. If Jacob said anything about Marah, she quickly changed the subject, and soon, Nora, Ian, and Sam were all doing the same thing. They all joined the children in the living room, the food put away and the kitchen clean. Sam poured everyone an after dinner Tawny Port and they talked about football and the snow just starting to fall. Bree and Brian begged to play in the snow, but Delia thought better of it. "Let's wait till tomorrow and we'll build a snowman," she told them. And they did. Six inches fell in the night and more fell Friday afternoon as predicted. The snow lasted until Saturday afternoon when the New Mexico sun beat down and melted the snow, turning the many dirt roads into a slushy mess.

Jacob and Nora left mid-day on Saturday to return to Llano, and Ian and Delia planned to leave Sunday morning. Saturday evening, as they finished dinner, a car pulled into the drive. Isobel looked out to see a young woman and an older couple get out of their car and walk up the stairs to her door. She opened before they had time to knock.

"Hello," she greeted them.

"Isobel Allen?" the man asked.

"Yes, that's me."

"Hello, I'm Dustin Cable, my wife, Emma, and our daughter, Callie."

Isobel stood puzzled looking at them, then her hand rose to her mouth. "Oh my, God. Callie. You, you're the girl Alec saved." By then, Ian joined her, at the door, and he reached around Isobel and opening the door for them.

"Come in," he said and Isobel stepped back for them to enter.

"We hope you don't mind us coming by. We were in Santa Fe for Thanksgiving and remembered you lived here. I'm sorry we didn't call. We weren't sure we could come."

"That's ok. I'm glad you did. Have a seat," and all three sat on the couch together.

Callie then spoke up, "Ms. Allen, I wanted to tell you how sorry I am about the loss of your son. Mr. Davis was the best. He was my favorite teacher," she started to tear up and choked out, "He saved me."

Isobel felt tears pooling in her eyes. She looked at this family and her heart ached. Her Alec died and their daughter lived. For a moment she did not know what to say. Ian, too, had teared up and couldn't speak. Then Isobel choked back the tears and stood, walking over to Callie. Callie stood up and Isobel hugged her, hugged her tightly. Then she stepped back, held onto her arms and looked her in the eyes. "I am so glad you are alive, Callie" and she meant it. "Thank you for coming. I have wanted to meet you, and after the attack," she swallowed, "I called the hospital several times, but they wouldn't let me speak to you."

"Yes, they told me you called." Isobel stepped back now, and Callie looked down at the floor, "I am ashamed I didn't contact you before now, but I felt so guilty I lived. I couldn't. I just couldn't."

"Don't you feel guilty. Don't you dare. You are alive and I hope you will celebrate that every moment of your life."

Callie softly whimpered, then raised her face to Isobel again. "He was such a great person."

"I know sweetheart. I know," and they both wiped at their tears.

Ian stepped over to his Mom now and put his arm around her shoulders. "Callie, I'm so sorry, this is Ian, Alec's older brother," and she pointed at him. Then he stepped up to Callie and hugged her.

"I'm glad you're alive, too," Ian said.

Callie's parents then stood up, "We didn't mean to intrude," said Mrs. Cable.

"No, no, I'm so glad you came by. Would you like some dessert and coffee? We have plenty left."

"Oh, thank you, but we really must go. We are getting an early start tomorrow and hoping the roads stay clear all the way home."

"Well, then, thank you again for coming."

Mr. Cable then said, as he put his arm around his wife, "I know your son is in heaven for his actions, Ms. Allen."

Isobel replied, "Mr. Cable, thank you, I think his spirit lives on in all of us who knew him." She reached out to shake his hand, but he was stunned by what she said and didn't notice.

"You don't believe in heaven, in God?" Mr. Cable asked.

"Well, no. I don't. And neither did Alec."

"I'm sorry to hear that."

"It's ok, Mr. Cable. We each have our own beliefs."

"But God is the only way for Salvation. To not believe in God, means an afterlife in Hell."

"I grew up in a fundamentalist Christian home, Mr. Cable. I'm very aware of your beliefs and respect your right to them. I just don't see things that way anymore."

"What about Alec?"

"What about him? What do you mean?"

"Without God, there is no salvation. That's all."

"Thank you, Mr. Cable," Isobel said through a forced smile. "Two men killed my son because of their religious beliefs, I do not need you to condemn him to hell because of yours."

The room grew quiet. Callie looked down at the floor, Mrs. Cable clung to her husband's arm and stared in disbelief at Isobel. Ian and Delia stood to the side, Ian slightly shaking his head, his hand resting on his chin, half covering his mouth. Then Mr. Cable stepped around her, followed by his wife, and

Callie, but Callie paused and grabbed Isobel's hand and whispered, "I'm sorry," as she stepped by Isobel and followed her parents out the door.

# Chapter 11

When Isobel's alarm sounded Monday morning, she turned on the light and lay staring at the ceiling. The long weekend had been wonderful, but she felt exhausted. Tears inexplicably rolled down the side of her face and soaked into the pillow. She closed her eyes again. An hour later, she looked at the clock. 'No problem, I can still make work on time,' she thought. Her eyes wandered around her room, the closed blinds, the framed Strindberg print, her great grandfather's tobacco table, her clothes from yesterday thrown over the chair in the corner, and then her vision blurred as tears again formed and rolled out the corners of her eyes. 'Get up. Come on, get going.' When she again looked at the clock, another hour had passed.

Isobel felt as if her body weighed a thousand pounds. With great effort she sat up, slid to the side of the bed to slip on her house shoes, and pull on her robe. Shuffling to the bathroom, she opened the shade on one of her windows, and watched the snow, still coming down hard, calculating another six inches had fallen. Before she left the bathroom, she picked up her cellphone and turning it on noticed a text message from Jorge Martinez. "Looks like an extended holiday. Stay home. No need to come in. See you tomorrow." Administration was required to come into work, even on snow days, but Jorge didn't want his staff on the roads and usually gave them the option to stay in. Relief flooded her as she crawled back into bed. Later, she woke when her phone buzzed with a text message, but she didn't bother to look. She rolled over and pulled the covers up tight around her neck.

Isobel woke again and picked up the phone. "Hey, I saw school is closed. Lunch?" It was from Diane. She hadn't seen Diane since the night she told Isobel to move on. Isobel, stared at the screen, then noticed the time was 12:30. She quickly texted Diane, "I'm sorry, just saw this. I went back to sleep this morning. Another time?" Diane wrote back almost immediately. "Sure." Isobel tried not to read anything into the curt reply, but knew her relationship with Diane had drastically changed. She sighed, and forced herself from bed.

"Okay, I'm getting up now," she said out-loud to herself, and threw back the covers to make sure she didn't drift off to sleep again. Pulling her robe snuggly around herself, she tied the belt as she walked down the hall to the kitchen. She glanced out the kitchen window and noticed the snow had stopped. Maybe another two inches fell while she slept. The sun might still show and melt most of the snow, then tomorrow there would be a delayed schedule avoiding buses being out on morning icy roads. By Wednesday, all would be gone. That's how snow came and went in Santa Fe. The beauty of sunny days, even in the winter. She made an espresso and went to her chair in the living room, where she cuddled up under a blanket and sat staring out the window at the beautiful scene.

An hour later, Isobel found herself still sitting in the chair, still staring out the window. She took her cup back to the kitchen and found the novel she was reading, from her bedside table. Bringing the book back to her chair, she opened to her marked place and looked at the page. Reading the first paragraph of the chapter, her eyes went to the next line, then she realized she couldn't remember what she read. She tried again, but replaced the bookmark and closed the book after a couple of minutes. 'Maybe later,' she thought.

Isobel sent most of the leftovers, from the weekend, home with Delia and Ian, but kept a bit for herself. She felt she should eat something, and shuffled into the kitchen. She opened the refrigerator and pulled out the Shoepeg Corn casserole and leftover mushroom stuffing and heated up a small serving of each. Again, she returned to her chair, and after a few bites, found herself mindlessly pushing the food around on her plate. She laid the plate on the floor and moved to the couch where she laid down and fell asleep. Dusk darkened the room by the time she woke, making her thankful the day came to an end. She carried her plate to the sink and dumped out the cold leftovers.

She warmed up some broth and stood at the sink sipping from the bowl. She forced herself to drink it all. Then she made a cup of hot chocolate, poured in two shots of whiskey and went back to her chair and stared into the deepening darkness.

Isobel replayed the weekend in her head. Bree and Brian made her smile, and even laugh, with their antics, a much needed reprieve from the black hole of sadness she felt. She enjoyed seeing Nora and Jacob, and once they put the topic of Marah to bed, the rest of the day had gone well. The visit by Callie and her parents though, left her with mixed feelings. She wanted people to just say, "Sorry for your loss." That's it. But time after time, people told her how to grieve based on their own beliefs. 'None of us can presume to understand the feelings of another,' she thought. Had that not been one of the major complaints she had had with Jacob when she was married to him? If she said, 'I feel like…' he would tell her she was wrong and she didn't feel that way. Crazy making. And now she felt like that again.

The cold in the house crept around her feet. She picked up her empty cup, wrapped the blanket around her shoulders and headed to her bedroom, dropping the cup off in the sink with the dirty dishes from lunch. She shuffled down the hall, dropped the blanket at the foot of the bed, climbed in and turned off the light. When she woke, the clock said two a.m. She had not brushed her teeth or even bothered to go to the bathroom, and now felt the urgency of both. Dreadfully cold in the house, she pulled back the blind on the door to her bedroom porch and saw the world lit up with the light of the moon reflecting off the snow covered landscape. Not a cloud in the sky, which meant the temperature probably dropped into the single digits. She kept the thermostat low at night, but she knew long before daylight, the heat would kick on because of this cold. Without turning on the light, she went to the bathroom, brushed her teeth and then peed, before hurrying back to bed and pulling up the covers tight around her shoulders. 'I will feel better in the morning. I will,' and then she dozed back into a dreamless sleep.

Daylight began to seep in around the blinds, Isobel woke with a start. She'd forgotten to set her alarm and looked at the clock now to see she slept till seven. Her phone lay on the bedside table, and she saw the message from Jorge, 'Two hour delay; see you at nine.' She sunk back into bed and meant only to stay a few minutes, but drifted back to sleep for almost two hours. Realizing the late hour, she messaged Jorge, 'I'm sick. Won't be in today.' He wrote back, 'Take it easy then. No problem.' She promptly fell asleep. Finally waking, with a repeat of the previous day. Before bed that night, Isobel messaged Jorge, "I'm still not feeling well. I'll see you on Thursday."

Isobel called in sick the entire week. Friday afternoon, catching a whiff of her own body odor, she realized her pajamas were the same she donned Sunday night for bed. Her uncombed hair and unbrushed teeth felt terrible. Isobel forced herself off the couch where she still lay at four, and went to her bathroom and stripped. The mirror spoke the truth: hollows in her face, pale skin and too thin. Isobel stepped into the shower and turned the hot water on full force, allowing the water to pour down her face and aching body. Finished, she towel dried her hair, dried herself off, and lay on the bed. The covers pulled up tightly around her naked body, she shivered against the coolness of the sheets, until warmed up, then Isobel drifted off to sleep again.

Startled awake, Isobel sat up in bed. Looking out her window, the looming night, held an eerie glow that confused her until she heard the pounding on the front door that fully woke her. She grabbed her robe from the end of the bed and went to the living room, turning on lights as she walked through the house. At the front door, she flipped on the porch light and saw Sam standing there with a grocery bag and wine bottle. She opened the door and Sam blew inside, followed by the cold wind. "My God, Isobel, I have been worried about you. I've tried to call you several times this week." He kissed her on the cheek as he breezed by her to the kitchen and she followed, flipping on the kitchen light for him as he sat his load on the counter.

"Sorry, I was asleep."

"All week?"

"I meant to call you."

"Ian's been calling too, and you haven't returned his calls either, so he called me this afternoon."

"I'm sorry."

"I called your office today and they said you hadn't been in all week." He stared at her now, seeing her disheveled hair and her food stained robe, he asked, "What's up, Isobel?"

"I don't know. I haven't been able to get out of bed. I think seeing Callie, the girl Alec protected, triggered something in me."

"Why didn't you call me?"

"I don't want to bother anyone."

"Isobel, you're never a bother, my friend."

She gave him a half-hearted smile. "Thanks, Sam. I'm ok."

"You're not okay, or you wouldn't be in your dirty bathrobe, with your hair sticking out all over, at seven o'clock at night."

Isobel looked down at her robe. Dry food of some kind stuck to the front and a wine stain streaked where she wiped her glass against her robe one evening. "Oh," she said, looking back up at Sam.

"I brought food. I'm cooking, you get dressed." She turned and started down the hall, "and call Ian while you're back there. Let him know you're alive. He is worried."

"Okay."

Isobel went to her room and closed the door. She sat on the side of her bed, picked up her phone and dialed Ian.

"Mom!" The relief in his voice was evident.

"I'm sorry I haven't called you back." Her voice trembled as she spoke.

"Mom, what's going on? You don't sound so good."

"I don't know," and the tears started again. "I just keep crying and sleeping. I haven't been to work all week." Saying that out-loud startled her. "I couldn't get out of bed." Then her tears became harder and he could hear her weeping.

"Mom? You okay?"

"Yes, sorry," she said through her sniffles.

"No need to apologize. I've been there too. Have you thought about seeing a counselor?"

"No."

"I had to find one. It's helped a lot to just be able to talk about Alec with someone. He's a grief counselor. I kept losing my temper with Delia and the kids, so she suggested it."

"Good for you, Ian. And Delia."

"Yeah, but Mom, I think you need to do the same thing. You're not as tough as you think you are."

She pulled a tissue from the box and wiped her eyes and nose. "Ok. Maybe."

"No maybe. Don't make me come up there," he said in a mock authoritative voice, a phrase she used on Ian and Alec when she heard them fighting in their room. She smiled and almost laughed.

"Alright. I'll see if I can find someone."

"What are you doing tonight?"

"Well, I would have been sleeping some more, I guess, but Sam is here. He got really worried after you called him and came by."

"That's good. I'm glad he's there."

"He's making me some dinner. I don't think I've eaten much this week."

"Then go eat."

The tears began to well up in her eyes again, "I love you, Ian."

"I love you too, Mom. Please take care of yourself. For me. For the kids."

"Ok. Ok. I will."

"Enjoy your dinner. I'll call you tomorrow and you better answer or I'm getting in the car and coming up there."

"I will." And they hung up. Isobel pulled on sweats and a sweater, then went back to the kitchen, the smell of sauteing onions and garlic, luring her back. Sam stood at the stove, stirring, and she came up behind him, placing her arm around him and leaning into his shoulder, watching his hand and the spoon methodically stirring the mixture. Always a good friend, he turned out to understand more closely than anyone else in her group, how she felt. Though he hadn't physically lost a child, he lost his children through what a research psychologist termed as divorce poisoning.

"This too shall pass, my friend," he said to her. "Depression is a mean companion, but I know you, and you will get through this." He continued to stir as he heard her sniffle. "Don't think I'm discounting what you're going through, it's real and it's painful, and overwhelming. But it is part of the grieving process for sure."

"Thanks. And thanks for coming tonight."

"You bet."

She stepped away from him as he added more chopped vegetables to the mix in the pan and picked up the glass of wine he had poured for her. "I don't know what to do, Sam. I feel like a lead weight is crushing me all the time and I just want to sleep so I don't have to feel this pain." The tears started again. "And I hate that I can't stop crying," she said, and wiped her eyes with her sweatshirt covered arm.

Sam covered the pan and picked up his wine glass, joining her at the kitchen bar. He took her hand and looked her in the eyes, "I can't tell you how long this will last, Isobel, but I can tell you the pain will ease and fade. The pain of losing Alec will never go away, but it will become a dull ache instead of a crushing one. It will."

She couldn't speak, but nodded her head in understanding. He hugged her to his chest, and holding her tightly there for a few moments. When she pulled away he said, "Have you thought about counseling?"

"Ian just asked me the same thing. He said he started seeing someone."

"That's good. What about you? I know someone who works specifically with people in grief. I'll look up her number and text you."

"Yeah, okay. Thanks."

Sam went back to the stove to finish dinner. He told her of the happenings in the world this week while she cloistered in her grief. Isobel listened, clinging to his discourse like a life raft sent to save her from roiling seas. When he finished with the curry and fluffed the rice, he set a hearty bowl in front of her. They sat side by side, looking out the window at the lights of the city. They talked about Thanksgiving and she told him about her visitors. "I think that's what precipitated this funk I've been in all week. Her father's comment really got to me and even seeing her alive hit me hard. I'm glad she lived. So glad, but it ripped me apart feeling jealous that Alec wasn't the one who lived. I felt terrible even having a thought like that."

"I think that's probably pretty normal. Of course you wanted Alec to live."

"I guess her being here made me realize he's not coming back. This is permanent. And I knew that, but seeing her made it real beyond what I imagined. I have never felt such despair." Tears rolled down her cheeks. She sat staring out into the night.

Sam picked up her hand and squeezed it. He knew nothing he could say made her pain better. He let her hand slip from his grasp and gathered up their dishes. He cleaned the kitchen, including the items she left in the sink over the week. In the living room he picked up the dishes scattered there, several coffee cups and a plate with dried food of some kind, and when finished, he poured them each a whiskey. "Come on, let's move to the living room," and she dutifully stood up and followed. Snow started to fall as they sat down, and they watched the flakes, small and sparse, turn thick and heavy. They talked some, but mostly just watched the snow. When they finished and Sam put their glasses in the dishwasher, he took her hand and pulled her off the couch.

"Go to bed now. I'll come by tomorrow. Let's say, 9:30, and we'll walk down to the coffee house."

"Okay. Sounds good."

"I'm coming no matter what."

"Gotcha," and she half-heartedly smiled at him.

"Good night, then." He kissed her on the forehead and hugged her. She closed the door and went to bed.

True to his word, Sam showed up Saturday morning and again on Sunday. Isobel knew he wanted to be sure she didn't stay in bed all day. He respected she had to work through this at her own pace. Monday morning he checked she went to work. Each day a struggle, but she knew she had to keep going. She called the counselor Sam suggested and made an appointment. Madge Renfro saw clients only two days a week, but because Sam recommended her, Madge fit her into her tight schedule.

Isobel felt relief after Madge explained the ins and outs of grief. "Just when you thought you should be feeling better, depression hit you. Don't let anyone talk you out of this. Use this time to reflect on your life and your time with Alec. This is all part of the process, Isobel. And coming to see me gives you an uninvolved person to talk to with no judgement or expectations." She suggested *Resilient Grieving* by Lucy Hone and Isobel ordered it as soon as she left the office.

Isobel followed Madge's advice to write her feelings in her journal, something Isobel generally did, but she had slacked off the last few months. She realized how much she missed her morning ritual of reading and writing, and made herself rise early the next day, and opened her journal, her purple pen gliding across the page. She let the words come and didn't stop for two pages. Grief poured from her, as did the tears, but she felt a release as she finished.

Isobel marked each day leading up to winter holiday off her calendar. Ian, Delia and the children expected her for the vacation. Seeing Madge helped lift the black fog clouding her mind all those weeks and helped her see she didn't need feel guilty closing her door to her colleagues. She needed the space and she took it. The Thursday before Christmas finally arrived and as soon as she left the office at noon, she hurried home, changed her clothes, loaded the car with her things and headed to Lubbock. She would shop there over the coming weekend for presents, something she had not felt up to before. Now she felt the excitement of the holiday and being with family would give her the peace she needed to think about what to buy. Smiling for the first time in what seemed like a long time, she pulled out of her drive and headed for Texas.

# Chapter 12

Marah plodded through the days following Thanksgiving, her colleagues and patients gearing up for their Christmas holiday. Though she did not celebrate Christmas, she looked forward to a time off work. The holiday fell on Tuesday, giving her almost a week and a half off and she planned to find a good book to read. She also thought a hike would be nice if the weather allowed. She attempted one hike on her own since her day with Isobel, and looked forward to trying another. Maybe she would drive to Santa Fe, she thought.

Two days before holiday, Marah had a young patient who kept staring at her throughout the exam. Marah attempted to get the young woman to communicate with her, but she sat stoney faced with her arms crossed. As Marah finished the exam, she noticed the expression on the young woman's face turn to an ugly scowl. "Are you a Muslim?" the girl asked.

"I'm not sure why that matters, but yes, I am."

"I thought so." She sat up quickly from the examining table and wrapped the paper cover around herself, sliding off the table as she did. "You're that kid's mother. I saw you. On the news. I was a student at Llano." Her face become contorted with rage as she spat her words at Marah. "Get out of here. I don't want you touching me ever again."

"Please calm down," Marah said, "I need to go over a few things with you."

The young woman then began screaming, "Get out! Get away from me!"

Marah's assistant ran into the room. "Calm her down, please. I'm going to see the Colonel." Marah headed down the corridor to Colonel Powell's office. Walking into her office as Marah approached, she asked the Colonel, "Can I speak with you a moment?"

"You've got five, that's it. I'm out of here at noon."

Marah followed her in and closed the door. "I just completed an exam on a young woman who recognized me. She became hysterical. Sergeant Mueller is in with her now trying to calm her down." She went on to explain what had happened. The Colonel nodded her head, but Marah felt like she had already left on her vacation.

"Alright Marah. We'll talk about this after the holidays. There's nothing to worry about."

"But this is precisely why I had to transfer here. My patients quit seeing me." On the verge of tears now, Marah felt she might become hysterical as her patient had only a moment ago. "Did you hear her screaming?"

"I wondered what that was about. No need to worry. We'll talk about this after New Years. I'll be back on the third. Is that all?"

"Yes, Ma'am," she managed to say before she left her office and walked down the hall to her own. She shut the door and stood there staring off out the window, her arms wrapped around herself. A tap on her door, brought her back to herself. "Yes?" she called out.

"Marah, can I come in?" her assistant softly asked as she opened the door a crack.

Marah turned around to face Sergeant Louise Mueller. "Louise, I'm sorry I had to ask you to calm her down, but she wouldn't listen to me."

"Is it true? What she said? Are you that boy's mother?"

"I am."

"Oh." They stood there for a moment. Neither knowing what to say. Then Marah pointed to the chairs in front of her desk, and they both sat down.

"Louise, I transferred here because my patients at Bellview quit coming to see me. I'm sorry I couldn't tell you anything, but I want to finish out my last year and retire. The general at Bellview gave me that chance by coming here. The only ones who know here, or at least knew, were Colonel Powell and General Black. Now, well..." Marah trailed off as she felt her face flush. "That boy was not the son I knew."

"Marah, I don't know what to say. This is...weird," Louise said. "At least now I understand why you keep to yourself so much. I thought you didn't want anything to do with us because you're Muslim, but it's your son?"

Marah could only nod.

"Wow."

Marah composed herself and asked, "Did you manage to calm Mrs. Gamble?"

"Yeah, she's a nutcase. I'd say she's pretty racist too. I'm sorry, but I'm afraid it won't be long till at least all the enlisted personnel know your story. She's got a big mouth."

"Yes. Then I'll have no patients and I'll be in the same situation."

"Marah, my God, I haven't even said how sorry I am. I mean, this is weird, ya know, but…" she paused for a moment, "but you had a son. How have you coped with all this? I mean, I can't believe you've gone through all this. You are like the nicest person."

"Thank you, Louise." Marah sat there for a moment, thinking of all the implications this might mean for her. She knew there would not be another transfer. She knew there would be questions from her colleagues and maybe even patients. She suddenly felt a sense of relief pass through her. She looked at Louise, "I think I'm glad this happened. I have hated having this secret hanging over my head. I can't even talk about my son, my life, my family, because everything is tied up together. At least now, I don't have to pretend any longer."

Louise looked at her watch, "Do you want to go to lunch? We still have enough time to grab something."

Marah started to say no, but caught herself and said, "Sure. Why not?"

At the commissary, they both selected something from the prepackaged section, made their purchases then headed back to Louise's car where they sat with the heater running and ate their lunch. Marah told Louise about Raheem, what a sweet boy she raised, and how in the end he changed, yet she barely recognized the differences until too late. Raheem received many calls from his father, but he always left the room and closed his bedroom door. She thought he didn't want to upset her by talking to Zaqui in front of her. Secrets had been their undoing. Secrets stole him from her. And now, secrets kept her from living her life.

"I go back and forth between missing him and actually despising him, which makes me feel like a terrible mother. A terrible person."

"Marah, you are one of the nicest people I know. I have watched how you care for our patients. You are always kind. You have every right to feel the way you feel."

Marah glanced at the time, "We better get back in there."

Patients had started to come in and were being directed to the waiting room after signing in. The receptionist motioned to Louise to come to her desk, as Marah went to her office. She put on her lab coat and took a seat at her desk to peruse the afternoon line up. Scheduled to be finished by three a short afternoon lay ahead of her. Louise tapped on her door and stuck her head in.

"Marah, Anne says two of your patients have canceled." She stepped into Marah's office and closed the door. "She said they requested to be rescheduled with someone else. Small-minded idiots."

"I knew this was coming." Marah frowned. "Let's not worry. I'll go see if I have anyone left. If not, I'm going home. I don't care today. I've had enough."

"Good idea. I knew that bitch would be on the phone the minute she left here."

"Louise, refrain from that word, please."

"Oh, sure. I just really find intolerant people... quite... intolerable."

Marah smiled at Louise, young and impulsive, but kind to stand up for her. "Thanks for standing up for me."

"Of course. You're welcome."

"I may take tomorrow off under the circumstances. Seems pointless to come in to no patients and the Colonel left at noon today."

"Do that. You should."

"What are you doing for the holidays?"

"Going to go see my parents in California. Can't wait!"

"Good for you," and Marah came from behind her desk and went to Louise. "Thank you again for being so kind."

"Sure thing."

"I hope you enjoy Christmas."

"You too. Wait, you don't celebrate, do you?"

"No, but I'm going to enjoy the days off." Marah leaned in and gave Louise a hug. "Have fun. I'll see you in the new year."

"Thanks! You too!"

They could hear Major Doerr calling for Louise. "Better run," Marah said, as she opened the door for Louise. "Bye then." Louise slipped out into the hall and was gone. Marah went to her desk and called the receptionist.

"Do I have anyone left on the books this afternoon?"

"Just one at three."

"Would you call her and reschedule her, please? I'm going home."

"You're leaving?"

"Yes. And I won't be in tomorrow either." With that, Marah hung up, took off her lab coat, picked up her purse and bag and left for home. There was nothing left for her here. At least not today. And she doubted there would be in the future. The snow had begun to fall when she stepped out of the building. Perfect, she thought. Fire, book, and hot chocolate coming up. And she headed for home feeling lighter than she had in months.

# Chapter 13

M arah woke to the call for prayer and looked outside to see a winter wonderland. The deepest snow the city had received in decades covered everything. The city had come to a standstill, closing the all but essential services at the base. Leaving behind a night of tossing and turning, thinking about that woman's response to her, she had felt guilty for saying she wouldn't be coming into work today, but now she could let that part go. After prayer, she made a pot of tea, curled up on the couch and turned on the television. Mindlessly, she watched the morning news show and sipped her tea. As the sky began to lighten outside, Marah pulled a blanket over herself and drifted off to sleep.

"Marah Jabrayah Dalal, mother of Raheem Zaqui Fatah and wife of Zaqui Muhammad Fatah who committed the April terrorist attack…"

Marah opened her eyes and looked at the television screen to see a picture of herself alongside that of Raheem and Zaqui.

"...on the campus of Llano University earlier this year, is now living in Albuquerque. We have learned she received a transfer from Bellview to Kirtland Air Force base in July. She is a nurse practitioner and has been working at the women's clinic on base. She has maintained her innocence in the wake of the shootings, claiming she knew nothing about her son and husband's actions. The FBI has cleared her of any involvement. The Air Force has cleared her of suspicion as well. A patient reported being surprised yesterday when she realized she was being examined by the mother of the murderer and felt she should have been informed of Ms. Dalal's connection to the terrorists. The woman, who has asked to remain anonymous, was a student at Llano at the time of the attack and felt traumatized by the visit to the clinic."

Marah stared at the television. She watched as her picture filled the screen, as the newscaster read her script, and only disappeared when she moved onto the next story. She picked up the remote and turned off the television. 'What next?' she thought.

She didn't know how long she sat there, what time the piece had run, or rather it ran again in the next hour of news, but the time was nine o'clock now. She retrieved her phone and turned it on. When the screen came up, she found several messages waiting for her. Apparently everyone in New Mexico, and even west Texas knew where to find her now. A message from Joe asked, 'Are you okay? Need me to come up?' another from a colleague at the clinic, 'Why didn't you tell us?' and one from Isobel, 'You've been outed. I know you must be upset. Call me.' Then she scanned the voice messages where she found one from the base, she tapped and listened, "This is General Black's office. He would like to speak with you ASAP. Please call me at…." and Marah jotted down the phone number on a napkin.

"Raheem," she said out-loud to no one but herself. She dropped the phone on the cabinet and went down the hall to her room. She sat on the edge of the bed and dropped her head into her hands, her elbows propped up on her knees. Waves of anger and then despair passed through her. Her life had been getting back on track and retirement in six months seemed like a good thing. The relief she felt yesterday, washed away in the embarrassment and anger she felt this morning. She fell to her knees beside the bed, "'You who believe, seek help through steadfastness and prayer, for God is with the steadfast.' Oh God, I am steadfast. I will pray every prayer. I just want my life back." She could hear Pa in her head, telling her she has the life Allah has given her and she must endure. "Why? Why? Why?" she said aloud to no one. When her tears subsided, she knew what she had to do. She knew the time had come. She would not wait till after retirement. She went to find her phone in the kitchen.

# Chapter 14

Isobel's phone buzzed as she helped Delia finish the breakfast dishes. She pulled the phone from her hip pocket and looked to see the caller's name. Marah. "I'm going to go take this in the bedroom," she said as she hit the answer button. "Hello Marah," Delia nodded at Isobel as she stole away to her room. "We saw the news this morning. Lubbock picked up the story, but we never saw anything on the national news front."

"Well, give them time," Marah sadly said.

"Yes. I know." Isobel paused for a moment, "Are you okay? I've been worried about you this morning."

"I've cried, I've yelled, I've prayed, I've worn myself out, and I tell you, I am sick of this. Yesterday, I was completing an exam on a young woman when she got this terrible look on her face and asked if I was a Muslim. When I said yes, she came unglued and said she knew who I was. She started screaming and my assistant had to calm her down. I felt humiliated, but then I had this wonderful moment of freedom, like if the secret were known, my life would go back to normal," she paused. "But obviously, that's not going to happen. I don't' even know why I would think such a thing."

"Because we all want normal back, Marah."

"I'm sorry. That sounded so selfish."

"No, you're fine. But what now?"

"I'm ready to talk. I'm taking my story to the news and I'm going to tell them about this book."

"Oh, Marah. That's good. You are doing the right thing. A good thing. I'm sure of it."

"Thanks. I hoped you would think so, but..." she grew silent. Isobel could hear her breathing deeply, then... "would you go with me?"

"Me? Why?"

"You have the other key, I think. You know kids. You know what parents should be doing."

"Thanks for the confidence, Marah, but I'm not sure."

"I was hoping we could get together this weekend, but with all this snow," Isobel cut her off.

"I'm in Lubbock until the twenty-seventh. I'll be back then. At least if there isn't another storm."

"Okay."

"I'll be in touch and you can always email or text me."

"Yeah, that's good."

"Do you have plans for Christmas?"

"No. I don't, I mean, we don't celebrate the holiday, so I'm just going to try and read. Watch some movies maybe. Run if I can get to the gym on base."

"Run. Do that. Good for us to stay active my therapist says."

"You're seeing someone?"

"I had to," Isobel confided. "I had to admit, I needed help because after Thanksgiving I got so depressed I couldn't function. I'm doing much better now. Just a few sessions with her, as well as the book she recommended, have helped tremendously."

"That's good," Marah, said hesitantly. "Really good, Isobel."

"She's helping me a lot. I mean, I feel better everyday. What about you? Have you thought about counseling?"

"No, no, I don't think I could" she said softly. "I should let you get back to your family. You'll call me when you're home?"

"I will," Isobel assured her, "and we'll get together. I'll come down there if you'd like."

"Okay. Thanks. I'll look forward to seeing you. Merry Christmas."

"Thanks, Marah. Enjoy your time off. And think about seeing someone. Okay?"

"Thanks, Isobel. I will. Bye now."

Marah stood at the kitchen sink looking out at the falling snow. She went to the back door and slipped on her boots, then stepped outside. She pulled her sweater tightly around her as she stepped into the yard, turning her face up, the flakes of snow felt like feathers tickling her skin. She let the cold air seep into her warm body, and the snow leave a coating on her skin and clothes, until she started to shiver. She stomped the snow off her boots and stepped back into the warm kitchen, her hair and face wet from the melting snow. She removed her sweater and hung it from the peg behind the door, then went through the house to her room where she toweled off her face and combed her hair. She dressed in leggings and a warm tunic, then went to call the General.

# Chapter 15

Isobel left Lubbock in a harsh northern wind. Arriving home, she walked into her cold house, hands full of grocery bags and her suitcase. She turned up the heat and thought she would make a fire as soon as she unpacked the groceries and her suitcase. The pre-Christmas snow, which she had missed, ushered in a bitter cold front plunging temperatures into the teens, and left snow in the yards and on the hillsides unmelted. Laying the grocery bags on the counter, she then rolled her suitcase to the bedroom to unpack. Ian, Delia and the children bought her a beautiful cashmere sweater for Christmas that she now laid on the bed and smoothed out. She donned flannel lined jeans, pulled on a thermal t-shirt and the deep v-neck, oversized sweater in her favorite color, blue. She walked into the bathroom and admired how the color of the sweater made her blue eyes seem brighter.

Then she bit her lip, and frowned. For a second, she forgot Alec's death. Her face flushed and a rush of guilt washed over her for a thought so frivolous. Moving on with life felt undoable at times, yet her therapist kept pointing out the necessity. She shook her head to dispel the thought and went to the kitchen to make herself some lunch.

Isobel sent Marah a text later that day. 'I'm home. When shall we get together?' They agreed to meet Saturday. Isobel arrived mid-morning and Marah came out on the porch as Isobel pulled into the drive, her arms wrapped around herself against the cold. Most of the snow had melted, and the sun shone brightly through the limbs of the tree in the yard, but cold temperature remained. Isobel hurried to the door and gave Marah a quick hug, before they stepped inside to Marah's warm living room.

"Thanks for inviting me down." Isobel still felt awkward in being friends with Marah and stumbled over what to say.

"I'm glad you came. Come in, come in. Tea?"

"Sure."

Marah walked toward the kitchen and Isobel followed. Marah had hot water ready to pour and carried the pot to the table. Marah placed cups and saucers in front of each of them, and set a plate of almond cookies with dates in the middle of the table.

"Your home is lovely, Marah. The pillows on your couch and on these chairs," she picked up the table cushion next to her to admire, "are really beautiful. Did you make them?" she said as she set the cushion back in place.

"My Mum did. The fabric all from Bangladesh where she used to live."

"Well, they are beautiful. I'm sorry I didn't notice them when I came last time," Isobel paused, and then to avoid an awkward silence, "How are your parents holding up from this?"

"Good, I think. They are all so far removed from here, I think that has made the loss easier for them. They worry about me though."

"Of course. I know they must miss you."

"Yes. Mum wants me to move in with them when I retire. I jokingly said I might, and she latched onto that and won't let it go." Marah smiled, then laughed out loud at the thought. "I love them dearly, but could never live with them. I've been on my own far too long."

"So, when do you retire? Did you tell me July?"

"Yes, but there's been a change of plans." Marah hesitated, then rushed on, "General Black is applying for a General Discharge for me, to take place as soon as possible, though he doesn't think the board convenes until February, so he's putting me on leave until then."

"But what about your retirement benefits?"

"I don't lose them. And it does not reflect poorly on me. They use this to cut back on personnel, generally, but under the circumstances, he feels this is best for everyone. 'We can't have women screaming in the clinic, or going to the media every time they see you,' is what he told me. He also told me he will recommend me as a GS14 for civil service, which gives me the option to apply for jobs back east, hopefully in Philly."

"What does that GS14 mean? Is that the pay grade?"

"Yes, that's what GS14 refers to. It's really good."

"Wow. How do you feel about retiring? I mean it sounds so drastic after you've been in the service almost twenty years."

"I'm ready. I was planning to retire anyway, and now I can go back to Philly. But I will be here until July. I signed a year lease and can't afford to walk away."

"Yeah, I guess that would be difficult." Isobel took a bite of cookie. "These are delicious, Marah. Did you make them?"

"Thanks. Yes. I don't bake a lot, but I know this recipe because it's so easy. I'm glad you like them. I wasn't sure they turned out well at all. They seem too crunchy this time."

Isobel noticed Marah's self-deprecating manner and rushed to reassure her, "No, no, they are perfect." She looked at the cookie, then at Marah, "Now I lost my train of thought I got so caught up in your cookies," she laughed at herself and Marah laughed too. "Oh, I know, I was going to ask you what you are going to do in Philadelphia."

"There are a lot of civil service jobs in that area. Also, there's a large Muslim population there and Muslim women are required to see a woman unless no other option is available and her life is in danger. I think I would have a good practice. There are few Muslim female nurse practitioners."

"It's great you can retire so young and still have another career."

"But you could do the same, couldn't you? Don't you just have to put in twenty-five years?"

"Yes. I got a late start though and I've thought, up until now that I want to keep going. I was hoping to have the Superintendent's job in a couple of years. But now I can't decide if I want that or not. Everything has changed." They both sat in their own thoughts for a moment. Isobel turned and looked at Marah now, "I mean, nothing really seems very important anymore, except my family and friends. Maybe I want to slow down. I," she paused, "I just don't know."

"I'm taking a year off before I start applying for jobs," Marah said. "My sister wants me to come stay with her in London for a month, in September, though now, I might be able to go earlier under the circumstances."

"Are you close?"

"Yes. I miss her terribly."

"Have you seen her since?" Isobel looked away and couldn't finish her sentence.

Marah felt her face flush and rushed to answer, "Yes. She came to my parents, in Philly, right after, while I was there, and she came for Thanksgiving. But I haven't seen her family in well over a year."

Isobel sighed, "I always imagined what it would be like to have siblings."

"You don't have any?"

"No, but I've always had friends I've considered as family. However, my best friend, wants me to 'just get over it already.' And I can't, of course. My friend, Sam, though has been an angel. He's pulled me off the cliff several times now."

"I'm glad you have someone."

"Thanks. Me too."

"I email and talk to my friend Joe now and then. He's been a big help."

A silence again engulfed them. They finished their tea, and each took another cookie then Marah got up and left the room. Isobel, puzzled, watched her go. She returned with Raheem's book in her hand. She tossed it on the table between them.

"I'm ready, Isobel. What do I have to lose now? Parents need to know this textbook is not good. And if their school is using it, they've got to ask for something else."

"I think you're doing the right thing, Marah."

"Pa told me not to, but I think Mum is for me. She understands."

"Maybe he will come around?"

"No. He won't. He'll be upset with me."

"What are you planning to do?"

Marah didn't say anything. She looked down at the book, then back up to Isobel. She did this several times before she finally choked out, "The local news station called me after that story last week and they asked if I would do an interview, and..." Again she paused and looked around before continuing, "and I told them I had been talking to you and so they want us both to come."

"Oh. I don't know." Isobel shook her head.

"I think our doing this together sends even a louder message, Isobel."

"Yes, but I don't know much about Islam. I mean, I've been doing research and trying to understand, but I'm not sure what I can offer."

"I think they are mostly interested in our," she paused, "our knowing each other."

"Hmm. Maybe so." She took the book from Marah and looked at the publishing info. "This is from Saudi Arabia."

"Yes. I think they supply textbooks to several countries besides their own."

They grew quiet again.

Isobel broke the silence, "I read the other day about a group of mothers whose children were recruited to training by ISIS and ended up dead. They go around to schools and talk to mother's groups. Seems like they are in Canada though."

"Really? Will you send me the link? I should tell them about this book."

"Sure."

"Isobel, maybe if we do this together, people will see us as a symbol of peace. I mean, that Muslims and non-Muslims can get along."

"I don't understand, Marah. One time you tell me we can't be friends because it makes you a bad Muslim, then now, we can?"

"I'm sorry. I know. I felt so responsible for what happened to Alec. So guilty. And you know, the pain is tremendous. I acted on that guilt and I know that's not true. We can be friends. I'm sorry."

"Thanks, Marah. I think I understand." She smiled at Marah. "My grief counselor says guilt is common when a loved one dies. I kept thinking early on, 'Why

Alec? Why him and not me?' I felt guilty for being alive."

"I'm glad to hear that. Maybe I'm not completely crazy."

"No, you're not." She smiled at Marah, then laid her hand on top of hers. "I'll go with you."

"Thank you. I'll give them a call later and let them know."

"Can I ask you something personal? About being a Muslim?"

"Sure."

"Why don't you wear a hijab?"

"Mum and Pa came to the US from East Pakistan, Bangladesh now actually, and well, they don't wear them there, at least they didn't back then. I think in some areas though, where Islamization has hit hard, the women are forced to wear them. But Mum never did, so we grew up that way. I think it's a personal choice."

"That's interesting. Thanks. I mean for explaining."

"Don't be afraid to ask me anything. I don't mind. If people would ask questions maybe we wouldn't have so much craziness." Then her animated voice grew quiet and she said in almost a whisper, "Raheem wanted me to wear hijab after he got so interested in Islam. And I didn't even bother to explain to him why I don't wear one."

"Please stop beating yourself up, Marah. You didn't know."

"I am trying. I am."

"So do you think no one should wear one?"

"Oh, no. I think everyone has to choose for herself no matter where she lives."

"I think my feminist white-woman self has trouble understanding why anyone would choose to cover herself like that. I'm all for modesty, seriously I think young women are not liberated in exposing themselves the way they do these days, but I'm not for the extreme." She paused for a moment, "I sound like an old lady now."

Marah laughed. "Yeah, kind of."

Isobel looked in surprise at Marah, then broke out laughing. "Thanks a lot!"

"You asked for it."

"Okay, okay."

Marah stood up, "Let's move to the couch. I'll start a fire."

They moved to the living room and Isobel watched from the couch as Marah built a fire in the small kiva fireplace. The sun shone brightly through the windows warming Isobel's shoulders. She leaned her head back and let her face be warmed as well. Marah soon had a strong flame going and the logs were catching fire. She sat on the hearth facing Isobel.

"Maybe we should ask to set the parameters for the interview," Isobel said after Marah had settled in place. "I don't want them to ambush us with some political agenda they might have. What do you think?"

"Do they let you do that?" Marah asked. Isobel shrugged her shoulders and made a questioning face. "They seemed to be mostly interested in our relationship after I mentioned we had met."

"I'm not sure, but, I know, when you talk to the reporter, ask what she is interested in covering and then mention we want to talk about the book."

"Okay. I will. I'll let you know what I find out."

Isobel realized she felt comfortable with Marah now. Though different in their beliefs, Isobel now saw how much more they had in common. She also realized, the burden the death of their sons created, lay on Marah the heaviest. Not only had she lost Raheem to death, but also felt she'd never known him. Isobel would always have the memories of Alec, and he remained vivid in her memory as he had been in life, but for Marah, her son had become an enigma.

# Chapter 16

Marah and Isobel arrived at the TV station of the local morning talk show. The host of the show met them in the green room.

"Hi, ladies. I'm Kim Wells, and you must be Ms. Dalal?" She reached out her hand to Marah, shook her hand briefly, then turned to Isobel, "And Ms. Allen," again reaching out her hand, but when she took Isobel's, she added, "I'm so sorry for your loss, Ms. Allen." Stunned for a moment, Isobel didn't say anything. Kim quickly moved on and asked, "Are you okay with me addressing you by your first names?"

"Sure," Isobel replied and Marah shook her head yes.

"Great, then I'll see you on the set. Someone will come to get you right before we go on." She turned to leave, but Isobel stopped her.

"Kim, I'm sorry, but Marah lost her son as well."

"Oh, yes. Yes, she did." And with that, she turned on her very high platform heels and left the room. Isobel looked at Marah and saw the tears lining her eyes.

"You okay?" Isobel asked.

Marah nodded her head yes, then wiped briefly at her eyes. "I'm okay. I am going to have to be tough, that's all." She sat up straighter, as if to indicate her tough spirit. They sat side by side on the tiny couch in the green room, each with a bottle of water an assistant had handed to them after Kim left the room.

"You're going to be great out there," Isobel said.

"Yes. I am." Marah smiled at Isobel, grateful for the moral support. "Thanks for standing up for me."

"Her rudeness is uncalled for. I hope she will be more sensitive in front of the camera."

"Yes. Me too," she said with resignation.

Kim's assistant popped her head in the room, "You're on in five. Follow me." She took them down the hall where a tech attached a small microphone to each of them and placed a small box on their backs. "I'm going to switch these on in a minute. Then, when I tell you, go have a seat on the couch and watch for the director's signal. He'll do a three countdown, then you're live. Just follow Kim's lead and you'll be fine." They waited while the weatherman finished his spiel. As he was finishing, they saw Kim step out from behind the set and take a seat in her chair.

"Alright, ladies. Go take your places. Smile. Keeps you from being nervous." They walked to their places and took a seat, Marah, clutching her book, sat on the end closest to Kim. Isobel beside her.

They saw the director holding up three fingers, and watched his silent countdown. They both smiled. Kim looked directly into the camera, "Good morning, Albuquerque. Today my guests are Marah Dalal and Isobel Allen. Welcome, ladies." She smiled, and they nodded their heads and smiled. Then she turned back to the camera, her face becoming extremely serious, and said, "Marah and Isobel have an unusual relationship. Marah is the mother of Raheem Fatah and the wife of Zaqui Fatah, the two men who attacked the public broadcasting station at Llano last year in April, killing Isobel's son, Alec Davis. They are joining me today to talk about some information they have learned that might prevent young people, like Raheem, from being radicalized. But first, I'd like to ask, how did you two meet?"

Isobel explained how she had found Marah and called her. "I wanted to know why. I thought how could a mother raise a killer. I wanted to confront her. I had this picture of a woman in a burqa, praising Allah, her son had killed infidels, and I hated myself for having created such a stereotype in my head." She glanced over at Marah, and they both smiled slightly, "but instead, I found a mother like me, grieving the loss of her son." Isobel reached over and took Marah's hand.

"Meeting Marah must have been difficult for you."

"Yes, but I felt compelled to go. My friends and Alec's father were against my meeting her, but my son Ian, Alec's brother, encouraged me to do what I needed to find peace."

"I admire your courage, Isobel." Kim paused only for a moment, then, "Now, Marah, I know you have been cleared by the FBI and the Air Force. You're a Lieutenant Colonel, is that correct? A nurse practitioner?"

"Yes, and yes, they have both cleared me of any suspicion."

"But I think we all want to know, how can a mom not know her son is becoming radicalized? Were you really unaware?"

Isobel felt herself becoming angry. 'What right did this woman have to put Marah on the spot like this,' she thought. But Marah remained calm. She didn't flinch.

"My son was a freshman at Llano Universtiy and had chosen to rent a place off campus. His father, Zaqui, came back into his life a few years ago and offered to pay for the apartment. I only felt grateful that his father had taken an interest after deserting us when Raheem was five. Believe me Kim, I have asked myself over and over, how did I miss the signs, but all I saw was a young man who was finally taking an interest in Islam and becoming passionate about his beliefs. And nothing you, or anyone else can say, can make me feel more guilty for missing the signs, and for what he has done, than I already feel." Her voice had risen a pitch.

Kim paused only for a moment, knowing she didn't want to turn her audience against her, and asked, "Tell us about the book you're holding, Marah."

Marah held it up to the camera. "This is a book Raheem's father gave him. I only saw it when the FBI returned his things to me after, after...what happened. I discovered some Muslim schools in the USA are using this Saudi published book in their classrooms. I want to warn parents against some of the teachings here," she said, tapping the book. "There are commentaries on Jews and Christians that are wrong, also about Jihad that are not what a peaceful Muslim would want his or her child to learn. I want parents to know. They have to be involved in what their children are learning."

"In what ways?" Kim asked.

"Read their textbooks. Have conversations. Learn the warning signs of radicalism. There are websites with information. But the thing is this, my son was radicalized by his own father. I wish I had known about what he was studying. As his Mum, I might have made a difference." Tears filled Marah's eyes, and she blinked hard to keep them from running down her face. Kim said nothing, but abruptly moved to Isobel.

"Isobel, as a high school principal, how do you feel about this?"

"I'm actually now the Literacy Director for the Santa Fe district, Kim, but as a former principal, I agree with Marah. Parents need to be involved with their kids. However, that doesn't mean a parent is always going to know what's going on in their child's life."

"But what if Marah had been following what her son was learning, do you think that would have saved your son?"

"Kim, there are no easy answers. Parents constantly walk a fine line between being over involved or not involved enough. And for single parents, I think that becomes much more difficult, especially for mothers, as they oftentimes are working more than one job to keep their heads above water. I do, however, think the most important thing any parent can do for their children is to talk to them and give them a vision for their future."

"Such as college?"

"Well, yes, but not just college. That seems to be the default vision, but I mean expose them to ideas and the arts, to other cultures to other people's way of doing things." Isobel sighed. "There is no easy answer unfortunately. Poverty is our greatest scourge, and I don't mean just poverty of money, but a poverty of spirit. I'm not sure this relates to what happened though with Raheem. He got caught up in the attention of a father who had deserted him and came back into his life."

"I believe your friendship with the mother of your son's killer is admirable. I'm not sure many people could pull that off."

"There's nothing to 'pull off,' Kim. Marah lost her son too. There is nothing more difficult than the loss of a child."

Kim kept her smile as she abruptly cut Isobel off, "Thank you for coming in today, Marah and Isobel." Kim turned back to the camera, "If you have questions about this book, you will find the information on our website. We'll be back with cooking gluten free, after these messages." She kept a steady smile till the camera turned off, then pursed her lips and left the set without saying anything to Isobel and Marah. Kim's assistant motioned for them to come to her, and she removed their audio equipment. "Don't let her bother you ladies. She's kind of in her own self-important world."

"Thanks," they both said almost simultaneously. They went back to the green room to retrieve their coats and purses.

"Wow, that was surreal," Isobel said. "You were awesome, how you stayed so cool and calm with her."

"Thanks. I almost broke down though and now I feel like I want to burst into tears" and Marah sat down hard on the couch, placing her head in her hands. "This is my life. I will ask myself till the day I die, *WHY*?"

Isobel sat down next to her and rubbed her back. She waited while Marah gathered herself. She felt her breathing deeply, then she lifted her head and sighed.

Isobel said, when she felt Marah was ready, "Come on, then. Let's get out of here and go have coffee."

"Tea sounds good," Marah said. Then she put on her coat and picked up her bag.

"Tea it is for you, and coffee for me."

The two of them walked down the hall and slipped out the door into the cold, icy parking lot.

# Chapter 17

A week later, Isobel received a call from one of the major networks in New York City. Someone there saw a blurb about their appearance on Kim's show in Albuquerque. "We are doing a show on unusual friendships during the week leading up to Valentine's Day and we would like to have you and Ms. Dalal join us."

"I can't speak for both of us, but if Marah is willing and interested, I will be glad to join you. We want to keep getting the message out about the book we believe helped radicalize her son."

"Great, I'll let the ladies know you're in and get back to you with all the specifics."

"Okay. Then you'll call Marah?"

"Yes. I have her number."

"Thanks."

Marah and Isobel both, found themselves researching radicalization, and gathering resources to help parents, after their appearance on the local morning show. The Canadian group of mothers had been helpful to them, providing them with links to de-radicalization sources and how they worked with parents to identify patterns, hopefully stopping radicalization in its tracks. However, no one answer fit all situations. And Marah felt part of the problem came from the harsh interpretation of some of the hadiths among some Muslims. Raheem's book displayed a prime example of the abuse of the hadiths.

Basically unemployed, Marah bided her time searching the internet, adding to their pile of information. Isobel suggested to Marah that she write a handbook for parents. "I'm not a writer, Isobel," she protested. However, Isobel assured her she would help.

"You have a perspective that could benefit other parents. You know the pain first hand of losing Raheem. Your story is also unique. We'll make it part memoir, part handbook."

"My perspective though is totally American Muslim. I'm not sure how helpful that can be in the greater scheme of things."

"That doesn't matter. We target the small enclaves across the country who have high concentrations of Muslim immigrants and the larger Mosques. I think you can have an impact, Marah."

Marah felt better now that she seemed to have a purpose again. Mum noticed and remarked on how much better she sounded. Marah told Mum what she and Isobel had been working on and the upcoming appearance they would be making in New York. Her Mum asked questions and encouraged her. Neither of them mentioned Pa, still angry she had spoken out against the book, against his wishes. "Mum, what if Isobel and I come visit you after our appearance?"

"Ah, yes, Marah. That will be good. We will be happy for you to come."

"Even Pa?"

"I will make him be happy. He will understand someday, daughter. You must keep going."

"Thank you, Mum." She loved her parents, and her mother's support touched her deeply. "I hope you're right about Pa. Maybe our visit will help him see and he'll change his mind," Marah said.

"I think so, daughter. He is a good man."

Yes, Mum, he is. Okay. We will see you February 15."

Isobel still talked to Ian daily and he recently remarked to her, "Mom, I think what you and Marah are doing is great. You sound better."

"I feel better for sure. I feel like Marah and I, especially Marah, can make a difference. Maybe keep something like this from happening to another family."

"I can't believe you two are going to New York. What a great opportunity."

"Well, they definitely are more interested in mine and Marah's relationship than anything else, but this gives her a moment to make a statement about knowing what children are reading and maybe a national audience will make parents sit up and listen."

"Mom, people always listen to you," he said half joking. "Alec and I always did."

"Yeah, right." They both laughed. "It's nice we can laugh again without breaking into tears," she said.

"Yeah, it is."

"I miss you guys."

"We miss you too."

"I'm glad we have the same dates for spring break this year. Have you and Delia decided what we're doing yet?"

"Not yet, but I'll let you know soon."

"Ok, sweetheart. I love you."

"Love you too, Mom."

They hung up and Isobel returned to her computer screen, the statistics on test scores in the Santa Fe district called to her. The tedious part of her existence seemed so inane now. So small. She glanced at her watch and realized she should be heading to a meeting with Jorge. She grabbed her laptop and headed for his office. She also needed to talk to him about time off to do this show.

# Chapter 18

Isobel glanced at Marah for a moment, seated next to her on the first leg of their flight to New York. Her eyes were closed, head leaned forward, bobbing with the motion of the plane. Isobel leaned her head back on the seat and closed her eyes. The last few weeks were difficult. After their interview with Kim, the school website had been inundated with comments about her appearance with the mother of her son's murderer. Some were supportive and positive, others spewed hate. She felt unnerved by one comment, 'You deserve to die for betraying your own son,' a message Jorge regretted having to tell her about. "Be careful Isobel," he had cautioned her that night before leaving work. The next day, he hired an extra security guard for the building and closed down messaging on the website. She spent a number of sleepless nights since then, jumping at every little noise. Sam came over and slept on her couch one night when she felt especially jumpy. But she finally settled back into routine and started sleeping again.

"Would you like something to drink?" the flight attendant was speaking to her.

"Coffee, please. Black."

She reached for her cup over Marah's head, then settled back into her thoughts. Almost ten months without Alec. A surreal feeling even now. She looked out into the blue sky, the sun becoming brighter as they flew east. 'What will happen after this interview?' She tried to concentrate on enjoying her coffee and thinking about being in New York again. They bought tickets to see a show, planned to visit the MOMA, and another museum or two. Isobel loved the vibrancy of the city and looked forward to being there, but she admitted to herself this television appearance probably meant more commentary by strangers on her relationship with Marah. What she dealt with back in Santa Fe had been hard to take. She didn't regret their decision to keep moving forward, but celebrity of this kind made her uncomfortable.

Isobel and Marah made their way through the Atlanta airport, stopping for a coffee and tea before boarding their second flight. They quietly talked about their plans and their upcoming appearance during the two hour flight. Once they landed, they were picked up in a limo and then deposited at a hotel near Times Square. "This is amazing being here. I still can't believe we are doing this," Marah said, as they walked into the lobby and checked into their adjoining rooms. Once settled in, they opened the connecting doors.

Isobel walked into Marah's and pulled her over to the window.

"I love the city," Isobel said. They stood side by side looking out over the rooftops. Isobel pointed out the water tanks that dotted the tops of buildings. "I used to think the water tanks were antiques, but they still use them."

"My parents would always bring us to New York in December to see the city decorated. Even if we didn't celebrate Christmas, we still liked looking at the lights and the store windows all decked out."

"What did you do on Christmas? Was it just like any other day?"

"No. Mum and Pa would read us the story of Mary and Jesus, peace be upon him, from the Qur'an. And we always fasted on Christmas Day, but Mum would make a feast dinner for late in the evening and we would each receive a little gift by our plate. We also had to clean out our rooms and make a pile of things to give away."

"Really? That's a great tradition."

"Yes. They did that to teach us about zakat, the required giving of Muslim peoples to help the less fortunate."

"I like that."

"What about you? What was your Christmas like?"

Isobel laughed, "Our religion didn't believe in celebrating the birth of Christ, so ours was just mild commercialism Christmas."

"But you were Christian? And you didn't celebrate the birth of Jesus, peace be upon him."

"Nope. His death mattered, nothing else in the eyes of our religion, since he died for our sins. His birth, I guess, seemed unimportant, which made no sense to me, as you can't have his death without his birth."

"That seems so odd."

"Yes, and that's only one reason I don't follow any religious body these days."

Marah looked at her and smiled. "We do have an unlikely friendship, don't we?"

"I think we do." Isobel put her arm around Marah's shoulders and Marah slipped her own around Isobel's waist.

They stood there for a moment. The sun was beginning to set, the shadows deepening across the skyline. Marah leaned her head onto Isobel's shoulder and hugged her. "Thanks, Isobel. I don't know how I could have made it through these months without your patience and your friendship."

"No need to thank me. You've helped me too. But hey, what are we doing? Let's get going! I'm starving!"

"Me too."

"Okay then, ten minutes and we're out of here." Isobel went to her room and as she started to pull the door shut behind her, "Tap on my door when you're ready," and she pulled the door closed.

Marah quickly changed clothes. She pulled a deep blue sweater dress over her head and black wool leggings on then pulled on her black boots. She grabbed her bag and coat, then tapped on the adjoining door. In a few seconds, Isobel opened her side. She had donned a pair of skinny jeans, black boots and her light blue cashmere sweater. She held her coat and bag, a large black leather tote. "Alrighty then, let's hit the town," she said. They left through Marah's room and headed out to find dinner.

The next day, Marah and Isobel walked the city. They went to the MOMA as planned then the Frick Museum. After dinner, early enough that they felt like senior citizens, they walked back to their hotel. "What a day," Marah exclaimed when they arrived back at their rooms. "This was great, Isobel. I don't think I've ever enjoyed New York this much before, even though my feet are killing me."

"Mine too, but it was a lovely day. I'm glad we're turning in early though. Are you nervous about tomorrow?"

"No, I actually feel at peace about it now. I am doing the right thing."

"Yes, you are," Isobel agreed. "I know it's been tough on you, but you'll be great."

"And you too."

"Want to look at our notes again?" Isobel asked.

"Sure. Let's get on our pajamas and order hot chocolate from room service," Marah said.

"Perfect."

They spent the next hour talking about the interview ahead. They knew they needed to sleep though, when they started laughing about the interview in Albuquerque. "I loved how she practically stomped her attitude with those ridiculously high heels," said Isobel. They had both been upset when they had left that day, but came to realize, they would have many more people like Kim to deal with and the sooner they could let go, the better they would be, and now they couldn't stop giggling. "Okay, okay," Isobel managed to say, "bedtime."

Marah leaned over and gave Isobel a hug. "Good night. I'll see you in the morning. Picking us up at 4:30, right?"

"Yup, that's like 2:30 for us, my friend."

"Yikes! Hadn't thought of that. Good thing we ate dinner with the cotton heads."

"Careful now, I'm not that far away."

"Maybe in age, but in no other."

"Thanks."

They smiled and Marah waved as she went to her own room and closed the door.

# Chapter 19

Isobel tapped lightly on Marah's door just before 4:30. Marah opened, brush in hand and toothbrush in her mouth. Isobel laughed, "Brushing everything at once?" Marah ran back to the bathroom and threw down the hairbrush and simultaneously removed the toothbrush, spit and rinsed. She quickly wrapped her hair into a bun at the nape of her neck and went to hug Isobel.

"I'm so nervous. I just started doing everything at once, and getting nothing accomplished." She picked up her bag and coat. "Okay, I'm ready."

"You're going to be fine."

"Yes. Yes, you're right. Ready?"

"Yeah, let's go."

When they arrived in the lobby, the driver greeted them and escorted them to the limo, holding the door for them as they scrambled into the seat. "I could get used to this," Marah said.

"Pretty nice being driven about." They laughed and settled in for the drive. Though the streets were still fairly empty, there were signs of life here and there, as they made their way to the studio. Only a few blocks, but the blocked portion of Times Square, required a much longer route than the ten minutes they could have walked it. When they arrived, he held the door again and escorted them into the lobby where they were met by an intern who escorted them up the elevator and through the halls to make-up.

"Good morning, ladies," a young woman dressed in black, wearing a black apron, approached them and showed them to a chair. "You both look great, but I'm going to apply a little more makeup so you don't wash out under the lights. Is that okay?"

"Sure," Isobel said, and Marah nodded agreement. She wrapped a white paper bib around each of them, then went to work, starting with Isobel.

"You have gorgeous skin," the girl exclaimed as she worked away adding a bit more base and blush.

"Thanks." Isobel smiled.

She finished with Isobel and turned to Marah. Isobel removed the makeup bib and sat watching the woman work on Marah. "You both have lovely skin," she said as she brushed blush onto Marah's cheekbones. "You're too easy," she exclaimed, making them both laugh.

"Thanks," Marah said. "I'm not used to this attention. I kind of like it."

"Alright ladies, I'm done. The intern," she paused, "damn, I can't think of her name, anyway, she will be back in a minute to escort you to the green room. Bye, bye." She turned and left them, and at the same time, the intern came in.

"Hi, I'm Lisa." She thrust out her hand to Marah, then Isobel. Isobel thought she couldn't be more than 20, but she oozed confidence. "I'm here to escort you to the Green Room. If you'll follow me ladies."

They followed her down the corridor to an open door, where she indicated they were to go. She then stuck her head in, "Help yourself to waters and the fruit and muffins on the table." She cocked her head towards the wall behind the door. "Sorry you have to come in so early and then sit around waiting, but someone will be back to get you at air time," Lisa said. "Need anything else?"

They both simply shook their heads no, looked at each other and broke out laughing as soon as Lisa had walked away.

"Wow, I never had that kind of confidence at her age," Marah said.

"Me either."

They both took a water from the cooler, and Isobel took some fruit. "You should eat a little something, Marah."

"I can't. I'm so nervous."

"Well then, I guess you'll have plenty of room for breakfast at The Smith when we're finished."

"That's exactly right. Cinnamon rolls, yum."

"I need a coffee. Hmmm." Isobel stood up and went to the cupboards on the far wall. She started opening them one by one, until she found the coffee pod machine and an electric kettle. "I knew they had to have coffee in here." She turned and looked over her shoulder at Marah, "Want a tea?"

"Yes, please."

Isobel checked the kettle for water and plugged it in. She dropped a pod in the coffee maker and made herself a cup, then handed Marah her cup of tea. "Hope they don't mind I helped myself," she said as she returned to the couch, coffee in hand.

"I have a feeling Miss Confidence was supposed to ask us and forgot."

"No one gets it all right, all the time."

"That is true."

Their idle chatter kept them from coming unnerved. Talking about their sons still felt difficult and raw. Talking about what they were doing together was easier.

They looked over their notes as they sipped their drinks. "Isobel, you'll help me if I freeze?"

"Of course, but you're going to be fine."

They had no idea how much time had passed. Other more important guests had come and gone. Lisa had remembered with the subsequent guests to offer coffee once she saw the cupboard door open. Isobel and Marah had sat side by side on the couch, waiting their turn. Then Lisa appeared again, and motioned for them to follow her. "Okay ladies, I'm going to have our sound crew mic you and get you ready to go on. I'll tell you when to walk out. The lights will blind you at first, but in five steps you'll see the stools across from Kathie Lee and Hoda. Take a seat and they'll take it from there."

"Thanks," Isobel and Marah said at the same time.

"Sure, no problem. Okay, here we go." A young man from the sound crew gave them wireless mics and asked them to attach the mic to the front of their clothes. Isobel wore a wrap dress and easily attached it to her collar. Marah wore her signature tunic style dress with leggings. She attached her mic and they were ready. Lisa stood at the edge of the stage entrance waiting for the cue.

Isobel and Marah could hear Kathie Lee, "Today's unlikely friendship is between two mothers. One mother whose son was killed by a terrorist, and the mother of the terrorist who killed her son." Lisa prodded them forward. Isobel reached down and impulsively took Marah's hand, then led the way onto the stage.

Blinded by the intense lights, Isobel remembered to count five steps and then she saw the stools in front of her. She let Marah's hand slip from hers as they each took a seat. Isobel sat across from Hoda and Marah from Kathie Lee.

Kathie Lee started the conversation, "Isobel, Marah, thanks for coming today. When we heard about your unlikely friendship, we said 'we have to talk to these two amazing women.'"

"Thanks," they both said simultaneously, and took a quick glance at each other.

"Isobel," Hoda began, "this seems especially difficult on your part, how did this friendship come about?"

"I'm embarrassed now to say, but I kept thinking 'How does a mother raise such a monster?' and I felt I had to meet her, ask her, Why? How? I managed to get her phone number when I found she had moved to Albuquerque. I called and sort of blackmailed her into talking to me." She glanced at Marah and smiled.

"Marah, what were you thinking?" Kathie Lee asked.

"Frankly, she surprised me by calling. I had become a pariah everywhere and I was worried she would tell people where I had moved, but it really came down to I just wanted to talk to someone."

"You had no friends to turn to? Family?"

"All but one friend deserted me, and my family lives across the country from me. They were of course grieving too, but living so removed from what had happened, they couldn't see on a daily basis what I was going through."

"Isobel, what happened next?" Hoda said.

"We talked for an hour, maybe two?" she glanced at Marah and continued, "And what I found, was another mother grieving just like me. I knew she had no idea what was happening to her son, how he was radicalized by his father. I could see it in her utter devastation."

"Marah, explain to us what happened to your son?" Kathie Lee interjected.

"His father," she paused, "my husband, Zaqui, had deserted us when Raheem was five, after he attained US citizenship. I think, well I know now, he used me for that purpose. I never filed for divorce because I knew Zaqui could take Raheem away from me."

"You didn't think the courts would find in your favor?"

"In Islam, fathers generally get their children in divorce. Boys by age nine. I couldn't risk it, even in an American court I foolishly thought they might decide in his favor."

"I didn't know that," Kathie Lee said.

"He came back into Raheem's life a couple of years ago, when he started working in D.C. I was glad. I really encouraged Raheem to see his father. He spent a couple of summers with his dad out there, but before his freshman year in college, he really started changing."

"Tell us about that."

"He started wearing long tunics and ankle length pants, and he grew a beard. These are true signs of devoutness, but they seemed out of character for him. He told me to wear a hijab, but I had never worn one. My parents were from what was East Pakistan, but now Bangladesh, and that wasn't done there. He started getting up every day for prayers and harassing me if I missed. And he started going to the mosque on a regular basis, though once he went to school, that stopped. So I started seeing these changes, but I thought they were good for him. To be closer to Allah." Isobel could hear the stress in Marah's voice.

"In the research Marah and I have done, we found this is often the case with young men who radicalize. Their mother's think this is good for them, then there turns out to be an underlying driver. In Raheem's case, we think he wanted to please this man who had deserted him. Finding out that driver is probably the most important thing a parent can explore with their child."

"Tell us about your son Alec, Isobel," Hoda asked.

"He was remarkable. He was kind and caring. A producer at a small public television station and he taught classes on the campus. His students loved him." Isobel felt the tears start to surface and she forced herself to hold them back. "Really, everyone loved him," she choked out. Marah reached over and took her hand.

"And Marah, what about Raheem?"

"He was a good boy. He loved his family and his friends. He was smart too. He thought he would study International Law, at least that's what he thought before his father came back. Then he seemed to lose direction where his studies were concerned." Isobel squeezed her hand.

"And now the two of you have become activists of a sort?" Kathie Lee said.

"Yes," Isobel said and Marah nodded, trying to collect herself again. "We don't want this to happen to other mothers, families." Isobel looked at Marah.

"Tell us about what you're doing," Hoda said.

Marah, hesitantly began, "When the FBI returned Raheem's personal belongings to me, I found a book I had never seen before, a commentary on Tawhid, which is our concept of Allah as one; unlike Christians who believe God is three, we do not. We believe in Jesus as a prophet, peace be upon him, but God is one being. This book took the hadiths of Muhammad, peace be upon him, and perverted them. I read it in horror. My son was receiving a twisted version of the meaning of the hadiths. I found things underlined and notes his father made to him and things he wrote himself, that were not how he had been taught. When I looked up the man who wrote the commentary, he is Arabic and is considered a fundamentalist."

"Do you think others are reading this?" Kathie Lee asked.

"Yes. It's available on the internet to download. I think parents sometimes don't know what their children are being taught, possibly in Muslim classes they attend after school, or in Muslim private schools. We have to protect our children from this fundamentalism. We need to monitor what they do on the internet. What sites they are perusing. We need to fight these manifestations of extremism. I know...," she trailed off and couldn't go on.

Isobel picked up the story, "We learned that many parents have no idea what their children are studying. And you know, you can apply this to all of us, not just Muslims. We have to stay active and aware in our children's lives. I saw it every day as a principal, parents who gave up control to their kids, the media, their devices, it's heart breaking. And I think it's hardest for single parents. That's not to blame them, it's just they are doing everything on their own. They need our help."

"Wow, ladies, this is such a difficult task you've set for yourselves," Kathie Lee said.

"I hope this helps get out the word," Hoda added.

"Thank you." Again, Isobel and Marah said simultaneously and then smiled at each other.

"Thank you for joining us today," said Kathie Lee.

Hoda turned toward the camera and said, "Next up, we have Peanut Butter and Janey, sharing her organic peanut butter and chocolate."

"Sounds great, Hoda. Yum," Kathie Lee smiled, "We'll be right back."

The camera lights went off and Isobel and Marah, slid from their chairs.

"Thanks again, ladies for sharing your story with us," Hoda said, as she extended her hand to each of them. "Lisa is here to take you back to collect your things." They shook hands with Kathie Lee, then turned to follow Lisa. She stepped up, headphones on, iPad in hand and motioned for them to follow. Hoda and Kathie Lee started talking to each other and Isobel and Marah followed Lisa off stage.

"Good job, ladies. I don't always watch every segment, but I caught yours today. I'm very sorry about the loss of your sons. But it is great to see you both trying to make a difference."

"Thanks, Lisa," Marah said. "It's hard, but we think it's necessary."

"Okay then, here you are." They followed her into the green room where they collected their belongings. Then she led them to the elevators. "When you get to the lobby, your driver will be waiting."

"Thanks," they both said as they stepped into the elevator. The doors slid shut and they were soon back in the lobby.

# Chapter 20

The driver stood by the revolving door waiting. He nodded his head towards them and led the way out of the building to the waiting limo. Isobel and Marah relaxed when they got in the back of the car. "That went great, Marah. You were awesome."

"And so were you."

"Well, thanks, but I'm most concerned about you and what you have to say. This is great. I hope we get some good feedback on this."

"Yeah, me too. After the Albuquerque appearance, I've been a bit worried."

"What do you mean?"

"Well, I didn't want to tell you, but I got a few threatening emails about being an apostate for speaking out and even some white supremacist from Virginia sent a hateful message."

"You did? Why didn't you tell me?"

"I thought if I said it out loud, I might get scared and not be able to continue. I think what we are doing is right and I refuse to be intimidated. I knew you had been harassed and I didn't think you needed to hear more. Besides, it's all good, right?"

"Right!" Isobel bit her lip and turned to look out the window, watching the crowds on the street streaming by as they sat in traffic. She did worry about Marah's safety and this revelation made her a bit nervous. She turned back to Marah, "Okay then, let's change and go to The Smith for breakfast. It's only a ten minute walk from our hotel. Then we can decide what to do the rest of the day. Like maybe some shopping."

Marah laughed, "Yes to food, and shopping."

Thirty minutes later they were stepping out of the hotel to a sunlit winter's day. Snow had been in the forecast, but for now there was nothing but glorious sunshine, and with no wind to speak of, the air almost felt warm. "First things first," Marah grabbed Isobel's arm and steered her towards Times Square. "Let's get a selfie in front of the jumbotron thingy."

"Okay, let's." Arm and arm they walked towards the middle of the square. "I love that it's all pedestrian friendly now. The first time I came to New York, I almost got run over for walking around looking up."

They stood in the center of the square, each of them turning around and around looking at the different signs. The whole place was almost one huge digital billboard. M&M's waved at them, and Walgreen's beckoned them to buy, buy, buy. The Naked Cowboy played guitar and posed with tourists for selfies. Everywhere they looked there were people, and looking up, digital wizardry advertising anything and everything.

"I love the energy of the city," Isobel exclaimed, "but I wouldn't want to live here."

"Me too," Marah said. "Okay, which sign?"

"I think it has to be One Times Square, for sure."

"Agreed." They turned their backs to the big sign and Marah held her phone out in front of them. "Okay, smile." Isobel smiled and then made a goofy face. Marah laughed at her, then made one herself. "Serious now," and as Isobel put on a seriously straight face, out of the corner of her eye she saw a man running towards them and turned her face in time to see him grab Marah. He lashed out at Isobel with a knife and before Isobel could respond, he had slashed her coat and she looked down to see blood oozing from her coat sleeve, then all she could hear was Marah screaming. The man yelled as he stabbed Marah, over and over, "Muslim bitch! You can't have our country." He stabbed her with each word.

Someone had grabbed Isobel and had her by the hand, tugging her away, but she couldn't stop screaming, "Stop him! Please! Someone make him stop!" The man had Marah around the waist now and took his knife, plunging into her neck. Isobel's eyes locked with Marah's, and she saw the last flicker of light there as the knife hit an artery and Marah began to choke on her own blood. Then he dropped her on the ground and looked around for Isobel.

What seemed like hours, had only been a minute or two, and a police officer was running at the man, yelling at him to stop, but the man just looked with wild eyes at the police officer and ran at Isobel. The officer stopped and pointed his gun at the man and fired. He hit him in the arm, causing him to drop his knife, spinning him around just a few feet from where Isobel stood, stunned. People were running and screaming, and the couple who had pulled Isobel away, dragged her along with them. The police officer then shot the man again, hitting him in the head and chest. The man dropped to his knees and fell forward to the ground. Isobel yanked herself away from the couple holding her and went to Marah, sobbing as she lifted her into her arms. Marah's eyes stared blankly up at Isobel. The paramedics were there, taking Marah from her, the policeman helped Isobel to her feet and led her in a daze to a police car that had arrived.

"Please, I have to stay with her. Where are they taking her. Please let me go." She sobbed and yelled as they made her sit in the back seat of the car.

"Ma'am, I'm going to take you as soon as they get her loaded in the ambulance. It's okay. Hang tight."

As soon as the doors of the ambulance were closed, the officer told Isobel, as he closed her door, they would follow. He turned on the siren and stayed within a few feet of the ambulance all the way to the hospital. When they arrived, he jumped out and opened the door for Isobel. She ran to the ambulance, and stood on the curb while they unloaded her and wheeled her into the hospital. She was whisked away down a corridor, where doors opened then closed behind her. Isobel stood in the hall watching. She realized the officer was speaking to her, but she leaned up against the wall and felt herself sliding to the floor as she passed out. The officer then noticed the blood running out of Isobel's sleeve and called for help.

Isobel woke to find herself on an examining table. Her coat had been removed and her shirt sleeve cut off, her arm stretched out away from her body, a young woman leaned over her arm. She looked up and noticed Isobel looking at her. "I just have a few more stitches here. You okay?"

Isobel nodded her head yes. "Do you know what happened to my friend? Is she going to be okay?"

"I'll send someone in to talk to you, I really don't know. I got the call you had passed out and were bleeding on our spotlessly clean floors and we can't have that." She smiled at Isobel. "I'm Doctor Phillips, by the way."

Isobel felt the tears sliding down her face as she watched the young doctor stitch up her arm. She closed her eyes and saw Marah being attacked. She began to shiver. Dr. Phillips stood and took a blanket from a chest in the wall, covering Isobel with a heated blanket. "This will help," and went back to stitching her arm.

"I'm going to prescribe you a pain med. This is going to hurt when the shot I gave you wears off. There is a huge crowd out there waiting to talk to you. I understand you witnessed an attack on your friend?"

"Yes, Marah." She closed her eyes again. "It was awful. And I couldn't do anything to make him stop. He just kept stabbing and stabbing her, and people were holding me back. Then he ran at me, but a policeman shot him," she stopped and took a deep breath.

"I'm finished, Isobel." Dr. Phillips stood up and patted Isobel on the shoulder, then she placed her hand on Isobel's forehead, brushing back the hair from Isobel's face. Isobel felt herself calming down. "Would you like to sit up?"

Isobel nodded her head and Dr. Phillips raised the back of the bed up. "Sit there for a few minutes. I'll let you step down as soon as I'm sure you're not going to pass out again."

"Okay." Isobel said. She sat there watching the doctor move things aside and then wash her hands. The shivering had stopped, but she pulled the blanket tight around herself.

"Listen, I don't want to send you into the melee out there. I'm going to grab a wheel chair and get an intern to take you to a waiting area. I'll let your friend's doctor know where you are and he'll come find you."

"Thank you."

She stuck her head into the hall and told the intern what she wanted, then turned back to Isobel. "Okay, here we go." She put her hand out and helped Isobel step down from the table and move to a chair. "He'll be right in to take you away. Your prescription will be waiting at the nurse's station when you're ready to leave. All good?"

Isobel nodded again. She was fighting a feeling of hysteria. She could feel herself wanting to scream and never stop.

"Hey there, I'm Mark," the intern said as he entered the room. "I've got a chariot waiting for you in the hall. Shall we?" He bent down and put his arm under Isobel's and helped her out of the chair. Tears streamed down her face, as he eased her into the waiting wheelchair. He rolled her down to the surgical waiting room. He bent down in front of her, "Doctor Walters will be in to see you in a minute. I saw you and Ms. Dalal on television this morning. She was very brave to speak out. I'm sorry it has ended like this."

Isobel could only nod her head in agreement. The tears wouldn't stop. She reached out and squeezed his hand as he stood up again.

"I've got to go." As he turned towards the door, a man entered. "Here's Dr. Walters."

Dr. Walters walked to her and sat down on the adjacent couch. No one else was in the room at the moment. He looked at Isobel. "I'm sorry, Ms. Allen. Ms. Dalal's attacker slashed through the main artery on her neck. She bled out before she arrived at the hospital. Our EMT's did all they could, but a cut like that generally results in death. We found her emergency contact information in her bag and her parents have been notified. They are on their way here."

Isobel cried, her shoulders shaking, as she listened. "May I see her?"

"Yes. I'll have someone come take you in soon."

"Thank you."

The doctor found a box of tissues on a chair across the room and brought them to Isobel. "Just stay here. It will be a few minutes yet. I'm sorry for your loss." He patted her shoulder as he left the room.

Isobel's purse was slung over the back of the chair. She hadn't noticed it until she heard her phone ringing.

She fumbled to grab her bag and find her phone, the throbbing in her left arm hampering her every move. She saw Ian's name and answered. "Mom, you and Marah were great. We loved it."

"Ian, I'm at the hospital."

"Are you okay? What happened? Mom?" He could hear her crying, as he waited for her to respond.

"Oh, Ian. It was horrible. I...we were taking a picture, and, and I saw this man rushing at us," she choked and then struggled on, "He grabbed Marah, and he...," she was crying hard now, she couldn't say anything. A nurse came into the room and came to Isobel's side. Isobel saw only the bright pink scrubs through her tears. "Marah is dead."

"Oh my God. Mom, are you okay?"

Isobel could hear the panic in his voice.

"Are you ready to go, Ms. Allen?"

She nodded her head yes, and willed herself to stop crying. "Ian, I'm okay, but the nurse is here to take me to see Marah. I will call you."

"Mom, I'm coming out."

"No, Ian. No. I'll call you back shortly."

"I love you, Mom."

"I love you, too, honey," she said as she was being wheeled down the hall. She hung up and closed her eyes as the nurse rolled her towards Marah. When they came to the door, the nurse pushed open the door and wheeled Isobel inside. Marah lay on the gurney completely covered. The nurse set the brake on the chair and helped Isobel stand. She felt wobbly as she walked to Marah's side.

"Ms. Allen, I'm only going to pull this back to her chin."

Isobel nodded as the nurse pulled back the sheet. All the color was drained from Marah's beautiful face, her eyes closed, her hair matted around her head. Isobel reached over and ran her fingertip across Marah's cheek, then stroked her forehead. "You were so brave, Marah. I won't let this stop. I promise." Isobel felt the tears rolling down her cheeks and saw one drop onto Marah's face. She wiped it off, then bent and kissed her friend. "Goodbye, Marah."

# Chapter 21

Isobel waited at the hospital for Marah's parents to arrive. She called Ian back and assured him she was safe. A security officer, assigned to watch over Isobel, stood close by. They found her a place to wait, away from the media detail who had crowded the emergency room with their cameras and microphones, waiting for Marah's parents to arrive or for her to leave.

The attending physician had a nurse call Mr. Dalal and asked them to come to the physician's entrance, where they were escorted to the morgue. They held hands as they entered the room. Marah still lay on the gurney and the attendant pulled back the sheet for them to see their daughter.

"Why, Marah, why?" Her father shook his head as he looked at his daughter. Tears filled his eyes and he turned away.

Dara took Marah's hand in her own and then kissed Marah's cheeks. She pushed loose strands of hair back from her head. "You were a good daughter. So good. I am proud of you." She kissed her again, then went to Shariq and hugged him to her. "Tell her goodbye, now."

Shariq's face revealed his anguish. Dara knew how conflicted he felt. "I knew something like this could happen. I knew." Tears streamed down his face as he went to Marah and kissed her cheeks. He pulled the sheet back over her face. He took Dara's hand and they went back into the hall. The funeral home director from Philadelphia had brought them with him in his transport vehicle. He stood in the hall talking to the morgue administrator, making arrangements to take the body. The hospital knew the needs of the Muslims who came through their doors, and knew time was important.

"They need you to sign some paperwork, Shariq, and they will release your daughter to me."

He followed the director into his office. Dara sat in a chair outside the office. She looked up when she realized someone was coming down the hall towards her. She recognized Isobel right away and stood up, walking towards her. She immediately took Isobel into her arms and hugged her. Startled and overwhelmed with emotion, Isobel clung to Dara. They stood there, two women who had never met, crying and hugging, holding onto each other for dear life. When they both calmed, Dara stood back and looked at Isobel. "Thank you for staying with my Marah. You meant so much to her."

"I am so sorry for your loss. So so sorry. I couldn't stop him. He just came at us."

"There, there. Allah wills things we do not understand." Isobel watched Dara's face, and though she was distraught, there was at the same time a look of acceptance. Isobel stood with Dara while Shariq finished the necessary paperwork.

"I need to pack up Marah's things for you. I…" Isobel hadn't thought through what to do next, but now realized she needed to go to Philadelphia to be with Marah's parents for the funeral. "I'll take the train to Philadelphia and bring her suitcase. The funeral will be in a few days?"

"No, dear, it will be tomorrow morning. That is our custom. But you must come."

Isobel nodded her head. "Okay." The tears flowed again when she realized tomorrow is when she and Marah would have been in Philly together. "We would have been there tomorrow. Marah and I."

"Yes." Tears also flowed down Dara's cheeks. She reached over and took Isobel's hand. "You will stay with us."

"I can't impose on you at this time."

"You are not imposing. You will give me peace knowing you are safe. You are Marah's friend."

"Thank you, Mrs. Dalal. That's so kind of you. Thank you."

"Please call me Dara and my name is actually Patil. Women keep their family name, even when they marry."

"I'm sorry. I didn't know. Thank you, Dara. What about her friend, Joe? I don't know how to contact him."

"I will be sure Shariq calls him, dear. Thank you for mentioning him. He was so kind to us," Dara said.

Shariq and the funeral home director came out of the office together. Shariq came to Dara and took her hand. "Shariq, this is Isobel."

He did not acknowledge her. "We must go, Dara. Khadijah is loading...," he paused, "taking Marah... outside."

"Shariq, you will acknowledge Marah's dear friend. She did not kill our daughter."

Isobel stood next to Dara, embarrassed and in shock at Shariq's response.

"Dara," he said sharply, "we must go." But Dara stood her ground and did not move.

Shariq looked at Isobel then. He tipped his head in acknowledgement. "Hello. I'm Shariq Dalal. I apologize for my rudeness."

"I'm Isobel. Thank you. I know what you are going through, Mr. Dalal. I do. I'm so sorry."

"Thank you. We must go now." He took Dara by the arm.

"Wait. Isobel, you need my phone number. Please call when you get to the station and we'll pick you up. The early morning train might be best. It's getting late now and I will be preparing...be taking care of Marah tonight. Is that alright, dear?"

"Yes. I will see you then." They exchanged numbers, then Dara took Isobel into her arms again and hugged her close. She then let Shariq lead her away.

When Isobel finally left the hospital, the security guard escorted her to a department store to purchase a new coat, then took her back to the hotel and stood outside her door. The hotel manager sent up a bottle of wine and dinner for her. Though she could hardly eat, she welcomed the wine. She stood at the window looking at the city, as she and Marah had done their first night. The entire day had been surreal.

Isobel opened the door between hers and Marah's room. She found all of Marah's clothes neatly stacked and folded in the bureau drawers. Isobel put them neatly into her suitcase, then packed her toiletries on top. She rolled the suitcase into her own room and closed their adjoining doors. Exhausted, she climbed into bed and switched on the television. Scrolling through the channels, she saw every news station talking about what had happened and Isobel couldn't watch. She found it too close. Too personal. She talked to Ian several times throughout the evening and her friends called. Nora and Jacob called to check on her. too. Now she lay on the bed, hoping for sleep.

She looked at her phone and decided to call Sam, though he had called her earlier in the day. "Hey you," Sam said when he answered. "Are you okay? Why aren't you sleeping?"

"I can't fall asleep. When I close my eyes I see it all again. Marah's face. Her agony. My God, Sam, it was so awful."

"Oh, Isobel. I can only imagine. I'm sorry."

"I wish you were here. You always calm me so."

"I can be on an early flight."

"No, no. I'll be home in three days. I'm okay. It's the thought of you."

"I miss you. I've grown accustomed to seeing you often and I'm missing that."

"Me too." Isobel said. She had felt herself growing closer to Sam this year and she realized, she really did miss him.

"I'm picking you up at the airport. No riding the train home."

"Thanks, Sam. That will be good."

"Call me tomorrow?"

"Yes. I'll call you after the service."

"Okay. Go to sleep now."

"Thanks, Sam. Hearing your voice helped. My arm is throbbing and I took a pain pill and I'm finally starting to feel drowsy. Okay then. Good night."

"Good night, Isobel."

# Chapter 22

Dara texted Isobel to take the 7:17 train the next morning. She would be waiting for her at 8:46 when she arrived. Isobel took a cab to Penn Station, the security guard riding along with her, and when they arrived he escorted her to the platform and waited for the train with her. After walking her to her seat and putting both hers and Marah's suitcases in the luggage racks, he said goodbye, and left her. She had been grateful for the security guard the police had provided, but now felt a bit anxious being on her own.

Isobel glanced nervously around at the other passengers, but no one looked in her direction. She settled into her seat and felt herself relax as the train began to roll. She tried to close her eyes, but the vision of Marah still played there and she could feel the panic and tears begin. She took out a magazine she had picked up a couple of days earlier and thumbed through it, trying to read a random article or two, anything to keep her mind occupied. When the train pulled into Philadelphia, she realized she had drifted off for a bit, her mouth wide open and possibly drool on her cheek. She jumped up, startled, and scrambled to throw her backpack over her shoulder and drag hers and Marah's bags off the train, her stitched up arm, throbbing. She pulled the bags to the center of the platform and got her bearings. She headed to the elevator and just as she pushed the button, the doors opened and Dara stepped out.

Dara hugged Isobel to her, holding her tight. Isobel heard her take a deep choking breath and felt her shoulders shaking from crying. Other passengers crowded around them to get into the elevator, but they stood there, neither one able to let go. When Dara finally released Isobel, she said, "I'm so happy you have come. We must go now. Let me help you." Isobel handed over Marah's bag and followed Dara into the elevator that had just returned.

Dara showed Isobel into Marah's room. "Please, make yourself at home. We will go to the mosque in an hour. Oh, and you will need a head scarf. Marah has several in this drawer," she said as she pulled it open. "Choose one that suits you, as you must keep it when you leave. I'll let you unpack, but come have tea when you're ready."

"Thank you, Dara." Isobel unpacked and changed into the dress she had worn for their interview. She found a scarf that covered her head and the front of the dress, which she thought might be too low cut.

Isobel then went to find Dara in the kitchen making tea for them. Isobel could hear a television, muffled behind a closed door somewhere. "Is Shariq here?"

"Yes, but he is dealing with this by shutting himself away. He will show his face when we must leave."

Isobel nodded her head. "I can only imagine how difficult this is for you both, to lose your grandson and now your daughter."

Dara couldn't say anything, but she took Isobel's hand in hers as she sat at the table beside her. Isobel saw tears filling Dara's eyes. "Yes. But we will survive, inshallah." They drank their tea, Dara telling Isobel stories of Marah growing up. She also told her she never liked Zaqui, but had bowed to both Shariq and Marah's opinion. "I felt he was too, what's a good word, smooth. Yes, smooth. It did not surprise me when he left, but my heart broke for Marah and Raheem." She sighed and blinked back tears. They finished their tea in silence. Then they heard the television shut off in the other room and both Isobel and Dara turned as Shariq appeared in the doorway of the kitchen.

"Hello, Isobel." He nodded his head towards her, "We will be leaving shortly," he said, his eyes directed to Dara.

They carried their tea cups to the sink and both went to find coats and scarves. The day was bitter cold. Isobel pulled on black leggings before putting on her boots and wrapped the scarf around her head and chest before pulling on her coat. When they arrived at the mosque, the women went into a side room and Isobel dutifully followed Dara. There were few women in attendance, and those there, huddled around Dara, hugging and kissing her. They sat in a small group and listened to the Imam.

When the service finished, they all filed out and loaded into cars, following the hearse. As each car pulled into the cemetery, everyone unloaded. Isobel stood with the other women. She watched the men pull a box from the back of the hearse, then open it. Four men lifted Marah's shrouded body from the box.

The men then began the procession to the graveside. All the men fell in behind the men carrying Marah. Then the women waited together and after all the men began to walk down the road, the women followed at a distance, Isobel following at the back of the group. The cold wind cut through her like a knife. She wrapped her scarf tightly around her head and shoved her gloved hands into her coat pockets. When they reached the gravesite, the men lowered Marah into the grave, not on her back, but on her side. Isobel watched as someone climbed into the grave and stones were handed down. Next there were prayers and then all said together, "In the name of Allah and in the faith of the Messenger of Allah." Then the men took turns shoveling three shovels full of dirt into the grave. When the men finished, the women stepped forward and each threw three handfuls of dirt into the grave. Isobel stood at a distance and watched. When they finished, the men again led the procession out and the handful of women followed behind.

Dara sat between Isobel and Shariq in the car back to the mosque. When the driver pulled out of the cemetery, Dara broke into tears, and Shariq put his arm around her and let her cry. He rubbed her shoulder and made a shushing sound, as to a baby. Their intimacy made Isobel feel like an intruder. She looked out the window as they made their way through the streets. The sun shown, belying the fact it was ice-cold weather, and the sun had no effect. She pulled her sunglasses from her bag and put them on, folding herself tightly into the corner of the car, arms wrapped around herself. She closed her eyes, and concentrated on not seeing images of Marah's last moments. But she couldn't push them from her head. They haunted her and reminded her of losing Alec. Tears trickled down the side of her nose. She wiped them away with the back of her glove. Dara reached over and took Isobel's hand in her own. They each rode in silence now, engulfed in their own private pain.

Isobel went to Marah's room to lie down when they returned to the house. She closed the door and curled up on the bed, pulling a small blanket over her shoulders. She drifted into a restless sleep. When she woke, she heard voices murmuring in the living room. There was a moment when she didn't remember anything that had happened in the last year, and then the floodgate opened and she felt herself back at Jacob and Nora's. Back where it all had begun almost a year ago. She slipped her feet into the slippers Dara had left for her, and walked into the living room crammed full of people.

Dara saw her and rushed over. She escorted her around the room, introducing her to the friends who had brought food and stayed to be with Dara and

Shariq in their sadness. Isobel's head spun as she made her way around each room. Women thrust food into her hands, and told her how they knew Marah, or Dara and Shariq. Hours passed and yet people stayed on. Everyone finally left around ten. Isobel and Dara sat down at the kitchen table again and Shariq locked himself away in his study.

Dara made a pot of herbal tea and poured them each a cup. "Thank you for the tea, but aren't you ready to collapse? Don't feel like you have to sit with me," Isobel said.

"I am very tired. And drained. But this is what I need right now." Dara managed a sad smile.

"Your friends were all very nice to be here for you all day."

"That is our custom. They will return tomorrow and the next day too. We are allowed three days of mourning, so friends and family spend those days with you."

"Three days? There's a limit?"

"Yes. Then one must accept Allah's verdict. Inshallah."

"But, but she's your daughter. I am still so sad from losing Alec." Isobel blinked back tears when she said his name, the emotions of the past two days still ran high.

"I will always be sad. But I must let her go. She is with Allah now. I will be happy for that and not let my sadness be too much. I will see her again in heaven. Inshallah."

"I see where Marah got her braveness from." Isobel looked down into her cup and paused for a moment.

When she looked back up, she looked into Dara's eyes. "I've never known someone so brave."

"I think so too."

# Chapter 23

Isobel woke early the next morning. She lay in bed thinking about everything that had happened this week. The senselessness of Marah's murder. The media had found them yesterday and stood outside the front door as friends and neighbors came and went from the house. No one spoke to them. Isobel anxiously awaited the arrival of Marah's sister. She hoped her sister would be accepting of her being here. For now, though, she wanted to lay here for a few more minutes under the warm covers, oblivious to the media and to the house that would soon fill with people again.

When Isobel finally rose and dressed, she heard voices coming from the kitchen and went to find Dara. A neighbor had already arrived with a traditional Indian rice bread and fruit for their breakfast. The two of them sat at the table having tea. "Ah, here she is," Dara said and poured Isobel a cup of tea. "You met Cora yesterday, yes?"

"Yes, we did. Good morning."

"Hello again. Did you get any sleep?"

"Yes, thank you. I think exhaustion took over." She turned towards Dara, "What about you?"

"No, not much."

They chatted and nibbled on the breads that Cora brought. Shariq came in and joined them briefly, then returned to his study.

"I don't think Shariq slept much either. I heard him up long before Fajr prayers, roaming around the house."

Soon the house filled with people. They brought food and the women congregated in the kitchen and the men joined Shariq in his study or sat in the living room watching television. The party atmosphere felt foreign to Isobel, but at the same time healing. They laughed and told stories. They even made Dara laugh some. The women dressed in many different styles. Some wore head scarves, others did not. Some wore what Isobel thought of as a kaftan, and others wore purely American style clothing. Though no one spent a great deal of time talking to her, she still felt welcome in their midst. Everyone felt welcome with Dara. Her genuine, loving, and kind nature welcomed all who came into her home.

When Suraiya arrived that afternoon, she and Dara disappeared into a bedroom. Isobel decided to slip away into her bedroom and take a nap. When she returned, she found Dara and Suraiya at the center of activity in the kitchen. She stepped into the melee, more crowded than it had been all day. Before Dara even had a chance to introduce her, Suraiya had come and hugged her, "I'm Suraiya. Thank you for being so kind to Marah. She told me often how much your friendship helped her through those dark months."

Taken aback by Suraiya's greeting, Isobel stood like a deer in the headlights, all eyes on her. "I'm so sorry for your loss," she managed to say. Then, "We helped each other, truly, but thank you." Suraiya took her hand and led her to the table.

"Here, sit with me." They sat down together and Suraiya leaned in to talk to her. In spite of the outward exuberance in her greeting, Isobel saw the weight of sadness in her face. She peppered Isobel with questions about what she and Marah had been planning to do once the television appearance was over.

"Marah planned to write a book. I promised to help her. I suggested a memoir type style and a sort of handbook for parents. I think she had so much to share. I'm sorry we won't get the chance." Isobel felt the tightness in her throat, and saw the tears gathering in Suraiya's eyes.

"Me too."

They were interrupted when old school friends of Suraiya's arrived to see her and offer their condolences. Isobel faded into the background and silently watched the comings and goings, the hugs and tears, and the laughter. Isobel's Granny told her when her Papa died, and the night before the funeral she had overheard all the cousins laughing and telling stories at bedtime, that nothing healed the heart better than remembering the good times we've had with those who leave before us. Isobel saw the wisdom in that here, and thought about how much hearing the stories of Alec's life from friends and family had meant to her during the early, most painful days after his death. Maybe the idea of mourning only three days held a wisdom. Celebrating the lives of Alec, and now Marah, seemed far more healing, and living her own life with love and kindness, and no regrets the most important thing she could do. Isobel slipped off to her room and closed the door, hoping to sleep before she left for home in the morning.

The next day, she again found the kitchen filling up with people by seven. She booked a ride to the airport for eight and wanted to spend her last hour with Suraiya and Dara, but she would have to share them. She sat with them one last time and soaked in their loving spirits. She felt at home with them, as she always had with her own little family. This is what love looks like, regardless of culture and customs. This is love.

# Chapter 24

Sam picked up Isobel at the airport as promised. She broke down as he hugged her against his chest. Relief flooded over her at being back safely in Albuquerque and headed home. The pent-up tension released at being back in her familiar. Isobel told Sam everything as they drove to Santa Fe. Sam carried her bag inside and to her surprise, he had dinner prepared, a fire laid and the table set. "Sam, this is perfect. I could get used to this treatment."

"I like hearing that," he said as he carried her bag to her bedroom at the back of the house and came back to start the fire. "Here, come sit," he pointed at the couch as she stood thumbing through her mail, "I'll pour us a glass of wine."

"Okay, then. I will." She sat watching him light the fire and leaned her head back on the couch. The last bit of sunlight was fading from the sky above the mountains and she watched as the sky turned to darkest night. Sam had the fire blazing in a matter of minutes, then went to the kitchen and poured them both a glass of a Napa cabernet sauvignon. When he came back, Isobel's eyes were closed. He sat down next to her and put her glass on the coffee table. She breathed deeply, her eyelids flickered as if she had fallen into a deep sleep, but then she suddenly sat up, startled to find herself at home. Images of Marah still filled her head each time she drifted off and had the power to wake her, afraid for her own life.

"Oh, sorry. I think I drifted off." Isobel wiped at her mouth, "Hope I wasn't drooling."

"No," Sam laughed, "you weren't. We'll eat soon so you can go to bed early and get some sleep."

"I can't seem to sleep. I see Marah every time I close my eyes. I'm re-living the loss of Alec over and over each time I see her and I feel heartbroken at losing her too."

Sam took her hand and she leaned on his shoulder. She always felt safe with Sam, knowing he didn't judge her feelings and just let her be. Her friendship with Diane had waned as the distance between them had grown vast and Isobel didn't see how they could mend that rift. With Sam she could relax. Isobel sighed, then reached for her wine.

"I think I'm going to quit work at the end of this year. I'm going to take my retirement and find a way to continue what Marah and I started."

"You'll give yourself time to think about it before you tell Jorge?"

"Yes. I'm going to wait till the end of March, but I'm pretty certain, this is what I want."

"That's great, Iso. Really great."

"I also have to write about Marah. She had a bravery she didn't even realize. She told me after we were in New York she'd had some death threats, but she didn't take them seriously. I wish I had when she told me. I didn't take the ones I got seriously either. But I am now." She told Sam about the emails that Jorge had fielded on the school website.

"I don't like you being here by yourself, Isobel. I'm staying tonight. No protests."

"Oh, I'm not going to protest. I'm happy for you to stay. Please do." She smiled at him. "Thank you for being such a great friend."

"You're welcome. Now let's eat." He stood and kissed her on the top of the head and went to the kitchen to finish their meal. They spent the rest of the evening talking about her plans. And also about her safety. Sam wanted her to keep a low profile while she figured out her strategy to continue what she and Marah had begun. She agreed with him on that. She saw first hand what it meant to ignore the threat. She went to bed that night with a sense of calm, but mostly the strong sense of purpose that she had begun to feel before Marah's death, but now seemed even more real. Her life in public education had run its course. She would stick to her March deadline for her final decision, but she knew in her heart, she would retire.

Isobel found herself highly distracted for the next month, waiting for spring break to arrive. She, Ian,

Delia and the kids had decided to go to Padre Island for the holiday. She would turn in her intent to retire at the end of the break. She hadn't told Ian her plans yet. She wanted to tell him in person, especially since her plans were much greater than retirement. Isobel realized he might not like her idea. He had been shaken by what happened to Marah, and lived in fear something would happen to Isobel. She had assured him of her precautions and told him there had been no more threats. Jorge had hired extra security at the building and Sam lived down the street. Isobel hadn't mentioned to Ian, since she returned home, she and Sam spent the night at each other's house almost nightly. Spring break with Ian would give them a chance to talk this all through.

Isobel flew to Galveston and drove to the island. Ian and Delia had driven down. For Isobel and Delia, their stressful school years gave them little time to be together, but spring break allowed them time to put the daily grind behind them. Isobel enjoyed playing with Bree and Brian, digging in the sand, building castles with elaborate moats. They all laughed a lot, the medicine they needed most.

One afternoon on the beach, Ian sat by Isobel in their row of beach chairs, "Mom, the anniversary of Alec's death is coming up. Can you meet us in Llano? Dad wants to have some kind of memorial for him. I think the University is planning something too."

"Let me know the details. I'll be there. Of course. I already knew I had to be with you that day. This will be good."

"I think so too. It will be good for everyone."

"I have some news too. I'm planning to go to Scotland this summer and hike to the top of Ben Nevis. Alec loved our hike and that's where I'm spreading my box of his ashes."

Ian looked at her with tears in his eyes. They both then teared up and Ian reached over and took Isobel's hand. "I can think of nothing better, Mom. He would love that you are doing that. He'll be in a place he loved."

Isobel put off telling Ian and Delia her plans, but when Ian brought up the anniversary she knew she had to fill them in that night after the kids were in bed. She laid out what she intended, from speaking engagements and writing Marah's life story, and how she felt she could make a difference. Delia immediately jumped on board, but Ian threw up protest after protest.

"Mom, I don't want you putting your life at risk. I can't lose you too."

"Honey, after what I witnessed, believe me, I will be cautious. I will. But none of us get any guarantees and I have to do something. My main objective is to write about Marah and Alec. I just want to get the conversation started about radicalization and hopefully someone will run with it. I also know a thing or two about fundamentalism, and it can be just as dangerous." They argued back and forth, until Ian realized he couldn't stop her .

"Mom, I'm proud of you. I know you will make a difference."

"Thanks, Ian. I love you, sweetheart. And I'll be around for a long time to come."

"Yeah, I think you will."

They sadly said their goodbye's the next day, with plans for the anniversary the next month, they knew they would see each other again soon.

# Chapter 25

I sobel drove to Llano a month later and joined Ian and family at Jacob's house for a party to celebrate Alec's life. He invited everyone they knew in Llano, so it seemed, as the house and both front and back yards were full of people. Isobel snaked her way through the crowd to find Ian and Delia sitting with a group of their friends on the back porch. Bree and Brian were on Jacob's putting green with their plastic golf clubs, Bree instructing her little brother, as he kept inching away from her and taking wild swings at his ball. She loved watching the two of them. Such different personalities, just as Alec and Ian had been.

Isobel moved from group to group. She knew a lot of the people who were there. She found herself in random conversations throughout the evening, everyone skirting the topic of Alec, the reason they were all actually there, and no one brought up Marah's death. When people finally started to clear out, Ian and Isobel sat on the couch together talking.

"Did you finally turn in your retirement notice?" he asked her. She had ended up putting it off until right before this trip.

"I did, and of course Jorge tried to talk me out of leaving. I knew he would. I felt bad that he made a special allowance for me this last year, giving me a different job, but life changes. And I had no idea it would change so drastically in one year."

"You're good then? Ready to go?"

"I am. I've never felt so sure about anything in my life. I've already started outlining my book on Marah, and I'm hoping I can still make it a handbook of sorts as we planned. I'm actually, excited. For the first time in a long time."

"That's great, Mom. When do you leave for Scotland?"

"Looking like mid-July. I know I have to deal with the crowds on the trail, but I still think Ben Nevis is where Alec would want to go again."

"I wish I could make the trip with you."

"I know, sweetheart. I wish you could too. Thanks." She gave him a hug. "Okay then, I'm going back to the hotel."

"You should have stayed here. Nora truly loves having us all together."

"Thanks, but this way the kids have their own room and so do you two. I'll see you at the memorial tomorrow at the University."

"Okay, good night Mom." He kissed her and gave her a hug.

"Good night then. Love you." Isobel said, as Ian held the door and she left.

The next day, the memorial held by the University recognized Alec and the four students who had been killed. The day was difficult for them all, but the tribute to Alec had been lovely, Isobel thought, and Claire's speech thanking Alec for his bravery had been amazing. Now she headed back to Santa Fe, the wide open road before her. She didn't mind the drive, really. The skies were blue, the clouds hung like huge cotton balls glued onto a child's sky painting. She used the time to think about her future. About writing a book. And about giving up her responsibility for students and what that would mean for her. She felt nothing but joy.

# *Epilogue*

July 23, Isobel stood on the top of Ben Nevis. The last time she had been there, she and Alec had taken turns taking pictures of themselves on the highest point. Today the line stretched in a circle around the top, and people laughed and joked as they waited their turn to stand there and have their picture taken. Isobel walked to the edge where she and Alec had once stood, and slipped her backpack off. She pulled a small box from the deepest section and held it in her hands. She looked out over the highlands, thankful that a cloud had not rolled in yet, and remembered when she and Alec had stood there together. They had been lucky enough to have a clear view then, as well, and had chosen this spot for their picnic lunch. They had pulled out their box lunches, purchased from the inn where they had stayed, and eaten, while gazing at this incredible view.

"My dear Alec, my life was made better the day you entered this world, and a light was stolen from this world the day you died. I give you this view for eternity where I know your spirit must be dwelling even now. I will love you forever, my baby, my sweet, sweet son." Tears poured down her cheeks as she stood there with Alec in her hands. Then she opened the box and poured him out, where he caught in the wind and swept away towards the highlands.

Isobel watched the ashes float away in the breeze, her face damp with tears. She wiped her eyes with her hands and a smile formed on her lips. "No more tears. No more tears. I love you," and she blew a kiss into the wind before slipping her backpack on her shoulders and walking away. When she reached the cairn marking the way down, Sam stood there waiting for her. He took her in his arms and held her tight. She took his hand and they began the descent.

# Author's Note to Readers

I began this book sometime around early 2015 when there was a great deal of rhetoric about all Muslims being terrorists. An act of terrorism, is just that, one act. It does not condemn a whole group of people because of one or two people's actions. If it did, then all Americans would need to be condemned for the collective acts of terrorism perpetrated now and in the past on whole groups of people. And when a group is condemned, where does it stop? I wanted to tell a story to reveal our similarities, rather than our differences, as people of different beliefs and backgrounds, because we are all human and so similar down to but the smallest bits of DNA, that we need to open our eyes and really see others. We also need to see ourselves for who we are and reflect deeply, to put away our preconceived notions of 'Other.'

I dived deep into researching all elements of my story. I wanted to portray these mothers to the best of my ability in the proper light. I researched specific traditions of Muslims in the place of Marah's parents birth, and traditions for American Muslim women as they traverse two different cultures. I engaged Muslim beta readers to be sure I had the story right and made changes based on recommendations. I also engaged a friend who lost her daughter in a scuba accident to read for grief after I had done extensive research. She said I had portrayed the mother's grief well.

Tragically, two months after completing my first draft, my oldest son unexpectedly died. The grieving process I went through after his death was surreal. Many times I found myself thinking, 'I've done this before, I know this part.' Losing my son has profoundly affected my life. I now know the worst possible tragedy a mother can know. Moving on with life is essential, but there is a sadness wrapped around my heart that is ever present. I am more grateful for my loved ones and much more tolerant of the ups and downs of everyday life. Life is fragile and precious. As I write this, we are in the eighth month of Covid-19 and though it has been trying at times, it is not the end of the world. I know what the end of the world feels like and am able to put this in perspective for me.

The book I mention in the novel that Isobel's counselor recommends is, *Resilient Grieving: Finding Strength and Embracing Life After a Loss That Changes Everything,* by Lucy Hone, PhD; 2017, a book that helped me and others in our family. I am ever grateful to her for this work and recommend this to anyone who has lost a child or a close family member.

The book Marah finds in her son's belongings is also a real book, found on the internet and controversially used in some Muslim classrooms in America at the time of this writing.

If you are grieving a loved one and feel hopeless, please seek help. The Compassionate Friends is an organization for parents grieving the loss of a child. Thank you for reading.

# Acknowledgements

I am deeply grateful to the following people for their encouragement, assistance, and presence in my life: My editor, Nina Bjornsson, who sifted through my story and made it better with her suggestions and thoughtful edits. After the death of my son, I had a hard time getting back to work, and she gently pushed me forward. To those who read for certain perspectives and feedback: Julie Simmonds, Jenn Hunter, Heather Fadida, Susan Tucker, Jim Johnston, Betty Williamson and my many Beta Readers of whom I know not their names. My father, Retired AF Major Glen A. Thompson (deceased) and Retired Army Colonel Rich Whitaker who answered numerous questions on military protocol. Sam Porter for answering questions regarding hand guns. My many friends who have asked about my progress along the way and shored me up with their encouragement and love. My sons, Paul Hunton and Matt Hunton, for their love and the many years of laughter they've provided me. My son Shawn Hunton, who died two months after I finished the first draft. He read large portions of the book as I worked. He will forever be missed. And most of all to my most critical reader and my greatest supporter, my husband, Steve Hasenmueller. I couldn't have done this without him.

# About the Author

Jane Thompson Hasenmueller, a former English Educator and Education Administrator, as well as a former lobbyist for the New Mexico Fellows of the National Writing Project, published her first book, *Choosing Happiness After Divorce*, in 2009 after stepping back from her education career. She went on to become a Certified Health and Integrative Nutrition coach, starting *Radical Aging,* a website about living healthy no matter one's age.

*The Grief of Wisdom* is her debut novel. You can find her, when she is not writing, hiking the Sangre de Cristo mountains of Santa Fe, New Mexico, or eating a croissant and drinking wine (not at the same time) in France.